Novels by Ib Melchior

EVA

THE TOMBSTONE CIPHER

THE MARCUS DEVICE

THE WATCHDOGS OF ABADDON

THE HAIGERLOCH PROJECT

SLEEPER AGENT

ORDER OF BATTLE

by

IB MELCHIOR

DODD, MEAD & COMPANY • NEW YORK

To Cleo

Who brings beauty to the world in so many ways

V-3 is a work of fiction. Any similarity to any person, living or dead, is purely coincidental.

Published by Dodd, Mead & Company, Inc.
79 Madison Avenue, New York, N.Y. 10016

Distributed in Canada by
McClelland and Stewart Limited, Toronto

Manufactured in the United States of America

Designed by Jeramiah B. Lighter

First Edition

Library of Congress Cataloging in Publication Data

Melchior, Ib.
V-3.

Bibliography: p.
1. World War, 1939–1945—Fiction. I. Title.
PS3563.E435V2 1985 813′.54 85-10247
ISBN 0-396-08483-4

V-1—*Abbreviation of Vengeance Weapon One, the propaganda name given the unmanned aircraft, Fiesler 103, the* Kirschkern *(Cherry Pit) flying bomb. As of June 1942, created especially for the bombing of London. First employment under the code name* Rumpelkammer *(Lumber Room) took place June 12, 1944.*

V-2—*Abbreviation of Vengeance Weapon Two, the propaganda name given the ballistic long-distance rocket, A-4, developed at the Rocket Research Center of the German Army at Peenemünde. Bombarded London from September 8, 1944 to March 27, 1945.*

Lexikon des 2. Weltkrieges
"Das Dritte Reich"
(*Encyclopedia of World War II*
"The Third Reich")

CONTENTS

ACKNOWLEDGMENTS

The author wishes to express his appreciation for the valuable assistance given him in the research for this book by:

Dr. Robert T. Fitzgerald, Director, Emergency Services, Brotman Medical Center, Culver City, CA

Mr. George Bennette, Director, Arts and Leisure Education, the New York Association for the Blind, New York, NY

The Gorham Division of Textron, San Dimas, CA

The Chamber of Commerce, Weiden, West Germany

Bundesarchiv, Militärarchiv, Freiburg, West Germany

Frihedsmuseet (The Freedom Museum), Copenhagen, Denmark

The Modern Military Branch, Military Archives Division, National Archives and Records Service, Washington, D.C.

The U.S. Army Information Service, Los Angeles, CA

Department of the Navy, DTV Elk River, San Diego, CA

Rear Admiral Paul A. Peck, USN, ex-Commander Carrier Group Three

Lieutenant James J. Fenwick, USN, Ret., Naval School of Deep Diving Systems

Captain H. L. Matthews, USN, Ret.

PART

May 1985 and April 1945

1

His mind was filled with it.

He felt exhilarated. Triumphant. He hadn't felt like that for—how many years? Forty? Forty-five? He gloried in it. Even his steps on the hard New York sidewalk felt lighter than usual. *Any day now,* the message had read. *Any day!* He smiled with secret satisfaction, a thin, bitter smile, as he walked down the street. *Any day.*

And the world would tremble . . .

At 3:17 P.M. on any given day, the traffic on Manhattan's Second Avenue near Forty-seventh Street is heavy and fast. It was no different on this, the ninth day of May, when Karl Johann Thompson stepped off the curb to cross the avenue as he'd done thousands of times before.

He was crossing against the light, for like many New Yorkers, Thompson paid little attention to such minor irritations as traffic lights. As was his wont, he crossed each lane of traffic in turn, waiting between them for a lull in the flow of cars and trucks that sped by on either side of him, neither slowing nor swerving and paying him no attention. He was almost across when for a moment his eyes left the oncoming traffic to look ahead. On the curb in front of him, two lanes away, stood a man. Average in every way, he appeared to be about Thompson's own age, somewhere in his sixties. The only unusual thing about him was a deep, jagged scar that ran from the middle of his forehead, across his right eye, to the heel of his jaw. It had obviously been there for a long time. For a brief moment the eyes of the two men met, and there was no mistaking the sudden glint of recognition with which the stranger stared at Thompson.

Startled, Thompson, as if pushed by an invisible hand, took a step backward.

The taxi that hit him struck his left thigh, instantly breaking it. The impact spun him around, and he fell to the ground directly in the path of a van from a Second Avenue cleaning establishment. Unable to stop or swerve in the heavy traffic, the van ran over him, one wheel crushing his pelvis. His scream was drowned out by the squeals of tires as the cars came to a stop around him.

The scarred stranger across the avenue stood frozen, but only for a moment. Then, abruptly, he turned and without looking back strode away.

Thompson lay motionless, sprawled on the pavement. He had heard the splintering, crunching sound when his pelvic bones were crushed, the vibration conducted up through his vertebrae and his cranial vault to his inner ear. He had not known it for what it was. He felt no pain—only the sensation of a heavy weight pressing down across his hips. It puzzled him. He looked. There was nothing to see. He tried to sit up—and sudden, blinding pain lanced through him. Again he screamed, but this time the searing agony would not leave him . . .

Student nurse Rita Sandoval had to half-run to keep up with the gurney as the orderlies hurriedly pushed it down the hospital corridor toward the emergency room. She held the half-full plastic IV bag high, watching the clear, lactated ringer's solution slosh in time with her steps. The gurney, she noted, had one of its front wheels slightly out of alignment, and it rolled along the corridor floor with a decided bump. Like a beat-up market basket, she thought.

Her eyes were drawn to the patient's torn shirt-sleeve, which dangled over the edge of the gurney, swinging free. The paramedics at the site of the accident had ripped it open to administer the IV. The cloth, mangled and slashed, flapped below the gurney, and to Rita it became a visible symbol of the mangled body hidden from view.

The man lying on the wheeled stretcher was obviously seriously injured, but he was still conscious. Furtively Rita kept glancing at him as she hurried along. It was the first time she'd seen an accident victim come in, wrapped in the inflated military antishock trousers, the MAST suit, as she knew it was called, and she was startled at the man's appearance. He looked curiously alien, like someone from outer space, she thought, not at all like the bloody mess she'd expected when she first heard the paramedics radio in to the emergency department their report of the massive injuries the victim had sustained. The man was encased in bloated, brown vinyl trousers from just below the ribs all the way down to his ankles. Cocooned as in an inflated space suit from *Star Wars*, she thought. A thick cloth collar was fixed around his neck to immobilize it, and looking like some unearthly facial appendages, two nasal cannulae ran from his nostrils to the green oxygen bottle lying next to him on the gurney. The skin on his exposed chest looked waxen and drained of color. If it had been green, she thought, she would have sworn he was a man from Mars.

He stared up at Rita. His face was ashen, his eyes unblinking. His gaze made her feel uneasy. She tried to smile at him, but she knew her attempt was only moderately successful.

Suddenly the man spoke, looking directly at her.

"You!" he rasped in an intense whisper, a ghastly grimace of a grin contorting his pallid face. "You! One . . . One thousand . . . One thousand . . ."

Rita stared at him. What did he mean? His eyes were hot with a strange intensity. Pain? Hate? Hunger? Involuntarily she shuddered. She looked away. But she could not avoid hearing the man hissing his meaningless words at her. Again. And again. It disturbed her.

Closely trailed by the two police officers who'd followed the ambulance from the scene of the accident, the orderlies wheeled the gurney into the trauma room. Dr. Mark Elliott and two nurses, Hawkins and that big redheaded one whose name Rita could never remember, were already waiting along with Adams, the physician's assistant, and Metcalf, the scribe. As the orderlies lifted the backboard with the patient on it and transferred it from the gurney to the trauma table, Rita hung the IV bag on the wall hook, and Adams, the PA, connected the nasal cannulae to the wall oxygen and removed the portable tank from the backboard.

Rita stepped back next to the X-ray view box, out of the way. She watched. After all, that's what she was there for. She knew she had to remain calm and cool, but she couldn't help feeling excited. A man's life was at stake. Right there in front of her.

Dr. Elliott quickly walked to the head of the table. He began to examine the patient. Without looking up, he said, "Nurse?"

"Blood pressure 90 over 50," Hawkins sang out. "Pulse 120."

Elliott nodded. "Male Caucasian," he said evenly. "Approximately sixty-five." The scribe quickly entered the information on the chart. "Blunt abdominal and left extremity trauma," Elliott continued. "Start a second peripheral IV and set up for a central line." The trauma team moved automatically even as Elliott urgently called out his orders. "Get the phlebotomist in here. I want surgical labs. Type and cross him for six units." He glanced at the victim's abdomen. "He'll need a Foley catheter." He turned to the PA. "Have X-ray on standby. Call the surgical team, and tell OR we have a possible laparotomy."

Rita listened attentively, filing away every word, every action. She watched nurse Hawkins prepare the patient for the second IV. As she swabbed the man's arm, he suddenly looked up at her.

"Zero!" he cried clearly. "One. Zero. Zero. Zero. Any day now!"

"Sure," nurse Hawkins nodded. She put the catheter into his vein. He seemed not to notice.

Intently Rita watched the members of the trauma team go through their well-choreographed routine as the doctor continued his rapid physical examination of the patient, calling his findings to the scribe in a clipped voice. Was he a little more tense than she'd seen him before? Rita thought so.

Quickly and efficiently, the team members performed their jobs. They made it all look easy. Rita knew it was not. And she wondered if she'd ever be that good.

The lab technician drew the needed blood from the patient's arm; the PA placed the Foley catheter to drain the man's bladder; and the X-ray technician positioned the film cassette. He winked at Rita, as she watched him gravely.

"Bp is 130 over 80," Hawkins announced briskly. "Pulse 100."

Good, Rita thought. He's got a chance.

The man suddenly turned his head and fixed his eyes on Hawkins. "Find!" he rasped hoarsely. "Find!" Hatefully he glared up at the busy nurse. *"Find!"*

Rita looked at him in wonder. Find? What did he mean? Find—what? Who? The man who ran him down?

"Deflate the MAST abdominal compartment," Elliott ordered. "I think we've got him stable enough now. And prep him for a peritoneal lavage. We might as well see how much internal bleeding we're up against. The surgical team will need to know." He looked up at Hawkins. "When will the OR team get here?"

"Ten minutes," Hawkins answered as she deflated the antishock trousers. She ripped open the Velcro straps. The tearing sound made Rita start.

"Any day!" the man called out, his voice suddenly strong and vibrant. "Any day now!"

Rita frowned at him. What did he mean? No one paid him any attention. Of course, there were other more pressing matters to be attended to than listening to the delirious cries and mutterings of an injured old man.

But someone should pay attention, shouldn't they? Concerned, she looked at the scribe. Was she taking down anything the patient said? No. She had her hands full, entering on the record everything that was being done.

"All die!" the old man breathed, staring at nurse Hawkins. "Rache. Rache. *Rache!* Bald . . ."

Resolutely Rita took a small notebook from a skirt pocket. It had a green cover with a red rose in one corner. She fished out a pencil. She began to write: Rah-her. Rah-her. Bald . . .

Hawkins had exposed the man's hips. The area looked curiously flattened, the matted clothing moist with blood. From the compound fracture, Rita thought. She could see the bone sticking through the skin and cloth. The MAST lay limp and soggy under the patient. Quickly yet carefully, the redhead and the PA began to cut the blood-soaked clothing away.

The old man glared at them, his eyes fiery. "Gift!" Venemously he spat out the word. He tried to sit up. "Gift!" Elliott gently restrained him. "Easy," he soothed. "Easy . . ."

The injured man called out again. It sounded like gibberish to Rita. He cackled unpleasantly. He seemed to mutter, "Room. Bell. Karma." Dutifully Rita wrote it down: Room. Bell. Karma . . . *Karma?* Was the man a Buddhist?

The man rambled on. His cries made no sense to her. Some of the words—if they *were* words at all—were incomprehensible. Maybe foreign? Hindu—or something? She wrote them down phonetically as best she could. Words like "fair-ghel-toong" and "fair-nick-toong." She looked at what she'd written. It made no sense. No sense at all.

The scribe was going through the contents of the pockets of the man's cutoff pants. She put the things she found—keys, a comb, a roll of Life Savers, some change (mostly pennies, it seemed), a blood-soaked handkerchief—into the patient's belongings bag. She wiped the blood from a worn black wallet and handed it to one of the police officers. Gingerly he took it. Even more gingerly he opened it, looking for any kind of ID.

Hawkins cleaned the patient's abdomen. "Looks distended," she said, troubled. She swabbed it with iodine, and the PA placed a sterile drape over the area. Elliott injected lidocaine and epinephrine. With a scalpel he made a small incision and inserted the peritoneal lavage trochar into the peritoneum. He attached a syringe to the catheter. Squinting, he examined the fluid he withdrew. He frowned. "Dammit," he said. "Grossly bloody."

The man's breathing began to sound labored. He started to toss with increasing agitation. Elliott at once turned back to him. With a worried frown he peered searchingly into his eyes.

Suddenly Hawkins called out. "Pressure dropping!" She sounded tense. "70 over 40."

"Get the MAST back on," Elliott snapped. "Move it! Get me an endotracheal tube. Quickly!"

"Pulse 150!"

Elliott glanced at the cardiac monitor.

"Pressure dropping!" Hawkins called.

"He's becoming bradycardiac," Elliott cried out. "Atropine. One milligram. Now!"

The trauma crew galvanized into action.

Rita watched nurse Hawkins feverishly refasten the MAST around the injured man's pelvic area. "We're losing him," the woman muttered angrily. "Dammit! We're losing him . . ."

Rita put away her little green notebook with the red rose.

She would have no further use for it.

Not here.

Not now . . .

The nicotine-stained finger that dialed the international access code, 011, linking metropolitan New York with the little town of Weiden in West Germany, twelve miles from the Iron Curtain as the ballistic missile flies, trembled slightly as it turned the disc on the old-fashioned telephone. The string of numbers was impressively long, and after the customary clicks and pauses, the ringing began. Several seconds went by; it was 3:14 A.M. in Weiden. Finally a man's sleepy voice answered.

"Bitte?"

The caller, his voice taut, simply said, "One. Zero. Zero. Zero."

There was only the slightest hesitation, and the man on the other side of the ocean, instantly alert, replied, "Four. Nine. One. Two."

The caller sighed. "Karl Johann is dead," he said.

"When?" The query was sharp.

"Today."

"How do you know?"

"Felix told me."

The gasp was felt rather than heard. "Felix! He is in New York?"

"Yes."

"*Verflucht!* Dammit!" The exclamation seemed unconscious. "You *saw* him?"

"No. He called. He told me Karl Johann had been killed. Finally."

"By him?"

"No. It was an accident."

"How?"

"He was crossing a street. Second Avenue. It is a busy thoroughfare. He saw Felix. He was hit."

"Did Felix . . . plan it?"

"No. He had not found Karl Johann yet. It was . . . it just happened."

"Scheissdreck!" There was a sudden urgency in the man's voice. "Did Karl Johann talk?"

"That is not known. Assume he has. Any orders?"

There was a pause, then, "No. None. It will make no difference. Now."

"*Schon gut.* I will arrange for—"

"You will do nothing!" The voice on the phone was sharp, a voice used to giving orders and being obeyed. "Keep yourself completely divorced from Karl Johann and any affairs that concern him. Understood?"

"Understood. What about Felix?"

"There is nothing we can do. He will no longer be a menace. He has had his revenge."

"As you wish."

"It will not be long, *mein lieber Herr Doktor.*" The voice was chillingly silken. "Any day. Any day now . . ."

2

"Birte! You got the double-stick tape?" Einar Munk's voice sounded slightly aggrieved. He pronounced her name the Danish way to rhyme with "beer-tea"—with emphasis on the "beer," of course.

Birte Munk dipped the last pair of panty hose into the suds in the bathroom sink. "Sorry!" she called. "I was using it at my desk. Wrapping that gift for the Galpers. I'll get it." She'd done it again, she thought. She knew Einar didn't like his things not to be in their proper places. She wiped her hands and headed for the kitchen. The tape was lying next to a roll of brightly colored paper on the little desk standing in a corner of the kitchen, where she kept her recipes and cookbooks, her household accounts, and the box with newspaper coupons. She picked it up.

Einar Munk was sitting at his desk in his little office, a pair of scissors in his hand. The desk top was strewn with newspaper clippings, snapshots, stickers, and party invitations. A clutter of mementos. At sixty-four Einar was eyeing senior citizenship and Medicare—but with no thought of retiring. As far as he was concerned, that was something to be eyed through the wrong end of a telescope.

"What're you doing?" Birte asked, although she knew the answer quite well. She handed her husband the tape.

"Finishing the US book," Einar answered—knowing that an answer wasn't really necessary. "It's half-past April already. About time we got out of 1984."

He took the tape. Birte watched him cut off a small piece and stick it on the back of a colorful matchbook cover, which he placed on an album page next to a snapshot of a smiling Birte standing in front of a picturesque country inn. She knew where it was: the Beekman Arms in Rhinebeck, upstate New York, which billed itself as "America's Oldest Inn." George Washington slept here, that sort of thing. They'd taken Amtrak up there, riding along the Hudson River, to celebrate New Year's Eve. Just the two of them. It had been lovely. Obviously the 1984 US book was nearly finished.

There were forty-two of the albums now. They formed a solid black base on the two-shelved bookcases under the windows in the living room. One book for each of the thirty-seven years they'd been married and a few extras for special trips. Each combination scrapbook and photo album was filled with the pictures they'd taken of events through the year, with little pertinent souvenirs: ticket stubs and programs, name tags and place cards, and—of course—matchbook covers, pasted in among the photos. Each book—originally called "The Two of Us," but quickly shortened to US when after only one volume it became "The Three of Us"—each book was a colorful minirecord of their life together. Einar loved to make them. And she loved to have them. They say nostalgia is a seducer. So what's wrong with being seduced?

Many a rainy night she'd pulled out one of them and glanced through it, reliving the year in memory. There was the very first one: 1947. The year Einar had brought her over from her native Denmark, with pictures from their wedding in the little Danish church, Salems Kirke, in Brooklyn, which had opened just a few years before. The choir had sung Grieg's *"Jeg Elsker Dig"*—"I Love You"—with the lovely words by Hans Christian Andersen. And there was the honeymoon at Niagara Falls. Kitschy, of course, but she'd wanted a real American honeymoon. And the following year when Sven was born. She always got a kick out of the superproud expression on Einar's face as he stood holding his son as if he were a fragile Ming vase.

There was the Bermuda trip in 1953. They'd splurged to celebrate Einar's first published paper with a byline in the publish-or-perish rat race. In *Scientific American,* no less. By then he'd been an associate professor of chemistry at Columbia University for a few years, and they'd already moved into their cozy little second-floor apartment on West 119th Street between Morningside Heights and Amsterdam Avenue, only a few blocks from the university campus. In Bermuda they'd stayed at the St. George Hotel and scuba dived among the colorful fish on the reefs offshore. She'd loved the trip, and she especially liked a snapshot Einar had taken of her gingerly holding a huge starfish. There was a picture, slightly out of focus (Einar had said, No wonder—that's how he felt the whole trip!) of Einar sleeping on the sand on his way to a glorious sunburn. And, of course, a matchbook cover from the hotel, only it wasn't a matchbook but a little flattened box.

There were a couple of favorite years: 1962 and 1963. Sven was a teenager, and she'd had a lot of time on her hands. She'd used it to work with a group of blind actors and actresses, the Lighthouse Players of the New York Association for the Blind. It had been one of the most challenging and rewarding times of her life—and it was all there in the US books.

Photos of the blind players familiarizing themselves with the set by feeling a miniature scale model; writing out their sides in Braille and memorizing the positions of every piece of furniture on the stage, always kept in exactly the same spot, as were all props. She still marveled at all the little ingenious tricks cooked up to aid the blind players in their performances. Tricks like placing a thumbtack in the upper right-hand corner of a book so the blind player wouldn't hold it upside down, or dog-earing a corner of a magazine; the clicking of a cup on its saucer when handing it to another blind player, who unerringly would reach for the sound; and putting the stage telephone bell directly under the telephone for the same reason. Or always speaking a line when two players were passing one another on the stage so they wouldn't get in each other's way. And the rubber runners. The all-important rubber runners that crisscrossed the stage to mark the way to doors and furniture. The players could feel the texture under their feet, and they had memorized the exact distances in steps. That way an actress could enter the stage, walk directly to a chair, and sit down without groping for it. Although she had to be taught to "look" at the chair first. A sighted person always does. Birte remembered at first being afraid the players would bump into each other or fall off the stage. She quickly learned such fears were totally unfounded. At each performance the audience invariably, within a few minutes, completely forgot that the players were blind.

It had been wondrous for her to see the blind players "learn" the expressions, the reactions and mannerisms of sighted people, gestures that they had never seen. And she came to understand fully what the famous actor, Otis Skinner, had meant when he said of the Lighthouse Players, "Those eyes of theirs see many things—fine things—ideal things—they taught my eyes to see." She often tried to see certain things with the eyes of those blind actors and actresses.

She still went regularly to the performances at the Lighthouse Theater on East Fifty-ninth Street, where the players had had their home for sixty-two years. She always came away enriched.

But there was one book she rarely took out. US 1968. Because of February 15, two days before her fortieth birthday.

On that day there were two items in the book. She did not have to open it to see them. They were indelibly etched on her mind. A photograph of Sven in the uniform of a sergeant in the army of the United States. And a letter.

She had known. When she opened the door on that fateful day so many years ago and saw the solemn young officer standing outside, she had known.

The "Tet Offensive," they'd called it. Somewhere in Vietnam. Sven had been killed while on patrol. They said he had died instantly.

She hoped it was true.

There were no pictures when she and Einar had claimed the flag-draped coffin with the body of their son at Andover Air Force Base.

The letter from Sven's commanding officer had arrived later.

But she often looked at 1982. A banner year for Einar. That year he'd been elected to the prestigious National Academy of Science. She'd taken his picture as he stood on the broad steps of the campus buildings. He looked as if he owned the whole kit and caboodle. And then some.

And just recently, at the Beekman Arms in Rhinebeck—the snow outside had been gorgeous—they'd been sitting in the charming Pewter Room, having dinner and enjoying the historical atmosphere so faithfully recreated; Einar had picked up the coat-of-arms coaster—he'd probably put it in the book; he'd have to split it, though, it was that thick—and he'd asked that little waitress he'd found so cute if . . .

Her reveries were abruptly shattered as the doorbell rang. It startled her. It always did. They'd made the bell ring extra loud, and Einar had connected it to a contact breaker on the front door so it would ring if the door was opened. They turned it on at night.

"Who in the world could that be?" Birte exclaimed. She glanced at the nineteenth-century grandfather clock in the corner, the only really good piece of furniture they had in the apartment. They felt safe owning it. Too big for a burglar to carry off. Einar had inherited it from his uncle. "It's already past nine o'clock," she finished.

"No idea," Einar said. He got up. "I'll get it."

"Keep the chain on."

"Oh, Birte, for Pete's sake," he protested. "I can take care of myself."

"You're not twenty anymore, darling."

"Three times that," he countered with a grin. "And three times as good!"

"I may have to ask you to prove that," she called after him, mischief in her voice. "Later."

The two men who stood in the hallway outside the door looked grim. Both wore conservative clothes.

"Professor Munk?" the older man inquired. "Professor Einar Munk?"

"I'm Einar Munk."

"Captain Martin, sir." The officer indicated his younger companion. "Lieutenant Hensley. CIC."

Einar frowned at the two men. CIC? The Counter Intelligence Corps? He'd served in the CIC. For five years. During World War II. He was puzzled. What was up?

"You *are* Major Einar Munk, retired, serial number 034 . . ." Martin rattled off the army serial number tonelessly.

"I am."

"May we come in?" Martin said. He started through the door. Einar effectively blocked his way. "May I see some identification?" he asked pointedly.

"Of course, sir. Sorry." Both men held out their ID cards. Einar glanced at them. He held the door open. "Come in."

Birte, looking concerned, joined her husband as the two officers stepped into the front hall. Einar turned to her. "These gentlemen are from the CIC," he said. "Why don't you put some coffee water on?"

"Thank you, sir," Martin said quickly. "We appreciate it, but I'm afraid there's no time. What we're here for is urgent."

"Urgent?" Birte looked at the officer in alarm.

"Yes, ma'am."

Martin turned back to Einar. "You hold a special, extended Army Reserve commission in the Military Intelligence Group. Is that correct?" he asked, not as a question but for confirmation. "With the rank of major?"

"I do."

Martin drew himself up. "I must ask you to come with us, sir."

Einar was taken aback. "Come with you?" he exclaimed. "Where to?"

"To Washington, sir."

Einar looked startled. "Why?"

"I am not able to tell you that, sir."

"Are you placing me on active duty, Captain? Pulling me back just like that? With no warning at all?'' Einar was beginning to sound a little annoyed.

''No, sir,'' Martin said soberly. ''No, we are not. We are simply requesting—strongly requesting that you agree to accompany us to the Pentagon for an interview with Colonel Henderson. Jonathan Henderson.''

Einar had a sudden flash of déjà vu. Once before, years ago during the war, he'd been peremptorily summoned to the office of a superior officer. Big brass. That summons had launched one of the most dangerous and traumatic ventures of his life. Was history about to repeat itself?

Martin looked at him gravely. ''It *is* a matter of the utmost importance, sir,'' he said portentously. ''Your cooperation will be . . . appreciated.''

Was that little pause in the nature of a veiled hint of a threat?

''Colonel Henderson is the assistant chief of staff, intelligence, sir, the Counter Intelligence Directorate. He asked us to convey to you that the matter he wishes to discuss with you is vital,'' Martin added. ''National security may well be at stake. I—I strongly suggest that you do comply with our request, Major.''

Einar thought quickly. Of course, he'd go. If he could be of any help at all, of course, he'd do whatever he could. But for the life of him, he couldn't imagine what it could possibly be. He dismissed it. He'd long since learned not to dwell on the wrong things at the wrong times. When the time was right, he'd find out.

''I'll pack a few things,'' he said.

''That won't be necessary,'' Martin said. ''We'll have you back here tomorrow morning.''

Einar raised an eyebrow. ''How are we traveling?'' he asked. ''Teleportation?''

''By military jet, sir. We have a Saberliner standing by at La Guardia.''

Einar nodded. ''Okay,'' he said. He turned to Birte. ''Lock the door after us,'' he said. ''And keep it locked.''

3

It was 11:47 P.M. when Einar and the two CIC officers arrived at the Pentagon. Einar was at once whisked to the office of Colonel Jonathan Henderson, hurrying through the brightly lit corridors, which he knew stretched on literally for miles. He'd been amazed at the activity in the place. It might as well have been a few minutes before noon as a few minutes before midnight.

He was sitting on a hard, straight-backed chair in the colonel's office, watching the grim officer across the desk. He still had not the vaguest idea of why he was there. Henderson, his graying hair closely cropped, was a man apparently in his fifties, although with military men it was sometimes difficult to tell. Could go a decade one way or the other. So far, the officer had offered no explanation, only proffered a perfunctory thanks for Einar's cooperation. Einar was dead certain the man would have been genuinely startled had his summons not been heeded. He was also aware that the officer was deeply concerned about something.

Henderson looked up at him. "Tell me, Major, briefly if you please, how did you enter the service? The CIC? You were a Danish subject at the time?"

It wasn't what the man said, Einar decided, it was the way the words seemed to taste sour to him. He certainly didn't seem to be overly friendly, his manner just short of being antagonistic. Einar decided to play it straight. Straight—but warily.

"Yes, sir," he said. "I was naturalized in the army."

Henderson nodded. It was somehow a patronizing gesture. "Go on," he said.

"I was born in Denmark," Einar began. "In Copenhagen. My father died in 1931 when I was eleven, and my mother, who was in ill health, placed me in a private school, a boarding school, where I was educated and grew up. I graduated in 1938 and went on to study chemistry at the University of Copenhagen. In the late summer of 1939, when I was nineteen, I came to New York to visit my uncle who lived there, and to attend a special course in chemistry at New York University. My uncle died several years ago. I was in New York when the war broke out in Europe, and when my native country was occupied by the Nazis in April of 1940, I stayed in the States, and after Pearl Harbor I volunteered my services to the armed forces. Because of my knowledge of languages—I speak four fluently and have a good knowledge of two more—I was placed in the Military Intelligence Service, ending up in the CIC. I was accepted for OCS a—"

"I know your military record, Major," Henderson interrupted. He put his hand on a file folder on the desk before him. It was open. "Have it right here." He looked soberly at Einar. "I suppose you are wondering why we asked you here on such damned short notice."

Einar nodded, a wry little smile on his lips. "Wondering?" he said. "More like totally mystified."

Henderson contemplated him pensively for a moment. "What I'm about to tell you, Munk, will remain strictly confidential. Is that understood?"

"Yes, sir."

"Yesterday afternoon," Henderson said, glancing at his watch. It was just past midnight. "Or rather on May 9," he corrected himself, "at about 1500 hours, an elderly man was run over on Second Avenue in New York City. He was taken to an emergency facility, where he died. His name was Karl Johann Thompson."

Einar stared at the colonel. He was thoroughly puzzled. It was not at all what he'd expected to hear. Although, what *had* he expected? He was intrigued. What had a traffic accident to do with the CIC? With him? Did they think *he* ran the man down? If so, why the CIC involvement? Was the man one of theirs? It still didn't make sense. Who the hell was Karl Johann Thompson?

"I don't know the man," he said.

Henderson waved an impatient hand. "Didn't expect you to," he said. "Hear me out."

"All right."

"The man was conscious when he was admitted to the emergency room," Henderson went on, his voice clipped and direct. "But he was apparently incoherent. He rambled. Some of what he said could be understood, other words were—incomprehensible." He picked up a little notebook and showed it to Einar. It had a green cover with a red rose in one corner. "A student nurse took down the . . . eh . . . ramblings of the man before he died. She copied the unintelligible words phonetically."

Henderson paused. He looked at the notebook in his hand, a worried frown on his face. He replaced the notebook on his desk with curious wariness, as if it were somehow fragile. Or dangerous.

"The nurse gave her notebook to one of the police officers who brought the victim in," he proceeded. "The officer glanced through it, and because some of the phrases it contained were . . . disturbing, he turned the book over to his sergeant."

"How . . . disturbing?" Einar asked, intrigued despite himself.

"There seemed to be a . . . a threat," Henderson answered. "The man called out things like, 'Any day now! All die!' He seemed to intimate that some dreadful, large-scale catastrophe was about to happen. A disaster against which there'd be no hope of resistance. A terror of unimagined scope. Or so it seemed."

A bomb, Einar thought. A terrorist bomb. They think this guy has planted a powerful bomb somewhere. In New York. "Have you—"

Henderson interrupted him. "Let me finish," he said curtly. He looked straight at Einar. "The precinct sergeant—because of the implied threat of violence—turned the notebook over to the FBI."

Einar stared at him. The damned plot is thickening, he thought. The FBI?

"In analyzing the . . . the phonetic words in the notebook," the colonel went on, "the FBI language experts determined that the man spoke partly in German."

"German!" Einar exclaimed. He stopped himself.

"Certain words the man uttered and which had been written down phonetically by the nurse—or as English words—could be German words, such as *find*—"

"The German word *Feind,*" Einar nodded. "Enemy!"

"Exactly. And there were others. *Bald.* It may not have meant a hairless pate," Henderson continued. "According to the FBI."

"In German *bald* means soon," Einar agreed. "If the man spoke with any kind of accent, it could easily have been taken for the English bald."

The colonel eyed him. "You mean, the man may have meant: All die, soon."

Einar nodded. He gazed intently at the officer. The damned plot *was* indeed thickening. Practically solidifying.

"There's more," the colonel resumed dryly. "Phonetic words. The nurse had written, room-bell-karma, for instance. Mean anything to you?"

Einar frowned. He shook his head.

"Think back, Major. To the early 1940s. And the Nazi war effort at that time. If you—"

"Rumpelkammer!" Einar almost shouted the word. "*Rumpelkammer.* I'll be damned. It does sound like room-bell-karma." He gave the colonel a hard look. "It was the German code word for the damned buzz bomb. In 1944. The V-1."

Henderson nodded. "Exactly. And the nurse had also spelled out: fair-ghel-toong—"

"Vergeltung," Einar breathed. "Reprisal."

"—and fair-nick-toong."

"*Vernichtung.* Annihilation!" Einar felt a cold shiver go through him. Forgotten words. Words from the past. "I'll be damned," he whispered.

"She'd jotted down other things," Henderson continued briskly. "A number. The number one thousand."

"As in Thousand Year Reich?" Einar suggested.

"Perhaps. And phonetically, rah-her, which the FBI linguists interpreted as the German *Rache.*"

"Revenge," Einar said. He was totally engrossed. It was a long time since he'd felt so alive, he realized.

"Because of this . . . this apparent threat, the man's residence was searched with more than usual diligence," Henderson continued. "In a wall-socket safe—" He looked at Einar. "You are familiar with the wall-socket safe?"

Einar nodded. "It's a popular stash spot for small items," he said. "A special box in the wall behind an electric outlet. To get to it, all you have to do is loosen the screw that holds the cover plate in place. Usually the outlet is live."

Henderson nodded. "They found a recent telegram. It read: *Any day now!* It was unsigned." He paused. He looked closely at Einar. "There's more," he said. "Another hidden safe was found. In the bathroom door."

"Behind the latch plate," Einar nodded. "A small receptacle set into the hollow-core door. Harder to get at than the outlet stash. Good for permanent or semipermanent stash items." He grinned a crooked little smile. "Not too imaginative. Both stash spots are on a par with the hollow book, or the fake water pipe fitting."

"There was a medal hidden in the door safe," Henderson said. "The Knights Cross with Oakleaves and Swords."

Einar whistled. "Pretty rich."

"Damn near as high as they come," Henderson agreed. "And there was a citation. Made out in Thompson's *real* name. Karl Johann Tollmann."

Einar shook his head. "The name is not familiar," he stated.

"I did not think it would be," Henderson said dryly. "But it *was* familiar to investigators from the Immigration and Naturalization Service. The man was a wanted war criminal."

Einar was startled. "A war criminal!" he exclaimed.

Henderson nodded. "A real SOB, apparently. His case came up in one of the less star-studded Nürnberg trials following the Goering-Hess show. He was a Nazi naval officer. Served in the *Kriegsmarine*. Seems that early in the war, when he was in charge of a detail of men assigned to pick up the crew of an English freighter, sunk in the Channel, he ordered his men to machine-gun the sailors as they clung to their lifeboats and floundered in the water. There were no survivors." He gave Einar a narrow look. "He was convicted in absentia at Nürnberg and sentenced to death."

Einar frowned at the officer. "Sir," he said slowly. "I still don't see how I come into all this. How I can . . . help?" He looked searchingly at Henderson. "Why me?"

"The telegram," Henderson said. "The unsigned telegram, which simply said: *Any day now.* It was sent from a town called Weiden. In Germany. Ring a bell?"

Einar sat up. "It does. I was stationed near Weiden. During the final weeks of the war. When I was with the CIC."

Henderson nodded. "When the Immigration people were notified of the case, because of the involvement of a former Nazi officer, someone over there remembered Weiden. And a certain case near there. Toward the end of the war. It involved a factory. A chemical factory."

Einar remained silent. He just stared at the colonel. He could feel the surge of adrenaline course through him. It was a feeling he hadn't experienced for many years. He suddenly knew he'd missed it.

"A report had been forwarded to the Army Interrogation Center of the Third Army," Henderson was saying. "A report from an agent in the field. It was located. It was yours."

Einar let his breath out slowly. He'd known what the colonel would say—and yet, unconsciously, he'd held his breath.

"Colonel, I—"

Henderson held up his hand. "Let me finish. Then you can have your say."

Einar fell silent.

"To summarize," Henderson said crisply. "The incoherent ravings of a delirious accident victim seem to hint at an impending cataclysm. The victim turns out to be a fugitive Nazi war criminal." The officer looked Einar directly in the eyes. "Mind you, I personally think it's all a lot of nonsense. I think it was simply the deranged babblings of a man in deep shock. Out of his mind. But some little undersecretary of defense—" Einar raised an eyebrow. "Yes," Henderson acknowledged, "it's gone all the way. Some eager beaver at the department, hoping to prove his worth by discovering doomsday in vivid decorator colors, ordered a full investigation. That's why you are here." He peered at Einar. "And we are, of course, working closely with Fort Mead. The National Security Agency," he explained loftily, as if Einar obviously wouldn't know.

Einar nodded. "Well and good, Colonel," he said. "But . . . once again. Why me?"

Henderson sat back in his chair. "Because of one more word jotted down as an English word by the student nurse," he said soberly. "A word that has many different meanings in different languages. A word that I think will have a special meaning for you, Munk." He leaned forward. He locked eyes with Einar.

"The word is—*gift!*"

Instantly Einar was catapulted forty years back into the past. He could see the emaciated body of the Polish slave worker he was questioning. In Weiden. He could see the man's drawn face and the sunken, haunted eyes that somehow looked too big for the face, regarding him fearfully—and he could see the thin, bloodless lips mouthing the word—*gift!*

The German word for *poison.*

4

Rigid and appalled, Einar sat staring at the colonel, but his mind was back in Weiden, a small German town hard on the Czechoslovakian border, forty years before, April 22, 1945 . . .

Then, too, he'd sat rigid and appalled, listening to the terrifying tale told to him by a frightened Polish forced laborer. The man had been working in the huge dump of Nazi CWS munitions discovered near Grafenwöhr three days before when American troops overran the place. The colossal depot, hidden in a forest, had contained over three million poison gas projectiles, mines, and storage drums. The boys from Chemical Warfare had had their hands full. But that was not what had grabbed his attention. It was the man's description of where he had worked before he'd been sent to the CWS dump. It had been in a factory manufacturing chemicals, located in the mountains a few miles east of Weiden in the Sudetenland, still in German hands.

It was a secret plant, he'd said. A plant that had developed and produced poison gas. A new type of a lethal poison gas with hideous, undreamt-of capacities of annihilation, stored in specially constructed metal drums of an unusual design. He'd told of foreign scientists forced to work on the project. He'd told of one such scientist who had killed himself rather than do so. And he'd told of the whispered rumors of the unspeakable horrors the gas could inflict. . . .

Einar stared at the colonel. "Poison," he said. "Poison gas . . ." Even to himself, his voice sounded curiously constricted, as if loath to utter the dreaded words.

"That's what your report stated." Henderson pulled a sheet of yellowed paper from the file folder in front of him. "A new and deadly poison gas," he quoted.

Slowly Einar nodded. His thoughts were awhirl. Poison gas. Dear God! Did they suspect that the dead Nazi war criminal had threatened that some sort of poison gas would be released? In New York? He shuddered. It sounded incredible. But then, so did many of the reported acts of terrorism carried out all over the world.

"I have orders to go over your report with you," Henderson said, a touch of resentment coloring his voice. "In detail." He looked questioningly at Einar. "How well do you remember the incident, Munk?" he asked. "And the subsequent mission? It's a long time ago."

Einar looked at the officer, his gaze solemn. Some things even time cannot erase.

"I remember it, Colonel," he said quietly. "I remember it well . . ."

* * *

The scribbled heading on his notepad read: "Weiden, 23 April 45. GRUBER, HEINRICH." The page was already half-filled with notes, points to press with the interrogation subject standing stiffly before him—points to check in the *Order of Battle* book. Weiden had been taken only two days before, and there were still plenty of fish in the barrel—such as this one in front of him, so desperately trying to appear confident. Ten to one, the bastard had something to hide. Something at least *he* thought important. Einar had that hunch every CIC agent in the field had developed. He *knew* when a subject was lying. In every instance when he'd thought so, he'd been right. Of course, he admitted to himself, if to no one else, there was no way of knowing how many times a Kraut shithead had slipped through because his hunch hadn't been aroused at all. But this guy, his papers in order, his story plausible, had something to hide. He'd stake his left ball on it.

He was just about to shoot a biting question at the prisoner when the door to the interrogation room opened. He looked up in annoyance. It was Sergeant Murphy. Dammit! The guy should know better than to barge in on an interrogation. He might blow the whole damned thing. He was about to tell the noncom off, when the man said, "Sorry, sir. It's urgent!" He handed Einar a piece of paper.

Einar glanced at it. He frowned. "Take the prisoner away, Murph," he said. "Keep him on ice for me."

"Sure thing, sir."

As the two men left the room, Einar once again looked at the paper. A TWX. Orders. From XII Corps HQ:

REPORT CIC HQ ICEBERG FORWARD IMMEDIATELY REPEAT IMMEDIATELY. LEE.

Einar stared at it. What the hell did that mean? Immediately? And the signature. Lee. Not Major Herbert Lee, CO, CIC, Det. 212. Just—Lee. Herb must have been in one hell of a hurry.

He'd take the jeep. Iceberg Forward, the forward headquarters echelon of XII Corps, was at the moment located in Bayreuth, less than fifty miles to the northwest. He'd be there in an hour and a half. At most.

It was 1745 hours when Einar barreled into Bayreuth. He'd taken the route over Neustadt-Kemnath and made good time. Bayreuth. The home of Richard Wagner and the famous Wagnerian Opera Festivals. He'd always been interested in opera. Especially Wagner. Although he at times found him a little bombastic.

When he'd been in Bayreuth before, just after the burg had been taken on April 14, he'd shot through and seen none of the sights. And now, dammit! His orders read: "Immediately!"

He drove past Villa Wahnfried, the celebrated home of Richard Wagner and later his son, Siegfried. Shit! It was chow time, and Herb would probably be feeding his face anyway. A couple of minutes wouldn't hurt, and he might never get a second chance. So why not pull the steel-helmet-tourist bit? He hardly ever did.

He stopped the jeep.

Villa Wahnfried seemed to have escaped damage. It wasn't until he walked to the rear of the house that he saw that half of it had collapsed. He couldn't resist going inside. Booby traps? Hell, it was possible, but chances were the place had been cleared.

He went in.

In the wreckage of a large room, he found Wagner's grand piano, miraculously undamaged. He looked it over and got a kick out of discovering that the great German opera composer had used an American-made Steinway piano. The big, black instrument with its intricately carved legs was dated New York, 1876! *Parsifal,* created between 1877 and 1882, he knew, might have been composed on it. He touched the keys and felt just a little bit awed.

When he left the place a few minutes later, he felt somehow fortified, ready to face anything old Herb had to dish out.

But all the same he was brought up short when he walked into his CO's office without knocking. Streeter himself, the Corps AC of S, G-2, Colonel Richard F. Streeter, was sitting with Lee, both men looking grim. And there was a third man present. A captain. A pilot.

"What kept you?" Lee growled.

"Sir. I—" Einar was taken aback. What the hell was up?

"Never mind," Streeter snapped. He rose from his chair. "Let's go!"

Led by the G-2, the four men hurriedly walked down the corridor from the CIC office. Once again Einar was startled when they stopped at the office of the Corps Chief of Staff, Brigadier General Ralph E. Maxwell. They went right into the outer office and were at once ushered into the inner sanctum of the Chief of Staff by an aide.

General Maxwell was seated behind his desk. He looked up as the officers entered. He glanced with curiosity at Einar.

"Is this the man?" he asked.

"Yes, sir," Colonel Streeter answered.

"Has he been briefed?"

"Not yet."

Maxwell got up. He walked to a group of chairs around a square table in a corner of the room. "Pull up a chair," he said.

They all sat down. Einar, increasingly puzzled, watched the general. This has got to be pretty high-powered stuff, he thought. Maxwell does not involve himself personally in the lesser doings of CIC agents.

Maxwell indicated the pilot. "Have you met Captain Williams?" he asked Einar.

"No, sir."

"He'll be flying you to SHAEF," Maxwell said. "Within the hour."

Einar nodded at the captain. He was startled as hell, trying not to show it. SHAEF! he thought. Supreme Headquarters Allied Expeditionary Forces. Were they kidding? What in the name of Little King Shit on Earth would he be doing at Ike's Supreme Headquarters?

"You will leave directly from here," Maxwell went on. "Don't worry about your gear. You will be issued anything you need at SHAEF."

"Yes, sir," Einar acknowledged.

"Your orders have already been cut," the general continued crisply. "Over my signature." He nodded toward the officer who had shown them in. "Smitty, here, my aide, will give them to you." He gave Einar a penetrating look. "You will receive your final briefing at SHAEF," he said. "From Colonel Lawrence Schneider. No need for you to know anything more at this point."

He stood up. The others followed suit. Maxwell turned to Einar. "I just wanted to meet you before you left," he said. He held out his hand. "And to wish you good luck."

Einar shook his hand. "Thank you, sir."

"Do the damned best you can, son," Maxwell finished. "Make the corps proud of you."

"Yes, sir."

The thoughts raced about in Einar's mind, tripping over each other. Good luck—with what? Do your best—up against what? Final briefing—on what? It was beginning to get to him, all that crap about no NTK—no need to know.

Outside in the corridor, he buttonholed his CO.

"What the hell is going on, Herb?" he asked. "SHAEF, for crissake! Why? What am I supposed to do there? Some kind of glorified latrine duty?"

"Calm down," Lee tried to pacify him. "I know no more than you. All I know is that your presence at SHAEF was ordered—by top brass—and pronto." He looked at Einar.

"I have no idea if they want to canonize you—or castrate you. You'll find out when you get there."

5

The Forward Command Post of SHAEF had been established by General Eisenhower only a few months before in the cathedral city of Rheims. This ancient town lies eighty-five miles northeast of Paris on the Vesle River and the Marne-Aisle Canal in the heart of France's Champagne country. Tunneled into the chalk formations that underlie the district is a labyrinth of cellars for storing the wine. Since the fifth century the kings of France had been crowned in the city, including Charles VII, at whose coronation another, earlier military commander, fighting on French soil, stood by his side—Joan of Arc.

The town had been badly damaged during the war, but the thirteenth-century cathedral and most of the other important historical buildings had escaped unscathed, and so had a large technical school, the College Moderne, where SHAEF was located in a big, red-brick building. The office of Colonel Lawrence Schneider was on the second floor, overlooking a courtyard.

Einar was taken to him immediately.

Schneider was a large, ruddy-faced man, who somehow looked out of place behind a desk. His eyebrows almost met across the bridge of his nose; his eyes were searching and penetrating as they regarded Einar, standing before him. There was another officer in the room, but Schneider did not introduce him. Einar noticed that the man was a British officer, a crown and a pip on his shoulder strap. A lieutenant colonel.

"Sit down, Lieutenant," the colonel said. "*I* have some questions to ask. *You* will answer them."

Schneider had a reputation for getting things done without any waste of time because he always came straight to the point. No one was better at unraveling red tape. And any really knotty problem got what he called his "Alexander treatment"; it was cut through as ruthlessly as Alexander's Gordian knot.

Schneider fixed Einar with his piercing eyes. "First, your knowledge of chemistry?" he snapped.

"Three years of study, sir," Einar answered promptly. "University of Copenhagen and New York University."

Schneider made a brief note.

"Your language abilities?" he asked briskly. "Besides English, what languages do you speak fluently?"

"German, French, and Danish," Einar answered.

"You were born in Denmark? Educated there?"

"Yes, sir. I graduated from a boys' boarding school. Bavnehøj Kostskole."

"You have any family in Denmark? Father? Mother?"

"Both dead, sir."

"Brothers? Sisters?"

"None, sir."

"Well?"

Einar shrugged. "A couple of cousins," he said. "We never saw each other much. We were never close."

Schneider nodded. His penetrating eyes bored into Einar. "Do you still have friends in Denmark?"

"Yes, sir."

"Friends you can trust?"

"Yes, sir. Two friends from my school days. We've kept in touch until the war made it impossible."

"Their names?"

Einar was startled. He had not expected that question. No reason not to answer, though. "Torben Kvistholm and Lars Olesen." And what the hell did a SHAEF chicken colonel want with *that* bit of hot information?

"Where do they live?" Schneider persisted.

"In Copenhagen, sir. Both of them."

Again Schneider nodded, apparently satisfied. Again he made a notation.

"You volunteered your services after Pearl Harbor?" he continued. "You were recruited for the OSS?"

"Yes, sir."

"Which branch? SI or SO? Or was it . . . research?" There seemed to be a hint of disdain in Schneider's voice. It was not lost on Einar.

"Secret Intelligence, sir," he answered stiffly. "Although I was trained for both SI and Special Operations."

"I see." Schneider consulted the papers in front of him.

Papers, Einar thought, always papers. The lifeblood of intelligence.

Schneider suddenly frowned. He looked up at Einar, narrow-eyed.

"You . . . left OSS shortly after your training period was completed." His eyes were cold as they regarded Einar. "Before you could be assigned a mission. And you were inducted into the army. I want to know why you found it necessary to leave the OSS. Your full reason." He paused. "Even though it may be . . . distasteful for you to discuss it."

No, you bastard, Einar thought, it wasn't because I couldn't cut the mustard. "Sir," he said, looking straight ahead to show his affront at the colonel's intimation. "As you know, the Office of Strategic Services was not a military operation. Wild Bill Don—I mean, General William Donovan formed it—"

"Your reason for leaving OSS, Lieutenant!" Schneider broke in sharply. "You seem to find it difficult to answer that question." Schneider's voice was icy with ill-disguised scorn. "Why?"

Give me a chance, Einar thought. I was just about to answer it, dammit! He was getting angry. What the hell was going on? The damned colonel was goading him. Deliberately goading him. Why? He was about to protest—but controlled himself.

"I was trained for operations in my native country, Denmark, sir," he answered evenly, his tone of voice matter-of-fact. "After my training, before I was assigned to my first mission, operations in the Scandinavian countries became the province of the SOE, the British counterpart of the OSS." It was all he could do not to glance toward the silent British officer observer, who sat motionless to his right, out of his line of sight. "I was given the choice of transferring to British jurisdiction as an OSS agent or entering the U.S. armed forces. I had just become a U.S. citizen, and I elected to remain in the service of the United States. I was inducted into the army—the Military Intelligence Service."

"Sounds very . . . admirable, Lieutenant Munk." Schneider's voice dripped sarcasm.

Einar kept staring straight ahead. Damn that bastard if he was going to get a rise out of him. The ass-breath probably spent most of his time sitting on his brain behind a desk. Probably couldn't find his own shadow if they put him in the field.

"Go on, Lieutenant," Schneider prodded.

"After my MIS training I was sent to Officer Candidate School and was commissioned," Einar went on, his voice cold but controlled. "I was assigned to the CIC, and after additional training I was shipped to the ETO, assigned to CIC Detachment 212, XII Corps."

Schneider nodded. He studied the junior officer before him. So far so good. The young man could keep himself under control. Didn't rile easily.

"In the OSS," he said, continuing his questioning. "What were some of the courses you took?"

Once again Einar was surprised. What the hell *was* that damned chicken colonel driving at? From schoolboy friends to OSS training? With a sprinkling of chemistry and linguistics thrown in.

"High explosives," he answered. "Demolition. Parachute jumping and infiltration. Cryptology. Communications. Morse code. The X-35.

Firearms—ours and theirs. Close combat. Interrogation." He thought for a moment. What the hell else? "Orientation—maps. Chemical warfare. Surveillance—and how to avoid it. Sabotage. Lock picking, that sort of thing. Booby traps." He stopped. Enough was enough.

Schneider picked up a piece of paper. He handed it to Einar. "That yours?" he asked.

Einar took the paper. It was a copy of his report concerning a chemical plant in the Sudetenland and a possible new type of poison gas developed there. He'd forwarded it to the Army Interrogation Center. How the hell did it get to SHAEF? And why? He was puzzled.

"Yes, sir," he said. "It is."

Schneider looked at him speculatively. "I've read it. Was your informant telling the truth?" he asked quietly.

For a moment Einar was silent.

"I believed him," he answered evenly.

Schneider seemed to relax. He closed the file that had been lying open before him. For a brief moment he contemplated Einar.

"Lieutenant," he said with Ciceronian rhetoric, "I need not remind you that everything said here is classified. Top secret."

"Yes, sir."

"Let me put you in the picture," the colonel went on, his abrasiveness gone. "That report of yours. We have had others. They seem to corroborate what your informant stated. Intelligence has been able to identify only one of the foreign scientists mentioned. The man who committed suicide. An act that fortunately left records that could be traced. He was a Dane, Lieutenant. A Professor Aksel Eigil Meyer. He may have been a former coworker of Niels Bohr's." He gave Einar a questioning look. "You know who Bohr is?"

"Yes, sir," Einar answered. "A top Danish scientist. A physicist."

"Correct," Schneider said. "What else do you know about him?"

Einar frowned in concentration. Quite a bit, actually. Bohr was, after all, a fellow Dane, and he'd been interested in reading about him. "I know he received the Nobel Prize in physics when he was only thirty-seven," he said. "Some time in the early 1920s. I know he had his laboratory in Copenhagen, and I know he escaped to Sweden from the Nazis occupying my coun—occupying Denmark. And I remember reading that he'd gone to England. In 1943, I think it was. They said he made the trip strapped in the bomb bay of a Mosquito bomber."

Schneider nodded. "You are well informed," he acknowledged.

Again he fixed Einar with his penetrating eyes. "Bohr is now in the

United States,'' he told him. ''Working on a top-secret project they call the Manhattan Project. He's virtually impossible to reach.''

He sat back in his chair. ''And that is where our problem lies, Lieutenant.'' He paused for a moment, as if formulating what he was about to say.

''Here's the situation,'' he finally said. ''There have been reports that Hitler and his gang are planning a last-ditch effort to turn the war around. A last-minute, all-destructive secret weapon that will make his V-1 and V-2 reprisal weapons look like children's toys, with the destructive power of a paper kite.'' He took a deep breath. He suddenly looked grim—and tired.

''Ordinarily we'd dismiss such rumors as typical Goebbels hogwash,'' he said, ''except for a series of several separate yet related events. Your report, Lieutenant, about that possible new poison gas, and other reports corroborating it. The plant described in your report is just across the border to Czechoslovakia. You know the restraining lines directives. We can't cross—yet. Anyone's guess when we can get in there. There was a sudden brief spurt of unusually heavy radio traffic in the area around Weiden, which stopped completely some weeks ago. And finally, the identification of the Danish scientist.'' He gazed at Einar, who was watching him intently.

''It is possible,'' Schneider continued. ''It is possible that we do face a last-minute act of desperation by the Nazis. Their war is all but lost now. If—*if* there is a Nazi undertaking involving poison gas, especially a new type of gas that we may not know how to combat, it may indeed be catastrophic. Certainly Hitler is not above unleashing a death that could destroy all of England and half the continent—if he could. The question is—can he?''

Again he leaned forward, his eyes fixed on Einar.

''That Danish scientist who was possibly Bohr's associate might well be the key. If we can find out exactly what his background is, his special field, what he was working on when the Nazis abducted him and shipped him to that plant in Germany. If we knew that, we might have the missing piece of the damned puzzle.''

He paused. He frowned. ''It is not possible for us to contact Bohr for the answers. If, in fact, he has them. By the time we could penetrate his cover and that of the project he's working on, it would be too late. But the answers may lie in Denmark. In Copenhagen. It is too late to mount and brief either an OSS or an SOE mission and provide it with effective underground contacts in Denmark.''

Again he paused. He looked straight at Einar.

"What we need is someone who is trained as an agent, capable of operating clandestinely. Someone who has a good grip on himself and doesn't easily get his balls in an uproar." He had a slight smile on his face, a smile that was quickly extinguished as he went on. "Someone who has a working knowledge of chemistry and who can speak Danish well enough to pass for a Dane. Someone who already has reliable contacts in Copenhagen—and who would be willing to undertake the mission. At once."

For a moment Einar stood silent. He felt the colonel watching him intently. He was aware of the unseen British officer's eyes upon him.

"Sir," he said finally. "If I am acceptable, I'd like to take it on."

He'd done it. For the second time he'd volunteered—flying directly in the face of the sound GI adage: never volunteer!

Colonel Schneider turned to the British lieutenant colonel. "Stokeley," he said brightly. "He's all yours."

Einar shifted his eyes to the British officer.

What the hell had he gotten himself into now?

Lieutenant Colonel John Stokeley stood up. He walked over to Einar. "Come along, then," he said pleasantly. "Next stop, London." He grinned. "By tomorrow we'll have you back in your native Copenhagen!"

Einar stopped his narrative. He was surprised how vivid his recollections were. Colonel Henderson watched him through steepled fingers as he finished his story.

"Well and good, Munk," he said. "What we want now is an exact account of what went on during that mission to Denmark back in 1945." He slapped his open hand down on the file folder on his desk. "Of course, I've read your official report written at the time. A bit—truncated," he observed condescendingly. "What I want now are details, intimate details. Details that may not have seemed sufficiently significant to you then for inclusion in your report, but may now in the light of today's happenings." He looked sour. "At least, that is the opinion of—" He stopped. "It is felt," he corrected himself, "that if—and I repeat *if*—there is any substance whatsoever to the crazy ravings of the ex-Nazi accident victim, it may tie in with the . . . eh . . . the supposed poison gas you reported and that was never located," he finished pointedly.

"I understand."

"And you think you *can* remember?" It was abundantly obvious that Henderson didn't think so.

Einar nodded. He was beginning to get annoyed with the officer's supercilious attitude.

"Colonel," he said quietly. "That mission was one of the most intense experiences of my life. In more ways than one. I remember."

Henderson sighed. He sat back in his chair, resigned.

"I hope it'll give us something to go on," he said dubiously. "As I told you, I personally consider the whole mess a lot of bullshit." He spread his hands. "But . . . you might as well go ahead."

Einar had had enough. He stood up.

"Sir," he said evenly. "As a reserve officer, have I been placed on active duty?"

"No." Henderson frowned at him.

"I am here strictly as a civilian?"

"Yes."

"Then, Colonel Henderson, let me tell you that I do not appreciate your overbearing attitude. It was not my idea to come here. I was brought here. Since you obviously feel it is all a wasted effort, and since I have no desire to take up your time nor waste my own with something you consider bullshit, if you will arrange for my transportation, I shall return home. Right now."

Henderson had slowly colored until he glowed noticeably crimson. Two veins in his temples stood out like pale blue snakes. He took a deep breath.

"Sit down!" he snapped. He caught himself. "Please." For a moment he was quiet. "If there *is* a threat," he said slowly. "If that man was not just raving. If something . . . catastrophic *is* about to happen, we must know. I am sure you will want to cooperate."

Slowly Einar sat down again. I'll cooperate, you overbearing bastard, he thought.

It *was* a long time ago. But he had not forgotten. He never would.

He wondered. A decades-old case had been resurrected from oblivion. Was it a piece of history that came to naught?

Or was it still alive? And dangerous?

Perhaps the past *would* provide a clue.

6

The drive from the airfield to one of the old manor houses north of London taken over by "the firm" had been a bit hairy, as Einar's companion, Lieutenant Colonel Stokeley, put it. Blackout regulations were strictly enforced in wartime England but hadn't inhibited the driver of the staff car who had been waiting for them, as he sped down the dark, narrow country roads. And to make it even more hairy for Einar—they drove on the wrong side of the road. "The firm" was, of course, the SOE—the Special Operations Executive—the British espionage organization, or as the operatives were known in the *in* circles, the Baker Street Irregulars, in a sort of left-handed tribute to the original, legendary inhabitant of Baker Street, Sherlock Holmes.

As they passed through the sentry post, drove into the cobblestoned manor house courtyard, and stopped next to an ancient stone-stepped horse mount, the dawn of an overcast day was just beginning to tint the trees with a gray-green pallor. It was 0447 hours, 24 April 1945. Einar had been able to catnap on the way over. After twenty-one hours of no sleep, he'd grabbed a few winks, and he felt refreshed enough to face the hours of intensive briefing he knew awaited him. It was one of the greatest feats his CO, Major Lee, had taught him. Lee never slept. At least not the way normal people did it, at a given length of time during the night. Lee catnapped. Anywhere, at any time, under any conditions. Available for duty twenty-four hours a day, he rested and dozed whenever there was a moment that did not demand his attention. He just closed his eyes and instantly sacked out. Sitting at his desk, lying on the floor in a corner of the war room, or riding in his jeep. Anywhere. Any time. Some said he could even log a few Z's when he stood and pissed at a slit trench.

Einar had learned the trick—except for the slit-trench accomplishment—and it had kept him going through many hectic operations.

He had a strong hunch this would be one time he'd need to make use of it.

As he and Stokeley strode across the spacious, high-beamed entrance hall of the manor house, they passed a uniformed noncom sitting at a desk and looking totally out of place in the atmosphere of historical grandeur. Stokeley waved casually at him as they went by, and the noncom merely nodded. Einar was pleased to see that military formalities were as easygoing in the SOE as they'd been in the OSS. Stokeley turned to him.

"Your conducting officer on the operation," he said, "your control, I believe you chaps call him, will be one of our best. Sergeant Major Ballymore. Roger Ballymore. He has a Pemberley rating of Double A," he added, a touch of awe in his voice. "Chap is cream of the crop. Let me fill you in about him."

They started up a flight of well-worn wooden steps bordered by an intricately carved railing.

"Bally had already completed two missions in France, accomplishing wizard things, when he was parachuted into occupied Holland. A freak gust of wind sent him crashing into a stand of trees, and his right leg got wedged in a fork. The pull of the chute was so strong that it broke his leg, bloody nearly tearing it off.'' He glanced at Einar, who was giving him his full attention. ''Bally managed to free himself from his harness and let himself fall to the ground. He made a tourniquet to staunch the bleeding and managed to crawl to the nearest farmhouse. The farmer, shocked half out of his wits, took him in—but it was obvious the leg had to go.''

Stokeley paused as they entered a sparsely furnished room with big, lead-paned bay windows. A man in civilian clothes, who was sitting at a desk, looked up.

''Scare up Bally, will you, James?'' Stokeley asked.

The man nodded, and with only a glance at Einar, left the room.

''Where was I?'' Stokeley said. ''Ah, yes. It was, of course, imperative that Bally get to a hospital as fast as possible.'' He looked at Einar. ''He also knew that the Dutch hospitals were closely checked by the Germans and that he'd have a deuced difficult time pulling the inconspicuous act. So . . . he had the cheek to have the farmer cart him to the nearest German Army hospital and had the bloody Nazis perform the amputation! Gave them a ruddy cock-and-bull story about being caught in some construction machinery while building fortifications for that Nazi construction crew, the *Organisation Todt.* He knew foreign workers wore civilian clothes, so he was all right on that score, and he told the hospital staff that the armband he was supposed to wear, showing his OT battalion number, had been torn off in the accident. The Heinies swallowed his story and never did catch on. Quite a chap. Tops, actually.''

He gave Einar a sidelong glance. ''You'll get along fine with the fellow,'' he said. ''Sounds a bit rum at times, but don't let that bother you. He's the best.''

The door suddenly was flung open, and a man on crutches came swinging through. Where most amputees wore the empty trouser leg pinned up or cut off, Sergeant Major Roger Ballymore left his hanging free, full length, flapping flamboyantly as he rapidly swung himself along with the agility of a circus acrobat. Most members of the SOE, or the OSS for that matter, were by no stretch of the imagination conformists. Sergeant Major Ballymore went at it with a vengeance.

He swung up to Einar, held out a ham-sized fist, and in a booming voice barked, ''Cheers, mate! Can you swim?''

Einar grinned. He knew at once what the big sergeant major was trying to pull. It was an old, albeit effective, trick. Say something totally unexpected to put your counterpart off balance and observe how he reacts. A sort of one-upmanship game. He grabbed the sergeant's outstretched hand and shook it. It felt like shaking hands with a grizzly.

"I'm Danish," he said brightly. "Haven't you heard?"

He saw the big man size him up in a quick, speculative glance. He didn't know if he passed muster.

"Heard what, mate?" Ballymore asked reluctantly, as if he knew he was being suckered in, but was too curious to let it go.

"I thought everyone knew," Einar said innocently. "All Danes are born on bicycles and immediately tossed into the water to learn to swim."

Ballymore regarded him blandly. "Unless you were born with shoes and knickers on, you might still muck it up, old chap," he stated dryly. "For that's actually how you may get tossed into the drink."

It was a weak comeback. One-up for me, Einar thought. "How so?" he asked.

"Instead of being dropped by parachute, you'll be put ashore from a sub," Ballymore told him.

"Hold on!" Einar protested. "I was told I'd be dropped in. I got my wings. I don't know a damned thing about subs."

"Don't have to, mate," Ballymore said tersely. "The Royal Navy makes a fair go at it."

Einar turned to Stokeley. "What's going on?" he asked. "I thought the mission had a top urgent classification. Why the change? I thought it was imperative for me to get to Copenhagen as fast as possible. A damned sub will take . . . it'll take—"

"Thirty-eight hours," Ballymore supplied calmly.

"Thirty-eight hours—as against, what? Two?" Einar looked at Stokeley. "It doesn't make any damned sense." He glared at Ballymore. "I want to be dropped in!"

"Sorry, mate," Ballymore said firmly. "The decision is—no chute."

Einar scowled at him. He wondered if the sergeant's stubborn stand against parachuting had anything to do with his own aversion to jumping. And his missing leg. Was the man vicariously gun-shy? "How about it, Colonel?" he asked, turning to Stokeley.

The officer looked at Ballymore. "What's up, Bally?" he inquired.

"While you were in the air," the sergeant major replied, "the firm sent its recommendation for the operation to SHAEF. It was approved."

"Fill us in."

"Analysis and evaluation showed it would take a minimum of twenty-four hours to select a proper drop zone, alert the appropriate contacts and set up a safe reception committee,'' Ballymore replied. ''A blind drop was ruled out. Too bloody dicey.''

''Twenty-four is still better than thirty-eight,'' Einar commented sourly.

''You're absolutely right, mate,'' Ballymore agreed. ''It was a contest between safety and urgency, you might say, and safety won out. It would do no bloody good to get you to Denmark in record time—if it meant jeopardizing your safety to the point of probable mission termination. No bloody good to have you caught bang to rights, what?''

''I can take care of myself!'' Einar snapped.

''No doubt you can. If given a chance. It's that chance we're going to give you.''

''How? By dumping me in the water?''

Ballymore grinned. ''The dumping'll be up to you, chum—to some extent, at least.'' He grew sober. ''The sub landings have proved the safest, most efficient method of infiltrating a special loner agent. No need to alert anyone. No need for local preparations. No telltale radio traffic. All sources of possible muck-ups.''

''We'll do it my way,'' Einar said stubbornly. ''Or you can get yourself another boy!''

''Crikey, you're a balky bloke,'' Ballymore observed blandly. ''At least hear me out.'' He turned to Stokeley.

''We'll be using the fisherman,'' he said.

Stokeley nodded. ''Thought so. Optimum safety margin.''

''And who the hell is . . . the fisherman?'' Einar asked.

''Not who,'' Ballymore said. ''What.''

''Then—*what* the hell is it?''

For a moment Sergeant Major Ballymore regarded him.

Then he told him.

When he was finished, Einar nodded soberly. Despite himself he was impressed. Convinced. It was a damned ingenious ploy. In depth. ''Okay,'' he said. ''The fisherman it is.''

''Good show,'' Ballymore beamed. ''Now—before we send you off for your fitting out and to have some pretty pictures taken for your IDs, there're a few things to settle. I want a record of your fist so I can recognize it when you transmit, right?''

''Right,'' Einar nodded.

''We have to select the exact spot for the landing,'' Ballymore went on. He looked at Einar. ''We thought you'd like to pick it, mate. We've selected a general area that's believed to be only lightly patrolled, and it's only forty miles from Copenhagen. Somewhere on the north coast of Zealand.''

''Sjaelland,'' Einar said.

''What?''

''Sjaelland. That's what it's called in Danish.''

''Right. Sjaelland. Any favorite spot?''

''As a matter of fact, there is,'' Einar said. ''Liseleje. It's a small fishing village, a summer resort. On the coast just a few miles north of the town of Frederiksvaerk.''

''You know the place?''

''Sure do. Friends of ours had a cottage four miles up the coast from there. At a place called Tisvildeleje. I spent many summers there as a kid. Helped with the gardening.'' He grinned. ''I didn't exactly have a green thumb. I took care of a little rock garden. Three of them died.''

''You ought to try out for the Brighton Music Hall, chum,'' Ballymore laughed. ''Might make a go of that.''

''How about Liseleje?''

''Liseleje it is, then,'' Ballymore said brightly. ''All that remains now is to give this little outing of yours a code name.'' He looked at Einar. ''What would you suggest, Lieutenant? You're the chap what's going to beat the Danish bushes and drum up the information you're after.''

''You just named it, Sergeant Major,'' Einar grinned.

''What?''

''Drumbeat!''

Ballymore chuckled. ''Operation Drumbeat. Bloody damned right! And you'll be the drummer. That'll be your code name.''

''Deal,'' Einar said.

Sergeant Major Ballymore turned to Stokeley, all business. ''Sir,'' he said. ''If you will arrange for air transportation to the Scapa Flow naval base, I'll take Lieutenant Munk to the haberdasher's. We shall be ready to leave here,'' he said as he consulted his watch, ''in two hours. 0900.''

''Will do, Sergeant Major,'' Stokeley agreed. He turned to Einar. ''If I do not see you before you take off, good hunting!''

Einar shook his hand. ''Thank you, Colonel.''

Stokeley left the room.

''Come along then, Lieutenant,'' Ballymore said as he swung himself toward the door. ''Let's go get you into some clean clothes.''

''Not too clean, I hope. I don't want to stand out like a gigolo among a bunch of stevedores.''

"Clean as far as the operation goes, mate. The muftis we'll be giving you come straight off the backs of Danish refugees." He eyed Einar. "Actually, they may be a bit raunchy. But whatever is found in them will be pure Danish. And that's bloody important. A bit of American tobacco in the lint from a pocket could cost you your bleeding life."

It was drizzling steadily from a leaden sky as Sergeant Major Ballymore and Einar were driven onto the Royal Naval Base at Scapa Flow, situated in the shelter of the Orkney Islands, north of the tip of Scotland. From here many of the operations against the German forces in the North Sea and occupied Scandinavia were launched. Ballymore and Einar had landed only minutes before at the RAF airport, where their ground transportation had been waiting for them. They were taken directly to the submarine pens. There, waiting for them, ready to put to sea, was the HMS *Vanir,* a 545-ton, "V" class submarine, one of the smallest subs in the Royal Navy, with a crew of only thirty-three.

"You'll like the skipper of the *Vanir,*" Ballymore said as he swung along side by side with Einar and they made their way along the wharf to the submarine. "You've got to be a bit bonkers to volunteer to serve in a bloody tin can, but Barney, Lieutenant Commander Bernard Cummings, is a bit of all right."

"You know him?"

"Trained together once," Ballymore nodded. "For a hush-hush caper. Never came off. But we did do a lot of pub crawling, getting noggy. Barney used to muck about with the X-craft at Rothesay. He was in the 12th Submarine Flotilla then. A bloody Coppist."

"You lost me, buddy," said Einar. "X-craft? Coppist?"

Ballymore laughed. "Forgot," he said. "You are a colonial. A coppist is a member of the Combined Operations Assault Pilotry Party. The X-craft is a midget sub. Fifty-two footer. Used to land reconnaissance parties. That sort of operation." He eyed Einar. "You are lucky the bloody things are too slow and the distance you have to go is too great, or you might have ended up in one of the bleeding things. And if you think you'll be crowded on the *Vanir*—the quarters on the X-craft are really confined."

Einar squinted at the submarine he was about to board. Already he felt . . . cooped up. "Guess those contraptions *are* cramped as hell," he said.

"Cramped!" Ballymore boomed, raising an eyebrow. "Listen, mate. They're so bloody cramped that if you have company at the urinal, you can't be sure you're shaking your own cock!"

They had arrived at the gangplank to the *Vanir.* On the bridge stood two officers leaning on the railing. One of them, his cap jauntily perched over his mustachioed face, waved casually at them. On his sleeve Einar could make out the two-and-a-half braid stripes under the loop. That would be Lieutenant Commander Cummings. He was startled to see how young the man looked. A teenager. Twenty at most. He knew he had to be older—and looked it when you got closer. But then—the Royal Navy was probably no different from the U.S. Navy, where submarine crews ranged in age from eighteen to twenty-two. And the officers not much older.

Ballymore waved at the bridge. "Ahoy, Barney!" he shouted. "Here's your man!"

"Bring him aboard," Lieutenant Commander Cummings called.

Ballymore turned to Einar. He rested himself on his crutches and stuck out his hand.

"On your way, then, Lieutenant," he said. "And keep your pecker up!"

Einar shook his hand. "I'll be in touch," he promised.

It was 1217 hours, April 24, when the HMS *Vanir* slipped away from the wharf.

As Einar stood at the hatch ready to climb down into the steel womb that would be his home for the next thirty-eight hours, he glimpsed the odd metal housing bolted to the deck of the sub, just aft of the conning tower.

In a few short hours he'd have to trust it with his life.

It held—the fisherman . . .

It was 0237 hours, April 26, when the HMS *Vanir*, like a smooth, gray leviathan from the deep, surfaced six hundred yards off the coast of northern Sjaelland, directly opposite Liseleje. The sea was calm and the night clear. Running on the surface most of the time for maximum speed, submerging only for the final approach, the *Vanir* had made excellent time.

Einar had used the interim to store up sleep as a camel stores water and he was impatient to get going. He had also familiarized himself with his transmitter, relieved to find that it was not unlike the X-35 on which he'd been trained, only smaller and lighter, the size and shape of a telephone book and weighing a mere three pounds. They'd told him it had been developed by the Danish resistance people. He'd memorized the SOE version of the coded abbreviations for often-used phrases, some of which were different from the ones used by the OSS: QRB—message understood; QRM—interference bad; GRIMI—repeat indicated group. There were dozens of them, including one group he hoped he'd never have to use, the ominous QUO—forced to stop transmitting because of imminent danger! And, of course, the SMB, which was totally meaningless, unless you realized it stood for Sergeant Major Ballymore; a group he would insert in all his transmissions. If he omitted it, no one would notice, but Ballymore would know something was wrong; that Einar might have been burned and was sending under duress by the Germans.

There were dozens of other facts and procedures he'd had to memorize. His cover identity. All his papers were made out in his own name; the address given was an address where he'd actually lived—Sankt Knuds Vej No. 5, st. tv. in the Frederiksberg district of Copenhagen. He remembered well the bicycle sheds in the rear courtyard and the little garden where he'd built a "fort" out of old packing cases when he was a boy. By sticking close to the truth, the risk of slipping up during questioning was kept to a minimum. His occupation was listed as clerk in an *Apotek*—a drugstore—on Gammel Kongevej, not too far from where he "lived." His knowledge of chemistry would enable him to talk a fairly convincing game. His papers also included ration stamps and the necessary passes and permits, such as his *Passértilladelse*—his travel permit—all supplied by the SOE Danish Section.

Clad in his Danish clothes, Einar climbed up on deck just in time to see the crew hauling the fisherman from the special housing.

It was a plain little rowboat, weathered and scuffed, a pair of chipped oars sticking out from the sides. Authentic Danish. It was, in fact, a dinghy from one of the Danish fishing boats that had escaped and was interned in England, supplied by the SOE Danish Section. The fisherman infiltration operation was as simple as it was foolproof. Protection from the word go. Fish were as scarce in Denmark as they were in Germany, and the Danes would often try to catch a few in the early morning hours to augment their daily diet. The Germans were used to this and seldom bothered anyone, except, perhaps, to confiscate a fish or two. Ordinarily the Danes were not stopped and searched unless there was a special reason. And Einar had no intention of supplying one.

He would simply row ashore. In his boat would be a large basket of fish; his transmitter on the bottom of the pile wrapped in a wet, foul-smelling Danish newspaper of a recent date, again courtesy of the SOE Danish Section. If he was intercepted at sea, he'd simply slip the transmitter overboard, and there would be nothing to incriminate him. He would, of course, be unarmed. If he was stopped on shore, his explanation was obvious and commonplace—and few German soldiers relished searching through a basket of smelly fish. It was a snap. No need to play hide-and-seek. He'd be right out in the open, always the best place to hide.

His plan was to walk the four miles to the town of Frederiksvaerk and take the train down to Copenhagen. They'd told him only a few miserably crowded trains were still running—and those were on erratic schedules, but he was optimistic that he could swing it. Alternate plan—steal a bicycle.

It all seemed so straightforward, so easy. Only in the back of his mind stirred the nagging thought that it might not be.

It just might not . . .

But there was not the slightest sign of trouble as Einar hauled the dinghy up on shore. It was 0419 hours, and as far as he could see in the misty twilight, the beach was quiet and peaceful. And deserted. Wavelets lapped lazily at the white sand, and a short distance up from the water's edge stood a shadowy beech forest.

He lifted the fish basket from the boat, slung it over his arm, and started up the beach toward the forest and the country road he knew lay beyond.

Liseleje was about a mile to his right. He'd skirt the village and join the road to Frederiksvaerk just to the south.

He felt buoyed. He was home. For the first time in years, he was once again walking on the soil of his native country. The memories of many happy days spent right on this beach cascaded through his mind, and he felt transported years back in time. With a conscious effort he shook the feeling off.

He was on enemy-occupied ground. It was not the time for daydreaming or reminiscing. It was a time to stay alert.

The forest was soundless and still as Einar rapidly walked along a narrow path. Thanks to the fisherman, Operation Drumbeat was off to a good start.

He rounded a bend in the path—and froze.

In a small clearing directly in front of him, no more than twenty feet away, loomed a massive German tank, the long, ugly-snouted barrel of its 88mm cannon pointing straight down the path.

And straight at Einar.

7

Even in the pale dawn light there was no mistaking what it was.

A P-VI Tiger Tank.

Einar stood stock-still, the fish basket suddenly heavy on his arm.

There was not a sound from the tank. Not a hint of movement. It was unmistakably a Tiger I, but somehow it looked different. Had the Nazis come up with a new model?

Still no sound from it.

Had they seen him?

Slowly, almost imperceptibly, he began to back off the path, inching toward the shadowy protection of the trees, his eyes never leaving the waiting tank. The sweat pooled in his armpits. He breathed through his open mouth to make as little sound as possible.

A few more feet—and he'd be out of sight. His full attention was riveted on the tank. It straddled the path, forbidding, threatening, and impassive before him.

He stepped behind a tree.

Safe.

Suddenly he felt the hard muzzle of a gun pressed into his back. A voice hissed in his ear.

"Stand quite still! Do not make a sound!"

With a shock he realized the voice had spoken in Danish!

A tidal wave of impressions and thoughts instantly assaulted his mind, each clear and crisp, each immediately evaluated and instantaneously decided upon.

Who was his ambusher? Danish police? A HIPO traitor? A German who could speak the language? A sentry from the tank crew? . . . Dismissed. Not of immediate importance. Was the man alone? Probably not. Assume not . . . And chagrin. Not ten minutes into the mission and already he'd made mistake number one. A beaut. He'd been so damned intent on the menace of the German tank that he'd neglected to look out for another. He could only hope it would not be a fatal mistake. For the mission. And for him. And one startling realization. His captor was an amateur. A rank amateur. No professional would push his gun into a subject's back. You never got that close with your weapon. One quick twist by your captive—and you could end up being shot with your own gun. You always kept your distance. If you were a professional.

Should he take him? It would be easy. No. If the man was not alone, it would be fruitless. Play the role. Stick to the cover. Stay in character.

"Don't shoot!" he cried in Danish, obviously terrified. "Please!" He dropped the basket of fish to the ground and shot his hands into the air. "I have done nothing! *Jeg vilde jo bare fange nogen fisk!*—I only wanted to catch some fish!"

The pressure of the gun eased from his back.

"*Vend dig om!*—Turn around!" the voice commanded. "Keep your hands up."

Einar did as he was told, and once again he was shocked by what he saw.

Facing him were four civilians. Children. Boys. The oldest no more than fifteen.

But each had a British-made Sten gun in his hands, cocked and aimed at Einar's gut, and their young faces, still untouched by razors, were hard and grim.

"Who are you?" the oldest demanded, his voice loud and sharp, with the tiniest edge of hysteria.

Einar cringed. Hadn't they seen the damned tank up ahead? "My name is Einar Munk," he answered, keeping his voice low. "There's—keep it down!—there's a German tank, right back there!" He nodded with his head.

To his surprise the boys sniggered. They actually giggled!

"He means *Kakkelovnstanken*—the stovepipe tank," one of them chortled. The others laughed.

Einar was totally puzzled. "What do you mean—stovepipe tank?" he had to ask.

"It's just one of those dummy tanks the Germans have built," the leader told him. "It's nothing but wood and cement. And a stovepipe for a cannon. It's supposed to fool the English reconnaissance planes."

"And they've got a broom handle for a machine gun," one of the others tittered.

Einar cursed himself. He was off to a terrific start. Fooled by a damned stovepipe and a broom handle, and waylaid by a bunch of giggling kids.

The leader looked at him suspiciously. "If you were from around here," he said, "you would know about the *Kakkelovnstank.*" Nervously he fingered the trigger on his gun.

"I'm from Copenhagen," Einar said quickly. "I'm on my way back."

The boy eyed him. "Even in Copenhagen they know about the dummy tanks," he said.

"Han ku' vaere en forbandet Stikker," one of the boys suggested. "He could be a damned informer."

"Or HIPO," another chimed in.

"He could be a German," the first one frowned. "Some of those bastards speak Danish." He stared at Einar. "Maybe even . . . Gestapo."

"I'm not!" Einar exclaimed. "Believe me. I *am* what I say I am."

The boys stood silent, staring at him. They did not seem convinced.

"What'll we do, Peter?" the youngest boy asked the leader. "We can't just leave him here. He'll give us away."

"Shut up, you dumb idiot!" Peter snapped. "I'll think of something."

"Harald is right," one of the boys said. He glared at Einar, his eyes cold. "We . . . we've got to get rid of him."

"I can prove who I am," Einar said quickly. He was getting worried. Kids were unpredictable. You never knew what they might do. Not the best of situations if they also had loaded submachine guns in their hands—and itchy trigger fingers. "I have papers," he added.

"So do the Nazi spies," the leader said. "That means nothing."

"Come on, Peter," one of the boys urged. "We have to do something. We've got less than half an hour to get there."

The fifteen-year-old stared at Einar, his eyes cloudy, showing fear and indecision. Einar realized it would be only seconds before he'd make up his mind. The wrong way. His frustration threatened to choke him. How the hell could he prove that he did come from England—when everything on him had been geared to prove he was a Dane? He had a sudden, desperate idea.

"Wait!" he said, his voice suddenly authoritative. It was not lost on the boys. "Turn that fish basket upside down." The boys looked at the forgotten basket with sudden mistrust. "Go ahead," Einar coaxed.

The youngest, Harald, gingerly toed the basket, as if he were afraid it would blow up in his face.

"Spill out the fish," Einar urged.

Harald did.

With the mess of slithery, shiny fish, Einar's newspaper-wrapped transmitter flopped to the ground. The boys stared at it.

"Unwrap it," Einar instructed them.

One of the boys did. Carefully. He stood with the transmitter in his hand. No one said a word.

"I am a British agent," Einar said calmly. "I am here on a mission. An important mission. What you have in your hands is my transmitter. My radio. My lifeline to my contacts in England. It's up to you what you do with it. And with me. But . . . consider your actions well."

He grew silent. He'd made his pitch.

For a moment the boys looked from the transmitter to Einar and back again. Then Peter spoke.

"You could still be lying," he said uncertainly.

"And I could be telling the truth," Einar countered firmly.

"Then why were you spying on us?"

Einar was genuinely taken aback. "Spying?" he exclaimed. "Hell, I didn't even know you were there!"

From their expressions it was obvious the boys did not believe him.

He looked hard at Peter. "You pointed out yourself that if I was from around here, or from anywhere in Denmark, I should have known about those dummy tanks the Germans have put up. You know I didn't. Doesn't that show you I'm telling you the truth? That I haven't lived in Denmark for a long time? That I come as a friend? From England?"

"Or Germany!" the belligerent boy shot back. He glared at Einar, hate in his eyes. "My brother was in the resistance. In Copenhagen. Someone joined his group. Someone who said he was a friend." He swallowed. "He . . . wasn't. My brother was shot!" His Sten gun trembled in his hands.

"Listen—"

"We've listened enough!"

"Hold it, Valdemar," Peter broke in. "Let him talk."

"I am not lying to you," Einar said earnestly. "I—"

"You don't even *sound* English." It was Valdemar again.

Einar looked up sharply. Shit!

"I'm not," he acknowledged. "I am an American. Born in Denmark. I am working with the English."

"Another clever . . . explanation," Valdemar said. "They sure come easy to you."

"I'm telling you the damned truth," Einar said. "You've got my transmitter. Look at it. I got it in England."

Peter took the transmitter from his comrade. He examined it. He looked up at Einar, his eyes angry.

"It was made right here in Denmark," he said flatly. "It is one of the Duus-Hansen transmitters. I recognize it. The resistance use it." He regarded Einar with hostile eyes. "Anyone . . . any German could have gotten hold of one. Easily. Especially the Gestapo!"

With a sinking feeling Einar knew the boy was right. The damned transmitter *was* Danish. Although that particular one had been made in England, it was modeled after the special, compact transmitter developed by the Danish resistance. They'd told him. A prototype had been smuggled to England for duplication. Dammit! He'd waded right into mistake number two.

"We'd better get rid of him," said Valdemar.

Peter seemed hesitant.

Einar decided it was time to take the offensive. "If you do," he said harshly, "London will have your hides!" He scowled at the four boys. "What are you doing here, anyway? And where did you get those Stens?"

"They were dropped," Peter said defiantly. "By the English. They were for the resistance." He looked uncomfortable. "They . . . they missed picking up one of the canisters," he explained, "and we found it." He looked at Einar, rebelliously. "We have formed our own resistance group," he declared. "We are the Rolf Krake group."

"He was a great Viking hero," Harald, the youngest boy, interjected proudly.

"We have as much right to the guns as anyone else," Peter finished.

"We're going to do a job," Harald said excitedly. "Tonight."

"Shut up, you idiot!" Valdemar warned him.

A job? Einar thought. What the hell were the damned kids up to? "Are you?" he asked. "What kind of a . . . job?" He looked straight at Peter. He lowered his hands. No one objected.

The boy hesitated.

"Go ahead," Valdemar mocked. "Blow the whole damned thing! You might as well. It won't make a shit of difference. Either he's okay—or we kill him. He won't do much talking either way."

"There's an airfield," Peter told Einar.

"An airfield?" Einar frowned. It had not been in his briefing.

"Just a small one. Up in Tisvilde Hegn. Not far from here." He pointed. "That way. It's not much of a field, but there's a radio tower there. The Germans get weather reports and things like that. It's important to them." Peter drew himself up. "Tonight we are going to blow it up!" he declared. "We have the explosives, too. Satchel charges."

Oh, shit! Einar thought. Kid saboteurs. Get themselves killed or caught. And put the whole damned area on the alert in the process. He needed that like he needed fat Goering for a partner.

"Maybe you'd better give that a second thought," he suggested. "Besides, London might not want you to do it."

"Why not?" Peter exclaimed, offended. "The freedom fighters carry out sabotage actions all the time!"

Better back off, Einar thought. Or the damned, hepped-up kids might clamor for his head again.

"What makes you think you can pull it off?" he asked.

"We've watched them," Peter told him. "The best time to hit them is five o'clock in the morning. There are only two guards then. And they're tired. Just waiting for their relief at six. Between midnight and four, the hours they think are the most dangerous, there are four guards. So five o'clock is best."

Einar looked with new respect at the boy. The fellow seemed to know what he was doing.

"If five o'clock is the time," he suggested, "you'd better get going."

"Yeah."

"What about him?" Valdemar objected. "We can't just leave him here. He knows too much."

Peter looked undecided.

"We could . . . tie him up," Harald said.

"Idiot!" the belligerent one shouted. "He *knows* us, doesn't he?"

Harald looked crestfallen.

Peter slowly backed away from Einar.

Einar had no choice. "I will come with you," he said. "I can be of help. I was trained for this sort of thing."

Peter looked at him speculatively. "Okay," he said.

"Are you crazy?" Valdemar exclaimed. "Suppose he *is* a *Stikker?* Or Gestapo?"

"Suppose he is not?" Peter bristled. "Suppose he really *is* from England?"

"We can't take him along." Valdemar was adamant.

"Okay," Peter said. "Then *you* kill him! Or *hold Kaeft!*—or shut up!"

For a moment Valdemar stood silent. His fingers spasmodically crawled on the steel of his Sten gun. None of the boys seemed to breathe. Einar locked the boy's eyes with his, as the seconds ticked by. The boy looked away.

"Awrh, the devil with it!" he spat out. "You are an idiot, Peter, but . . . let him come along. He can prove he really *is* a British agent."

"You can watch him," Peter suggested.

"Damn right!" Valdemar agreed. "You bet I'll watch him."

It was just after five when the group arrived at the airport. In a corner of the little field, near a row of barrackslike huts, stood the radio tower, reaching its iron limbs into the overcast sky.

They stopped at a tall, heavy wire fence topped with barbed wire.

"You have wire clippers?" Einar whispered.

"No," Peter shook his head. "We couldn't get any."

"Dammit! You can't get over that fence."

"I know that," Peter said. "But we can get under it." He looked at Einar. "We tried it. I read an English manual," he went on. "It was in the drop canister. It said—always look for the obvious. Look for the key under the mat and see if the door is unlocked before you break it down to get in, that sort of thing. It seemed obvious to me that if you couldn't get over the fence—maybe you could get under it. The ground is mostly sand around here. It's easy to dig. The Germans didn't think of that."

Einar stared at the boy. He suddenly understood why he had become the leader of the group. Dammit! The guy might even do well at B-2. Or Pemberley.

Peter was right. Less than ten minutes later, the boys had dug a small tunnel under the fence, big enough to wiggle through.

The morning mist was rolling in from the sea and gave them a modicum of concealment as they cautiously and silently headed for the shadowy radio tower.

They had just passed a small building, its windows dark, when suddenly the powerful beams of two strong torches imprisoned them. A gruff, gutteral voice called, "*Halt! Oder ich schiesse!*—Halt! Or I shoot!"

They were caught. Bang to rights, as Sergeant Major Ballymore would have put it.

Einar's mind raced wildly. This was the real thing. The real enemy. He wasn't playing with kids now. What to do? Shoot it out? Impossible. He was unarmed—the boys would be mowed down. And so would he. *Ballymore!* The thought literally exploded in his mind. Audacity! Pull something brazen, totally unexpected. Like Sergeant Major Ballymore. Hagerstown! That OSS training mission at Fairchild Aircraft. He'd nearly botched that one. He'd make it work now.

Quickly he turned to the four boys who stood petrified behind him. "Do exactly as I say," he hissed. "No questions!"

He turned back into the bright beams of the flashlights. They effectively blinded him. He could not see his enemies. He drew himself up, clicked his heels, and flinging up his right arm in the Nazi salute, he cried, "Heil Hitler!"

He turned to the boys. In a loud, authoritative voice he ordered, "You know the routine. Put your weapons down—carefully this time. We'll need them again. And hands on top of your heads. *Los!*"

For a brief moment the boys stood staring at him. Then Peter put his Sten gun on the ground. The others quickly followed suit. They all placed their hands on their heads.

Einar turned back toward the flashlight beams.

"Well done!" he called. He looked at his watch. "Three minutes and twenty seconds. *Prima!*"

"What the devil is going on?" the gruff, gutteral voice demanded. The flashlight beams were turned toward the ground, and two German *Wehrmacht* soldiers, MP-38 Schmeisser submachine guns on the ready, appeared to the group.

"I am *Hauptman* Leopold Richter," Einar said. He was speaking perfect German, a touch of arrogance in his voice. He took his wallet from his hip pocket, flipped it open for a second and put it back. "*Abwehr III*—counterintelligence, *Sicherheitsabteilung Zealand*—Security Section Zealand. We are conducting a vulnerability test. Probing the alertness factor of your station." He nodded imperiously. "You are to be commended," he said. He peered at the shoulder strap of the soldier apparently in charge. "*Obergefreiter*—what is your name?"

"Pregler, Gerhardt." The response was automatic.

The corporal stared at Einar. "Herr *Hauptman*," he said uncertainly. "Vulnerability test? I . . . I have not—"

"Are you telling me you have not been briefed on the project?" Einar interrupted in outrage. "*Scheissdreck nochmal!* Who is your commanding officer, Pregler? What is his name? Answer me! *Sofort!*—At once!"

The corporal was quick to see his chance and grab it. Better his CO should get his ass caught in a meat grinder than he. "*Leutnant* Wendros," he answered smartly. "Heinz Wendros." He stared speculatively at Einar. "Herr *Hauptman*," he said hesitantly, "may I see—"

Brusquely Einar broke in. "I want Wendros brought here immediately. *Sofort! Verstanden?* Understood? I want him to see for himself what he has neglected to inform his command about. Get him! *Los!*"

"Herr *Hauptman*, I—"

"Don't keep me waiting, Pregler!" Einar warned him coldly.

The corporal turned to his companion. "Go get the *Leutnant*," he growled.

"He'll be asleep."

"*Du Trottel!*—You nitwit! I know that. Get him!"

The soldier took off. Pregler stayed. His Schmeisser had not been lowered one inch. It still covered Einar and the boys behind him.

Einar impatiently slapped an invisible riding crop on the side of his leg. He glanced at his watch. "I presume I will not have to wait long," he said imperiously.

"Sorry, Herr *Hauptman*," Pregler said. "The officers' quarters are in the administration building on the other side of the field. It may take a few minutes. And the Herr *Leutnant* is asleep," he added.

Einar made a snorting sound of impatience. Inside he exulted. It had worked. So far. He had cut the number of adversaries in half and had bought a little time. Precious time. Now—to gain the corporal's confidence, enough to be able to execute the next phase. He contemplated the man. His accent? It was German regional. He had it. Bavarian. He took out a cigarette and lit it. He held out the pack and took a step toward the German.

"*Schpreiz'n?*" He used the Bavarian idiom for cigarette.

The corporal almost accepted. "*Danke,*" he said regretfully. "No thank you."

Einar was acutely aware of time rushing on. How much did he have? Five minutes? Ten? He needed time, dammit! As much as he could get. If he tried to rush matters, he might screw up completely. He contemplated the corporal.

"You are Bavarian, aren't you, Pregler?" he said casually. "Munich area?"

"Regensburg, Herr *Hauptman.* Little town called Abensberg."

"You are a long way from home."

Pregler shrugged. "We all are, Herr *Hauptman.*"

Einar turned back toward the four boys standing with their hands on their heads, watching the two men wide-eyed.

"You may sit down," he called to them curtly. "We may have to wait awhile."

The boys obeyed. Pregler did not object. Einar indicated the four boys behind him.

"They, too, are learning," he said. "*Hitler Jugend*—Hitler youths. From NAPOLA. They're in a training program at the Reichsschule at Maastricht in Holland. You have heard of it?"

"*Nein,* Herr *Hauptman.*"

Einar shrugged. "It is all a little *spinnat,*" he said, using the Bavarian dialect expression for crazy. "Those sow Prussians in Berlin can come up with the most idiotic schemes, *nicht wahr?* Right?"

Pregler grinned. He was flattered that an officer would be so—*kameradlich*—so companionable with an enlisted man. But then, those officers in the *Jagdverbände*—the commandos—were different.

"Like those boys," Einar continued. "Having to use them on important security is *dof*—stupid." He lowered his voice and leaned toward the German. "They're nothing but bluster and piss. Can't find their own shadows in bright sunlight!"

Pregler grinned. He relaxed a little. The Schmeisser was held less tightly.

Now? he wondered. He could take him. But probably not before he got off a volley. There was another way.

"Night before last," he confided, "we tested the security alertness of a factory. Ball bearings." He laughed. "It was all totally *versaut*—totally messed up." He lowered his voice and stepped a little closer. "The little one back there," he said, "he stepped in a bucket of rejects, and before you could say *leck' mi kreuzweis,* ball bearings were rolling all over the damned place." He laughed again. "It took three minutes and eighteen seconds before anyone showed up. Their security was far from *erstklassig*—first rate." He looked at the corporal. "Not like here."

Pregler grinned broadly. "We do our duty, Herr *Hauptman.*"

"You have obviously had good training, Pregler," Einar observed. He nodded at the Schmeisser in the corporal's hands. "The way you keep us covered until your superior arrives, it is the proper thing to do. It is good soldiering. You are indeed to be commended!"

"*Jawohl,* Herr *Hauptman. Danke,* Herr *Hauptman.* Thank you," Pregler said, pleased. He held his Schmeisser at the ready, but it was more show than caution.

"I know guard duty, especially at night, is *scheisslangweilig*—dull as hell. But you fellows were on your toes all the same." He seemed to get a sudden idea. "Say, I'd like to give you a written commendation, Pregler, for the job you've been doing here. What is your army serial number?"

Pregler rattled it off.

"*Prima.* I'd better write it down," Einar said. He fished a piece of paper from his pocket. "Do you have a pencil?" he asked as he stepped a little closer to the corporal.

"Sorry, Herr *Hauptman.*"

Einar patted his pockets. "I may," he said. "Ah, yes." He pulled a pencil from his jacket pocket. It was an ordinary pencil, about seven inches long and well sharpened. "Give me that number again," he said, the pencil poised over the paper.

Once again Pregler began to recite his serial number.

With explosive suddenness Einar made a vicious stabbing motion to the man's midriff, at the same time uttering a hoarse cry. In the same split second he put his left hand on the submachine gun and pushed it back. Startled, with uncontrollable reflex motion, Pregler jerked forward, sticking his neck out; ineffectually he tried to pull the trigger on his gun as it was being pushed back and his finger was being forced from the trigger guard. Completing the sudden stabbing motion with the sharply pointed pencil, Einar brought it up toward the man's outstretched neck and jabbed it into his exposed jugular vein, piercing it.

Pregler was unconscious before he hit the dirt.

Dead, before his Schmeisser clattered to the ground beside him.

Einar whirled on the boys. They sat shaken, petrified, gaping at him.

"Get going!" he shouted at them. "You've got your damned satchel charges. Place the fucking things!"

The boys scrambled to their feet. They ran to the radio tower, Einar with them.

"All of them around two of the legs," Einar ordered. "On one side." The boys hurried to obey.

Finished. Vehemently Einar motioned to the boys.

"Let's get the hell out of here!"

They were a few hundred feet away, running through the forest, when they heard the blast.

The boys whooped.

"Stow it!" Einar snapped at them. "It's not over yet."

They quieted down. They hurried on, talking fitfully as they ran.

"What are your plans now?" Einar asked. "Where are you going?"

"To Valdemar's place," Peter answered. "He lives close by."

Einar looked worried. "All of you?"

Peter nodded. "I know what you think," he said. "But it is all right. We are expected to. We have a . . . a study group. We often stay with Valdemar overnight. Like tonight. Because of the curfew."

"Okay."

"What about you, sir?"

"I'll be going on to Copenhagen," Einar answered. "I'll take the train from Frederiksvaerk."

Peter stopped, the others with him. He looked at Einar. "You had better not," he said soberly.

"Why not?"

"Because of the *razzias,*" Harald explained.

"What . . . *razzias?*"

"Ever since Erik Petersen was killed by the Holger Danske resistance group a few days ago, the HIPO's have been carrying out surprise raids on trains and in restaurants," Peter told him. "Trying to find the killers."

"Petersen was the chief of the HIPOs," Valdemar said.

"You wouldn't be safe on the train." It was the worried voice of Harald.

Valdemar stepped up to Einar. "Hr. Munk," he said. "If you will come home with us, I will give you my bicycle. You can use it to ride down to Copenhagen. It would be much safer."

Peter stared at his friend. The bike was his prize possession.

Einar looked at Valdemar. "Thanks . . . buddy," he said.

It was just after 0714 hours when Einar pedaled Valdemar's bike toward Frederiksvaerk, blending in with all the other bike riders on their way to work. On the baggage rack over the rear wheel were his fish and his transmitter, all wrapped in fresh newspaper.

He passed the railroad station. Ironic, he thought. If it hadn't been for his goofs that delivered him into the hands of the young resistance saboteurs, he might well have delivered himself into the hands of his real enemies, while jam-packed into a train compartment.

Somewhere there was a moral in it all.

Damned if he knew what it was.

He pumped on. He would take the country roads over Gørløse and Farum, coming into town through Gladsaxe. It was some forty miles to Copenhagen that way. He should be there before nightfall.

Operation Drumbeat was just beginning.

8

It was dusk—about an hour before curfew—when Einar pedaled into the Copenhagen suburb of Gladsaxe.

His butt and the inside of his thighs were chafed and his leg muscles sore, but he had made good time, stopping only twice to eat. Mindful of Peter's warning about the HIPO raids, he'd eaten in a couple of small, out-of-the-way inns along the road. The fish were gone from his bike rack. Judging from the smell, it had been doubtful if they would have lasted all the way. At the first place he'd stopped to eat, he'd traded most of them for a dozen eggs and some carrots. At the second place the rest had been traded for some real Danish dark *Rugbrød*—rye bread—which he had not had for years, and some butter. His transmitter was carefully packed with these provisions.

Traffic was relatively light, not bustling and alive as he had remembered it. Mostly bicycles and trucks, some of them clumsily converted to woodburners. And, of course, the yellow streetcars.

He had just passed through the traffic circle, Torvet, and was pedaling down Søborg Hovedgade, coming up on the library, when he noticed a commotion up ahead. With the other bikers he stopped and dismounted.

The sight that met him turned his stomach.

HIPOs!

The *Hilfspolizei*—the infamous Danish-German Auxiliary Police Force, an organization of brutish, traitorous Danes who preyed upon their countrymen, busily living up to their reputation.

They were carrying out a raid on a streetcar. Several of them—their guns drawn, their black uniforms with a single row of metal buttons down the front of their tunics, sturdy laced boots and black caps standing out obscenely in the crowd—were herding the frightened passengers together, shoving and shouting. Two HIPOs were dragging a young man from the tram. One of them pushed him roughly, and the youth tumbled from the steps to the street. Another kicked him savagely in the face, smashing his mouth, which suddenly looked like a crimson clown's grin smeared grotesquely on his face. The young man put both his hands over his mouth and doubled up into a pitiful fetal position as another HIPO sadistically booted him in the groin.

Einar was shaken. He stared at the black-uniformed brutes. His countrymen? He was shocked to witness such brutality and realized that even as friendly and peace-loving a people as the Danes could produce such beasts. Is there a little "Nazi" in us all? he thought. No. He refused to believe so. But he was deeply disturbed. One thing is to hear about such atrocities. Another is to see them happen.

Shaken, he turned around and quickly wheeled his bike away from the ugly scene.

A short detour through some side streets quickly brought him back to the main road, which would take him to the section of town where his friend, Lars Olesen, lived. On Wesselsgade near Peblinge Lake.

His mind seethed with frustrated anger and disgust at what he had just witnessed. He found it difficult to think dispassionately, as he knew he must. He cast about for something to cleanse his raging thoughts.

Lars . . .

There had been three of them. Lars, Torben Kvistholm, and he, Einar. For six years they had been inseparable, sharing with each other the joys and pains of growing up. Experiencing together their first awareness of their own maleness and sexuality, their first interest in girls—a subject that was strictly taboo at the school—and their need to exert themselves and rebel against conventional authority. They had fancied themselves akin to the Three Musketeers they had read about in Fru Ring's French class, and they were going to name themselves after the three adventurers. But after one of their capers, when the headmaster had called Einar a black spot on the school's reputation, they'd decided to call themselves the Three Black Spots. They'd solemnly sworn always to be true, one black spot to the others. And to seal their vow, they had tattooed three tiny black spots on their upper arms, using a razor blade and China ink. Einar still had the three little blue-black spots near his shoulder; Lars only had two, as he recalled. His cuts had gotten infected, and only two of them took. By the time Lars could have scratched in the third, they'd had other ideas and other interests.

Lars had had a vivid imagination and a flair for intrigue. Like the time they got even with Baggesen, their German teacher. Baggesen had been the only really unpopular teacher at the school, and for some reason he'd taken a special dislike to Einar, Lars, and Torben, always riding them mercilessly.

He also rewarded his favorites, however, and on Saturday afternoons he would give such lucky ones special permission to bicycle to the nearby town and attend a matinee at the local movie house. Needless to say, Einar, Lars, and Torben were never among those lucky ones. And Lars had cooked up a scheme to get even with the unjust taskmaster.

One Saturday, after lunch, as Baggesen stood watching them from his window, they conspicuously joined the group of favored moviegoers and boisterously rode their bikes with them as they left the campus for town.

They'd made sure Baggesen was at his window again when they and the movie-going group returned, laughing up a storm and comparing opinions about the great film playing in town.

It was no surprise, therefore, when within the hour they had been summoned to the headmaster's office. Baggesen had been there, of course, alternately glowering at them with righteous wrath and gloating in anticipation of the dire consequences to be suffered by the rebellious trio.

It was not until the headmaster accused them of flagrant, deliberate disobedience that Lars—looking more innocent than one of Raphael's angels—had said, "But Headmaster, I don't know where Herr Baggesen gets the idea that we went to the movie. We had arranged with Fru Ring to go over some French texts with her at her house. That's where we were. All afternoon!"

The headmaster at once had made a call. The look he had given Baggesen when he hung up made the man squirm, and the boys had savored every minute of his embarrassment and discomfort, every expression of chagrin and frustration mirrored on his face, as they were summarily dismissed.

Baggesen had left them alone since that incident. They had been convinced it was because he hadn't wanted to invite another "get-even" escapade. Closer to the truth, Einar thought in retrospect, was probably the fact that Baggesen never could be sure if a particular prank apparently pulled by the trio was real—or another trap to sucker him in. In any case, they'd gotten away with murder . . .

Einar turned into Wesselsgade. He felt excited. It had been years since he had seen Lars. In fact, it had been five years since they had even been in touch. Since before the war.

The building Lars lived in was a modest, five-story apartment house, the lower two stories painted a soft pink. There was a little furniture store next to the entrance, and a bike rack just inside the portal that led to the courtyard. The rack was empty.

Einar placed his bike in the stand. He gave a fleeting thought to leaving the package with his transmitter and the food, wrapped in a current newspaper—but he thought better of it. He untied it from the rack. He caught a glimpse of the grim headline on the front page: HENRETTEDE—Executed. He knew what the whole headline read: 9 TERRORISTER HENRETTEDE! For terrorists read freedom fighters, he thought bitterly. He had read the story. The patriots had been caught with the help of HIPO informers. He put the package under his arm. Lars could probably use some of the fresh food.

A list of tenants was posted in the hall on the ground floor. Lars Olesen was on it. Second floor, left. That would be two flights up, according to European custom. Einar pushed the button that would give him a few minutes of light and started up the stairs. He was aware of his growing anticipation and excitement. It had been a long time. A very long time.

L. Olesen, read the porcelain sign on the front door, second floor, left.

Einar rang the bell.

Almost at once the door was opened.

In the doorway stood Lars. His eyes widened in astonishment. "*Hvad Fanden!* Einar!" he exclaimed. "What the devil! Einar!"

Einar stared at his friend. His world was suddenly filled with the chilling sight of a black uniform with a single row of metal buttons down the front and black breeches tucked into sturdy, laced-up boots.

Lars Olesen was a HIPO.

A Nazi!

9

Without a word Einar turned and ran.

He bounded down the stairs, two steps at a time. Halfway down, the lights abruptly went out, and he found himself cocooned in blackness. Only his instant grip on the handrail with his one free hand kept him from stumbling on the steps and pitching headlong down the stairs. Clutching his parcel with the transmitter to him with the other hand, he felt his way down the few remaining steps to the bottom.

He was down. He pushed the door open, just as the lights went on again, turned on by Lars.

He was outside. He rushed to the bike rack in the courtyard.

His bicycle was gone!

For the span of a heartbeat, realization swept over him. Someone had stolen his bike, and he had thought of leaving his package with the transmitter on it. What if he had? He would have lost his all-important link with his control in England and found himself in enemy-occupied country, "blind" and without contacts. He cursed himself. He should have known. Wartime Denmark was not the Denmark he had known as a boy. Instinctively he took a firmer grip on his package as he whirled from the empty bike rack and sped from the courtyard into the deserted street.

The spring night was fairly bright, but curfew was in effect. There was nothing for it. He had to get as far away from Lars as he could, at once, before his erstwhile friend could collect himself and alert his Nazi friends—or give pursuit.

He ran.

He had been dealt a major setback. His presence in Copenhagen was now known. While his enemies did not know the nature of his mission, his description would be circulated quickly among the Nazis and their HIPO cronies. Lars was certainly familiar enough with it. His mission had suddenly become a hundred times more difficult. And more risky.

At a run he turned on Korsgade and raced toward the lake. He had not as yet formulated any plans of where to hide; the only thing in his mind was to get away to safety.

His "fort"!

That was it. In the garden behind his boyhood home on Sankt Knuds Vej No. 5.

As a boy it had meant a place of privacy and security from imagined enemies to him. And now, when he was threatened by real ones, his mind still sought it out.

Sankt Knuds Vej was about seven or eight blocks away, as he remembered. About a mile. He might just make it. No, dammit! He would! Of course, the fort would be long gone. After all, it had been almost fifteen years since he left Copenhagen for boarding school. But the bicycle sheds would most likely still be there. They would provide a hiding place. Temporarily, at least. As a boy he had constantly lost the key to the padlock on his stall, but it had been easy to get in. All the stalls had loose boards in the back.

He was running easily along Peblinge Dossering, the street next to Peblinge Lake, when he suddenly stopped short.

Ahead of him a German patrol car was turning from the Søpavillion causeway into Peblinge Dossering, a powerful searchlight tacking the street before it.

The light was still moving in a sweeping arc as the car turned. Any second it would blaze down the street, and he would be caught. There was no time to try to sprint across the street and hope to find refuge in a house. The beam would catch him.

Even as the thought crystallized in his mind, Einar vaulted over the low railing around the lake, hoping to be able to crouch down behind it and escape detection.

He almost cried out. The purchase on the other side was narrower than he had expected. Next to nonexistent. He lost his footing and nearly plunged into the lake below. Instinctively he grabbed the railing with both hands and hung on. The package with his transmitter fell from his grip, plummeted down, hit the water, and sank.

On the street above, the German patrol car lumbered by and disappeared around the corner of Nørrebrogade.

Einar hauled himself up over the railing. He was trembling. For a moment he sat leaning against it, spent.

The transmitter.

Gone.

He was fully aware it would be an utter impossibility to go fishing for it.

He was—"blind."

He stood up. He still had to get to Sankt Knuds Vej. He kept close to the buildings, melting into the shadows. He moved slowly, cautiously, so as not to run into anything unexpected. Once he saw a patrol ahead—and he waited, pressed into a doorway at a corner, ready to slip down a side street, should the Germans come his way. They turned off.

He found himself on Rosenørns Allé and was startled to see the stark, skeletal remains of a huge structure towering before him. He realized it was the Forum, the largest exhibition hall in the Scandinavian countries, in ruins, looking like a giant, three-dimensional X-ray in the black-and-white shades of the night. Only the metal framing, girders, and struts were left standing, silhouetted against the night sky. All the brickwork and all the cement blocks had been shattered into rubble that covered the ground.

He was shaken. He remembered the hall and the many exhibitions he had seen there. He had not known it had been destroyed. He wondered why. If there had been a reason.

He skirted the X-ray ruins and soon found himself on Sankt Knuds Vej.

He felt a pang of nostalgia as he stole up to No. 5 and quietly slipped down the driveway to the garden and courtyard behind the building.

The little garden was still there, and in the far corner he could make out a darker structure.

His "fort."

He entered the garden and crept up to the shelter. Amazed, he stared at it. Weathered, cracked, a couple of pieces of wood hanging loose, and obviously long forgotten, his little "fort" still stood in the corner, leaning against the back fence, splotched with peeling red paint. Someone must have painted it, he thought. After me. I never did.

He peered inside. He could barely make out a few garden tools, some pots, and a couple of cardboard boxes. His "fort" was now a toolshed, and he realized that the garden itself no longer was filled with flowers—but with vegetables. Memories crowding his mind, he gazed at the little "fort." It obviously must have shrunk, he thought. He remembered it as large and roomy. But now it would barely hold him.

It certainly was not a place to find privacy and safety any longer.

That left the bicycle sheds.

They, too, were still there.

He squeezed in behind them—had they moved them closer to the wall? Instinctively he found the one that had been his.

The boards were nailed fast, but not so solidly that he couldn't wrest one or two loose. He did. He forced them apart and pushed inside.

It was pitch dark. Carefully he felt around. One bicycle was hanging by its wheels from hooks in the low ceiling. It was a man's bike, both tires without air. Another bike stood leaning against the wall. A woman's bike. In a corner stood a pail filled with rags. There was just enough room for him to stretch out on the cement floor.

He fished the rags from the pail and spread them out on the rough floor. They might keep the chill down, at least give the illusion of a sleeping mat.

He eased himself down. He was suddenly painfully aware of the aching exhaustion that saturated him. He would rest a few hours. First thing in the morning he'd be on his way.

He had to find Torben. Torben Kvistholm. And hope that his friend could help him contact a resistance group in Copenhagen. A resistance group with a transmitter that could reach London. It was imperative that he make contact with Bally—before he was written off.

He fell asleep. . . .

Someone had stolen his eyes.

It was one of those eerie dreams where you know you are dreaming and where you impotently watch yourself struggle through the dream. Or nightmare.

He could see the thief who had taken his eyes, all of him except his face. He was clad completely in black, and his face, too, was black; ominous, empty, black space.

And he had Einar's eyes, wrapped in dirty newspaper, in his hands.

He was chasing the thief, but his legs were as heavy as lead, and every step hurt with an aching pain that got sharper and sharper as he tried to catch up with the figure in black.

Suddenly the thief stopped. He turned around, and Einar could see his face. It had a smear of red slashed across it, as if in a hideous crimson grin.

The man held up Einar's eyes—and all of a sudden he hurled them into the sky.

Higher and higher they rose. Up. Up toward the sun. All was light. White, searing, blinding light, and—

He woke with a start.

The first thing he became aware of was the sharp pain of the cramps in his legs. The second was the bright light streaming into the shed from the open door—and the figure silhouetted against it, towering over him, as he lay on the floor.

There was a quick gasp. *"Hvad gør De her?"* The startled voice was that of a woman. "What are you doing here?"

Slowly, stiffly, Einar got to his feet. Gradually his eyes got used to the light. The woman standing in the doorway to the bicycle shed looked to be in her late thirties. She was sensibly dressed, a minimum of makeup on her pleasant face. She carried a large, well-worn purse on a strap over her shoulder. As she got a closer look at Einar and saw his unkempt, bedraggled appearance, she inched away from him.

"Who are you?" she asked, apprehension darkening her voice. She answered herself. "You are . . . running," she breathed. "From the Germans."

Einar stepped toward the open door. The woman drew back in alarm.

"Please!" she said. "Please leave." Her eyes were wide and frightened. "I will say nothing. Please do not get me involved." She started to walk away.

"Wait!" Einar called.

She turned back to him. She looked at him with pleading eyes. "Please," she whispered miserably. "I . . . I cannot get involved with . . . with anyone underground. It is too dangerous. My—" She stopped. She bit her lip. "Just . . . let me have my bicycle," she begged. "So I can get to work. Please!"

Einar took hold of the bike. He wheeled it toward her.

"I don't want to get you in any trouble," he said quietly. "But . . . I am not in the resistance. I am not underground."

It was only a small white lie.

The woman looked at him, puzzled. "Then . . . what—"

"What am I doing here?" he finished for her. "Why am I . . . hiding?"

She nodded.

Earnestly he gazed at her. He needed her help. He had a hunch. "It is not important who I am," he said. "But it is true that I need help."

She shook her head, again alarmed.

"I will not ask you to give it," he said. "I know you are afraid someone else may suffer for anything you do."

She stared at him. "How . . . how do you know?" she whispered.

"You told me yourself," he said. "You began to refer to . . . someone else. And stopped." He glanced at the man's bike hanging from the ceiling. "That is his bike, isn't it?" he suggested. "Your husband? Your brother?"

"My husband," the woman acknowledged bleakly.

Einar nodded. "I shall not do anything to put either of you in jeopardy," he assured her. "As soon as you leave, I shall leave, too." He looked straight into her troubled eyes. "Take my chances," he finished.

The woman at once began to wheel her bicycle away. She stopped. She turned back to him.

"My husband is a policeman," she said, her voice trembling. "The Germans have taken him and all the others that did not manage to go underground to Germany. To a camp. It is called Buchenwald." She stopped, her eyes tormented. "Some of them were lucky," she continued. "They were sent to Sweden. Only just now. But . . . my husband was not among them. He is still there." She took a deep breath. "If . . . if the Germans find out that I helped someone they . . . they are after, they will take it out on my husband. He will not come back. Please understand."

Einar nodded solemnly. "I do understand," he said quietly.

She watched him. "You look . . . hungry," she said. "And you need to . . . to clean up." Resolutely she dug into her purse. She pressed a key into his hand.

"Our apartment is on the second floor to the right," she said quickly. "There is food in the kitchen. You can use my husband's things to clean up." She looked defiantly at him. "If they find out, I will swear that you found the key under the mat. You understand? I never saw you!"

He nodded.

She glanced toward the bike hanging from the ceiling. "You can use my husband's bicycle, if you want to," she said, her voice flat. "It is the safest way to get around."

Quickly she turned away. But not quickly enough for him not to see the tears brimming in her eyes.

He watched her mount her bicycle and purposefully pedal from the courtyard.

He closed the door to the shed and started for the apartment on the second floor to the right.

He passed by the apartment where he'd lived as a boy. *Stuen til venstre*—ground floor, left. He glanced at the nameplate on the door. *J. Haldby*. He felt a pang of resentment. Who were these Haldby people who lived in *his* apartment?

The layout of the apartment on the second floor, right, was just as he remembered his own, only in mirror image, and it had obviously been remodeled. The bathroom had a shower, a sort of hand-held shower head attached to the plumbing, and a tiled floor that slanted toward a drain.

He stripped, and while he showered, he washed out his socks and underwear. He'd quick-dry them in the oven. It was a trick he'd learned when he lived alone and constantly ran out of clean linen. He longed for a toothbrush, but he didn't want to use someone else's. The only toilet article he carried himself was a small pocket comb. It was obvious. People don't usually go about their daily routine with a full set of toilet articles in their pockets. He settled for rubbing some toothpaste on his teeth with his finger, and a good rinsing. He hunted around and found a safety razor and a well-used shaving brush in a drawer. No shaving soap. He used the ordinary soap he found on the washbowl. The lather was thin and watery but better than nothing.

In the sparkling clean kitchen, he found some cheese, some butter, and half a loaf of dark Danish rye bread. He gave a fleeting thought to the loaf he'd lost, lying at the bottom of Peblinge Lake, along with his transmitter. He also found some ersatz coffee but hadn't the courage to try it.

Refreshed, clad only in his shirt, he sat down to take stock.

He had to find Torben. His friend was his only chance, his only hope not only of completing his mission—but also of surviving.

He had memorized two addresses for Torben. One where he lived, on Sundevedsgade, the other where he worked, a bookstore, Pegasus Boghandel, on Maglekildevej. He found a telephone book, and after some searching he located both addresses. He contemplated calling Torben but thought better of it. He needed to make personal contact, not through a telephone operator, and he did not want to do anything that might compromise his hostess.

Finally he put on his warm underwear and dressed. He put a generous portion of his ration stamps on the kitchen counter and left the apartment as clean and sparkling as he'd found it, minus only several slices of bread and cheese, some butter, and a dab of toothpaste. He placed the key under the mat and made his way to the bicycle shed.

A bicycle pump was affixed to the frame of the bike. He pumped up the flat tires—and they held.

Wheeling the bike from the shed, he mounted it and rode from the courtyard of his boyhood home as he'd done thousands of times before.

Long ago.

All was well. The whole damned mess meant only a slight delay. Torben would be able to put him in touch with the right resistance people. He had no doubts. Torben had always been inventive. As Einar headed for Maglekildevej and Pegasus Boghandel, he eased his tension by letting his mind dwell on one of Torben's more memorable stunts in school . . .

★ ★ ★

They had been sixteen, perhaps seventeen, and they had chafed under the stern discipline of the school. It was only now, he thought, that he realized the importance of that discipline. If you do not learn discipline when you are young—how do you acquire the self-discipline that is necessary to function successfully as an adult?

Since it was strictly forbidden to drink or to have any kind of alcoholic beverages in your room, it had, of course, become mandatory for the Three Black Spots to do so, even though none of them liked the stuff.

Torben had been appointed bartender. The least obnoxious drink they could think of was a sweet port wine. Not unlike a strong fruit juice, they'd thought, and Torben had acquired a bottle. But where to keep it? Their rooms were subject to inspections that sometimes bordered on veritable searches at any time, whether they were there or not. So how do you conceal a bottle and three glasses to go with it?

Torben had come up with the answer.

He had a little stand next to his bed, with a front that rolled down into the base much like an upside-down rolltop desk. It could, of course, be locked, but the rules forbade any such attempts at privacy. Torben used the stand to keep his records and notes from past classes and studies, which he might need for future reference. On the top shelf was a row of notebooks neatly marked on the spine with the contents: German Grammar, Geography, History, and so on. There was only one catch. The notebooks were only two inches deep; the rest of them had been cut off. Firmly glued together, the backs of the books formed a sturdy, deceptive partition behind which stood Torben's port wine and glasses.

All had gone well. They had suffered through several sips of the forbidden liquid fruit, when one evening during the hours the students were allowed to visit each other and the Three Black Spots had been together in Torben's room, the headmaster himself had appeared. Luckily the port paraphernalia was safely hidden behind its concealing camouflage.

The headmaster was angry over some long-forgotten infraction, and as he'd scolded them, to emphasize his displeasure with them, he'd slammed his hand down on Torben's little stand, violently jarring it and its incriminating contents.

Almost in the same instant, apparently startled by the headmaster's gesture, Torben made a quick move and swept a framed photograph of his parents off his desk. It crashed to the floor, shattering the glass.

Only the three friends knew that the obvious tinkling of glass did not all come from the broken picture!

Torben was inventive—and he could think on his feet. Just what was needed now . . .

Einar had almost reached his destination. He turned the corner into Maglekildevej—and braked to an abrupt stop.

He stared.

The entire street that stretched out before him lay in ruins, every building an empty, burned-out shell rooted in rubble.

Torben's bookstore was nonexistent.

Perhaps Torben as well.

10

It was not there.

Again he checked the directory of tenants posted in the hall of the apartment house on Sundevedsgade where Torben was supposed to live. With the Pegasus bookstore destroyed, he'd gone there directly.

There was no Torben Kvistholm listed.

Had he remembered wrong? He checked his memory. He visualized the way he had written the address down. He visualized the printing in the telephone book. He *was* at the right place.

Then why no Torben Kvistholm?

Had he moved? Had he been killed in the bombing of his bookstore? Or injured? Was he lying in some hospital somewhere?

It made no difference, he thought bleakly. Torben was out of reach. His last contact was a bust.

A final, desperate time he checked the list of tenants. No Torben Kvistholm.

But something kept nagging at him. There was something odd about the directory. Once more he went over it carefully. And he found what had been bothering him.

Apartment 3-B had no tenant name listed.

It was a long shot, a damned long shot, but he had to try.

He walked up the three flights of stairs. There was no name on number 3-B. He rang the bell.

He listened. Presently he heard a shuffling sound behind the door. A man's voice called, "*Hvem er det?*—Who is it?"

Was it Torben? He could not be sure.

"Einar Munk," he answered.

The door was flung open.

In the hallway beyond, Torben Kvistholm stood gaping at Einar.

"Det var som bare Fanden!" he exclaimed. "That beats the devil himself!" With a quick, sharp glance past Einar to the stair landing, he pulled

his friend inside and closed the door. "How the hell did *you* get here, *din gamle skiderik*—you old bastard?"

He stood back and looked Einar over, a huge grin on his face.

Einar returned his grin. He noticed Torben limped a little and saw the soiled bandage around his left ankle.

"Torben!" he said fervently. He put his hands on his friend's shoulders. "Am I glad to see you!"

"Come in," Torben said, taking Einar by the arm. "Take a load off your feet. We've got about five years of talking to do."

He shuffled toward the living room.

"What happened to your leg?" Einar asked solicitously.

"It's nothing," Torben dismissed it. "Almost as good as new again."

"I went to Maglekildevej first," Einar told him. "To the Pegasus."

Torben nodded grimly. "Happened about a month ago." He tapped his leg. "That's a little souvenir."

They'd reached the living room. Torben pointed to a large, stuffed easy chair. "Sit," he said. He grinned at Einar. "How about a glass of port?"

Einar laughed. "You bet," he agreed. "It is an acquired taste. By now I have acquired it!"

Torben walked to a little cabinet and opened the glass-paned doors. Behind them was a little bar. He poured two glasses of port wine and brought one to Einar. "I was lucky," he said. "Over a dozen people were killed. Right next to the Pegasus."

"How?"

"It was an air raid," Torben told him. "A British air raid." He glanced at Einar. "The resistance had asked for it."

"On Maglekildevej? What the hell for?"

"That was by mistake," Torben said. He seemed reluctant to talk about it. Still gun-shy? Einar thought. But he wanted to know. "What do you mean, mistake?"

"The target was the Shell House," Torben said, his voice flat. "The Gestapo took over Shell Petroleum's offices about a year ago. A big, modern building. They occupied the lower floors along with HIPOs and certain informers and Danish Nazi translators. But to keep the English from bombing the hell out of the place, just as they had done in Aarhus, the Gestapo converted the attic into prison cells where they kept Danish patriot captives. The elite of the resistance. And they made damned sure everyone knew."

"The resistance asked for a bombing raid?" Einar asked incredulously. "On their own people?"

Torben nodded. "They considered it all-important. And the prisoners were doomed anyway. They would only be tortured before they died. The reason for the raid was that the Germans had come into possession of records that could cost the lives of thousands of freedom fighters." He looked at Einar. "They wanted those records destroyed before the Gestapo could act upon them." He looked down at his hands. "It was a special raid," he explained. "The bombers were supposed to kill only the Germans and their collaborators. Not the prisoners."

"How the hell could they do that?"

"They did," Einar said. "They skipped their bombs along the pavement into the two lower floors and opened up one side of the attic. They killed over two hundred Nazis and traitors, and burned the records. Most all the prisoners escaped."

"I'll be damned!" Einar shook his head in wonder. "But . . . what has that to do with Maglekildevej?" he asked, puzzled. "That's nowhere near the Shell House."

"That was the mistake," Torben said. "The bombers came in low, very low, in three waves. One of the planes in the second wave hit a railroad semaphore signal mast and crashed into a school in Frederiksberg. The French convent school, not far from Maglekildevej. Some of the planes that followed thought the fire and smoke from the crash was the target and dropped their bombs on it." He looked away. "They killed almost a hundred children. And their teachers."

Einar was stunned. "Oh . . . my God!" he whispered.

For a moment both men were silent, each with his own thoughts. Finally Torben turned to Einar.

"What about you?" he said. "What are you doing here? I thought you were in America."

Einar nodded. "I was." He looked soberly at his friend. "Torben," he said, "I need your help."

Torben frowned at him. "Help? What kind of help?" His eyes flitted toward the door. "I will do anything I can, of course."

For a moment Einar hesitated. A twinge of doubt nibbled at him. He was about to disclose his mission. Should he? Mentally he shook himself. This was Torben. His friend. If he couldn't trust him, who the hell could he trust? He deliberately suppressed the thought of Lars. He plowed on.

"I'm here on a mission," he told his friend. "For the Allied intelligence." Torben gaped at him. "I . . . lost my transmitter. I need to get in touch with someone in the Danish resistance movement." He looked closely at his friend. "Someone who has access to a transmitter. Do you know anyone? Can you help?"

Torben stared at him. "What . . . what kind of mission?" he asked.

Einar was about to tell him, but something stopped him. What was that idiot phrase? NTK—need to know. Torben had no need to know. At least not yet. He looked at his friend. "It's a long, dull story and not important," he shrugged. "What is important is that I make contact with the underground as quickly as possible. Preferably yesterday."

Torben rose. He hobbled over to the window and stood staring out for a moment.

"I . . . I am not in the resistance myself," he said finally. "But maybe I *can* help you. Why will you need a . . . a transmitter?"

"I have to make contact. With my control in London. Let him know the mission is still go."

Torben nodded. "Were you not given any names of resistance people here?"

"No. It was a case of rush, rush, rush. I told them I had two old friends here who would help. Who would trust me on sight without need to check me out with London. You and Lars Olesen." He gave a little snort. "Lars sure turned out to be a total loss," he added bitterly.

Torben turned to him, a fleeting look of alarm on his face. "You saw Lars?" he asked sharply.

"Yes."

"What did he say?"

Einar gave his friend a quick glance. Why the sudden apprehension? Was he afraid Lars would figure out he'd go to Torben next, and would pull a raid to nab him? Possible. He could do nothing about it. Not just yet. He shrugged.

"He said nothing. I took one look at that damned uniform he was wearing and ran. That's how I lost my transmitter." He looked at Torben, hurt darkening his eyes. "What the hell happened to him?" he asked. "Lars? A HIPO! How could he, Torben? Dammit! How could he?"

"I know," Torben nodded solemnly. "It is . . . difficult to accept." He looked away.

"Can you help me?" Einar persisted.

Slowly Torben nodded. "I . . . think so. I do know someone who is involved. I'll try to get to him."

"Now?"

"If it is that important."

"It is."

Resolutely Torben drew himself up. "Okay, Einar," he said firmly. "I will try." He limped toward the door. "You stay here. Don't go anywhere. I will be back within the hour."

Einar looked at the door closing behind his friend. He frowned. He'd made his contact. Soon he'd be in business. Then . . . why did he feel uneasy?

Was it . . . Torben?

Carefully he examined their conversation step by step. There were little things, he realized. Little things that had bothered him. Things that he had deliberately chosen to overlook or explain away, because he hadn't wanted to face them. Each by itself meant nothing, but . . . together?

Why was Torben not listed on the directory in the hall below? Who was it he did not want to know where he lived? And there was that . . . that strange, furtive look when he'd pulled Einar into his place. Who was he afraid to see? Why? And his questions—seeking to learn about the mission, were they just normal curiosity, or was there another reason? If so, what? The look of alarm he'd seen in his friend's face when he'd mentioned Lars. Why? Because of his HIPO connections?

He felt ashamed. Ashamed of suspecting a friend. But the uneasy feeling—the hunch—that something was askew would not leave him.

And he'd long since learned to trust such hunches. He looked at his watch. Torben had said one hour. Time enough.

He began in the kitchen. It was well stocked—including several imported delicacies. In a cupboard drawer he found several packs of cigarettes, a French make, worth their weight in gold in wartime Copenhagen. In the little bar were some fine wines. German. And a bottle of French cognac, nearly full.

He was becoming increasingly worried. How had Torben come into possession of such luxuries? There had to be an explanation. He continued searching.

There were papers lying on a desk, all routine: utility bills and such. He found not a single personal letter or document, no notebooks or even a private record of addresses and telephone numbers. Nothing. It was not—normal.

He examined the blotter on the desk pad. It was well used. He held it up to the light to see if he could make out any impressions. There were too many, all obliterating each other.

Except one.

In a corner of the blotter was the faint outline of a number. A telephone number. With a Copenhagen prefix. He could barely make it out.

For a moment he hesitated. Then he picked up the phone and asked the operator for the number.

It rang.

Einar almost put the receiver down. What was he doing? Doubting his friend? Spying on him?

And a voice, clipped and curt, heavily accented, came from the receiver. "*Sturmbannführer* Coblenz, Gestapo."

He hung up, dropping the receiver on its hook as if it had suddenly become red hot.

He stared at the phone as if it had all at once turned into a poisonous snake.

There had to be an explanation. Oh—please God—there had to be.

Not—both his friends?

Not—both of them . . .

But in his heart he knew that Torben was a *Stikker*—an informer. Worse than Lars. Plying his infamous treason in secret.

He ran down the stairs, two steps at a time. He grabbed his bike, hidden behind the stairs in the hall. He wanted only to get away from the house. Away from Torben. Get away as quickly and as far as possible.

He stopped.

He could not leave. He *had* to make sure. Absolutely sure. Torben was his friend. He owed him that much.

Quickly he wheeled the bike across the street. He hurried into a little courtyard and hid the bike behind a shed. He climbed the stairs to the second floor and crouched down on the landing at a small window facing the street.

He was there when a few minutes later two German trucks and a staff car came barreling down the street and stopped at Torben's house. German soldiers and HIPOs spilled from them and ran into the building.

In the staff car sat an SS officer—and Torben.

Einar's eyes started to burn as he stared at his friend, barely visible in the backseat of the staff car, sitting comfortably and complacently in the company of a Nazi officer.

He felt a great sadness, a bleak emptiness inside. Torben. His friend. As close as any friend could be for so many years. He would have trusted him with his life. He had. But within a few years of Nazi domination, both he and Lars, both his closest friends, had been subverted. Changed. He felt a great loss. There remained only an icy void within him.

It was late afternoon when Einar finally stirred from his place at the window. The Germans had long since left. And Torben with them. Einar had felt safe in staying put. The best hiding place is one already searched. The Nazis were not likely to return to Torben's neighborhood.

He felt numb, betrayed, ready to throw in the sponge. He thanked his lucky stars he hadn't told Torben more than he had. As it was, the Germans now knew with certainty that he, Einar Munk, an Allied spy, was in Copenhagen on an important mission.

Bad enough.

He was suddenly defiant. Dammit! He wasn't going to be licked before he even got started. Not by a bunch of traitors!

What could he do? Short of advertising for resistance contacts, what the hell could he do?

Two things.

He could bicycle back to Frederiksvaerk and look up Valdemar. The boy's brother had belonged to a Copenhagen resistance group. Valdemar might know some names. It was a long shot—and time-consuming.

Or he could go back to the woman on Sankt Knuds Vej. She had mentioned that a lot of the Danish policemen had gone underground. Some of her husband's colleagues. She might know someone.

He looked at his watch. If he started out in a few minutes, he'd be there by five o'clock. He wanted to be there when she returned from work.

It was still daylight as he rode into the courtyard of Sankt Knuds Vej No. 5. He wheeled the bike to the shed—out of habit?

He was still deeply disturbed as he walked to the back stairs that led to the apartments above.

As he stepped through the open door, his arms were suddenly grabbed by two men. Roughly he was slammed against the wall. A third man—holding a gun in his hand—a German Luger—stepped in front of him.

He thrust his face at Einar and said calmly, "Be perfectly quiet. Or we will silence you!"

11

Einar stared at the man. About his own age, clad in civilian clothes, obviously Danish. The two others as well.

Who were they?

They had been waiting for him. That was obvious. It was a deliberate ambush. But who the hell could have known that he'd go to Sankt Knuds Vej No. 5?

His mind raced. Lars? Torben? The only two people who knew he was in Copenhagen. Neither of them had ever been to Sankt Knuds Vej. He'd lived there before he'd ever met them. Had he ever told them about the place? About his "fort"? He searched his memory. He had no recollection of doing so, but he probably had. They'd held nothing back from one another.

Or the woman he'd come to see? Could she have informed the

Germans? He dismissed it. First of all, had she wanted to denounce him, she would have done so at once—and he'd have been nabbed when he was still in her apartment. Second, she could not possibly have known that he would return. He'd only known that himself for less than an hour.

Torben. It had to be.

When the raid on his apartment had been a flop and the Germans had found their quarry gone, Torben must have reasoned that Einar had found him out. He knew that Einar only had two contacts in Copenhagen—himself and Lars—and that he could go to neither of them. He must have remembered Sankt Knuds Vej as being Einar's home long ago—and played a hunch.

It had been a good one.

He glared at the man holding him at gunpoint.

"Who are you?" he asked.

"Shut up!" the man growled. "You will find out soon enough." He gun-gestured to his two companions. Their grips on Einar's arms tightened as they led him through the narrow corridor and the front hall to the street.

Across the street a coal delivery truck was parked. Einar had noticed it as he arrived. *DET DANSKE KULKOMPAGNI* was painted in big white letters on the side, and a telephone number on the cab door. Appropriately enough, the truck had been converted to coal burning. The awkward, cylindrical burner had been mounted on the side between the cab and the truck bed. They headed for the truck.

Einar frowned. A coal delivery truck? He'd expected a German car to drive up to collect them. Why the truck? What the hell was Torben up to? Why the civilians? Why not Germans? Who were these men? Torben's fellow informers?

A chilling thought stole into his mind and quickly raced to fill it with dread. It was not a pretty scenario that he suddenly evoked. Was his erstwhile friend out to take revenge? Or trying to save face? He had been shown up and humiliated before his Nazi friends when they'd found that their prey had flown the coop. Was Torben now going to prove to them that he could still deliver? And not only the fugitive's warm body, but also his full confession? The Gestapo had experts to make recalcitrant people talk. Torben may be a star pupil. Involuntarily he shivered. That would explain the civilians.

His inquisitors.

He sat wedged between the driver and the man who appeared to be the leader of the team, uncomfortably aware of the Luger jabbed into his side.

It was beginning to grow dark. He tried to orient himself as they drove through the streets.

They were driving down Gammel Kongevej. They passed a large building in ruins. With a shock he realized it was the Kino Palae, one of his favorite movie theaters as a child. A strange military target.

They were headed toward the center of town. They skirted Raadhuspladsen—the Town Hall Square—and crossed H. C. Andersen Boulevard. Finally they stopped at an old house on a small side street near the university.

For a moment they sat in the cab, watching the street.

There was no traffic; there were no pedestrians.

"Out!" the man with the gun ordered curtly.

Einar followed him out of the cab. The two others were waiting for him.

As the coal truck drove on down the narrow street, the men herded Einar into the building.

He didn't know exactly where he was. All he knew was that he was in an old part of town, where many of the students who attended the University of Copenhagen rented rooms and small apartments. He figured that perhaps the basement of one of those houses would be a preferred place for Torben's purposes. He was surprised when he was taken to a small, neat two-room apartment and shoved into a tiny room.

As the door was slammed shut behind him, he took in his surroundings.

It was a bedroom. Tidy, clean, one bed. And it was obviously a woman's room.

Puzzled, he sat down on the only chair available, in front of a little mirrored dressing table.

He waited.

The thoughts churned in his mind. What was in store for him? What would Torben do to him? Or his henchmen? Slowly he began to conjure up visions of torture, of horror, of agony . . .

Angrily he tried to dam the flood of sinister fantasies. It was always what happened when you were kept waiting. Waiting for some unknown danger or horror. The fear would grow. And grow, and grow. He knew that only too well. He'd used it himself, countless times, to soften up a stubborn interrogation subject. Insinuate a dire happening—and wait. After a few hours alone with his own mind, his own thoughts, his own imagination, the subject would usually be only too eager to talk.

And now it was happening to him, dammit! The fear. Fear is a formidable weapon. You can use it against your enemy. Or against yourself. He had to stop thinking, stop anticipating. He knew it was impossible. As impossible as being told *not* to think of a purple rhinoceros in the kitchen sink.

Once the thought had been planted in your mind, it was all but impossible to erase it. Especially on command.

Replace it? Think of a white lamb on the coffee table? It might do the trick. All he had to do was concentrate. Concentrate. That was what Felumb had said. Exactly that. He would never forget. Concentrate.

He let his mind remember, every impression, every detail . . .

Felumb had been their history teacher, his, Torben's, and Lars's. At Bavnehøj Kostskole. But he had not been an ordinary teacher. Somehow he had been able to breathe life into a subject that could have been deadly dull, a string of dates and places and events without meaning.

But he still had to teach within the system, and that system called for frequent tests and examinations.

Every week there was at least one formal test. He, Einar, and the two other Black Spots with the rest of the class would sit at their desks, a piece of paper before them, blank side up. On the other side would be a series of questions. They would have twenty minutes to answer them after the word to begin had been given, and the papers would then be collected and graded.

It was one of those tests. Felumb had started them on the quiz and gone to the back of the classroom.

Suddenly they had all been startled at a loud, ringing cock's crow coming from behind them. *Kyiy-ki-li-kyiy! Kyiy-ki-li-kyiy!* As one they had all turned around—and there was Felumb, flapping his elbows, hopping around, his head thrown back in a lusty cock-a-doodle-doo!

Spellbound, the boys watched him. Watched him turning from a cock to a cow with appropriate moos, to a quacking duck, waddling about, and a donkey, braying and kicking. It was an astounding show.

Most of the boys completely forgot about the test before them and only watched Felumb's antics. Others tried to concentrate on the test—more or less in vain. Only a few turned back to the task at hand and finished it as best they could. He, Einar, had been one of them—although his answers had been anything but perfect.

All of a sudden Felumb had looked at his watch. "That's it," he'd said. "Time is up!"

And he had collected all the test papers—blank or not.

Placing them on his desk, he'd turned to the class. "Lesson for today," he'd said. "If you have to concentrate on something important, let *nothing* distract you!"

He'd put his hand on the papers. "These tests, too," he'd said, "will be counted toward your grade average."

He had never forgotten . . .

* * *

Suddenly he heard footsteps outside the door. He was torn out of his reveries. He realized he was sitting in the dark. He stood up. He backed up against the wall. Let them come; he was ready for them.

Again he waited.

The door was opened.

Silhouetted in the doorway stood a man. He reached in and turned on the light.

Involuntarily Einar gasped.

The man standing in the open door, feet apart, firmly planted on the floor, wore a black HIPO uniform.

It was Lars.

12

Einar steeled himself. His wary eyes never left Lars.

A huge grin appeared on his friend's face. In two steps he stood before Einar. Impulsively he enfolded him in a crushing bear hug.

Einar stood speechless, thoroughly confused.

"Einar, you damned reprobate!" Lars exclaimed delightedly. He shrugged out of his HIPO tunic and threw it on the floor as he went on. "You are not an easy man to get hold of. Damned lucky I remembered your bragging about that Sankt Knuds Vej fort of yours."

Einar gaped at him. "But—" He glanced at the discarded HIPO uniform.

Lars followed his glance. "Oh, that," he said contemptuously. "Camouflage. A disguise. Distasteful—but necessary." He looked at Einar. "After seeing me in *det skidne Antraek*—that shitty getup," he said soberly, "I don't blame you for taking off. You couldn't know it wasn't for real. Fact is, we belong to a section in one of the largest sabotage groups, Holger Danske—Holger the Dane. For the last couple of days, we've been casing a factory that is forced to produce war material for the Germans. Only way we could get close to the areas we needed to know about was to masquerade as HIPOs. Pretending to check the workers." He grinned. "We got what we wanted. Day after tomorrow, Sunday, when there are no workers around, the damned place goes BOOM!"

Einar stared unashamedly at his friend. It's true, he thought. That old cliché about a weight being lifted from your shoulders. It's all so damned true.

"Lars," he said. His voice broke. "Lars . . . I . . ."

"Forget it, Einar," Lars said quietly. "I know what you want to say. No need to. I would have thought the same thing."

He struggled into a gray, woolen pullover. When his tousled head emerged through the neck opening, he added, "The important thing is we got you here."

"You sure did," Einar grinned. "But why the strong-arm tactics?"

Lars gave him a speculative look. "Would you have gone with Allan—that was the man who brought you here—would you have gone with him, if he'd simply told you that seeing me in a HIPO uniform was all a mistake?"

"I guess not."

"I didn't think so."

"I might—if you'd come yourself."

"I wanted to, but I couldn't. I *had* to be at that factory. The Sunday operation is too important. That's why I sent Allan. And told him to bring you in any which way short of in a box. I thought you might be a little . . . reluctant. Especially after your run-in with Torben. You know what they say: once burned—and all that. And you'd already been burned twice."

Einar looked at his friend. "You . . . know about Torben?"

Lars nodded soberly. "It tore me to pieces, Einar, so help me. He turned traitor about two years ago. Just couldn't resist the power, the privileges, the . . . the pageantry of the Nazis, I suppose. He joined the German-run Schalburg Corps and became part of their ET, the espionage unit of the corps. A bunch of damned informers."

Einar shook his head sadly. "It . . . it doesn't seem possible. Torben? *Han var paere Dansk*—he was apple-pure Danish." He looked at Lars. "He was our friend."

"Yes," Lars said tonelessly. "Was."

"He must have been bitter," Einar ventured. "Because of losing his shop. And being wounded by the British bombers."

Lars snorted in disdain. "Is that what he told you? Crap! He was injured in the raid on the Shell House. He was there, Einar, informing on his 'friends'!"

Einar looked stricken. "Informers," he muttered. "HIPOs. What has happened here, Lars?"

"Don't judge us all because of them," Lars said firmly. "For every one of them, there are thousands of us. With all the glamour-coated recruiting mounted by the Nazis, there are little more than five hundred HIPOs in the whole damned country."

He picked up the HIPO tunic from the floor, folded it, and began to wrap it in a newspaper.

"We tried to stop you before you went to Torben," he said. "I thought you'd go there. We staked out Sankt Knuds Vej that same night."

"I was there. I slept in a bicycle shed."

"Allan missed you. And he got to Torben's place just in time to see him arrive with his Nazi cronies. He stayed around to see them come out empty-handed and figured you'd made Torben and taken off."

"That's exactly what happened."

Lars nodded. "I was sure of it. That's why we are meeting here."

"Why?"

"Torben. By now he has denounced me to his German friends. He didn't know I was in the resistance. I figured you had told him about seeing me in a HIPO uniform, and I knew he'd put two and two together."

"Shit! I—"

"Don't worry about it. You couldn't possibly know. Anyway, all I had to do was get out of the place where I live. Believe me, it wasn't the first time."

"Would Torben have turned you in? You?"

Lars gave him a sidelong gaze. "Remember Niels?" he asked. "At Bavnehøj? One class below us? Torben kind of took him under his wing."

Einar nodded.

"Niels got himself involved with a BOPA sabotage unit. He and Torben were still seeing each other off and on . . . and Niels confided in him." He paused. He looked straight at Einar. "He was shot," he said. "After a week of . . . interrogation by the Gestapo. At Ryvangen. They said he was so weak he couldn't stand by himself, but had to be tied to the damned stake. Torben turned him in."

Lars gave an angry tug at the paper he was wrapping around the HIPO tunic. It tore. He ripped it off and began all over again.

For a bitter moment both men stood in silence, broken by Einar.

"Whose place is this?" he asked.

"My sister's. She's taking *Philosophicum* at the university. She became *Student* last year. Torben doesn't know about her place, but to take no chances, we'll find another safe house tomorrow."

He had finished. He placed the neatly wrapped package on the bed. "Now," he said, looking straight at Einar. "Why the hell are you here? What can I do to help?"

"I need a transmitter," Einar said. "I lost mine when I bolted from your place. I need to contact London as quickly as possible."

"No problem. We have access to a transmitter. Twenty-four-hour monitoring on their side."

"Great! Take me to it. The quicker the better. I'm my own pianist, so you don't need an operator."

Lars contemplated him, eyes momentarily hooded. "Better still," he said brightly. "Write your message, and I'll see that it gets off immediately.

Your fist will make no difference. We cannot contact your control directly. Your message will have to go through our contact. Allan can take care of that.'' He smiled at Einar. ''Then you and I can discuss where we go from here . . . and get something to eat. I happen to know there is a freshly made *Leverpostej* in the kitchen.''

In the span of a few heartbeats, a thousand thoughts sped through Einar's mind. He trusted Lars. But he had also trusted Torben—up to a point. Go slow. Be *certain* this time—absolutely certain that Lars and his group are totally reliable. London would know, if they are what Lars says they are. London could vouch for them. Wait. The message. It can say very little. He'd have to write it in clear text. His own cipher would not be understood by Lars's London contact.

As if reading his thoughts, Lars said, ''There's paper and a pencil on the night table.''

Einar sat down. How to word the damned thing? First, QSP—priority message. Then SMB—his personal verification group. No one but Bally would recognize it, but Bally would know the message was indeed from Einar, and not transmitted under duress. He wrote:

QSP SMB CONTACT BALLYMORE SOE INFORM AM OPERATIVE TRANSMITTER LOST NEED NEW TRANSMISSION INSTRUCTIONS DRUMMER

He looked it over. Not too long—but it was all Bally would need to know. For now. He knew the sergeant major would check out the source of the transmission, and if Lars and his group were on the up-and-up, he'd reply—including his own verification group. All he had to do now was wait.

He handed the slip of paper to Lars.

''Just send this,'' he said. ''You'll have to use your own enciphering.''

Lars glanced at the message. ''That's all?'' he asked.

''That's all.''

''Good as done.''

''When will we have an answer?''

''Two . . . three hours,'' Lars said. ''Depending on what action they have to take in London.''

Einar nodded. ''Of course.''

Lars picked up the package from the bed. ''Okay,'' he said. ''While I take care of this, my sister'll get you a bite to eat.''

He opened the door. He called.

''Bo! Come in here, will you?''

The girl who stepped into the little bedroom was about nineteen years old. Lithe and slender, but obviously a woman, she had that glowing, fresh complexion so common to the Scandinavians. Her short-cut hair was blond, and her gray-blue eyes had that ever-present twinkle of people with a sense of humor. Einar found her extremely attractive.

"Einar," Lars said, "I want you to meet my little sister. We call her Bo—her initials."

He smiled at the girl.

"Her name is Birte."

13

The *Leverpostej* looked delicious. It had been a long time since he'd had it last. His mouth actually started to water as he spread a generous helping of the creamy liver paté on the *Rugbrød*—the Danish rye bread. Lovingly he topped it with a slice of *Asie*—pickled cucumber rind. How long since he'd had *that?* He was aware of Birte watching him, her eyes amused.

"Did you make the *Leverpostej* yourself?" he asked. What a damned inane question, he thought, disgusted with himself.

"Yes," Birte answered. "Yesterday."

He glanced at her. Damned attractive girl. He wanted to get to know her, and that was all he could think of saying? He took a bite. It would give him a little time to come up with something more intelligent.

The *Leverpostej* was as delicious as he'd remembered it. More so.

"It's very good," he said. Oh, brilliant!

"It's mostly pork liver," Birte told him. "With egg yolks and spices—and a few other things. I bake it for one hour."

The conversation was becoming positively scintillating.

"Lars tells me you are studying for your *Philosophicum* at the university," he said. Not much better, he thought. "Do you find it interesting?"

"Much of it is fascinating," Birte said. "But philosophy is really just a fancy word for common sense, isn't it?" She smiled at him. "Unfortunately that seems to be in short supply these days."

"I got my *Cand. Phil.* in 1939," Einar told her. What the hell was the matter with him? He sounded like a retarded high school kid on a bad day. "From the university right here," he finished lamely.

"I know," Birte nodded. She gave him an enigmatic look. "Actually, I know quite a lot about you. At one time Lars never stopped talking about you." She sipped her milk.

"I'm glad you are still talking *to* me," he observed wryly.

Birte laughed. "He did have some rather . . . elaborate tales to tell about your schoolboy exploits," she acknowledged.

"I'll bet."

"Don't worry. I only believe half of what he told me."

"I sure hope it's the right half," he said fervently.

She laughed. He found her laughter delightful.

"That depends, doesn't it?" she teased him. "On what *you* consider the right half."

Luckily his mouth was full of *Leverpostej* so that he didn't have to think of a clever comeback. He wondered what Lars had told his sister about him. He was surprised to realize that it mattered to him. None of the . . . the girl escapades, he hoped. It made him vaguely uncomfortable to think Birte might know.

Birte lifted her glass of milk to him. "Here's mud in your eye," she said. "I learned that from an American movie with Humphrey Bogart."

He laughed. "I think I prefer the Danish *Skaal!*"

There were cheese snacks and a few butter cookies before Birte was through feeding him. The conversation gradually became less self-conscious and stiff, and by the time Einar was helping Birte clean up and put away the dishes, they were chatting easily like old friends.

He told her about going to America and about joining the army, and she filled him in about her activities with her brother and his group. Mostly as a courier, she told him. A young woman on a bicycle had an easier time with the police patrols than a young man. Especially, Einar thought, if she has the looks of a golden Viking princess and a smile that sets you tingling.

They were both startled when Lars returned. The nearly three hours had flown by.

"Sorry I didn't get back before so we could talk," he said to Einar. "Something came up that needed attending to." He glanced at his sister. "I hope Bo behaved herself," he grinned. "She has a tendency to talk your ears off."

"Mine are still on," Einar observed. "I don't know about hers."

Lars fished a piece of paper from his pocket. "Here's your answer from London," he said. He handed the message to Einar.

Einar read it at once:

DRUMMER CONTINUE TRANSMISSIONS VIA PRESENT LINK
GOOD LUCK

And there was the verification code of Sergeant Major Ballymore. The message was genuine. No one could have known Bally's personal code.

"Everything all right?" Lars asked.

"You bet."

"And we pass muster?"

Einar gave his friend a quick, embarrassed glance. Lars laughed. "I know you were checking us out," he said. "You had to. And don't forget—it worked both ways!"

He pulled up a chair and sat down.

"Now," he said soberly. "Tell me why you are here. What is it you have to do?" He glanced at Birte. "You don't mind if Bo stays?" he asked.

Einar smiled at Birte. "Please stay," he said. He looked at Lars.

And he outlined his mission for them. From the initial report about the poison gas to the need to find out what he could about the late scientist colleague of Niels Bohr.

For a moment Lars sat frowning in thought. "Professor Aksel Eigil Meyer," he mused. "I don't know of him." He glanced at his sister. She shook her head. "But that means nothing. We can certainly find out who he was. And possibly locate some of his coworkers, or friends."

"That's all I need," Einar said. "That—and being able to use your radio." He looked at the two of them. "Any suggestions where to begin?" he asked.

"The obvious," Lars said. "Biographical reference works in the library. He might even be listed in *Kraks Blaa Bog—Who's Who.* A listing might give us some leads."

"University records," Birte suggested. "Even if Professor Meyer was not on the staff, they might well have records of him. Certainly if he was in research."

Lars picked up a telephone book. He began to leaf through it. "The most obvious," he commented. "And the one source most people never think to use. This is an old directory. Professor Meyer may have been listed then. We might find out where he lived." He found the page he was looking for. His finger searched down the columns. "Only . . . Professor Aksel Eigil Meyer is not listed."

"Utility records," Birte said. "Electricity, water, gas, that sort of thing. I think they keep records for a few years back."

Lars nodded. "And licensing bureaus. First thing in the morning, I'll get my people on it." He nodded to Einar.

"We'll find out about your professor for you."

By noon the following day, Saturday, April 28, the reports from Lars's group were in.

Biographical reference works at the library—negative. Apparently Professor Meyer was not a prominent-enough scientist to merit a listing.

Utility records—negative. No Professor Meyer had availed himself of such services in greater Copenhagen. Licensing bureaus—similarly negative, as were postal box queries and queries to department stores—Illum and Magazin du Nord, where information could be obtained at all. All City Hall records were controlled by the Germans and not accessible without prior written request in triplicate.

The records of the university contained no mention of a Professor Aksel Eigil Meyer. Even discreet inquiries around Niels Bohr's Institute of Theoretical Physics under the university had yielded no information whatsoever. And the facilities themselves had already been thoroughly searched by the Germans, all remaining documents and papers removed.

It was a dead end.

Einar began to doubt that the man ever existed. Perhaps intelligence had come up with a wrong name?

It was Birte who hit pay dirt. She had gone to the home of Niels Bohr, the Jacobson House inside the grounds of the Carlsberg Brewery, a large residence that had been placed at Bohr's disposal by the Carlsberg Foundation, established to further the arts and sciences.

Birte had located a former caretaker, a woman, who remembered seeing Professor Meyer. He was, however, not a coworker of Bohr. She was positive of that. He was simply a friend, she believed. She had often seen them together, along with a third man, going off to lunch, she supposed, or to some other social affair; a man who was a pathologist at the Rigshospitalet—the national hospital. In the morgue, she shuddered. And she knew his name. It was Dr. Henrik V. Westphal.

And Dr. Henrik V. Westphal was listed in the telephone directory.

Dr. Westphal was a small, balding, middle-aged man with bad, tobacco-stained teeth, which might have accounted for the fact that he hardly ever smiled. It was Saturday, and he was home when the doorbell rang.

He peered suspiciously at Einar standing on the landing outside his apartment. Einar was alone. Lars had his hands full with preparations for the next day's sabotage action and had not been able to go with him, and Einar had not wanted to wait. But Birte had insisted on accompanying him. She was stationed in the hall below as lookout.

They had discussed how to get Westphal to tell them what they wanted to know, should he prove reluctant. Birte had persuaded Einar to use the completely frank approach rather than to try deception of some kind, rarely successful with intelligent people. Disarmingly frank, as she had put it, and Einar, although not convinced it was the best course to follow, had agreed—with only minor changes. Even if Westphal turned out to be a German sympathizer and talked, Einar could not be found. Revealing himself held only minor risks; certainly he could not be placed in greater jeopardy than he already was.

He looked at the man in the open doorway.

"Dr. Westphal?" he inquired.

"I am Westphal."

"Dr. Westphal," Einar went on earnestly. "My name is Einar Munk." He showed the man his SOE identification. "I am in the resistance movement—and I need some information only you can give me. It is of the utmost importance to our country, and it will, of course, be held in the strictest confidence." He looked directly at the wary man. "May I come in?"

Westphal did not answer, nor did he motion Einar inside.

"What do you mean . . . information?" he asked, his eyes filled with distrust. "I can tell you nothing."

"You can, Dr. Westphal," Einar persisted. "I need information about a . . . a friend of yours."

Westphal shrugged. "I am afraid I can tell you nothing, young man." He glared coldly at Einar. "Whether you are from the resistance, or the . . . authorities." The word sounded like a swearword.

"I am not an informer, Dr. Westphal. I am not a collaborator," Einar said emphatically. "I am working for the resistance."

"It makes no difference," Westphal said flatly. "I can tell you nothing." He began to close the door.

"Wait!" Einar stopped him. "You don't even know who it is I need to know about," he protested.

Dr. Westphal shrugged. "It can make no difference."

"At least, will you hear me out?"

"Of course," Westphal nodded indifferently. "I believe in being courteous to strangers."

"The man I need information about is Professor Aksel Eigil Meyer."

Westphal's eyes widened almost imperceptibly for a split second. He stared at Einar.

"Professor Meyer was arrested," he said tonelessly. "By the Gestapo. He was . . . deported."

"I know."

Westphal gave him a sharp look. He said nothing.

"Professor Meyer is dead," Einar said, watching the tiny twitch that tugged at Westphal's face. "He was sent to Germany to work for the Nazis. He killed himself rather than do so."

"You know more about Professor Meyer than I do," Westphal said slowly.

"But not what I need to know."

Westphal appraised him, eyes veiled. He stood silent.

"I need to know about Professor Meyer's work," Einar continued.

"As much detail as possible. His special field. Anything that can shed light on why the Germans wanted him." His eyes fixed the little man solemnly. "Professor Meyer sacrificed himself rather than work against his fatherland, Dr. Westphal. Can you debase his memory and the memory of your friendship by withholding information that could be of help to what he believed in and gave his life for?"

For a moment Westphal stood frowning at the door. Then he looked up, his eyes bleak but defiant.

"I . . . I regret the death of Professor Meyer," he said flatly. "But I cannot help you. He was merely a friend. We played cards together. Nothing else."

"With Niels Bohr," Einar nodded.

Westphal stared at him. "You know that, too?"

"But I need information about Professor Meyer's work," Einar pressed earnestly. "From you. Was his field pathology, like yours? Or physics, like Bohr's? Or what?"

Westphal slowly shook his head. "I know nothing to tell you," he said darkly. "I am afraid you will have to go back to your . . . superiors and tell them so. You will have to get your information elsewhere."

"Dr. Westphal, I know what you mean by my . . . superiors. But let me assure you, I am *not* a HIPO informer."

"I did not say you were."

"I do represent the resistance. The freedom fighters."

"So you are telling me."

"But you do not believe me?"

Westphal shrugged. "It is immaterial what I believe, young man. I have no information to give you." He closed his mouth, pressing his lips together with a look of defiant finality.

Einar realized he was getting nowhere. Westphal simply did not trust him. And there was no way he could force him to cooperate.

"Dr. Westphal," he said solemnly. "Please reconsider. You, as did your friend, Professor Meyer, have a duty to your fatherland. I shall contact you again."

"I shall be here," Westphal assured him. "I am a law-abiding subject." He gave Einar a cold glance. "But I shall still not have the knowledge you seek. Good day to you, young man."

And Dr. Westphal closed the door.

Einar joined Birte below. He said nothing. Quickly they retrieved their bikes and hurriedly pedaled away. Birte glanced at him. "Did you get what you wanted?" she asked.

He shook his head. "He would not believe me, Birte," he said. "I'm afraid he thinks I'm a HIPO informer, trying to trick him."

Birte nodded. "It would not be the first time," she agreed soberly.

"I've got to make him believe me," Einar said. "He's my only lead. And I know he has the information I need. I feel it in my bones. But he's afraid of something. That revealing what he knows about Meyer's work will get him in trouble? Or has he something to hide? Is he protecting someone? Dammit! How in hell can I make the bastard trust me?" he asked in frustration.

For a moment they rode in silence. Then Birte looked at him and said quietly, "I think I know how."

At exactly that same moment, across town, Torben Kvistholm walked out of the new Gestapo headquarters in Dagmar Hus. He was in deep thought. He was still seething with anger at the discredit he had suffered when Einar got away. He knew his star had sunk by several degrees in the eyes of the Germans, especially *Sturmbannführer* Coblenz, and he was determined to make it rise again. Perhaps to even greater heights than ever.

He mulled over what he had just learned. Reports from several informants infiltrated into a variety of official organizations indicated that someone, someone unknown and for unknown purposes, was attempting to elicit information about a certain scientist, a Professor Aksel Eigil Meyer, who had been conscripted to work in Germany for the Reich on some unknown project. A man who was now dead. Who was making these inquiries?

And why?

He thought he knew who, although he had said nothing to his German masters.

It was Einar.

It had all started at the time Einar had appeared. Just after he'd arrived from England. And it was Lars. The raid on Lars's flat had yielded absolutely nothing. Proof enough that Lars was a member of the resistance. He was convinced that Einar and Lars had somehow gotten together. They were behind the clandestine search for information about Meyer. He did not know why, but he would find out. Of Einar and Lars he was certain. The way the investigation was being conducted was exactly the way Lars would have done it. He smiled coldly to himself. He knew Lars. And he knew Einar. He was totally confident that he'd be able to anticipate their next moves. He drew himself up.

He walked rapidly down the street, his injured leg forgotten.

He knew exactly what they'd do next.

He would be ready for them.

14

It was still dark when Einar woke up with a start. For a panic-stricken split second, he did not know where he was. Then he remembered. He struck a match and looked at his watch: 5:00 A.M. Too early for a Sunday, he thought. But then, this would be no ordinary Sunday. This would be the day a machine-parts factory producing war material for the Germans would, as Lars had put it, go BOOM!

He was too keyed up to go back to sleep. For a moment he lay listening to the steady breathing of Lars, fast asleep on his cot in the attic of the house where Allan lived. They'd moved in with him soon after their meeting at Birte's place. They used his apartment below for their necessities and slept in the attic, where they also kept their few belongings. When you were underground, you moved a lot, he'd found out, and traveled light. In case of trouble, there were two escape routes prepared for them. Allan's apartment was located in an old part of town, and the houses were built shoulder to shoulder in the streets. By breaking through the walls in the attic on either side, access was gained to the attics next door. Allan's attic connected through three houses either way.

The night before, there'd been a meeting at which the freedom fighters of Lars's group had gone over the entire sabotage operation for the third and last time. There had been eight people gathered in Allan's little flat: Lars and Allan himself; the two men who had been with Allan when they'd picked Einar up at Sankt Knuds Vej, Per and Klaus; two more members of the group; and Birte and Einar.

Birte's idea of how to win the trust of Dr. Westphal was simple and undeniable. With some misgivings Lars had agreed to it.

Birte and Einar would join the operation. Birte would carry a small camera—and shoot pictures of Einar in compromising situations that identified him with the sabotage. The next day, when the papers carried the story of the raid, they'd show the pictures to Dr. Westphal. That should settle any doubts he might have about Einar.

Einar had been impressed with the plans for the sabotage operation. Any trained OSS team would have been proud of it. Nothing had been left to chance. The target was a big factory, and a lot of high explosives would be needed if any real damage was to be inflicted. The risk of carrying such large amounts of HE to the target site at one time, on the day of the action, would be considerable, and Lars had come up with a different and ingenious way of getting the explosives to the factory. As a matter of fact, they were already there. Fifty-two pounds of plastic high explosives. All that was left for the saboteurs to carry were the sensitive detonators and some lengths of time fuse. For the last two weeks a couple of factory workers, cooperating with Lars's group, had—as had all the workers at the plant—brought their lunch with them to work, *Smørrebrød*—open-faced sandwiches—individually wrapped in paper. Four each. The two top ones in their lunch buckets were topped with cheese, Danish salami, or *Leverpostej*. The two bottom ones were plastic high explosives shaped and wrapped as sandwiches. These *Smørrebrød* explosives had been carefully hidden in the workers' lockers in the common locker room. The lockers were private and safe, and the odor in the room of sweaty clothing and sour boots, and of strong soap, would disguise the distinct smell of the plastic high explosives.

At the time the factory would go up, the two workers would be fast asleep miles away with the most iron-clad alibis in the world.

The plant operated on *Skiftehold*—double shifts—closing only Sunday mornings. That would be the time of minimal risk to Danish workers. It would also be a time when few people were in the streets, always an important consideration for a successful strike. The sabotage operation was scheduled to take place at precisely 8:00 A.M. Lars would have preferred daybreak, but the saboteurs might have been stopped and searched if they were seen abroad too early on a Sunday morning.

The target factory was located opposite an office building on a street in the harbor district near Sydhavnen—the South Harbor. Allan and the other resistance men, each armed with a handgun, were already at the place of rendezvous, the courtyard of the office building, when Lars, Einar, and Birte arrived.

There were no greetings; there was no small talk. Only solemn, brief nods and necessary checks. In just minutes the lives of all of them would be on the line.

The bikes were placed against a wall facing the portal to the street, ready to be mounted on the run for a fast getaway once the action had been carried out.

Suddenly Lars looked up sharply. Tensely he watched two men—strangers—who came riding into the yard. They stopped in front of the group. All eyes were upon them, all hands near weapons.

One of them looked directly at Lars.

"Do you have a match?" he asked.

Lars nodded. "Yes. One that weighs fifty-two pounds," he answered.

"That should do it," the stranger said.

Lars grinned. He stuck out his hand. "Welcome," he said. "You can set up on the stairwell of the building. It overlooks the site of the action."

The two men nodded. They placed their bicycles with the others and quickly walked to the door that led to the stairs of the office building, carrying a couple of bags.

Einar looked after them, puzzled. He turned to Lars. "Who—?"

"They're from Holger Danske," he explained. "The umbrella resistance group. A photographic team. They'll film the operation."

"You're kidding!"

"Not at all. Most of the major sabotage actions are recorded on film by resistance photographers. They must have hundreds of thousands of feet of film by now." He grinned. "I hope this one will be one of their more spectacular numbers."

He glanced at his watch, suddenly sober. Quickly he issued his orders.

"Per, take your position at the south end of the street. Klaus, the north. No one gets through."

"Right." The two men grabbed their bikes and took off for their posts.

Lars turned to Einar and Birte. "Remember," he admonished. "You stick close to me."

They nodded.

"Let's go."

Carrying the detonators and the fuses, Lars and his three remaining group members hurried from the courtyard, closely followed by Einar and Birte.

It was exactly eight o'clock, Sunday morning, April 29. The operation had begun.

The little group hurried across the street. Their manner of gaining access to the plant was direct and effective. Lars simply banged loudly on the front door with all the arrogance of a HIPO or German officer. Presently the door was opened, and a sleepy watchman blinked at them.

Quickly Lars pushed him inside and held him at gunpoint. The others crowded in after him, closing the door behind them.

"We know there are two of you," Lars snapped sharply. "Where's the other one?"

"In the guard room," the watchman said, eyeing the gun.

Lars gestured impatiently. "Move!"

The man led the way to the little guard room. Another man was snoozing in a chair. He woke up with a start as his comrade was pushed in through the door. He stared at the gun held by Lars. He gave a quick glance toward his own, nestled in a holster on his belt, which was draped over the back of a chair, but he made no move to grab it.

"Get up!" Lars snapped. "If you don't want to get blown sky-high along with this whole damned building, you'd better get your ass out of here. You'll be safe in the courtyard across the street." He nodded to Allan. "All yours."

At gunpoint Allan herded the two security men from the room. The others at once hurried toward the locker room.

"Look for numbers 79 and 45," Lars called as they ran down the corridor.

Each locker had a neat stack of *Smørrebrød* explosives at the bottom, hidden under some rags. Quickly they were hauled out. There were fifty-two of them. Each of Einar's two comrades took seventeen packets, enough for three charges of five to six pounds each. Lars, whose targets were the most massive, took the remaining eighteen.

The next few minutes were a blur of activity for Einar. Working quickly, efficiently, every move rehearsed, the men shaped the charges and taped them together with the electrical tape left for them in the lockers. Einar worked right along with them:

Tape the plastic explosives tightly together. Crimp a detonator to a length of time fuse. Use your teeth if no pliers are available. He used his teeth. Birte was snapping away with her camera. The time fuse was red. Einar knew that meant it would burn forty seconds to the foot. Each length of fuse was six feet. They'd have just four minutes to get out of the plant to safety after the fuses were lit.

Lars talked urgently throughout, his voice taut. "You know your targets," he said. "Place your charges securely. Be sure the fuses are lit."

The detonators were number 6s. Not the more powerful number 8s. Use two for each charge—to make absolutely sure. Carefully he inserted them into the plastic, taping them in place.

"Six minutes to go!" Lars called.

Feverishly they worked.

They were finished.

Lars shot a glance at his watch.

"On time," he announced. "Four minutes left. In exactly four minutes, light your fuses—and get the hell out of here!"

He suddenly became worried. He always did. Were they taking too long—in case some kind of alarm had been given? He dismissed the thought as soon as it intruded. Stick to the damned plan.

They took off, carrying the prepared charges.

Lars, trailed by Einar and Birte, ran toward his targets. Two big transformers.

Two minutes left.

Einar took one of the charges and taped it firmly in place.

Birte snapped away.

Zero.

The fuses sputtered to life.

They ran.

All of them reached the door within seconds of each other. Together they sprinted across the empty street to the safety of the courtyard beyond.

Their breaths came quick and hard as they waited with Allan and his two prisoners. The tension was a tangible pressure in Einar's chest.

And it came.

The explosion was ear-shattering. A searing white light flashed through the portal. Almost immediately, a second explosion rent the air, instantly followed by a series of blasts. The ground trembled.

They grabbed their bikes. They ran to the street. The entire roadbed was littered with debris; shattered bricks and crumbled concrete; twisted chunks of metal that had once been intricate machinery; splintered glass. Not a window in the office building had survived. A broken water main gushed water.

The factory was gutted. The roof at one end had collapsed. Fire was roaring through the hole, and flames were licking through the empty openings that had been the windows. Thick, black smoke churned and billowed high into the air.

The two photographers came running with their bikes. Quickly they all mounted and sped from the scene. Any minute, perhaps any second, the Germans would come roaring. Already they could hear the wailing horns of the fire engines and police cars in the distance. They pumped the pedals as fast as they could, and their bicycles skittered over the cobblestones.

At the first street corner, one of the bikers peeled off. At each successive street crossing, someone else would leave the group. If there was any pursuit, there'd be no easy target to follow. In a short while, Einar and Birte found themselves alone. They pedaled sedately down the street. They knew where they were headed. Enghaven. A little park around a library. There they could be found—two lovers sitting on the lawn, enjoying the calm of a Sunday morning.

Impulsively they embraced as they sank down on the grass. Einar could feel his heart race as he held the girl in his arms. He was well aware it was not caused entirely by the excitement of the raid and the exertion of the bike ride.

Triumphantly Birte held up her little camera. She smiled at Einar. She looked radiant.

"I've got it," she exulted. "You can convince Dr. Westphal now. You can get your information!" She patted the camera affectionately. "Lars will have them developed right away. We can go see Westphal later this afternoon."

Torben Kvistholm stirred lazily in his bed. It wasn't even half past eight yet. He liked to lie and doze on Sunday mornings. Besides, his damned leg throbbed. He might have overdone it these past couple of days.

He wondered idly what the distant bang and rumble was. Early summer thunder? No matter. It had nothing to do with him.

He was pleased with himself. His hunch had paid off. He'd put himself in Lars's and Einar's place. What would they do to find out about Professor Meyer? Other than the inquiries he already knew about? On a hunch he'd queried about a dozen additional scientific organizations in Copenhagen, including the Technical College, the Carlsberg Scientific Laboratories, the Finsen Institute, and Bohr's Institute of Theoretical Physics. He knew that Lars was thorough, so he'd gone to Bohr's residence as well. And he'd found the caretaker, who'd told him he was the second person wanting to know about Professor Meyer, of all people. She could only tell him what she'd already told that nice young woman.

And now he knew about Dr. Westphal. Dr. Henrik V. Westphal.

The man's house was already under surveillance. By Torben's own men.

Sooner or later they'd show up there, Lars and Einar. It was only a matter of time.

A little time.

15

Birte's snapshots would not have won any prizes in a photo contest, but they would serve their intended purpose. There was Einar crimping a detonator; Einar moving among the machinery in the factory; Einar taping an explosive charge; Einar uncoiling a fuse; Einar placing a charge at a transformer. There was no mistaking Einar, and there was no mistaking the fact that he was actually in the target factory. The factory that had just been destroyed.

Birte was delighted. "It's only a little past five," she said. "Let's not wait until tomorrow. Westphal has probably heard all about the raid anyway. Let's go see him now."

"Easy, Bo," Lars laughed. He glanced at her with affection. He knew his little sister. Eager to show what she'd accomplished. He looked at Einar. "What do you want to do?" he asked.

"I want to get whatever information Westphal has as quickly as I can," Einar said. He frowned lightly. "But—"

Lars nodded. "But is right. You're thinking the same thing I am."

"Yes. Torben."

"What about Torben?" Birte asked.

"Look, Bo," her brother answered her. "Einar and I, we know Torben. We know how he operates. He doesn't let go. He follows through. On the smallest details. And he'll go off on the wildest tangents if he thinks there's the slightest hope it'll pay off." He looked earnestly at her. "What you could find out—what we could find out—Torben could, too. And probably did."

"Oh," Birte said, crestfallen. "Then you think he may know about Westphal? Where he lives? You think he may have set a trap for us there?"

"Possibly," Einar nodded.

"We also know where Westphal works," Birte said. "At the Rigshospitalet. We could go there. To the morgue."

"It's Sunday."

"People die on Sundays, too. Somebody's got to be there. It could be Westphal. We could find out."

"We could, Bo," Lars said. "You have an excellent idea. It would be better to contact Westphal at the hospital than at his home. We've already been there, at least you have, and you know my rule, never go to the same place twice." He looked at his friend. "Einar?"

"I agree; the hospital is a great idea. It will be a hell of a lot easier to figure a way to get to Westphal there, where there's a lot of people and activity, than walking up to his door, big as life. I think we have to assume that Torben also knows about Westphal's hospital job. However, at the man's home it would be easy to take us. At the hospital—another story. We'd have a damned better chance." He looked closely at Birte. "That's why I also vote to wait until tomorrow. The newspapers will be out. If Westphal hasn't read about the raid, we can show him. And more important, the hospital routine will be normal."

Birte nodded. "I see your point. Tomorrow, then."

"Tomorrow," Einar repeated. He was silent for a moment, then he looked gravely at Lars. His friend returned his somber look.

"It will have to be done," he said heavily.

Einar sighed. "I . . . agree."

"I . . . I'll alert Holger Danske. I am certain there will be no problem getting the go-ahead from the council."

"What are you talking about?" Birte wanted to know.

"Torben," her brother answered her soberly. "He is becoming very dangerous. To us. To Einar's mission. And to the resistance movement." He glanced at Einar before he continued. "The freedom council must okay any . . . eh, action taken against an informer. We'll get it. And Torben will be liquidated."

Birte was about to say something. She thought better of it. She bit her lip. Now was not the time. She knew how close the three friends had been. All through school. And the years after. She realized how very difficult it must have been for her brother and Einar to make the decision they had just made. She kept quiet.

For a brief moment they all sat in silence. Then Lars spoke.

"Go home, Bo," he said kindly. "Einar and I will turn in early tonight. It's been . . . quite a day. We'll pick you up tomorrow morning." He looked at his sister.

"I have an idea how we may lick the problem of getting to Westphal," he said. "And we'll need you."

It was midmorning when Einar, Lars, and Birte placed their bikes in one of the racks on the grounds of the Rigshospitalet.

It was Monday, April 30. Count Folke Bernadotte of the Swedish Red Cross was in Copenhagen on his way to Sweden. Already the city was abuzz with rumors. Bernadotte was returning from a secret meeting in South Jutland with *Reichsführer-SS* Heinrich Himmler. Was an armistice imminent? Or capitulation of the Nazi forces in Norway and Denmark? Einar felt the mood of the people tense in anticipation.

HIPO acts of terror were on the increase, and so were railroad sabotage by the resistance and the elimination of *Stikkere*—the hated informers. Eight of them had been killed the day before.

The end appeared to be near. And so, perhaps, Einar thought with a chill, was a desperate decision by Hitler to try to turn the inevitable tide with a last terrible stroke of horror.

The secret of Professor Aksel Eigil Meyer—and the Weiden project?

It brought a new urgency to their quest. An urgency that justified the risks they were taking.

For a short while they stood looking around, appraising their surroundings. Nothing untoward. They started to walk toward the main building.

The hospital was actually a large group of big brick buildings taking up the entire block on Tagensvej between Jagtvej and Nørre Allé. The morgue was located in the basement of the main building.

They entered on the ground floor at the opposite end of where the morgue was located. They moved in cautiously, closely observing everything around them. They saw nothing suspicious. The hospital staff, busy going about their errands, paid them no attention.

"Any idea where we can 'organize' the stuff?" Lars whispered.

"If you mean 'liberate,' as in steal," Einar whispered back, "the answer is no."

"How about a supply room?" Birte suggested.

"Sure," Lars said. "Where?"

"Back there." Birte pointed. "Down that corridor we just passed. I saw a sign on a door."

They turned and quickly walked back the way they'd come.

The attendant, who was sorting cards at a desk outside the area that held the pathological offices, labs, and storage vaults of the morgue, looked up as two white-smocked orderlies appeared, carrying a stretcher between them with a blanket-covered body. Only a shoeless foot and a slim ankle could be seen sticking out.

"HIPOs are at it again," Lars said. "Killed a woman over by Trianglen—the Triangle intersection. Real mess." He consulted a piece of paper. "Where's Dr. . . . eh, Westphal's lab?"

The attendant looked at him. His gaze traveled to the covered body on the stretcher, to the shapely ankle, to Einar—and back to Lars. He pointed.

"First corridor on the right," he said. "Two doors down. You can't miss it. Name's on the door."

"Thanks," Lars said. He hefted the stretcher. "He'll love this one!"

As they rounded the corner with their blanket-covered burden, neither Lars nor Einar saw the attendant reach for the telephone and vigorously crank the handle.

The swinging doors gave way as Einar and Lars pushed into the lab, carrying the stretcher. Einar, in the lead, at once took in the scene. Dr. Westphal was seated on a stool at a table, peering into a microscope. He was not alone. At a sink in the back of the room, an assistant, a young woman, was washing out some beakers and test tubes. Opposite Westphal stood a large cabinet, its contents of bottles and jars visible through glass-paned doors. On a table next to it stood a tray with surgical instruments.

Westphal barely looked up from his work. "On the table," he said, giving a quick nod toward a stainless-steel lab table standing in the middle of the room directly under a medical light fixture hanging from the ceiling.

Einar and Lars followed his instructions. They placed the stretcher with the covered body on the table. One end of it was overhanging the top.

The lab assistant was turning from the sink, a clean beaker in her hands, just as Birte sat up on the stretcher and tossed the blanket aside. The woman gave a short, startled cry, and the beaker crashed to the floor.

Alarmed, Westphal whirled around. He stood up abruptly, his stool toppling behind him. He stared at Birte, who was swinging her legs from the stretcher on the table.

"What—?" Recognition leaped into his eyes. "You!" he exclaimed. "What in hell are you doing here?"

"Dr. Westphal," Einar said, urgency tightening his voice, "we don't have much time. But we must talk with you." He looked around. The lab assistant stood pressed against the sink. But she looked more curious than frightened.

"Be quiet," Einar said to her. "Stay where you are and don't interfere, and you won't get hurt."

The woman nodded.

Einar pointed to a door, the only other door leading from the room. "What's in there?" he asked.

Westphal stared at him, his face flushed in outrage. "How . . . how dare you!" he sputtered.

"Records," the assistant broke in. "It's where we keep the records of the examinations and autopsies performed here."

Lars went to the door. He opened it. The large room beyond was filled from floor to ceiling with rows of shelves, holding hundreds of brown, flip-top cardboard record cases.

"Dr. Westphal," Einar addressed the pathologist. "Have you seen this morning's newspaper?"

"No," the man said curtly. "And I do not see what business it is of yours." He glared at Einar. "If you do not leave here at once, I shall summon the police!"

Without a word Birte handed him a paper she'd been holding. Westphal glanced at it. The banner headline read: DARING SABOTAGE RAID. And the subheading: Factory Totally Destroyed by Terrorist Action. Uncomprehendingly Westphal frowned at the paper and at the three people confronting him.

Lars pulled a packet of snapshots from his pocket. "Please look at these, Dr. Westphal," he asked quietly.

The pathologist took the snapshots. He leafed through them. Abruptly he stopped. Sharply he looked up at Einar. He returned to the snapshots, studying each one carefully. He steadied himself against the table and stood a moment in silence.

"What do you want?" he said at last. "How can I help?"

"We need to know about Professor Meyer," Einar said. "Anything you can tell us."

Westphal nodded. "It is not much, I am afraid," he began. "Aksel was somewhat of a recluse. He did not have many friends outside Niels and me. Niels Bohr. He lived with his widowed sister, a Fru Rasmussen—"

That explains why we couldn't find any utility records, Einar thought.

"—and he spent most of his time in his laboratory. He had a private research grant."

He looked at Einar. "You must understand, young man. After the German takeover here, and after the Nazis hammered nail after nail of hopelessness into the coffin that held our faith, our need for justice, our loyalty and our hope, after Norway fell to the Nazis, and Holland, Belgium, and France, Aksel concentrated more and more on his work, his science, to the exclusion of everything else. We all did. When he was arrested by the Gestapo and taken away, his laboratory was stripped bare."

"Why, Dr. Westphal?" Einar asked tautly. "Do you know why the Germans wanted him?"

Westphal shook his head.

"What was Professor Meyer working on?"

"He never discussed his project." Westphal looked thoughtful. "But it seemed . . . it seemed very important to him."

"What was his field? His speciality?"

"Professor Meyer was a toxicologist," Westphal said.

Einar felt a surge of dread.

There it was.

Westphal continued. "He studied poisons. Conducted experiments, I believe. There are thousands of substances known to be deadly poisonous. New ones are discovered or developed every day. One of the few times Aksel ever talked about his work, I remember he told us that there were potential antidotes to every poison imaginable, even the most virulent and horrible ones. Even to poisons as yet undreamed of. And he wanted to find and perfect such antidotes. He was a man of strong beliefs." He spread his hands. "I . . . I am afraid that is all I can tell you."

"Before his arrest," Einar asked, "did he talk to anyone? Do you know anyone else who was his confidant?"

Again Westphal shook his head. "Just before he was taken," he said, "he seemed . . . preoccupied. As if he knew something was about to happen to him. But I do not know—"

He suddenly stopped.

"Wait!" he cried. "There is something else." Excitedly he turned to his assistant.

"Lise," he said. "Get the file records of . . . of—" He thought hard. "Martens. Sophus Martens." He wrinkled his brow. "I made it easy to remember when I hid it. Nine. That's it." He brightened. "The date is 9. 9. 1939."

The assistant went into the records room. Lars followed. Einar turned to Westphal.

"What is it you have?" he asked.

"A package," Westphal said. "A small packet. Papers, I believe. Aksel asked me to keep them for him. I think he did not want them to fall into German hands. He did not say so. That is what I think."

The assistant returned with one of the brown record boxes. She handed it to Westphal. He examined the label.

"That's it," he said. "I think that for some reason Aksel did not want them to be associated with him. As far as the Germans were concerned. That is why he gave them to me."

"Thank you for that information, Dr. Westphal!"

The voice came from the door.They all whirled toward it.

In the open doorway stood Torben, a Luger, cocked and ready, trained on the group around Westphal. He was flanked by two burly HIPOs, each with a gun held firmly before them.

"That box, if you please, Dr. Westphal," Torben said with exaggerated affability, the smile on his face like a slit in a piece of sandpaper. "I shall take it!"

16

The moment hung frozen in time. Einar was the first to speak, his voice flat and bitter.

"Torben," he said, "do you know what you are doing? It's me. Einar. And Lars. We're your fellow Danes. We were your best friends. What happened? Why, Torben, why?"

Torben looked at him with a thin smile, the gun in his hand never wavering.

"Why?" he mocked. "Why? There is no . . . banal reason. The Germans are not holding my parents or my sweetheart hostage to force me to ally myself with them. If you are looking for such trite motivation, it is because you have seen too many gangster films in America."

"You are working with the damned enemy, Torben. Against your native country. How can you? How can you be a . . . a traitor?"

"Traitor?" Torben snapped scornfully. "Because I can see the future? Because I believe in it? Because I want to be part of it? Make something of myself?"

"Torben. Listen—"

"No, you listen, Einar, my friend. You don't understand. You were away in America, on your own sweet way to a promising future as a chemist." He nodded toward Lars. "And Lars was already making a successful career for himself in architecture. I was getting nowhere. Luck was always with you, never with me. I had to *make* mine. And now I have a chance to make something of myself. When the new order triumphs in Europe, *I* will be someone to reckon with!"

"There will be no . . . *new order,* Torben. Germany is losing the war."

"Churchill propaganda," Torben spat out. "The Führer will not be defeated. He has promised us a new weapon. A new and terrible weapon that will win the war in short shrift."

"Empty promises, Torben."

"Are they? Adolf Hitler promised us extraordinary weapons before. And he delivered! The V-1 and the V-2 have already brought the English to their knees. His final weapon, the weapon he has promised us, will finish them off. He will use it soon. Any day now!" He drew himself up. "And then *I* will be on top. If I have proved myself." He looked from Einar to Lars and back. "Of course, I regret that it is you who will be serving my purpose, you—a top Allied spy, and a top terrorist. But I shall see to it that you are treated with leniency. I shall personally speak to *Sturmbannführer* Coblenz."

He gestured with his gun. "Now, Einar, give me that box."

"Reconsider, Torben," Einar pleaded. "Please. You are throwing your life away."

"The box!" Torben held his gun out in front of him for emphasis.

Einar watched him. He suddenly knew there was no way for him to reach his friend. Torben *had* to believe himself right. Right without a shadow of a doubt. Or his whole world would come crashing down.

So be it.

He felt himself grow tense. He wanted to look at Lars, alert him, but he dared not do so, lest Torben should catch on. Resigned, he took the file case from Westphal. He started toward Torben. At the table with the cantilevered stretcher, he stopped.

"Torben," he said tentatively.

"Put it on the table," Torben said curtly. The gun in his hand pointed steadily at Einar. He stepped closer to the table.

Not yet.

Einar took one more step. He seemed to stumble. The box dropped to the floor. With all his might Einar thrust both his hands down on the end of the stretcher overhanging the table. The other end flew up like a teeter-totter—and struck Torben's gun arm at the wrist, sending the Luger flying.

For a split second the two HIPOs were distracted.

In the same split second, Lise, the lab assistant, grabbed a scalpel from the instrument tray and viciously sliced at the gun arm of the HIPO close to her. The razor-sharp knife bit through the black uniform tunic, through the skin and flesh, laying bare the bone from wrist to elbow, severing the artery. The man shrieked. His gun clattered to the floor, and he collapsed, unconscious, in shock—his life draining from him in oily rhythm.

Simultaneously Lars picked up a large glass beaker and hurled it at the other HIPO. The man fired. But in trying to protect himself, the shot went wild. The beaker struck him forcefully and squarely in the face, shattering into myriad razor-edged, stiletto-pointed glass shards that peppered his eyes. He screamed as he flung his hands to his bloody face.

As soon as the gun dropped by the blinded HIPO hit the floor, Einar lunged for it. He was aware of Torben diving to the floor on the other side of the table. Einar found the gun. He grabbed it. In the same motion he rose to a crouching position and whirled toward Torben, gun ready.

He froze. He found himself looking at the Luger held in Torben's hand, aimed straight at him.

Now!

Einar's finger froze on the trigger. He willed himself to pull it. He could not. Visions flashed before him: Torben, laughing and pedaling his bike into the school yard; Torben proudly pouring port wine; Torben helping him with his homemade tattoo; Torben, spellbound by Felumb's animal show. Torben . . .

Einar stared. He saw the hate, the rage, the desperation in his friend's eyes. He saw, and he understood. He had robbed his erstwhile friend of his imagined glory. He prepared to die.

There was a sudden sharp report. Torben shuddered. Uncomprehendingly he turned. But his eyes glazed over in death before they could register the sight of Birte, the gun dropped by the scalpel-slashed HIPO in her hand, standing staring at him, her face white.

It was over in the span of a few seconds.

Westphal picked up the file box from the floor. He pressed it into the hands of the dazed Einar.

"Take it!" he urged. "And leave. Quickly. Someone may have heard the shots. They will investigate." He nodded toward Lise. "Take her with you. I will tell the Germans my version of what happened. I shall be all right. But Lise—they will punish her for what she did. Hide her. It will all soon be over. The Allies will win the war. Any day now."

They hurried from the room. It had all happened so fast that Einar had trouble separating the acts.

He was alive. Because of Birte.

But Torben, once his friend, lay dead.

He felt a deep, dull sadness. Some of his innocence, the insouciance of youth, lay sprawled in death on the cement floor of a hospital morgue.

★ ★ ★

COUPLE DIES IN MOJAVE DESERT. LONDON DEVASTATED BY "V-1." AFRICAN ORDEAL. Einar frowned at the headlines. "I don't know what the hell it's all supposed to mean," he grumbled disgustedly. "It makes no damned sense."

He was perched on Allan's bed with Lars, Birte, and Lise, staring at the papers that had been in Professor Meyer's packet spread out on the covers.

Newspaper clippings. Magazine features. A few amateur snapshots. That was all.

The articles fell into two categories: dehydration and Nazi V-weapons.

There were accounts from English, German, French, Danish, and American sources. There was a piece about an elderly couple who had attempted to walk for help from their disabled car in the searing heat of the Mojave Desert in California, with detailed descriptions of the dehydrated condition of the corpses, when found.

There was a pitiful story from a paper in southern France about a child found locked up in a small windowless shed without water—including a picture of the shriveled, wasted appearance of the dehydrated little body.

There was an article from a picture magazine detailing the ravaging effects of dehydration on both cattle and people during a prolonged drought in Africa, with harrowing photographs of walking skeletons, sunken eyes, and cracked lips.

And there were others, including a few scientific articles from international science journals on dehydration, complete with charts and tables and medical terms such as diuresis, electrolyte deprivation, and renal failure, which meant nothing to them.

And there were the stories and pictures of Hitler's vengeance weapons, the V-1 and the V-2, and the damage they had caused.

VOLKSGENOSSE, SCHWEIGE!—Compatriot, Be Silent!—cried an article from the *Diepholzer Kreiszeitung* of August 21, 1944, admonishing people to give away none of the secrets of the V-1, accompanied by a picture of the "legendary bird of terror."

And a piece from the *Nordschleswigsche Zeitung* of November 8, 1944, *AUCH "V-2" EINGESETZT*—V-2 Also Employed—trumpeting the total lack of defense against the destructive vengeance weapon, as well as clippings of buzz bombs over London and the terrible devastation wreaked by them on the city . . .

And there was a feature from the Nazi propaganda magazine, *Signal*, from November 1944, about the V-1, calling the weapon a "turning point in warfare."

And finally, in an envelope, they'd found a few snapshots, obviously taken by an amateur in some hospital, showing patients suffering from dehydration, with file notations referring to the individual cases.

"Why on earth would Professor Meyer save those clippings?" Birte asked, puzzled. "Dehydration and vengeance weapons. What could possibly be his reason?"

"Beats me," Einar said. "They don't seem to have anything in common." He found it difficult to conceal his disappointment. The collection of clippings looked more like someone's hobby than the key to a secret project.

"I thought Westphal said Meyer was a toxicologist," Lars said. "What has all this to do with the study of poisons?"

"Not a damned thing," Einar said, "as far as I can see."

He gathered up the clippings and put them back in the file box.

"Back to square one," he said. "And we haven't even collected two hundred dollars for passing go."

The others looked at him, perplexed.

"Monopoly," he explained sheepishly. "Never mind. What I meant was, we've got to start from scratch." He looked at the others. "Any suggestions?"

"Fru Rasmussen," Birte said at once. "Professor Meyer's sister. You will have to talk to her."

"I can get the address," Lise said. "From Dr. Westphal."

Einar nodded at her. "Good. When?"

"I'm going home with Birte," Lise said. "For the night. I'll call Dr. Westphal at home this evening and give Birte the information for you."

"We can call on Fru Rasmussen first thing tomorrow morning," Lars said. "With Torben . . . gone, the pressure should be off."

"Meanwhile I'll cook up a report for London," Einar said. "I'm afraid it'll have to be fairly long." He looked at Lars. "Your radioman may have to break it down into two or three parts. Move around. You don't want to stay on the air in one place too damned long."

"No problem."

"How are you going to handle all that in your report?" Birte asked, pointing to the file box.

Einar shrugged. "I'll mention it," he said. "No details. I have none to give, anyway."

He stood up and stretched.

"Let's hope Fru Rasmussen turns out to be a gold mine of information. Tomorrow will tell . . ."

* * *

Einar had trouble falling asleep. The shadows in the dark attic took on the shapes of ominous, brooding figures silently watching him.

He could not get the image of Torben lying dead on the cold morgue floor out of his mind. With a pang of guilt, he realized he had been too shocked to thank Birte properly. She had saved his life. He promised to rectify this oversight. First opportunity he had.

Had it all been worthwhile? He *had* learned that Professor Meyer was a toxicologist. But he had expected that. It merely corroborated the ominous report the Polish slave laborer had given him—and made the search for *real* information that much more urgent. But outside of Meyer's sister, he had no idea where to find it. He had a nagging feeling that the strange collection of clippings in Meyer's package had some significance he was missing. But he had no idea what. Perhaps Meyer's sister would know.

For a while he lay on his cot and listened to Lars's regular breathing as his friend slept. Once aware of it, he could not shut it out. The sound of it became more and more intruding, louder and louder, and made it impossible for him to doze off. After each breath he found himself waiting for the next. Like waiting for the second shoe to drop, he thought mirthlessly. Only he was listening to a centipede. He *had* to get his mind off it. And off Torben.

Birte . . .

He tried to visualize her. It was not difficult. Her lithe, slender body and her delightful pixie face were clear in his mind. What would she be doing right now? She'd be asleep. He could see her. Lying peacefully in her bed, the one he had sat on, her short-cut, blond hair tousled on the pillow, her merry, gray-blue eyes closed, one deliciously bare arm stretched languidly over her head. He could see the exciting curve of her hip as she lay on her side under the thin blanket, her long legs drawn partly up.

He fantasized. Her breasts would be small and firm, easy to cup. Her skin cool and silken. Her scent . . . Her scent—

And he was asleep . . .

He was brought out of his deep sleep abruptly. Someone was shaking him. It was almost light outside. Allan and Lars stood at his cot.

"There's a message for you," Allan said. "Came in early, at first contact. From London." He looked gravely at Einar. "You had better read it."

17

Allan handed Einar a piece of folded paper. Einar unfolded it. The message had been written in penciled block letters on a piece of lined paper from a school composition book. It was unusually long.

The first letter group Einar saw was QSP—Accept Priority Message.

"Have you read it?" he asked Allan.

Allan nodded.

Carefully Einar read the message:

QSP DRUMMER REPORT ACKNOWLEDGED GOOD SHOW STOP HITLER DEAD WAR COMING TO END STOP ON SPOT INVESTIGATION INTERROGATION DETERMINE NO DANGER EXISTS RE WEIDEN PROJECT STOP ABORT REPEAT ABORT MISSION STOP AWAIT ARRIVAL ALLIED TROOPS IN SAFE PLACE STOP REPORT SENIOR INTELLIGENCE OFFICER FOR RETURN TO UNIT STOP TAKE NO RISKS REPEAT NO RISKS DURING DISSOLUTION GERMAN OCCUPATION STOP KEEP PECKER UP BALLY

And it was followed by Ballymore's personal verification letters and the letter group, QSL—Please Acknowledge.

For a moment Einar sat staring at the message in his hands. He didn't know whether to feel elated or let down. The whole damned operation was one colossal anticlimax.

But—the war was over!

He looked at Allan. "Will you acknowledge for me?"

Allan nodded.

"Is it true?" he asked Einar. "Is the damned bastard really dead? Do you really think it is true?" He seemed hardly to dare believe.

Einar nodded. "I'm sure it is," he stated. "Why the hell else would they put it in the message?"

Their mood gradually soared as realization sunk in, although there was still an edge of skepticism. Was the war really about to be over? Was the hoped-for, the longed-for day of liberation really near?

Lars turned to Einar. "Where are you going to go to wait for victory?" he asked. "Any ideas?"

"Yeah. I thought I'd go to Praestø. I haven't been there in years. Not since we left school. It'd be fun to see Bavnehøj again. And at least I know my way around there."

"Great idea," Lars agreed. He looked soberly at his friend. "I have a favor to ask of you."

"Anything."

"I'm afraid we're in for a rough time here in Copenhagen," Lars said. "General Lindemann has vowed to fight any insurrection. To the last minute, and the last man. The HIPOs will be desperate. They are already going crazy. Violence in the streets will rise. I am sure of that. We will have to round up every one of the bastards. Every damned informer. Every collaborator. Every lousy 'field mattress.' There will be fights. Bloodshed. Killings. If Birte stays here with us, she will insist on doing her part. You already know how strong-willed she can be. And she could easily be hurt. Or killed." He looked earnestly at his friend. "I want you to take her with you," he pleaded. "To our old stamping ground."

"Of course. You bet," Einar said at once. He was surprised at the fervor in his voice. Lars gave him an amused look.

"This time, *gamle Ven*—old friend—you are on your own!"

Einar knew at once what he meant. It had been back at Bavnehøj. They'd been two years from graduation. Sixteen years old. And their interest in girls had become acute—especially since any subject concerning the opposite sex was strictly taboo, and there were, of course, no girls at the boarding school.

None—except the household trainees, a dozen or so young women, eighteen or nineteen, who were there learning domestic household duties in the school kitchen. Of course, they lived in adamantly segregated quarters and were forbidden any contact with the male students.

One of them, a mischievous-looking blonde named Ellen, had become Einar's object of faraway worship and romantic fantasies. Totally unfulfilled until one day, by accident, his hand touched hers as she was serving him at the big common dining table. It had been like an electric current shooting through him, and he'd missed his plate with the mashed potatoes. After that day every time Ellen served him, their hands would briefly and excitedly touch. And soon their eyes would meet when Ellen entered the dining hall with her serving platter; fleetingly, lest anyone's suspicions should be aroused. Einar had written pages and pages about her in his secret diaries.

It was Lars who had come to his rescue and cooked up a plan for him to satisfy his desires.

Every night at nine o'clock, the three older classes would gather in the teachers' conference room, where there was a piano, to sing their vespers. Afterward the students would retire, while the headmaster and some of the teachers would have a late cup of coffee. In the corridor outside, the coffee tray would be waiting during the singing, held by one of the household trainees.

Ellen.

There were huge double doors between the corridor and the room, and when they stood open, anyone standing behind one of them would be totally hidden from view. In fact—even two.

And it was here Einar had stolen his first kiss, while Lars stood guard.

It had become a habit. A delicious, eagerly awaited habit. There had been something enormously exciting about it. While everyone else was singing a pious hymn, he, Einar, was enjoying the terribly immoral act of kissing a girl. And once, even, feeling a firm little breast.

Of course, one thing led to another, as they say, and at the age of sixteen and a half Einar had enthusiastically lost his virginity to Ellen, lying on the sunbaked grass at the lake in Faksinge Woods.

Ellen had been wonderful. But for weeks afterward, he'd anxiously looked for signs that she might have become pregnant.

It was long ago.

He grinned at Lars. "I won't need you this time," he asserted. "This time . . . it's different."

He suddenly remembered. "Talking about favors," he said, "I have one to ask of you."

"What?"

"There's a kid up near Liseleje. I got his address. His name is Valdemar. He saved my butt. I want you to see to it that he gets a new bike. Okay? I'll leave you the money."

"Will do," Lars nodded.

Birte had been torn between her desire to go with Einar and what she believed was her obligation to stay with her brother. She finally agreed to go, especially when she saw the look of pleasure on Lars's face when it was suggested that Lise stay in her flat while she was gone, and Lise agreed. Neither her brother nor Lise seemed the least displeased with the arrangement.

It was late in the afternoon of Tuesday, May 1, when Einar and Birte, sticking to side streets and byways, rode their bicycles south, out of the city on their way to Praestø.

The mood of the city was electrified, a volatile mixture of elation and fear of what was to come. Huge newspaper headlines screamed *HITLER FALDET!*—Hitler Fallen!—from every kiosk. The HIPOs were running amok in the streets, firing wildly without provocation, in a final frenzy of brutality. A notorious and dangerous traitor in the service of the Gestapo was shot down on Vester Boulevard by the freedom fighters, and several HIPOs were killed in the streets. Dozens of sabotage actions against the German-run railroads exploded all around the country, and the vengeful Schalburg Corps retaliated with the usual wanton *Schalburgtage* against popular landmarks. The Gestapo made as many arrests as their manpower would allow, and the German armed forces commandeered as many motor vehicles as they could lay their hands on, often with bloody results. In the midst of it, fourteen hundred women, emaciated and savaged, arrived in Copenhagen on their way to Sweden from the infamous Ravensbrück Concentration Camp, where close to one hundred thousand of the less fortunate had died, their rescue negotiated by Count Bernadotte. The city was seething, ready to explode.

And it was only the beginning.

It was difficult to reconcile the explosive atmosphere in the Copenhagen streets with the peaceful quiet around Praestø and Bavnehøj.

Praestø was a small provincial town of a couple of thousand souls, snugly situated on Praestø Fjord some seventy miles south of Copenhagen, known primarily for the nearby Nysø Castle and Bavnehøj Kostskole, which stood about three miles out of town. Einar and Birte had made the trip down in two days, stopping overnight in Køge.

Einar had enjoyed walking the still-familiar streets of the little town. He deliberately stayed away from the school. He might too easily have been recognized, and there was no sense in taking any risks, however remote. Besides, he had been ordered not to.

The mood of excitement and anticipation flourished here, too, and Einar and Birte enthusiastically joined the townspeople who gathered in squares and fields for *Alsange*—a sort of patriotic community singalong where everyone sang the beautiful old national songs.

Einar showed Birte the railroad station where he'd either arrived or departed so many times; *Badeanstalten*—the bathing pier, where the Bavnehøj boys went to swim in the summer, and the little sweets shop halfway between the school and town, where the larger part of the student allowances ended up.

But when he wanted to show her the motion picture theater of "get-even" fame, he got a shock. The theater was nothing but a hollow, burned-out shell.

He asked about it, and a nearby shopkeeper told him what had happened.

"*Schalburgtage*," the elderly man said bitterly. "The Schalburg boys set fire to it. They called it retaliation."

"Retaliation?" Einar asked. "For what?"

The man eyed him quizzically. It was obvious he realized that Einar was a stranger. It was equally obvious that he decided to take a chance on him.

"Most of our entertainment came from that movie house right there," he said. "That's why they selected it for their . . . revenge."

He waited for Einar to ask again.

"Revenge for what?" Einar obliged him.

"Well," the man said, beginning to enjoy his role as raconteur, "the Germans always insisted that one of their propaganda shorts be shown before each feature film. It was a fool notion, and we usually just sat through them, saying nothing of what was on our minds. But then, this time, as the propaganda film was showing a German ship, a freighter it was, unloading a whole lot of consumer goods in the harbor of Copenhagen, someone in the audience shouted, 'Hey! There's something wrong here. The film is running backward!' " He gave Einar a sidelong glance. "So . . . they burned the theater."

They'd laughed, of course, a sort of gallows-humor laugh. But afterward Birte had grown sober.

"They destroyed a lot," she said sadly. "In retaliation for the sabotage against the German war installations. And they always selected national landmarks or popular places, so people would really be hurt. All over the country they blew things up or burned them down. The beautiful concert hall in Tivoli, the Royal Yacht Club, Odin's Tower in Odense, the Tuborg Breweries," she called off the targets. "And theaters in Copenhagen, too. The Apollo and Kino."

"I saw it," Einar nodded. "So damned stupid. And the Forum."

"That was not *Schalburgtage*," Birte told him. "The Forum was destroyed by the resistance. They smuggled the explosives into the place in beer crates—and blew it up."

Einar stared at her in surprise. "Why?" he asked. "What the hell for?"

"The Forum was being remodeled," Birte answered. "By the Germans. It was to be the largest barracks building in the country for German troops. The resistance blew up that Nazi dream."

It had been one of their rare sober moments. Mostly they enjoyed their stay in the little town.

And each other.

The days flew by. And at 4:23 P.M. on May 5, the first Allied soldiers set foot on Danish soil, when a detachment of British troops under General Dewing landed at Kastrup Airport outside Copenhagen.

The day of liberation had arrived.

And Einar's stay in Denmark had come to an end. . . .

For a moment Einar sat silent. He found it difficult to return from his long journey into the past and accept the fact that he was sitting in the Pentagon office of a colonel in the Counter Intelligence Directorate. Recounting the time of forty years before had brought back so many memories and made them vivid and fresh once again; he had a little trouble getting back to the "now."

He looked at the officer sitting noncommittally across the desk from him.

"That's it," he said. "Now you know as much as I do, Colonel. Any ideas? Do you see any clues that might shed light on the present problem?"

Henderson eyed him indifferently. He answered Einar's question with other questions of his own. "That is all? There is nothing else you can tell me? Nothing left out?"

"Nothing," Einar said firmly.

It was, of course, a lie. But he didn't think it was any of Henderson's business.

But there had been—one more thing.

18

It was their second day in Praestø, his and Birte's. That Friday they'd taken a drive through the countryside on their bikes. Dusk was just settling comfortably over the rolling green fields and new-leafed woods when they stopped to rest. They were at the lake in Faksinge Woods.

They sat on the sweet-smelling, sunbaked grass, looking out over the still water, and Birte snuggled up to him.

"Einar," she whispered softly. "Is this the spot?"

He felt an instant flush course through him. He knew at once what she meant, but he asked, "What do you mean?"

"Ellen," Birte said. She looked up at him, merriment in her gray-blue eyes. "Lars told me all about it. A long time ago. Before he ever thought you and I . . ." She let the rest of the sentence trail off.

"No," Einar said. "It . . . it was somewhere else."

"Did you . . . love her?"

"I was sixteen."

It was not an answer, but she let it go. "Einar," she said softly. "What about . . . us?"

He looked down at her, at her tousled blond hair, and her big dreamy eyes gazing up at him.

"With you and me it must be very special," he said earnestly. "It will be something we will remember for the rest of our lives." He drew her to him. "Not here. Not where there is even the tiniest shadow of things past."

He kissed her. He looked into her questioning eyes.

"With you and me," he whispered, "it must be extra special."

It was.

They were walking on the beach far away from any houses, any shelter, when a sudden early summer thundersquall hit. The rain came down in torrents, and in no time they were drenched.

They spotted a small boat lying on its side a short distance up from the water's edge. They ran for it. Einar turned it over, bottom up, and they crept in under it. Their clothes were wringing wet. Einar shrugged out of his shirt, and Birte took off her skirt and blouse. They spread the wet clothes out on the soft sand and lay on them—listening together to the rain drumming on the boat planks above them.

They were lying closely side by side. He looked at her face so close to his. Her wide-open eyes gazed back at his. Her wet blond hair formed a cap of burnished gold over her rain-wet, glowing face.

And he loved her.

He found her lips, and their moist, soft coolness inflamed him. He buried his face in the secret cleft between her small, firm breasts and breathed the intoxicating fragrance of her clean, wet skin. And of her mounting excitement.

Neither he nor she was aware of slipping out of the rest of their clothing, only that their eager, naked bodies strained, one against the other. Aroused, they pressed together. Birte moved to receive him. Tightly he held her in his arms.

And he took her. And he moved with her until a flood of ultimate pleasure surged through him.

He had wanted the thundersquall to last forever. . . .

He looked at Henderson. "Nothing else," he said firmly. "I have told you everything. I was debriefed by a senior British intelligence officer. The debriefment lasted all of half an hour. I was put aboard a plane in Copenhagen and flown directly to SHAEF, where I reported to Colonel Schneider for another perfunctory debriefing. No one seemed remotely interested in the Weiden question. I was shipped back to my own outfit, which was in Grafenau by then, where I made my report. My detachment CO, Major Herbert Lee, wrote me up for a Bronze Star, which General

Maxwell promptly approved. They added up my ASR points, and I was in one of the first batches of junior officers to be sent back home."

He stopped. That was the whole kit and caboodle, dammit. As far as Henderson was concerned.

Henderson picked up Einar's XII Corps report about Operation Drumbeat. He glanced at it.

"Very well," he sighed, much put upon. "You have come up with nothing new." He looked at Einar, a snide little smile on his lips. "You did . . . eh, embellish the original report, of course, but there is nothing to tie in with the . . . eh, ravings of the old man in New York. As I thought." He was obviously pleased with himself. It was a moment he did not want to let go of quickly. "The dark mutterings, the twisted figments of a delirious mind," he intoned knowingly. "Probably giving voice to old emotions and desires. The man was, after all, an ex-Nazi. Mental wish-fulfillment, if you like, brought on by his trauma. No connection with Weiden, of course."

He closed the file. "I think we can safely let the matter rest."

Einar's mind whirled. Something was trying to surface in the sea of disjointed facts and impressions. What? With awe he realized it was his old "hunch," believed long forgotten, that insinuated itself on his thoughts, clamoring for attention.

There was something. What?

Henderson was watching him. "You agree, I take it," he said.

Slowly Einar shook his head.

"No," he said. "No, I do not."

Henderson raised an eyebrow. "Really, Munk?" He sounded slightly annoyed. "On what grounds?"

"Let's . . . analyze the events for a moment, Colonel. Facts are, there was a poison gas plant near Weiden; there was a report of a lethal new gas being developed; there was a scientist working on it, who committed suicide. I did determine in Copenhagen that he was a toxicologist."

"Agreed," Henderson nodded curtly. "So?"

"I also found a collection of strange clippings that had been owned by him and given to a colleague for safekeeping. Why? They were only briefly mentioned in my original report. And not by subject matter. That is something new." He frowned. "I . . . I have a feeling those clippings are important."

"Really?" Henderson's voice was ripe with condescension. "I think you just have a very fertile imagination, Munk."

"At least we should examine it," Einar persisted. Damn the man. Did he approach every problem with the vision of an Amtrak train conductor punching tickets?

"Suppose the plant in Weiden *was* developing a new type of poison gas. A gas that could be deployed by a delivery system such as the V-1 and the V-2 in Professor Meyer's collection of articles. Suppose that poison somehow was able to contaminate a city's water supply. With effects similar to dehydration, again as in Meyer's clippings. And finally, suppose that someone, some terrorist group today, got hold of a supply of this poison that survived the war, never mind how, and planned to use it to poison the New York water supply, for whatever insane reason."

Henderson sat back in his chair. He steepled his fingers. "As I said," he remarked, "you have an excellent imagination. But we have to act on facts, Munk. And only facts." He spread his hands. "There is nothing to indicate that your . . . eh, scenario has anything to do with facts."

"Will you at least bring it to the attention of the National Security people?"

Henderson gave a short, unpleasant laugh. "No, Munk, I will not. I'd be the laughingstock of the CID!"

He started to get up. "I think—"

"Colonel," Einar stopped him. "One thing. There was a report made of the Weiden plant investigation after it had been taken. Correct?"

"Of course."

"Do you have it?"

"Yes." Henderson placed his hand on the file in front of him.

"May I see it?"

Henderson frowned in irritation. He made a show of looking at his watch.

"Make it snappy!" he growled. He searched and pulled a couple of sheets of paper from the file. "We've already been here all night."

Einar took the report. Quickly he scanned it. It was routine. Nothing unusual was discovered at the Weiden-run chemical warfare factory. Moderate stockpiles of phosphorous, mustard gas, chlorine, and other conventional poison gases were found, housed in well-protected storage magazines, one of which had, in fact, been nearly empty except for a few large, sturdy metal drums of an unusual design, also empty. Nothing else. There were copies of the interrogation reports of three people with Weiden addresses who had worked at the plant. They had given no information about a new type of poison gas. No one had, in fact, ever heard of it. Einar made a note of the three names: Herta Siemens, Alois Hoffner, and Heinz Lohmann.

He looked up at Henderson. "It says here that the report was put together from on-the-scene inspection, interrogations, and 783 captured documents found at the plant. Where are those documents now?"

Henderson threw up his hands. "Certainly not here," he said in exasperation. "In storage, I suppose."

"There is usually a list of such documents attached to a report," Einar pointed out.

Henderson threw open the file folder. He was obviously irritated. "Here," he said. He tossed a list on the desk.

Einar picked it up. He let his fingers run down the list of documents, which were numbered and briefly described; dates, names, and other pertinent information.

Suddenly he stopped. He felt an icy stab shoot through him.

Document #479.

He stared at it. A treatise by a scientist at Berlin University: *Clinical Metabolism of Body Water and Electrolytes in Dehydrated Patients.*

There it was. The connection.

"Look, Colonel!" Einar said excitedly. He handed the document to Henderson. "Document #479."

Henderson took the list. He looked at it. His expression did not change. "What about it?"

"It's the connection, Colonel. Don't you see? The connection between Meyer's clippings on dehydration—and the Weiden project!"

"I fail to see how you arrive at that," Henderson said sourly. "I see a lot of different subject matters listed here. One of them happens to deal with dehydration. Not unusual in the line of the Weiden plant."

Einar found it difficult to conceal his exasperation with the officer. How damned obtuse can you get? He controlled himself.

"Don't you see?" he repeated. "The Nazis have a project going at Weiden. A secret and deadly project that somehow involves dehydration. They learn of Meyer in Copenhagen, who apparently is researching a similar subject. They cart him off to Weiden to work for them. When he finds out what they want him to do, he kills himself. Dammit, Colonel! We'd better find out what the hell that project was. And if in some way it is still alive!"

Henderson regarded him patronizingly. "Inference, Munk," he said. "Inference and conjecture, not facts. And we do not act on inference. There is nothing in the whole exercise that suggests you are correct in your . . . eh, rather imaginative assumptions."

"Dammit! Don't you see?" Einar exploded.

For a moment Henderson contemplated him, a slight frown on his forehead. He sighed.

"Look, Munk," he said, surprisingly calm. "I am not stupid. But what have you got? A coincidence, that's all. The facts are, there *was* no last desperate use of a new poison gas in 1945; there *was* no such gas found. Ever. No one could be located who had any knowledge of it." He looked closely at Einar. "Even if, and I say *if*, there was a connection between Professor Meyer's . . . eh, clippings and that document you saw on the list, it in no way proves that there is, as there must be for me to act, a clear and present danger. That is what I must be concerned with."

Einar stared at him. He said nothing. Henderson continued.

"What would you have me do, Munk? Mobilize the National Guard? Evacuate New York? Be reasonable. The chances that there is a real and present danger connected in any way with Weiden and that unfortunate old accident victim is so infinitesimal that . . . that we are in greater danger of Manhattan sliding into the ocean. And I am certain you don't advocate we issue water wings to every New Yorker!"

For a while Einar sat silent. Was the man right? Was it all nothing but a wild goose chase? Was it? Perhaps—

But his hunch would not die.

"You won't follow through?"

"That is correct, Munk. I see no reason to burden our investigative agencies with something that, in my opinion, is much ado about nothing, to put it politely."

Einar stared at him. One more try.

"Colonel," he said earnestly, "don't you realize what you so nonchalantly are dismissing? Suppose some terrorist group *has* gotten hold of a poison gas. Poison, dammit! As in death. Remember, only five short months ago? The catastrophe in Bhopal, India? When a deadly poison, leaking from a chemical plant manufacturing toxic substances, sent a cloud of horror over that city? More than two thousand people died, Colonel. Two thousand! And two hundred thousand were blinded and maimed. Dammit, Colonel! It would all be a ring-around-a-rosy in comparison to what would happen in New York if an odorless, lethal poison gas was spewed into the air."

He stopped.

Henderson contemplated him over steepled fingers.

"Very dramatic, Munk," he said dryly. "Very. But hardly to the point."

"Colonel—"

"I appreciate your terrorist speculation, Munk. But it makes no sense."

"Terrorists are always at their most effective when they do not make sense, Colonel. What sense is there in blowing up a chocolate soldier Horse Guard parade? Or the toy department in a department store? Senseless, purposeless killings are the most powerful psychological weapons of the terrorist."

"An interesting theory," Henderson said, obviously growing impatient. "But hardly applicable to what we have been discussing."

He stood up. "We want to thank you for your cooperation, Munk, even though your efforts turned out to be . . . eh, fruitless." He closed the file folder.

"Then . . . you consider the case closed," Einar said tightly.

"I do. Officially closed."

Henderson walked around the desk.

"I'll arrange for your flight back to New York right away." He smiled at Einar. "Let us be thankful that our little scare turned out to be a false alarm."

19

The egg yolk broke.

"Damn," Einar muttered under his breath. He liked his breakfast eggs sunny-side up and placed on top of a toasted English muffin. Unbroken. He picked at it, his thoughts miles away.

"I know I was under orders not to discuss the damned case with anyone," he said to Birte. "But you don't count."

"You'd better mean that the way I think you do," Birte said with a smile. She brought a spatula to the table and deftly lifted Einar's other egg on top of his second muffin. It did not break. "You did what you could, love. You gave that colonel the whole kettle of fish in a nutshell," she said, happily mixing metaphors.

Absentmindedly Einar picked at the second egg. "Dammit!" he exclaimed. "Everything makes sense, except those clippings we found in Meyer's package. They have to make sense, too. They've got to fit in."

"Maybe they do," Birte said. "In some way you don't know yet."

"That's just it, *yet!*" Einar at once pounced on the word. He looked earnestly at her. "Look," he said. "I have this nagging feeling that something is out of kilter. That damned hunch I developed. Back in the war. Like every other CIC."

Birte nodded. "I remember."

"Well, it's back. With a vengeance. Strong enough to make my damned hackles rise on the back of my neck—if I had any."

"What do you think it is?"

"Damned if I know." Einar frowned. "But something is wrong. Very wrong." He jabbed his fork into his egg. "And I am missing it. Everyone is missing it. The CID won't lift a finger. All my arguments fell on the deaf ears of a blasted Pentagon pencil pusher who'd left his hearing aid in his sewing basket." He looked up at her. "Why the hell is it that big brass always is so hard to sell? We're all supposed to be on the same side. It was that way in the war, too."

"You really feel strongly about this, don't you?"

"You bet. Strongly enough to—" He stopped. Resolutely he looked up at Birte. "Look. This thing is going to spook me till I go batty. I've got to do something. Find out. The winter quarter at the university is over, and I can cut loose for a week or so. If I can't find out anything in that time, my hunch, for once, was wrong. Or I will have been too late."

"What do you want to do?"

"I want to go to the only place where there may still be some answers," he said. "Weiden."

Birte nodded. "In Germany."

He looked at her. "I'm sorry," he declared. "I know we had planned on that Caribbean cruise this summer. But . . . if I go to Weiden, we can't swing both."

"I understand," Birte said. "And I agree you should go. Put your . . . hunch at ease. But on one condition."

"What?"

"That I go along."

Einar frowned at her. "I don't know what I'll be getting into," he professed. "If there is something to all this, there could be . . . danger."

"We've been there before," Birte countered quietly. "I can hold my own."

For a moment Einar contemplated her. He grinned. "In spades!" he agreed. "Okay, sold." He stood up, already planning the trip. Now that the decision had been made to take action, he suddenly felt impatient.

"Our passports are still valid," he said. "From our visit home two years ago. We can take off for Germany as soon as we get packed—and get our tickets."

"Give me a few minutes," Birte laughed. "I may want to take more than a toothbrush."

"Well, get moving," he said as he hurried her, good-naturedly. He walked rapidly toward the bedroom, leaving his broken eggs untouched on the plate. "I'll get a pair of socks."

Birte gazed after her husband with an affectionate smile. She knew him. Once he'd made up his mind to do something—it was *now.* It was a long time since she'd seen him so spirited, so aggressive. It was like old times. She was beginning to feel the excitement herself.

Einar headed straight for the closet that held their suitcases. He felt buoyed, full of vigor. That same high feeling he remembered from his CIC days when he had a case by the tail and knew it was a live one.

He welcomed it.

If there were any answers to be found to his premonition, his hunch of danger—a clear and present danger, dammit!—they were to be be found where he and Birte were headed.

Weiden.

And he was determined to find them.

PART

May 1985

20

At seventy miles per hour the little Volkswagen was tooling along Highway 22 toward Weiden. It was just past noon on Monday, May 13. Einar and Birte had caught Lufthansa Flight 401 in New York at six-thirty the previous evening and arrived in Frankfurt in time to take the connecting flight to Bayreuth. The local flight had taken one hour, and they'd picked up a rental car at the Bayreuth airport. It was a 1984 two-door Jetta, model 161-E42, and they'd gotten a good deal because it was a year-old model.

Einar liked the clean lines of the car and enjoyed the feel of it. The bucket seats, upholstered in plush velour, were comfortable, and even the digital clock worked. The car was a luxuriously far cry, he thought, from the awkward-looking, hard-riding captured German *Wehrmacht* Volkswagen, with its tin-can doors and spare wheel smack in the middle of the slanting hood, that he'd driven occasionally during the war. It hadn't been much of a rival for the U.S. Jeep, which he had greatly admired and often counted on to get him out of a tight spot.

He'd made an ambiguous, perhaps nostalgic choice. He'd picked out an FI/5 manual shift rather than an automatic—because it brought back the old times when he'd driven his Jeep all over the highways and byways of Germany, and he'd chosen a bright Gambia red color—to stay away from the drab gray of the military Volkswagen and the olive drab of the jeep.

He'd slept during most of the flight from the States, and he felt fine. Somehow the lost night's sleep at the Pentagon had been evened out by the jet lag and put his biological clock back on time. Or so confused it that it had given up. He glanced at Birte, dozing next to him. She'd catch up.

He looked at the peaceful countryside around him. He was driving the same route he'd driven forty years earlier, almost to the day, when he'd been summoned to his meeting with the brass at XII Corps, but he didn't recognize it. Where were the potholes gouged out by tanks and trucks? Where were the bomb craters, the burned-out shells that had been houses, the smoking wrecks of military vehicles at the wayside? It was all so neat and clean.

He felt vaguely uneasy, but he couldn't pinpoint why. The Jetta was behaving beautifully, and the traffic was light, although fast.

A BMW motorcycle, coming up behind him, flashed its Cyclops light and passed him with almost flying speed. Slowing before him, it backfired.

Instantly Einar's right hand flew to his left armpit. But there was no shoulder holster. No gun. And he knew what had made him feel uneasy. He was unarmed. He was in "enemy" country—and he had no weapon. It was the first time he had been back in Germany since the war, the first time he had driven once again on German soil. And he was without a gun. Sheepishly he placed his hand back on the steering wheel. Some reflexes sure die hard. He glanced at Birte. She hadn't noticed. She was still asleep.

They passed through a small village. He missed the signpost with its name. It looked familiar to him. Was it—? No, it couldn't be, but it sure looked like it. Being back in Germany brought memories rushing helter-skelter into his mind. All seen through the frosted glass of time.

Like that little village forty years ago . . .

Marberg had been the name. The burg had been taken late in the day before, and he'd been on his way there to clean up the local Nazi leadership. But the village had been one of several, printed right in the fold of his much-used map, and like a snafu goof-up in basic training, he'd misread it and ended up in a place called Marktberg instead. Only he hadn't known it.

It had been one of the few times he'd set out alone, strictly against SOP, of course, but what the hell. He'd barreled into the little village in his jeep, the guillotine wire cutter on the front bumper sticking up like the shaft of a horny bull. He'd stalked into the farmhouse office of the local *Ortsbauernführer*—the village Nazi leader—and heaved the man out on his ear. He'd summarily installed another farmer, who he'd found out was known as a reluctant Nazi, to serve until MG could place their own man in office, and he'd ordered the villagers at once to dismantle a Mickey Mouse barricade they'd thrown across the main drag. They'd hopped to it as if they had dynamite sticks up their collective ass. He'd wondered vaguely where the hell the GIs were holed up, but he'd been too busy throwing his weight around to worry about it, and it wasn't until he got back to Corps and made his report that he'd found out he'd gone to the wrong damned place; that Marktberg had not yet been taken, and that the village had been bursting at its manure-stinking seams with Krauts from a Waffen SS outfit armed to their eyeballs!

They'd kept out of sight, waiting to strike. For he had acted so cocky and so obnoxiously arrogant that they had been convinced half the U.S. Army was about to follow him—right into their ambush. Corps brass had known about the troops, and that was the reason the village had been left alone. But he'd blundered right in and taken the town—by drizzle rather than by storm.

He'd taken a lot of ribbing on that one. The guys at Corps had called him a one-man-blitzkrieg, a wrong-way Corrigan—and a lot less complimentary epithets. It had been less than his finest hour . . .

Birte stirred.

"Should be there in a few more minutes," he told her. He glanced at the digital clock on the dash. He'd covered the forty-five miles from Bayreuth in under an hour, including the crawls through Kemnath, Erbendorf, Neustadt, and the other villages along the road. In about half the time it had taken him forty years before.

Weiden, situated on the Naab River in the Bohemian Forest, was a medieval fortified city. On the old Town Hall a plaque can be seen: Anno 1241, the year the town was founded.

They came in on Highway B22 and passed a colorful sign, *WEIDEN i.d. OPF.*, above a bright-hued town coat-of-arms, with a crowned lion rampant next to a field of blue-and-white diamond checkers, above a green tree on a red field.

"What does *i.d. OPF.* mean?" Birte asked. "Sounds like someone upchucking."

"In der Oberpfalz," Einar grinned. "In the Upper Pfalz. It's the section of the Bohemian Forest we're in."

Below the coat-of-arms was written: *HERZLICH WILLKOMMEN IN DER MAX REGER STADT*—Cordially Welcome to Max Reger Town.

"I wish they'd make up their minds," Birte commented. "What is it? Weiden or Max Reger Town?"

Einar laughed. "Both, I guess. Max Reger spent his childhood in Weiden. And later he wrote some of his most famous works here."

"Never heard of him."

"You're not the only one."

"What did he write? Anything I might have read?"

"Not read. Heard. Reger was a composer. Mostly organ music. He died just before World War I. When I was here before, I saw the Max Reger house. Pretty run down, as I remember."

They turned off B22 at Friedrich Ebert Strasse and crossed the river. They were headed for a hotel called Hotel Schmid on Obere Bachgasse, right in the middle of the old town, a cat's leap from the old Rathaus—the old Town Hall. A pleasant young lady at the car rental agency at the Bayreuth airport had recommended the place to them. Clean and reasonable, she'd said; everything you will need except television in your room. They'd thought they could do without it. The hotel was their first objective; check in, get settled, and then go to work.

They turned into Unterer Markt, passing through the narrow "Eye of the Needle" in *Das Untere Tor*—the lower gate—to the old city.

Einar stared at the gate building. The damned thing sure looked different from when he first saw it, cracked and crumbling, defaced by the passage of war. Now it looked as if it had been built yesterday: pleasingly pale gray in color, with a darker gray for the beams in the half-timbered gatekeeper's house. The tower's steep, intricately designed red-tile roof, topped by the ornate, columned cupola with the inset clock, looked fresh and new.

Before them lay the main street of the old town, the Markt, lined with quaint, gabled, fifteenth-century houses in a painter's pallet of muted hues—pinks, blues, and yellows, greens, grays, and browns, a cobblestoned street cupped between two pastel rainbows of mortar and brick. A veritable fairyland town—incongruously surrounded by a skyline of modern buildings.

Birte looked around with pleasure. "If the word *picturesque* didn't already exist," she declared, "it would have to be invented for this place."

Einar nodded, bemused. Was this the same drab place he'd first entered forty years ago—when the only bright spots in the dismal, war-scarred town had been the white sheets of surrender that hung from every window in the same gabled houses, or were held by the sullen "Bürgers" as they stood silently before their battered homes? It was a different world.

It suddenly struck him. It would all be different. This case, this investigation would not be a repeat performance. It would be as different as the Weiden he'd known in 1945 was to the Weiden of today. This time he could not operate with the power of a conquerer in a conquered country, with the might of an occupation army behind him. This time he was strictly on his own.

The hotel was everything the rental car woman had said it would be, and Einar and Birte were quickly on their way to the first place of inquiry, the new Town Hall on the corner of Kurt Schumacher Allé and Dr. Pfleger Strasse next to the state school.

The town records and registers might yield some information about the three people whose names Einar had taken off the 1945 case report: Herta Siemens, Alois Hoffner, and Heinz Lohmann.

Einar watched the young Town Hall clerk explain to the woman in charge of the records department that two Americans wished to speak with her. Seated in her little glass-enclosed cubicle, protected from the outside world, yet able to keep tabs on it, the woman glanced incuriously toward them, as they stood waiting at the counter.

Einar sized her up. About forty. Plain. Lackluster hair of nondescript color. Sensibly dressed with a no-nonsense mien, neither friendly nor unfriendly. From the looks of her office, scrupulously neat. In other words, the toughest kind of bureaucrat to crack.

He turned to Birte. "By the way," he said out of the corner of his mouth, "don't be surprised at anything I say. Just go along with it. I usually play things like this by ear."

"Don't worry," Birte whispered back. "I can't read music anyway."

The woman in the little office rose, left her cubicle, and came over to the counter.

"May I help you?" she inquired, her tone of voice correct, but without any real desire to help evident in her manner.

"If you please," Einar said respectfully. "We are seeking information about three individuals who used to live in Weiden. And, of course, may still do," he smiled.

"May I ask why?" the woman inquired.

Einar pretended not to hear her. Pedantically he searched through his briefcase, coming up with a piece of paper. He placed it on the counter in front of the woman, saw it was upside down, and—flustered—turned it around.

"There," he said. "These are the names."

The woman merely glanced at the paper.

"Why?" she repeated. "Why do you want this information?"

Startled, Einar looked at her. "Oh!" he said. "Oh, of course. I am Einar Munk." He looked questioningly at the woman. "Frau—?"

"Fräulein Mossbach," the woman said stiffly.

"A thousand pardons!" Einar stammered. "Fräulein Mossbach." He indicated Birte. "This is my assistant." He leaned a little over the counter toward Mossbach. He glanced around him with a quick, almost furtive motion. His voice grew confidential.

"We . . . we represent a law firm in New York," he confided. "Specializing in tracing lost heirs. There is a possibility"—again he glanced stealthily about—"a possibility, mind you, that these three people or their heirs have an inheritance waiting for them in the United States. From a distant relative."

The woman looked interested. "I . . . see," she said. She looked at the paper with the names. She frowned. "This information goes back to the . . . goes back many years," she said.

Einar nodded regretfully. "Alas," he agreed. "But such is the nature of our business. Nothing but difficulties." He looked beguilingly at the woman.

"I think . . . if we could be permitted to go through whatever town records exist from that time, and current ones as well, of course, we might find some clues."

"The current records are possible," the woman nodded. "But it would be most difficult, and time-consuming, to locate the old ones in our archives. And regulations—"

"I know," Einar broke in earnestly. "It *is* an imposition. Unorthodox, to say the least. It is . . . difficult. That is why I always make it a point to go to the person in charge." He looked directly at her. "I have found that they usually can find a way, where others can't. You would be surprised how successful we have been dealing with the people of importance."

"Well—" Mossbach looked uncertain.

Einar smiled ingratiatingly at her. "I just know," he said, "that if *you*, for instance, if you wanted to make these records available to us, it would be done at once. And think how grateful the heirs would be, if we find them. And they would surely know whom to thank."

Birte was watching Einar raptly. She tried not to burst out laughing at his performance. Nothing subtle about that approach! Fortunately she succeeded in keeping a straight face. And she had to admit that Einar knew his German *Beamte*—his German functionaries—when the Mossbach woman hesitatingly said, "You will have to examine them here."

She nodded toward a door with a frosted glass pane. She looked at Einar. "It will take some time . . . for us to locate the records you seek, and for you to go through them."

"Understood, Fräulein Mossbach," Einar said gratefully. "And I thank you a thousand times for your courtesy. On both our parts, and on behalf of the possible heirs."

It was just before 5:00 P.M. when Einar closed the final records book. They'd been at it all day—with time out only for a quick bite of lunch at a restaurant a couple of blocks from the Town Hall. Knockwurst with sauerkraut and a boiled potato, thick brown mustard, and a stein of beer.

Mossbach had dug up all kinds of town records going back to 1943, and they'd gone through them all, as well as several current listings. Everything kept with true Teutonic thoroughness. They'd looked through town registers, birth certificates and real estate records, marriage licenses and drivers' licenses, telephone books, obituaries, a demographic study made by the government, and some records they didn't even know how to classify.

Mossbach had personally brought them some of the more precious old documents. She seemed to have become genuinely interested in the project. Einar once caught her eyeing them speculatively as she left the little office.

He looked at the mountain of record books and files before them. A picture *had* developed—although it was woefully lacking in detail. He'd made a chart. He studied it.

He could feel the uneasy urgency churn through him. He had forgotten how much time was spent in dull, plodding research when working on any case; how meager the results usually were. He was desperate for action. For something to happen that would bring matters to a head, so he could act. Too damned much time was being pissed down the drain just digging up basics. Time. How much time *did* he have? Dammit!—How much? He frowned in frustration at his meager chart:

HERTA SIEMENS
BORN: June 1924
AGE: 1945—21
Today—61
HISTORY: Listed in several town records
Last listing, 1945
No listing thereafter
QUESTIONS: Dead? Married? Moved?
No records found
ADDRESS: None available

HEINZ LOHMANN
BORN: No birth certificate on file
AGE: Unknown
HISTORY: Listed in town records
Marriage certificate, 1948 (Maria Hessler)
Widow listed 1952-54
No record of Lohmann's death
QUESTIONS: Lohmann born in town other than Weiden?
Died elsewhere?
ADDRESS: None available

ALOIS HOFFNER (1)
BORN: Aug. 1919
AGE: 1945-26
Today—66
HISTORY: Listed several town records
No marriage license found
ADDRESS: Hans Sachs Strasse (Tel. book listing)

ALOIS HOFFNER (2)
BORN: Mar. 1923
AGE: 1945—22
DIED: 1967

ALOIS HOFFNER (3)
BORN: Sept. 1922
AGE: 1945—23
Today—63
HISTORY: Listed current records
Marriage license 1943 (Paula Ross)
Son born 1944 (Hermann)
ADDRESS: Birkenweg (Tel. book listing)

Three damned Hoffners. It never rains . . . He bit his lip. It was not an encouraging picture. The Siemens woman would be impossible to trace within his time frame, even if she was still alive. Lohmann was dead, and so was one of the three Hoffners. He hoped he hadn't been the one he was looking for. That left two men he might find in Weiden, both of them named Hoffner. Both could have worked at the chemistry plant. One had been twenty-three at the time, the other twenty-six. He cursed the interrogator who'd made out the original interrogation report for not including more particulars about his subjects. The SOB could have made things so much easier if he'd only included their ages.

"Two Hoffners," he said to Birte. "Both of them possibles. We'll hit them both tonight."

"Which one first?" she asked.

"The one on Birkenweg. Near the industrial district. He seems the most likely candidate. He's the right age, and apparently has been in the Weiden area most of his life."

"What're we waiting for?" Birte asked. "The sooner, the quicker."

Birkenweg was in the northern part of town across from the *Am Forst* industrial complex. Einar and Birte, driving their rental Volkswagen, crossed over the B22 Highway on Hammerweg and turned left onto Birkenweg. They had no trouble finding the Hoffner house.

A pleasant-looking woman in her late fifties opened the door in response to Einar's knocking. She wore a stained apron—and a delicious aroma of cooking wafted out the door from behind her.

"Bitte?" she asked. "Yes, please?"

"Frau Hoffner?" Einar asked. "Frau Alois Hoffner?"

The woman nodded. "I am Paula Hoffner."

"Frau Hoffner, my name is Einar Munk. From New York," Einar said. "Fräulein Mossbach at the Town Hall suggested I speak to your husband. Is he at home?"

The woman looked puzzled. "Fräulein Mossbach? In records?" She smiled. "Yes, Alois is home." She opened the door wide. "Come in. Please come in." Self-consciously she removed her apron. "And please excuse the house smelling of food. I am cooking some *Bratkartoffeln*—some fried potatoes and onions."

"They smell scrumptious," Birte smiled.

"Please," the woman said. "Follow me. I will take you to Alois."

Einar knew that the man sitting in the wheelchair was only sixty-three, but he looked ten years older. He did not stir as they entered the room.

"Alois!" his wife said, her voice extra loud. "Alois! You have visitors. From America. A gentleman. And a nice lady." She turned to Einar and

Birte. "You must excuse, please. Alois does not hear very well. And . . . he is blind."

"Grüss Gott," Alois mumbled. "God's Greeting."

Einar felt uncomfortable. But he was here—so, on with it.

"Herr Hoffner," he said, speaking as loudly as he could without shouting. "I am seeking some information about the old chemical plant in Sudetenland, about fifteen miles from here. Fräulein Mossbach at the Town Hall suggested you might have worked there and would be able to give me some information about the place. For a study that is being done."

"Why would she do that?" the man demanded to know. "I never saw the place. I knew about it, but I never saw it. I certainly did not work there."

"We know that a man named Alois Hoffner worked at the place. In 1945. Fräulein Mossbach thought it might have been you."

"It was not me," the man said emphatically. He cackled. "I wish it had been. I was in the *Wehrmacht*—35th Panzer Regiment. From 1942 until I got hit." He lifted his hands and shook them in front of him. "If you ever wondered what it would be like to be inside a Tiger One tank during a direct hit by a *verdammte* Russian T34—just look at me!"

Automatically Einar's mind ticked off the information: 35th Panzer Regiment. A unit of the 4th Panzer Division, home station—Würzburg. Wehrkreis XIII; largely upper Bavarian personnel. Fought in Poland, Belgium, and France. Central Russian front . . . He was startled. Once he had known all the information—at least most of it—contained in the *Order of Battle* of the German Army. It had been his job to know. Then. He had no idea it was all still lurking somewhere deep in his mind, only waiting to be prodded to life.

"I regret," he said. "As you said, it must have been another Alois Hoffner who worked at the plant. Please accept my apologies for disturbing you."

"Would you like to stay and have some *Bratkartoffeln*?" the Hoffner woman asked. "You are welcome. We are just about to eat."

"Thank you, Frau Hoffner," Einar said. "You are very kind. But we have somewhere else to go. Otherwise it would have been a pleasure."

As he and Birte turned toward Hans Sachs Strasse, it was beginning to get dark.

One down—one to go, Einar thought bleakly. One last chance to find one of his only three leads . . .

Hans Sachs Strasse was situated in the western part of Weiden, not far from the State Forestry Office. The Alois Hoffner who lived there could be his man, Einar thought. He was the right age. Sixty-six.

The woman who opened the door looked tired and worn.

"Was wünschen Sie?" she asked. "What do you want?"

"I should like to speak with Herr Hoffner," Einar said politely. "Herr Alois Hoffner. Is he at home?"

"No."

"Do you expect him?"

"No."

The woman's voice was flat and weary. Einar was taken aback at her abruptness. "Do you . . . do you know where he is?" he asked. "Where I can find him?"

"Yes."

"Please tell me."

"At the Waldfriedhof."

Einar stared at her. "The—*Friedhof!*" he exclaimed.

The woman nodded.

"Yes. The Forest Cemetery. Alois died last month."

21

Einar felt shattered. Defeated. He shook it off. If one path leads to a stone wall, find another. Or a way around.

"Are you Frau Hoffner?" he asked.

The woman shook her head. "I am Alois' sister," she said. "My brother was not married."

"Did you keep house for him?"

"No. He lived alone."

"I wonder if I might ask you a couple of questions. It is of some importance."

The woman nodded. "You are the lawyer," she said. "From America."

They stared at her.

"Fräulein Mossbach at the Town Hall mentioned you." She eyed them. "Alois had no relatives in America."

Einar quickly recovered from his astonishment. "We may not be talking about a . . . a relative, Fräulein—it is Fräulein?"

The woman nodded. "Frieda Hoffner."

"Fräulein Hoffner," Einar continued. "So, with your kind permission we should like to determine if your brother is—or was—the Hoffner we are trying to locate. There *is* another Hoffner in Weiden, as you undoubtedly know."

Again the woman nodded.

"Well, then, do you remember a . . . a chemical factory located about fifteen miles from here, in the Sudeten? Back in 1945?"

The woman frowned. "You mean *Der Gestanktopf*—the Stinkpot? That is what everyone who worked there called it. It always smelled so bad. Like . . . rotten eggs, they said."

"That's the place," Einar said. "Did your brother work there?"

The woman gave a little nod. "For a while."

Einar stiffened in anticipation. "Do you know what he did? What his work was?"

The woman shrugged. "He never talked of it. I don't think he was supposed to. It was some sort of factory for the war effort. No one was allowed to talk about it. No one did."

Einar thought quickly. "Fräulein Hoffner," he said. "Do you live here now?"

"No. I am just packing up the last of Alois' things. Mostly kitchen utensils and dishes left. The house has been sold."

"The . . . the rest of Herr Hoffner's belongings are already gone?"

"It was not much. Nothing of value. Just some clothes, a little furniture, and a few books. The radio was nice. And the china." She sighed. "There are still some old papers and such left in his room. Just junk."

"Fräulein Hoffner," Einar said solemnly. "I know this is an imposition, but it is of some importance, as you know. Would you permit me to look through the papers that were left behind?"

The Hoffner woman shrugged. "If you like," she said. "Everyone else has gone through his things."

She stood aside to let them in. She pointed. "His room is over there. You will excuse me, but I will have to get on with packing up the dishes. It is getting late."

Birte gave the woman a quick look. "I'll give you a hand, Fräulein Hoffner," she said brightly. "While my . . . associate takes a look through Herr Hoffner's papers."

The woman nodded. "If you like," she sighed.

Birte followed her to the kitchen.

The room that had served as living room and study for Alois Hoffner was bare of furniture, except for a broken lamp, a stool with one leg missing, and a bug-eaten deer head with one antler broken off. A pile of papers had been swept into a corner, and three or four small wooden crates, which had once contained local wines, were stacked against one wall.

Einar went through the papers. Old bills and receipts; mailers and brochures from the local china factories, textile mills, and other merchants advertising their wares. A few old magazines, a couple of family snapshots faded beyond recognition, a few sheets of unused foolscap, and some Christmas wrapping paper, once used and carefully folded and saved. Nothing of even remote interest.

He turned his attention to the old wine crates. Apparently Alois had used them as file boxes; a couple of them still contained a few papers. Einar shook them out.

Nothing.

He examined the boxes.

Empty.

He removed and turned over the wooden covers made to slide shut in two grooves. On the inside of the third one, he found it.

A dog-eared, three-by-two-inch tag with an attached pin, rusted and bent, and a piece of coated material the size of a Band-Aid pulled through two slits in the cardboard. The material had grown sticky with age and adhered to the underside of the wooden lid.

Eagerly he pulled it off. He stared at it.

ACHTUNG!
WARNUNGSSTREIFE-ABTEILUNG B

VERFÄRBUNG SOFORT ANMELDEN!

W A R N I N G !
MONITOR STRIP DIVISION B
REPORT DISCOLORATION AT ONCE !

He knew immediately what it was. He'd seen such detection badges before, worn in areas of contamination risk and radiation danger.

Alois Hoffner *had* worked in the poison gas plant!

Einar fingered the tag. What he wouldn't give to be able to go take a look at that damned factory—if it were still standing. But this time an even greater barrier than restriction line directives prevented him: a naked barbed-wire fence, a freshly plowed field planted with mines and traps; trenches, guard towers, and men with submachine guns who would shoot to kill anyone who dared try to cross.

The Death Strip.

The Iron Curtain . . .

He put the tag in his pocket. There was a chance—a very slight chance—that analysis of the strip might give a clue to the kind of poison gas it was designed to detect. But as a chemist, he knew that chance was virtually nonexistent. Too much time had gone by.

He turned to leave and almost collided with Birte.

"Guess what?" she cried excitedly. "Frieda and I were talking. Her brother knew the Siemens woman. Herta Siemens. The one we thought we'd never find. She was a coworker of his. She's married now. Her name is Werner. Herta Werner. She doesn't live in Weiden. She lives in Schwarzenfeld. Only twenty miles from here!"

She stopped, out of breath.

Einar stared at her.

"Bingo," he said quietly.

They decided to drive to Schwarzenfeld first thing the next morning, Tuesday, May 14. They returned to the Hotel Schmid for a good night's rest.

Birte was lying in the big double bed, peering over the mountainous feather bed, watching her husband undress. It pleasured her.

A fine figure of a man, someone had once said of Einar. She'd been so right, Birte thought. Those broad shoulders, the deep chest—and those high, firm buns.

He was in good shape at sixty-four, she thought. And looked it. Einar was whistling a little tune as he finished undressing. He always slept in the raw. She didn't recognize the melody. She usually knew them all.

"What are you whistling?" she asked.

"It's a little ditty I suddenly remembered," he answered. "I guess it's being back here. It's an old Berlin tune."

"It's got words?"

"Sure." Softly he sang:

Heut' war ich bei der Frieda,
Da geh ich Morgen wieda'
Denn so was wie die Frieda,
War noch nie da!

Today I was with Frieda,
I'll go again tomorrow,
'Cause there was never anyone,
Like Frieda!

She threw a pillow at him. "You're impossible!" she laughed.

He walked over to the foot of the bed. He looked down at his wife, nearly swamped under the huge feather bed.

"I think I'll have to make up a ditty that rhymes with Birte," he grinned. He tugged at the feather bed. Birte held on to it and tugged back.

It became a tug-of-war.

Einar won.

It was just after seven, Tuesday morning, when Einar and Birte drove their Volkswagen Jetta through the village of Rothenstadt on Highway B15 just south of Weiden on their way to Schwarzenfeld and Herta Werner, née Siemens. They both felt marvelous, and it was not only because of the brisk, fresh spring day.

At that same moment, back in Weiden, a man completed the connection on a telephone call to New York.

"Yes?" The voice that answered was also that of a man.

"Four. Nine. One. Two," the caller said crisply.

The man who'd answered responded at once.

"One. Zero. Zero. Zero."

"There is a problem."

"Yes?"

"A woman, a functionary at the City Hall here, has been asking questions."

"What questions?"

"About . . . the plant."

"Why?"

"I checked. There are two Americans here. A man and a woman. They are the instigators."

"Who are they?"

"They claim to be investigators for a law firm. Here regarding an inheritance. I do not believe this to be true."

"Why not?"

"They are interested in only three people. All of them worked at the plant. In 1945."

"Could they be . . . government investigators? Military?"

"It is possible."

"*Verflucht!*—What can they find out?"

"That is difficult to answer."

"If they did learn about the . . . project, would it matter? It is already too late."

There was an uneasy pause.

"Well?" The man in New York sounded sharp. "They could not . . . interfere, could they? No one could, at this stage. You said—*any day*!"

"There . . . there is a margin for error, Herr Doktor." The Weiden man's voice was taut. "There are . . . too many variables for total accuracy."

"How great a margin? In time?"

"Weeks. Perhaps a month."

"Verflucht nochmal!" The man in New York spat the oath. "Nothing must interfere. No one!"

"I agree."

The voice on the other end of the line grew cold. "Then you must make certain the . . . inquirers learn nothing. Is that understood?"

"It is understood."

"The woman. At the Town Hall. Is she also a danger?"

"No. Only a harmless busybody."

"Then—it will be only the two Americans. Have you a name?"

"The man gives his name as Einar Munk. That is all I know."

"I will find out if he is in Weiden officially. In any case, he and the woman must be—stopped."

"I understand."

"You know what to do."

"I do. I shall have Kratzer take care of the matter. At once."

"*Prima!*—Excellent! Kratzer is a good man."

And the man in New York hung up.

Schwarzenfeld was a small town of under five thousand. It was one of the Iceberg Forward HQ towns Einar had missed. XII Corps had headquartered in a large housing development at the outskirts of the town during April 1945 when he had been in Denmark. It was here, he knew, while he had been away, his unit had been involved in the preliminary interrogation of two big-brass German officers, *Generalfeldmarschall* Ewald von Kleist and *Generalleutnant* von Russwurm. They told him how von Kleist had refused to pose for official Corps photos, and how the AC of S had given corps photographers the go-ahead anyway—at the urgings of a signal corps corporal. Being commanding officer of a German Army group had counted for very little against the persistence of a XII Corps corporal determined to take his pictures. He'd seen the shots. Von Kleist had sat, stiffly and sullenly, in a command car in the seat usually reserved for a PFC orderly, while the photographers had snapped away.

And it was here his buddies had found a fabulous treasure, accumulated by a Nazi overseer of slave laborers on the West Wall in France, amounting to some three million dollars in currency, gold, and jewelry, including a diamond ring even Elizabeth Taylor would have been proud to wear. It had all been found in an old trunk, hidden in the middle of a putrid manure pile on a farm in the nearby village of Tirschenreuth.

It sobered him to think that the treasure he was seeking now—the treasure of information—might well have an infinitely greater value. And he fervently hoped he wouldn't be stuck with an empty manure pile.

The address of the Werners given to Einar by Frieda Hoffner was in the eastern part of town. Einar parked the car a few houses away, and he and Birte walked to the house of Herta Werner.

Einar could feel the tension rise in him as they walked up to the door.

This was truly his last chance.

There was no bell, so he knocked on the door.

And waited.

Presently a woman opened the door.

"Grüss Gott," she said pleasantly. "What can I do for you?"

With a quick glance Einar sized her up. About sixty. Graying hair pulled up in a bun. Slightly overweight. A friendly, soft face.

"Frau Werner?" he asked. "Frau Herta Werner?"

"Yes," the woman nodded.

"Frau Werner," Einar said. From his pocket he fished the warning badge he'd found in Alois Hoffner's wine crate files. "I should very much like to ask you a few questions in connection with—this."

He held the badge up for her to see.

The woman's reaction was instantaneous and dramatic. Her hand flew to her mouth in a vain effort to stifle the little cry of horror that burst from her throat. Her eyes tore wide open as they stared at the badge; the blood drained from her face, leaving it white and drawn, and with a gasp of utter terror she collapsed, unconscious.

22

"In here!" Birte called. She pointed to a sofa in the little parlor room. "Put her down there."

Einar carried the unconscious woman to the sofa and put her down.

"Hello!" Birte shouted. "Anyone home? Hello!" She turned to her husband. "No one here," she said.

Einar felt the woman's pulse at her neck. "She's okay," he said. "Just out cold. What the hell happened?"

"It was the badge," Birte said. "She obviously recognized it."

"Hardly a reason to conk out like that."

Herta Werner moaned. She stirred, her eyes fluttered open, and she looked up into the face of Einar, hovering over her. The terror in her eyes came back; she pressed away from him.

"Bitte!" she whispered in obvious desperation. "No! *Bitte, bitte!*—Please, please! Not now. After so long. So very long. Please—don't . . ."

"Easy, Frau Werner," Einar said gently. "Everything's all right. No one's going to harm you. You just—fainted."

The woman stared at him.

"You . . . you are not German," she said.

"I'm American," Einar said. He pulled Birte next to him. "So is my wife."

Birte smiled at the frightened woman.

"You have no reason to be afraid of us," Einar assured her. "I'm sorry we startled you."

Herta Werner looked at him, wide-eyed. She sat up.

"You . . . you are not . . . from them?"

"Them?" Einar frowned. "What do you mean—them?"

"What do you want with me?"

"Them?" Einar asked again. "Who?"

Herta averted her eyes. *"Die Brüderschaft,"* she whispered. "The Brotherhood."

"You mean the organization of SS members?" Einar was startled. It was unexpected. "Gestapo?"

Herta flinched at the word. She nodded.

"That's all in the past, Frau Werner," Einar reassured her. "And certainly *we* have nothing to do with them. Anyway, they're long gone."

Herta shook her head. "No," she breathed. "They are back. They are here. . . . They are here."

"But—what has that got to do with you?" Einar asked.

Herta looked at him, her eyes dark with fear. "It is because of Anton," she whispered. "I should not have done it. They swore they would find me. They swore they would punish me. If it would take forever."

She placed her hands over her face and began to cry uncontrollably. Einar looked at her—at a loss what to do.

Birte touched his shoulder. "Leave her be," she said quietly. "Let her get it out—whatever it is. Let me stay with her. Maybe I can calm her down. We can't learn anything from her until she does." She nodded toward a door that led to a little garden. "Why don't you go walk in the garden or something. I'll do a little woman-to-woman crying with Herta."

Einar nodded. It made sense. As he left the room, Birte was putting her arm around Herta's heaving shoulders.

Questions whirled in Einar's mind. Who was Anton? What had Herta done to the guy? Why did she think the SS—the Gestapo—would punish her? Today? After forty years? Did it have anything to do with her work at the plant? He had that familiar feeling that he was about to get some answers. Some real answers. But not until Herta stopped seeing the past and could talk coherently to them. Birte would quiet her down.

He looked around the garden. It sloped down toward a little creek in the back of the house. It was well kept, growing gradually more wild as it neared the stream.

And suddenly, he too was in the past . . .

Another garden, another time—toward the end of the war. His CIC team had just pulled into some little burg and set up shop in a small house much like this one, on the edge of town. As usual they'd kicked out the Kraut family living there and moved in. They'd long since learned by bitter experience that if you moved into an empty house, it was usually booby-trapped—and you could blow yourself to kingdom come if you sat down on the john, flopped on a bed, or knocked a picture of the Führer off the wall. Not so if the Germans lived there. They could come back when the team moved on.

He'd been sitting in one of the rooms downstairs writing out a report. It was getting dark when he suddenly saw a shadow flit across one of the windows. Someone was in the garden outside. Someone who did not want to be seen.

He'd doused the light and grabbed his .45. He edged over to the window and looked out, just in time to catch a glimpse of a furtive figure disappearing into the shrubbery.

Cautiously he let himself out. He was on enemy ground and fully aware of it. There'd already been incidents of Werewolf activity—those fanatical Nazis, sworn to do as much damage to the U.S. armed forces as they could: assassinations, bombings, arson, and other such pleasantries.

The garden was ill-kempt and overgrown, a jungle of weeds and brush, sprinkled with broken masonry. Silently, watchfully, his gun at the ready, pressed against his abdomen, he stalked his way through the shrubbery—and suddenly he came upon him.

It was a little boy, perhaps eight or nine. He was kneeling in front of a small wooden cross, crudely put together and stuck into a little mound of dirt. On the earth before it lay a bunch of wildflowers.

Einar stood stock-still, taking in the sight. He felt sheepish and a little ashamed. This was his "Werewolf," his enemy: a small boy remembering happier days and a friend who had shared them. A pet, probably. A dog? A cat? Afraid of the new military masters of the house, the boy had chosen darkness in which to steal to the grave of his pet.

Einar put his gun away. Quietly he made his presence known. The boy jumped to his feet, startled, but he stood his ground. Einar talked to him, reassured him that he had nothing to fear. And he asked the boy who was lying in the grave. His dog?

Einar took a deep breath. Since his return to Germany, the past had been crowding in on him, too. He could still see the boy standing before him and hear his timid voice as he held out his right arm, the sleeve hanging loose from the elbow, and said, "No, sir. It is my hand."

He turned back toward the Werner house. He wondered what secret it was that Herta Werner had kept buried for so many years.

All he knew with absolute certainty was that it was a secret he had to unearth.

When he returned to the parlor, Birte and Herta were sitting together. Birte looked up.

"She understands now," she told him. "She knows who we are. She will tell us anything she can."

Einar nodded. He sat down opposite the apprehensive woman. "Frau Werner," he began. "We very much appreciate your cooperation." He smiled at her. "My wife has told you why we need to talk to you?"

Herta nodded.

"You did work at the plant we are interested in? Back in 1945?"

"Yes. I did."

"What did you do?"

"I was only a *Telephonistin*—a switchboard operator."

"What was manufactured at the plant?"

"Chemicals. For the war."

"Including poison gases?"

"Yes." Herta's voice was barely audible.

"Do you know what kind of gases?"

"Only in general." She thought. "Carbonyl chloride phosgene. Chlorine. Di-chlordi-ethylsulfide—mustard gas. White phosphorous. Tear gas—"

"All conventional agents, Frau Werner," Einar interrupted. "Anything else? Anything unusual?"

"There were some new ones," Herta said hesitantly. "They called them nerve gases. Their names were *Tabun* and *Sarin,* and the worst of them, *Soman.* They were supposed to be very much more toxic than the other casualty gases. But there was only a small amount of them produced at the plant."

Einar's thoughts flew ahead. Were these the gases his informant had referred to? They *had* been totally new at that time, back in 1945. And their effects *were* terrible. Convulsions. Coma. And death. By now, of course, those early German poisons were even more effective. But—they were known. Was there something else developed at the Sudeten plant? Or was he beating a dead horse—as that supercilious bastard, Henderson, had suggested?

"Frau Werner," he said earnestly. "Please think. Was there anything else made at the plant?"

"I . . . I do not know," she whispered, suddenly afraid again. "There were . . . rumors."

"What kind of rumors?"

"There was a place, a part of the plant, *Abteilung B*—Division B—where no one was ever allowed, except those who had to work there. And they never talked about their work. But there were rumors that they were working on something very secret." She shuddered almost imperceptibly. "They all wore the kind of badge you showed me."

"Do you know, did any of those badges ever change color?"

Herta nodded. "There were two or three of them that we knew of. The badges turned dark."

"What happened to the people who wore them?"

"I do not know. No one knew. They were taken away. We never saw them again. We never heard from them—nor about them. Not even their families." She paused, her face drawn. "That is why Anton—" She stopped.

"Who was Anton?" Einar asked quietly.

"A friend," Herta whispered.

"What happened to him?"

"He knew about the others. He was afraid to report it when his badge began to go dark."

"Did he know why it went dark?"

"No. He had done nothing he did not always do."

"What was that?"

"He was an *Ausputzer*—he cleaned out the metal containers and the instruments that were used in the laboratories of *Abteilung B*."

"But you don't know what they made there?"

Herta shook her head. "Only that they said it was something terrible. Something that would destroy the enemies of the Reich."

"Did you ever see what it was? What it looked like?"

"No."

"Did Anton?"

"I do not think so. He once said that someone had told him they were making 'brown sugar.' He was making a joke. But Anton said that every once in a while, very rarely, a tiny grain of some substance would adhere to one of the containers he was cleaning. He said it did look like brown sugar."

"What did he do with it?"

"He had a special solution they had given him. He used it to clean the containers."

"Did he say anything else?"

"He told me he wore some sort of protective clothing when he worked. Gloves. And a breathing mask." She frowned in thought. "He told me that on the day his badge changed color, he had discovered a tiny rip in one of his gloves. But he had not felt anything."

"But he didn't report it. What did he do?"

"He . . . he asked me to help him," Herta whispered. "Help him get home, instead of turning himself in—and being taken away . . ."

"And did you?"

"Yes." It was barely a sigh.

"What happened?"

"I . . . I gave him a new badge. I knew where they were kept. And he got through the *Kontrolle*—the Control Station—and went home to his wife. He did not feel good." She swallowed hard, holding back the tears. "They . . . they found out about it, and—"

"Who?"

"They. The Gestapo." Her voice trembled. "They came for me. To arrest me. For treason against the Reich and the Führer. But—I got away. They told everyone I was to be executed. They told them to turn me in if they saw me." She looked up at Einar. "They said they'd find me. One day. No matter how long it would take. And I would die." The tears brimmed in her eyes and rolled down her cheeks, unnoticed. "And, when you came and showed me the badge . . . I thought—" Her voice broke. She sobbed.

"But you know now," Einar said gently. "We mean you no harm. We only need your help."

She nodded, not trusting herself to speak.

"What happened to Anton?"

Herta shook her head. "I do not know. I was in hiding. I talked to no one. And then, when the war was over, I ran away . . ."

Einar put his hand on her arm. "Thank you, Frau Werner," he said. "We are grateful for your help. And, please believe me, you are quite safe."

She nodded, not quite believing him.

Einar stood up. "Good-bye, Frau Werner," he said.

"Good-bye," Birte echoed. She gave the woman a little hug. "You take care."

They started for the door.

"If . . . if you want to know about Anton," Herta Werner said, "he had a daughter. I know his wife is dead, but his daughter is still alive. She could perhaps tell you what happened to her father."

In one step Einar was back in front of the woman.

"Where is this daughter?" he asked urgently. "Do you know?"

Herta nodded.

"She is back in Weiden. Her name is Karla Moser. I do not know where she lives, but she works in one of the factories that make fine china, *Porzellanfabrik Arin.*"

The drive back to Weiden seemed to take ten times as long. Einar was impatient to find and talk to Karla Moser. He was frightened. Something deadly, something unknown, *had* been produced at the Sudeten plant. Something that looked like brown sugar. A poison in crystalline form, he thought, like adamsite, which was a greenish-yellow solid.

He knew about the other World War II poison gases that had been produced at the Sudeten plant. The phosgene, a colorless choking gas with the pleasant smell of new-mown hay. It caused such damage to the lungs, flooding the air cells, that the victims died of lack of oxygen . . . The chloride, a greenish-yellow gas with a smell as pungent as bleaching powder, a powerful irritant that severely inflamed the eyes as well as the bronchial tubes and the lungs . . . And mustard gas, a cruel vesicant or blister gas, a yellow liquid with the faint odor of garlic or horseradish; absorbed through the skin or mucous membranes, it burned and destroyed the tissues, crippling the victims . . . And the nerve gases, colorless liquids that inhibited the normal action of body enzymes with horrible and lethal results. One tiny drop on the skin would cause death within fifteen minutes.

And there were others. Many others. Some of them colorless and odorless, some with odors ranging from geraniums to bitter almonds. Some were gases, some liquids, some solids. Some of them with immediate action—others delayed.

What was the poison gas, so jealously kept secret, that had caused Anton's badge to turn dark?

And was it the threat the New York accident victim—known as Karl Johann Thompson—had referred to?

Perhaps Karla Moser would have part of the answer . . .

★ ★ ★

Porzellanfabrik Arin was located in an industrial park in the northwestern section of Weiden. It was just past noon when Einar parked his Volkswagen Jetta in the spacious parking lot surrounding the plant.

The factory produced porcelain, mostly for hotel use. Karla Moser worked in the decorating department, affixing colorful decal patterns to the chinaware before the deco firing, which would bond them on permanently. She was just about to begin her lunch hour when Einar and Birte were shown to her work station.

They watched her deftly place two decal halves with a flower pattern on the rim of a dinner plate fresh from the Glost kiln and lay them in place with a small squeegee. She turned the plate over and affixed the *Porzellanfabrik Arin, Weiden* logo on the bottom.

Karla Moser looked to be in her middle fifties, slender to the point of being gaunt, with short-cut mousy-blond hair and eyes that were curiously cold and expressionless. Apathetically she acknowledged Einar's introductions.

"Fräulein Moser," he said. "We understand you are about to break for lunch. It would give us great pleasure if you would join us. I'm sure there is a nice little restaurant nearby."

Dispassionately Karla looked at him. "I brought my lunch," she said.

"Then may we join you when you take your lunch break?"

Karla shrugged indifferently. "If you wish. I eat in the employees' lounge."

She stood up. From under her work table she pulled out a brown paper bag. Without a word she started to walk toward the lounge. Einar and Birte exchanged glances. Then they followed her.

Karla selected a small table in a corner, away from the main section and her coworkers. She sat down and opened her bag.

Uninvited, Einar and Birte joined her.

"You must forgive us for imposing on you like this," Einar said, "but we urgently need some information that only you can give us."

Karla brought out two sandwiches wrapped in transparent plastic paper, and a small thermos bottle. Incuriously she glanced at Einar.

"I have no information," she said flatly. "About anything."

"It has to do with your father," Einar explained.

Karla did not react. She did not look up at Einar. Birte was watching her. Did she stiffen? Almost imperceptibly?

Karla unwrapped the two sandwiches. One with liverwurst, one with cheese. She said nothing.

"That liverwurst looks wonderful," Birte said brightly. "Homemade? Did you make it yourself?"

"My neighbor," Karla said laconically.

"How terrific to have such a talented neighbor," Birte marveled. She chuckled. "Ours back home, the Newberrys, have trouble opening a can."

Einar kept silent. He knew exactly what his wife was up to. Trying to put Karla at ease. She was good at it, he thought, but that cold fish of a Moser woman was something else.

Karla took a bite of her liverwurst sandwich. She opened the thermos and poured some hot, black coffee into the cup lid. She literally took no notice of the two strangers at her table.

"It was a friend of your parents who suggested we look you up," Birte went on pleasantly. "Herta Werner. Herta Siemens then. Did you know her?"

Karla nodded curtly. "I was thirteen when she left town."

"Then you must surely remember her," Birte exclaimed. "Such a nice and friendly woman. She told us how she had helped your father."

Karla gave her a brief glance.

"Helped?"

Now that Birte had gotten them back on track, Einar stepped in.

"She told us about the accident your father had at the plant," he said. "She told us how she helped him get home to his family."

"Helped?" Karla repeated, her manner strangely impassive and remote. "I remember her . . . help." She could not hide the hint of bitterness that showed through her apathy.

"What we need to know—and it is of the utmost importance—what we need to know is, what happened to your father?"

For a moment Karla sat silent, not looking at them. Then she said, "He died."

"How, Fräulein Moser?" Einar asked. "How did he die?" He leaned toward her. "Please believe me, I would not ask such a painful and personal question if it were not of the greatest necessity that we know."

Karla looked at him, her eyes as dark and empty and cold as outer space.

"You want to know how my father died," she said, her voice flat and toneless. "I will tell you. He dried up. He vomited. His body fluids flowed from him. He could not control it. The sweat oozed from his pores. In hours his eyes shriveled, and he went blind. His skin wrinkled and cracked open, but there was no blood, only a brown slime. His lips turned black, and his tongue grew stiff and dry so he could not talk. Only scream. For a while. Until his lungs withered, and in agony he died."

She stopped. Her words hung in the air between them like a poisonous mist.

"That is how my father died, Herr Munk," she spat the words out at him. She was breathing rapidly. "The Gestapo came for his dried-up body. In secret. And took it away. My mother died quickly thereafter. She could not live with what she had seen . . . And I—"

Suddenly her rasping breath shattered into a series of sobs. Abruptly she stood up.

"Damn you!" she whispered venomously. "I did not want to remember. Damn you to hell!"

And she ran from the lounge.

They walked to the car and got in.

Einar sat stiffly, silently staring into space, his face white and drained, a film of tiny drops of perspiration covering his forehead.

Birte watched him. She was alarmed. She had never seen him like that before.

"Einar," she asked softly. "What is it?"

He blinked. He took a deep breath and turned to her. "I know what the poison is, Birte," he said, obviously deeply troubled. "I know what it can do. God help us, if it still exists—and is in the hands of men who will use it."

"What is it?" She was frightened.

"It's a virulent type of nerve gas, Birte. A poison that after it invades your system, through breathing or through the skin, seems to produce the effects of an immensely powerful exsiccator."

"What's that?" Birte asked. Even the word with its sound of finality chilled her.

"It's a chemical agent that exsiccates or draws out all moisture," Einar explained. "From the tissues of a living being, for instance, man or beast. In this case, it apparently causes the body to discharge or excrete all its fluids. Dramatically and effusively. It'll produce quick, total anhydration. Dehydration, if you will. And certain, agonizing death. From Karla's description, that's what that 'brown sugar' is."

"Oh, dear God," Birte whispered.

"It fits," Einar said grimly. "The Nazis did develop nerve gases during the war. *Soman*, for instance. It, too, induced vomiting, diarrhea, eye contractions, convulsions, and vasoparesis—a sort of paralysis of the blood vessels. It was the worst of those poisons. There were others."

"The . . . 'brown sugar'?"

Einar nodded. "Such a poison could well be produced in crystalline form—and look like brown sugar. In gaseous form it would be invisible and odorless. Undetectable—until too late. If it is as strong as indicated, a small amount could easily wipe out an entire metropolis. Such as New York. Kill everything alive."

He looked at Birte, the dread dark in his eyes. "And its special properties are unknown. There would be no antidote." He looked stricken. "There is no longer any doubt left," he said. "The Nazis did develop a new and terrible poison gas at that Sudeten plant. It *was* there. And it killed. Where is it now? In whose hands?"

He started the car. "We must get back to the hotel. I'll have to send Colonel Henderson a wire. Tell him everything we've found out. Dammit! He'll have to act now!"

Einar was deeply engrossed in composing a comprehensive telegram to the CID officer. He wanted to make certain he conveyed the full danger and urgency of his discoveries—without sounding melodramatic. It was not easy. He was startled when the telephone rang. He picked up the receiver.

"Hello?"

"Herr Munk?" a man asked. "Herr Einar Munk?" The caller's voice was low and guarded as if he was afraid of being overheard.

"Speaking," Einar said.

"Herr Munk, I can be of help to you."

Einar was at once alert.

"What do you mean? How?"

"Today I saw you speaking with Fräulein Moser," the man confided. "In the lounge at the *Fabrik*. I know you are seeking information about the plant in the Sudeten, and the . . . the 'brown sugar.' I can help." The man spoke hurriedly in a furtive half-whisper. "I was there. I saw it loaded, in heavy metal drums. Onto a train bound for northern Germany. It was during the final days, one of the last trains to have a chance of getting where it was going."

"Where?" Einar asked tensely. "What was the destination of the train? What else do you know?"

"Not on the telephone, Herr Munk. I cannot talk for long. You must meet me. Tonight."

"Of course. Where?"

"I, too, work at the *Fabrik*. Where you were today. I am a maintenance man. Keeping the kilns fired when the plant is closed down for the night. I will be here. Come to the door opposite the main entrance. I will wait for you. Come at 2300 hours. It will be safe then. Until later, Herr Munk."

"Wait!" Einar said quickly. "Who are you? What is your name?"

"I told you who I am," the man whispered. "My name is Kratzer."

23

Only a couple of cars were parked in the huge, brightly lit lot at *Porzellanfabrik Arin* when Einar drove his Jetta across it, getting a kick out of disregarding the painted parking lines. The windowless factory building was dark except for a light inside the main entrance. The security guard station, Einar guessed.

He parked his car close to the door on the opposite side of the building. In his pocket he had a long telegram to Colonel Henderson. He would add to it anything he learned from the man, Kratzer, before he sent it. He turned to Birte, sitting next to him. "Here goes," he said.

A light was burning over the entrance, and the figure of a man could be seen waiting in the shadows of the doorway. He stepped out to meet them as they walked up.

"I am Kratzer," he said, extending his hand. "I am pleased that you have come." He made a small bow toward Birte. *"Gnädige Frau,"* he said.

"We're anxious to learn what you know, Herr Kratzer," Einar said, shaking the man's hand. It was the kind of a handshake he loathed. A flabby, passive gesture with no firmness to it at all.

Kratzer, a man in his late fifties, perhaps sixty, appeared to be nervous.

"We will talk inside," he said. "I must keep an eye on the kilns. The temperature must be kept correct."

He turned and led the way into the plant.

Only work lights were burning in the huge, cavernous expanse of workshops, spilling pools of pale light among the giant pieces of machinery and stabbing thin beams through their convoluted forms.

Birte felt uneasy. Instinctively she walked close to Einar as they crossed hall after hall, department after department. The plant was oppressively hot, and the massive machinery seemed to press in on her. The place was peopled with weird, somehow ominous shadows that seemed to take on a dark life of their own as the three of them walked through the deserted factory.

Einar, too, felt on edge. There was nothing that appeared to be an obvious menace, yet he recognized the perceived need for wariness from his CIC days of long ago. His alert caution was not lost on Kratzer, who eyed him speculatively.

Power presses, dryers, and jiggering machines loomed over them as they walked through the darkened plant. Rows upon rows of wheeled metalware racks with stacks of chinaware in various stages of completion—from greenware to bisque-fired stock—stood like silent sentries, waiting for action. And like sleeping behemoths the enormous kilns, their searing breaths rumbling softly deep in their fiery steel throats, squatted in massive bulk on the concrete floors.

At last they reached their destination. Kratzer pointed to a colossal kiln more than a hundred feet long.

"It is the deco kiln," he explained. "It is where the ornamentation on the ware is fired. It has been acting up a bit. I have to keep an eye on it. I hope you do not mind. But I do not want the temperature to go below fourteen hundred forty or above fourteen sixty degrees Fahrenheit." He pointed to a small wooden table and a couple of benches nearby. "We can sit there."

He walked over to the table and sat down. Einar and Birte followed.

"You told me on the phone that you saw the . . . the 'brown sugar' being loaded on a train, Herr Kratzer," Einar said. "How can you be sure that's what it was?"

Kratzer licked his bloodless lips. "It was the drums," he said. "It was because of the drums. They were special. Only used for the *Abteilung B* product. The 'brown sugar.' "

"How were they special?"

"They were very heavy. I do not know what the metal alloy was, but it looked different from the regular drums. And they had two broad steel bands, painted red, circling them, and two more going lengthwise and fastened over the top with special latches."

"How many of them were loaded on the train?"

Kratzer shook his head. "A hundred. Two hundred. More. I do not know exactly. I do not know how many had already been placed in the cars before I began to watch."

Birte shuddered as she was listening. Two hundred drums. She remembered the terrible effects on Anton Moser, described to them by his daughter, after exposure to only one tiny grain in a detoxification solution. And through a pinpoint rip in his glove . . . Two hundred drums . . .

"Where were they going? Do you know?" Einar asked.

"North, as I told you. The stencils on the cars said *HAMBURG.* But that could mean anywhere in the region."

Einar looked earnestly at the German. "Herr Kratzer," he said. "Do you know what that 'brown sugar' was? What they were going to do with it? How they were going to use it?"

Slowly Kratzer shook his head. "It was a poison agent," he said. "I am sure of that. It was what the Sudeten factory produced." He paused. He looked at Einar. "They said . . . they said it was the final weapon that would win the war. It was Hitler's ultimate vengeance weapon. His V-1 flying bomb had failed. So had his V-2 rocket. But, they said that the Sudeten plant formula would succeed. It would be Adolf Hitler's *V-3*. And it was invincible."

He shrugged. "Only—they were wrong. The war was lost."

Einar was wholly engrossed in what Kratzer was telling him. He thought of the threat made by the ex-Nazi in New York. It suddenly loomed larger and more menacing than ever.

"What happened to the shipment?" he asked tensely. "What do you know about it?"

"Nothing. Only that—"

He stopped. He cocked an ear. "There she goes," he exclaimed with annoyance. "Scraping again. Hear it?" He picked up a crowbar that had been leaning against the wall. "Excuse me, please. I shall be only a minute."

He stood up and walked past Einar.

Suddenly he whirled. Viciously he swung the heavy crowbar directly at Einar's head.

With that instant reaction born of training, experience, and instinct, Einar brought up an arm to ward off the blow and ducked his head to one side. The heavy iron bar was minutely deflected and struck only a glancing blow to Einar's temple, or he would have been killed.

He was unconscious before he fell across the table.

Even as Kratzer dealt the savage blow to Einar's head, Birte was on him. She leaped on his back. She raked her nails down across his face, feeling the warm, oily blood smear her fingers.

Kratzer roared.

He let the crowbar fall. He grabbed Birte and flung her violently from him. She crashed to the floor and slid across the concrete, coming up hard against the cement block wall.

For a moment she lay stunned. In a haze she saw the German manhandle Einar's inert body from the table, haul it to the loading end of the deco kiln, and heave it up onto the rough steel-mesh conveyor belt, which steadily inched its way at a snail's pace toward the gaping opening to the mammoth furnace. She saw him reach for and twist a dial, and she saw the conveyor belt visibly pick up speed, moving inexorably toward the fiery maw of the kiln, carrying Einar's unconscious body along.

Groggily she struggled to her feet. She knew she would have to get Einar off the conveyor belt. Fast. In a minute, at the most two, it would be too late. She also knew she could not possibly fight the German. And win.

The security guard. At the main entrance. If she could reach him, he could help.

Where? How could she get to the guard station? With a sinking feeling she realized she would have to find her way through the maze of unfamiliar paths that crisscrossed the many work halls filled with machinery.

And she had less than a minute.

She turned. Out of the corner of her eye, she saw Kratzer whirl on her, his face contorted with rage.

She ran.

Pursued by Kratzer, she dashed through the convoluted, shadowy realm of looming ram presses, dryers, jiggering machines, bisque kilns, and glazing ovens, and in between workbenches.

She yelled and shouted, screaming for help whenever she could muster enough breath. But no one responded. Deliberately she knocked over storage rack after storage rack, shattering greenware in the path of her pursuer in a desperate effort to slow him down.

But he was gaining.

And the seconds were ticking by.

She tore headlong through a broad door opening into a dimly lit area, smaller than the others. It was filled with mechanisms she had not seen before. She raced past a bulky mixing tank, its square hopper towering above her. She sped beside a filter press and almost tripped over a sharp protrusion on a pug mill.

And Kratzer was gaining on her steadily.

She was getting desperate. Her heart pounded. Her breath wheezed through her open mouth.

Where was the guard station?

How much time did Einar have left?

Disjointed, incongruous thoughts tumbled about in her tortured mind. The funny slapping sound of her own running footsteps on the concrete floor, changing in pitch as she ran past the solid ball mills . . . Wondering if Kratzer's blood would ever wash out from under her nails . . . She had the weird feeling that she was outside her own body, watching herself. As in a nightmare. Or as in one of those old, melodramatic movie serials she'd watched as a child. Where the hero finds himself in some unimaginable danger—and intrepid help arrives in the nick of time. She used to laugh at them. She didn't now.

She bolted on.

In the half-light she skittered around a high-speed mixer and almost collided with a long, thick vertical metal shaft that reached down from the gloom above to end about a foot from the floor in a large, wicked-looking disc of steel blades twisted and angled to cut in all directions.

Quickly she looked around. Involuntarily she gasped.

She was cornered.

She stopped in dismay, her breath rapid and rasping in her throat. There was no way out—except back the way she'd come.

Past Kratzer.

She could hear his pounding footsteps nearing the dead end. Frantically her eyes flew about. Behind her was a panel on the wall. On it were several dials and two buttons. One red. One green.

And Kratzer came rushing around the tank. He saw her. Cornered. He skidded to a halt—triumphant.

But the floor was wet. He slipped. He lost his balance and fell against the greasy metal shaft.

Birte's thoughts raced. She knew she had to do something. Something that would give her a chance to get around her hunter. What? Her eyes found the green button on the panel behind her. Green. It would start something. Something that might distract Kratzer long enough for her to get away?

Or something that would imprison her even further?

She hit it.

Instantly the huge shaft began to spin, almost at once reaching a speed of a thousand RPM. Kratzer, just regaining his balance, screamed as the whirling, circular blades near the floor sliced through his right leg. The force of the spin hurled his severed foot through the air. It hit Birte's legs and bounced off into the darkness.

Losing his balance, unable to hold on to the spinning pole, screaming his terror, Kratzer slid down the shaft, his chest and neck hitting the savagely whirling blades.

At once Birte ran from the gruesome sight, not even taking the time to stop the spinning blades that bit into the splattering gore that a few seconds before had been her pursuer.

Perhaps Einar's killer.

She pounded back the way she'd come, guided by the havoc she'd wrought as she fled from Kratzer.

Was she too late?

She reached the deco kiln.

The feeder belt platform was at the far end.

She sped down the hundred-foot length of the monster kiln. She reached the feeder platform just in time to see Einar's shoes slowly disappearing into the gaping opening, carried on the inexorably moving steel-mesh conveyor belt toward the all-devouring flames that glowed bright red deep inside.

Her eyes flew to the control panel nearby. There was an array of buttons and switches, dials and knobs. Which one would stop the belt? There was no time to experiment.

Desperately she grabbed hold of Einar's feet. She could barely touch them, as they were slowly being drawn out of her reach. She leaned into the furnace-hot opening. Furiously she pulled. She strained. But even though her fear and desperation gave her superhuman strength, Einar would not budge. The rough steel mesh, imbedded in his clothing like a thousand shark's teeth, was holding him in a relentless grip, and Birte was unable to pull him out.

Soon she would not be able to reach him at all.

Feverishly she looked around. The belt crawled ponderously across two driver drums before going around the larger end roller.

Something to jam it with!

There. On the floor.

The crowbar Kratzer had used to knock Einar unconscious.

She grabbed it.

With all her might she jabbed it into the space between the belt and the upper driver drum.

With a sickening grating, grinding sound, the belt came to a stop, the driver drum still rotating, straining and screeching, against the steel-mesh belt.

At once she scrambled up on the feeder platform. On her hands and knees, she crawled to her husband, mindless of the cuts she inflicted on herself.

Disregarding the shimmering heat that belched from the kiln, she entered the opening. She tore and yanked and pulled at her husband's body, slowly, gradually loosening it from the grip of the conveyor belt.

She dragged him off the platform. He was limp. Still unconscious.

But he was alive.

She ripped a piece from her slip and wet it at a nearby water fountain. Gently she bathed her husband's flushed and burning face and daubed the wound on his temple.

Softly she called his name, again and again, knowing he could not hear her. Consciously she kept back her nausea at the faint stench of singed hair.

And Einar's eyes blinked open.

Struggling, he sat up. He leaned against the bench.

Tears streaming down her face, Birte threw her arms around him and held him tight.

There was no need for words.

Unsteadily Einar hauled himself to his feet. Still wobbly, he held on to the table.

"Where's that damned bastard?" he mumbled.

Birte put his arm around her shoulder. "Come on," she said. "I'll tell you on the way. We'll find the guard at the front entrance." She looked with concern at her husband. "We'll get a doctor to look at you."

As they slowly made their way through the factory, Birte told him what had happened to Kratzer. Einar said nothing, but his arm tightened across her shoulder. Gradually he seemed to regain his strength and clear his head.

He was disgusted with himself. Was he getting too damned old? He'd let that German bastard lull him into a false sense of security with his tales. He'd forgotten the most important edict of an agent in the field: the day you stop watching, suspicious of every detail, is the day you sign your own damned death warrant. Once he'd lived by it with an iron will. Was that iron will getting a bit rusty? Or was it just that he hadn't quite accepted the fact that the perils of today were just as deadly as those of forty years ago? Well, dammit!—He accepted it now. And he vowed that from now on, there would be a part of him that would never cease to watch.

They walked on, and presently they saw a glass-paneled door with a light behind it. They'd found the main entrance lobby.

Beyond the door was a lighted reception area. Another glass-paneled door, leading from it, stood ajar.

Birte knocked on it.

"Anyone here?" she called. "Hello!"

There was no answer.

Einar pushed past her and nudged the door open. Beyond it was a small security room; inside were a desk with an instrument panel and an array of small TV monitor sets showing different areas of the plant, including the deco kiln.

A man was lying on the floor, bound and gagged, unconscious.

The guard.

Einar bent over him. He felt his pulse. He tested the gag but did not remove it.

"He's all right," he said. "Just out cold." He examined the man's head. "Not a mark on him," he said. "They must have given him something." He pointed to a thermos and a cup half full of coffee. "Probably in that."

"We must call someone," Birte said. "We'll have to make a report. The police."

Seriously Einar looked at her. "No doctor," he said firmly. "No report. And no police. All would involve us in a lengthy investigation. We don't have time for that."

"What about him?" Birte nodded toward the unconscious guard.

"He'll be fine. He'll sleep it off. Someone will find him in a few hours.

And they'll find Kratzer. Let them try to figure out what happened without us. No one knows we were here. Let it stay at that."

He took her by the shoulders and looked seriously at her. "Look, Bo," he said. "We have just had proven to us that huge amounts of a deadly poisonous substance exist somewhere. And that there are men who intend to use it. I don't know how or where or when. Only that when it does happen, the results will be catastrophic. And we know now that those men, whoever they are, will kill to safeguard their operation. We have to find a way to stop them. We can't allow ourselves to be delayed. For any reason."

He turned to leave. "Let's get the hell out of this damned place before anyone else shows up."

On the way back to the Hotel Schmid, Einar soberly took stock.

"First thing in the morning, we send the wire to Henderson," he said. He looked grim. "And then I get myself a damned gun."

"How?" Birte looked at him. "If it's anything like back home, you can't just walk in and buy one. There's a waiting period before they let you have it."

"I know," Einar said, his jaw set in that determined way she knew so well. "I'll figure out something. And then we'll follow up the lead Kratzer gave us."

Birte looked puzzled. "What lead?"

"His name."

"What do you mean?"

"We'll make use of one of the most effective investigative research tools around," he said. "The telephone book. We'll find out where Kratzer lived. It'll give us a place to look for his cronies."

He looked at her.

"Where there's one louse, there're usually more. And, dammit! We'll scratch for them till we find them!"

24

The telegram to Henderson was two pages long. It contained everything they'd found out, cloaked in language that would not alert the uninitiated but would give the CID officer all the information he'd need. They left out only certain aspects of the Kratzer incident.

As soon as the shops opened, Einar and Birte set out to acquire a gun.

First they went to a hobby shop they'd seen on Max Reger Strasse when they were there before. In the window Einar had seen a collection of replicas of historic guns that looked astoundingly realistic. He bought a Walther, 7.65, Model PPK of World War II vintage that could do anything but shoot.

When they left the shop, Birte looked at her husband. "Looks terrific," she said caustically. "Make a good paperweight. But not much protection, unless you aim to throw it at somebody."

He laughed. And he told her the rest of his plan.

The little gun shop on Sedanstrasse a few blocks away sold everything from shotguns to used handguns, from daggers to *Hirschfängers,* the big, ornate Bavarian deer-hunting knives. Einar entered the shop by himself. The clerk greeted him deferentially.

"What may I do for the gentleman?" he asked.

"I'm interested in a small handgun," Einar said. "Something from the war years. Perhaps a Walther, 7.65, Model PPK, preferably."

The clerk nodded, pleased. The guns were expensive items. "Of course, sir. A very popular gun. An excellent weapon." He showed the way to a display under the glass-topped counter. "We have a couple of them, sir. Right here. They are not easy to find these days."

Einar bent over the counter and looked at the guns. He pointed to one of them that looked nearly new. "May I see that one?" he requested.

"Of course, sir. An excellent choice. As you can see, the gun is in exceptional condition." The clerk brought out the gun and gave it to Einar. Einar examined it critically.

"Exactly what I want," he said with satisfaction. "Do you have ammunition for it?"

"Of course, sir." The clerk brought out a box of 7.65 cartridges. Einar opened it and looked at the neat rows of rounds that filled it. He picked up the gun.

"When can I have it?" he asked.

"The gentleman is not German?"

"American."

"Ah, yes. It will take about a week, I am afraid. Five working days exactly, before the paperwork, the necessary permits, and licenses can be processed. I shall need your name, your passport number, and the address where you are staying in town. With a small deposit you may pick up the gun a week from today."

Einar lifted his hand and ran his fingers through his hair.

"It's cutting it pretty close," he said. "But I guess it'll be okay."

The door chimes sounded, and Birte entered the shop. She marched up to the counter. Imperiously she called to the clerk. "Young man. I am here for the *Hirschfänger.*"

"One moment, *gnädige Frau,*" the clerk called back.

"You promised it would be ready for me to pick up"—she looked at her watch—"right now. I don't have much time," she added petulantly.

The clerk looked puzzled and uncertain. "Excuse me one moment," he said to Einar. He started toward Birte. Einar got ready. At that moment another man came through the curtains to the back of the shop. "May I be of help?" he asked Birte.

Relieved, the clerk turned back to Einar.

Einar fumed inside. A second clerk was not according to the script, dammit! What the hell now? He spilled a few of the cartridges out on the counter. He picked up a round. "How old is this ammunition?" he asked.

"I assure you, sir, it—" He stopped and looked toward Birte. She was raising her voice in obvious annoyance.

"The *Hirschfänger*," she said loudly. She pointed to a long hunting knife with an ornate stag-antler handle and a carved leather sheath that hung in a display case. "It was that one, I think." The second clerk turned and got it for her.

The clerk with Einar once more gave him his full attention. "I assure you, sir, the ammunition is *erstklassig*—first rate."

"Well, then, you'd better go get the necessary papers."

"Have them right here," the clerk said brightly. He reached under the counter.

"That's *not* the one!" Birte said in loud indignation. "The etchings on the blade are quite different. Can't you see? All you had to do was glue that little silver whatever-you-call-it back on the hilt. That young man over there," she said, gesturing with the heavy hunting knife toward the clerk with Einar. "He promised me it would be ready today."

Suddenly the big *Hirschfänger* slipped from her hand. It crashed down on the glass countertop, cracking it.

For a moment everyone's attention was on Birte and her accident. A brief moment only, but long enough for Einar to switch his replica gun for the real one.

The clerk turned back to him. "Sorry, sir."

"Look," Einar said, slightly irritated. "I think I'll come back when there is less commotion." He handed the replica Walther PPK to the clerk. "Just keep it for me."

The clerk took the gun. Birte called loudly, "Young man! You!" She shook her finger at the clerk with Einar. Startled, he looked toward her. "Did you not promise me?" she shouted.

Distracted, with only a cursory glance at the Walther, the clerk put it back under the counter with the other guns.

"Excuse me, sir," he said to Einar. He hurried over to Birte, who was angrily berating his colleague.

Quickly Einar swept up a few rounds of ammunition, put them in his pocket, and walked from the shop.

He felt a hell of a lot better.

He was armed.

He waited for Birte around the corner.

"They thought I was crazy," she laughed. "I told them finally that I was in the wrong shop!" She looked at Einar. "Did you get it? I wasn't sure."

"You were terrific," he grinned. "And I got it."

"But not for nothing," Birte said. "I paid them for the broken countertop. Generously."

There were two Kratzers in the Weiden telephone book. Luckily it was not a common name. One was a woman. The other was one Julius A. Kratzer. He might be their man. His address was Pension Adler.

The woman who answered Einar's ring was ample and rosy-cheeked, with large underarm sweat stains on her blouse.

"Guten Tag," Einar said pleasantly. "We are looking for Herr Julius Kratzer."

The woman's pudgy hands flew to her mouth. *"Ach, du lieber!"* she exclaimed. "You have not heard?"

"Heard what?"

"Herr Kratzer is dead! He had a terrible accident. Last night. At *Porzellanfabrik Arin.* They found him this morning."

Birte looked shaken. "Oh no!" she whispered.

"You knew Herr Kratzer?"

Einar nodded. "We are old friends," he said, obviously dismayed. "We wanted to surprise him. We live now in America."

The woman brightened. *"Ach, so,"* she said. "You must be the people who have been writing to him. I saw he occasionally got a letter from America."

Einar nodded again. "That's right. We corresponded."

The woman stood aside. "Won't you please come in?" she suggested. "Perhaps I can tell you something of Herr Kratzer."

"You are very kind, Frau—?"

"Wasserman," the woman said. "Adele Wasserman. My husband, Joseph, died three years ago." She waved her hands around as they followed her to the downstairs parlor. "That is why I must now rent out some of my upstairs rooms. To nice people, like your friend."

"I'm glad he found such a pleasant place to live," Birte said. "And such a gracious landlady."

Adele Wasserman giggled and said, "Please sit down." She patted a seedy, overstuffed sofa with a row of gray-looking crocheted antimacassars, which stood under a shelf with Bavarian steins.

"Herr Kratzer was a good boarder," Adele Wasserman went on. "Always paid his rent on time, even though he was retired, of course. Never any trouble. Poor man. One wonders why he went to the *Fabrik* so late. He did not work there." Her eyes gleamed. Obviously she loved gossip. "And the guard." She threw up her hands. "They found him drugged. And tied up. He doesn't know what happened."

She looked conspiratorially at them. "One wonders what happened out there." She was plainly waiting for her guests to venture a guess. When none was forthcoming, she continued.

"It was such a dreadful shock. Such a tragedy, don't you think?"

Einar was disappointed. He'd hoped to get some concrete information about Kratzer from the woman, not just gossip, but he realized that Kratzer must have been aware of the fact that Adele Wasserman held secrets as a sieve holds water and would have told her nothing of consequence.

He nodded solemnly. "How did you find out, Frau Wasserman? If they found him only this morning?"

"Oh, it was on the radio already. Just an hour ago. The local station."

"Then . . . his friends will know, too."

The woman looked sad. "Poor Herr Kratzer," she sighed. "He did not have many friends. He was really a lonely man. I know of only one friend he had in Weiden."

"Who was that, Frau Wasserman?" Birte asked. "Perhaps we know him."

"Heinrich Mahler," the woman said. "He and Herr Kratzer had served together during the war. In the *Kriegsmarine*—the navy. Herr Mahler would call occasionally, and the two of them would go out. For a beer together, I'm sure." She drew herself up in vicarious pride. "Herr Kratzer had been executive officer on a U-boat."

"I know," Einar said. He looked thoughtful. "Mahler. Heinrich Mahler. We do not know him personally, but I do seem to remember Julius mentioning him in his letters." He looked questioningly at the woman. "It might be considerate if we called on him."

"Oh, yes, please do," Adele Wasserman enthused. "I am certain he would be delighted. He lives right here in town. I shall give you his address."

She walked to an old rolltop desk. Einar and Birte exchanged a quick glance.

They had found a second louse. . . .

* * *

The sign over the little shop read: HEINRICH MAHLER—PHOTOGRAPH.

Einar had thought long and hard, trying to decide how to handle Mahler. He realized he could not conduct an interrogation along the lines he'd used in his CIC investigations long ago, with its pressures, tricks, and threats. He had no power to do so. Mahler could toss him out on his ear any time he chose. He had decided on a different tack. Bluff. The big bluff. It was risky. He could do nothing to back it up. He could easily end up with a whole omelette on his face. Or he could get it served on a silver platter.

So bluff it was.

As he walked across the street with Birte, he pressed his left arm lightly against his side, feeling the comfort of the Walther PPK in his belt. If needed, it would be in his hand in less than a second.

It had been decided that Birte would wait outside. Somehow she didn't fit in the ploy.

A bell tinkled merrily as Einar entered the studio anteroom.

"Herein!" a man's voice called from the back. "I am in here. Please come in."

Einar followed the voice and walked through an open door. He found himself in a small studio.

A man was in the process of setting up a camera aimed at an array of colorful fabrics draped artistically over rich-looking furniture in a modern room setting. Lights and stands ringed the set, and small spots and floods were cleverly hidden from the camera behind accessories and furniture. The man was in his late sixties, bald, with a square jaw, cement-colored eyes, and no more than five foot six.

Heinrich Mahler.

He looked up as Einar entered the studio.

"Moment, bitte, mein Herr," he said. "I shall be right with you."

He steadied the camera on its tripod, checked a setting, and locked it in place.

"It's an advertisement shot for one of Weiden's finest textile houses," he explained. He waved a hand at the fabrics. "Beautiful, are they not?" He turned to Einar. "What can I do for you?"

Einar stood ramrod straight before the man, feet slightly apart. Sternly he said, "Herr Mahler? Herr Heinrich Mahler?"

Mahler nodded, a hint of apprehension in his eyes. "I am Heinrich Mahler," he acknowledged.

"I am Major Einar Munk," Einar said coldly. "NATO intelligence. We want to ask you a few questions."

"Questions?" Mahler exclaimed, an uneasy frown wrinkling his forehead. "About what?"

"About the exsiccator poison gas produced at and shipped from a certain chemical plant in the Sudeten. The so-called 'brown sugar.' "

Mahler grew visibly paler. He stared at Einar.

"I . . . I do not know what you are talking about," he protested.

Einar regarded the man through narrowed eyes.

"Don't make it any more difficult for yourself, Mahler," he said icily. "Or for me. We already have most of the information we need. From your comrades in the *Kriegsmarine.* Karl Johann Tollmann in New York and Julius Kratzer right here. All we need is your corroboration."

"Julius Kratzer is dead."

Einar smiled a thin smile. "I know," he said. "He was . . . uncooperative at first. And then he tried to get away from us. He took refuge in some pottery plant. It was a mistake."

For a moment Mahler regarded Einar, his eyes penetrating and calculating. Then he shrugged in resignation.

"Very well," he said. "I will go with you." He turned to his camera. "I will just put this away."

He touched it.

Instantly the entire room exploded in blinding, searing white light. As if a lightning bolt had struck his eyes, Einar was at once totally blinded.

The world around him was black.

25

Einar instinctively went for his gun. He knew at once what had happened, dammit! Mahler had had the entire studio set up with slave units, concealed flashbulbs set to blow at the instant the main flash on the camera went off.

Gradually his sight returned except for some black spots burned into his retinas. His eyes quickly searched the room.

Mahler was gone.

Einar raced from the room. He rushed out the front door, nearly colliding with Birte, who stood looking down at Mahler sprawled on the sidewalk.

She looked up at Einar. "Gee, I'm sorry," she said. "He came out in such a hurry he must have tripped over his own feet." Her eyes twinkled. "Or mine. I'm afraid he'll have quite a bump on his head."

Einar hauled the dazed Mahler to his feet. To the couple of people who'd stopped to look, he said, "It's all right. The gentleman fell. We'll take care of him."

He and Birte ushered Mahler into his shop. They plopped him down in one of the chairs on his set.

Mahler nursed a growing lump on his head. Sullenly he fixed his baleful eyes on Einar—and on the Walther PPK in his hand.

"You are not from NATO intelligence," he said testily. "You are the American who has been nosing around."

"Correct," Einar said, his voice arctic. "And therefore you will realize that I am not bound by official regulations." Suggestively he moved his gun minutely as he said, "If you don't give me the exact information I want, first I'll shoot off one kneecap, then the other, and then the family jewels. Understood?"

Mahler looked gray. "What is it you want to know?" he asked.

"I want to know all about the couple of hundred special drums filled with 'brown sugar' that were shipped from the Sudeten plant," Einar said crisply. "I want to know where they are now. Who controls them. What plans there are for using the poison in them. And your involvement in the entire affair. And I want it now!"

"I do not know everything," Mahler said tartly.

"You know enough. And I want all of it. So start talking."

Mahler sat in stony, silent thought for a moment, a slight, malicious smile, which never reached his eyes, playing on his lips.

"I will tell you what you want to know, American," he said scornfully. "It will make no difference now. There is nothing you can do."

"Talk!" Einar snapped. "You were in the *Kriegsmarine.* Start from there. Where did you serve?"

"In the U-boat service," Mahler said. The pride of the submariner was still there—in his voice. "We were a top crew. That is why we were chosen to carry out the Führer's Operation Ultimatum, it was—"

"Operation Ultimatum?" Einar asked. "What's that?"

"I will come to it," Mahler said testily. He continued. "We were given a whole week at a U-boat pasture at Oberammergau, and we—"

"U-boat pasture?"

"Rest camp. There were rest camps for U-boat crews only. We'd go there to recuperate from the *Blechkoller*—the tin-madness—as they used to call it. After months in a stinking steel coffin, crammed in like five dozen Jonahs in a giant iron fish, we needed a little holiday from hell." He picked up his narrative. "We were ordered to report to the pens in Kiel. It was in early March of 1945. We were to be given a special mission. We thought it might be another gray wolf outfitted with some new-type development, like the *Schnorchel.* We sure as hell hadn't anticipated it would be the U-1000. We—"

An alarm bell went off, clamoring in the back of Einar's mind. He was at once alert. *U-1000!* Where had he heard that before? When?

And he knew.

Thompson. The ex-Nazi accident victim. In New York. He'd kept mumbling: *You. One. Zero. Zero. Zero.* Only he hadn't. What he'd said was: *U. One. Zero. Zero. Zero*—U-1000. The number of a Nazi submarine!

"The U-1000?" he asked sharply.

"A type XX, oceangoing transport," Mahler said. He was warming to his subject. "She was built to carry rubber from the Far East. From Penang in Malaya. Tin, molybdenum, and tungsten. Materials needed for the war effort. She was 255 feet long, with a displacement of 2,962 tons. She had a lot of power. Two-shaft diesel/electric motors. But lightly armored. Only one 37mm AA gun and four 20mm's. She had a surface speed of—"

"Spare me the commercial," Einar interrupted. "Get on with it."

Mahler stopped. He glared at Einar. *"Scheissdreck, Mensch!"* he swore angrily. "If you don't let me talk, how the devil can I tell you what you want to know?"

Mahler suddenly realized that he *wanted* to talk. Tell everything he knew. Now that it could make no difference. He was proud of the U-boat service. Proud of his own achievements. He was proud of having kept his Führer's secret for all these years—so his plan could be fulfilled. He wanted to boast, to crow a little. See the terror on the faces of his enemies, once they knew the truth—and realized they were helpless. He looked around his drab little studio without really seeing it. There was an aching void inside him. He missed the old days. *Verflucht nochmal!* How he missed those times. The long days and nights in a tin boat, days and nights that ran into one another with no telling which was which. The cramped quarters, shared with the deadly eels—the torpedoes, their snouts packed with explosives; the foul air and the stench of bilge water, wet oilskins, sour rubber boots, stale sweat and engine fumes; the food that tasted like diesel oil flavored with rotting mold; and the heat, sometimes so hot that your nuts hung down to your knees; the constant moisture of condensation and the gray-green film of mildew that coated boots and belts; the black submariner underwear—the *whores' undies*—that wouldn't show the filth. And the *Kameradschaft*—the close, heart-clutching comradeship of his fellow crew members; the excitement, the adventure; seeing the English and American ships go down in flames and the hated enemies floundering in the oil-slicked water. Dammit!

How he missed it all. *Harte Zeiten, aber gute Zeiten*—hard times, but good times, they had been.

The damned American was asking him another question. What?

"—were your duties?"

"I was the *Stabsoberbootmann*—the bo'sun," he said with pride.

"And your cargo?" Einar had to ask—although he knew. He knew.

Mahler looked at him, a glint of triumph in his cement-colored eyes.

"Your 'brown sugar,' American," he gloated. "Not a couple of hundred drums. Six hundred! To be exact, 679 red-banded drums of the Führer's final vengeance weapon. His V-3!"

A chill coursed through Einar. A vision of unspeakable horror flitted through his mind.

Mahler regarded him speculatively. He sensed he was in control of the situation, despite the Walther PPK pointed at him. He decided to tell the *verfluchte* Ami everything. He would enjoy doing it.

"I will tell you all I know," he said arrogantly. "But I will tell it my way. Agreed?"

"Agreed," Einar nodded. "Go on. You were the *Stabsoberbootmann* aboard the U-1000. Your cargo was 679 drums of poison."

Mahler nodded. "On-loaded in Kiel."

It was yesterday. In his mind it was yesterday. It always would be.

"We were seven days out of Kiel," he began, "somewhere in the North Atlantic. There was only a sliver of a new moon when we were ready to surface. *Der Alte*—the Old Man—had searched the sea through the periscope, and all was clear. We went down to 250 feet to prepare for our mission. Operation Ultimatum."

It was yesterday . . .

. . . They were ready.

"To stations!" the Old Man called over the intercom, heard throughout the boat.

Fleischer, the chief engineer, stood watching the depth indicator. "Pump ballast to sea!" he ordered.

Slowly the boat began to rise.

"Fore planes hard arise!" Fleischer called. "Aft planes up four."

The depth gauge needles began to spin.

"Boat rising!" the chief called out. "200 feet . . . 150 feet . . ."

At eighty feet the Old Man, *Korvettenkapitän* Günter Wierdring, twenty-nine, called, "Hydrophone!"

There were no surface sounds. Forty feet.

"Up periscope!"

All was clear.

"Ready to surface," the chief reported.

"Surface!"

Wierdring began to mount the iron ladder that led from the control room through the lower hatch to the conning tower.

"Blow all main ballast tanks!" Fleischer ordered.

Compressed air hissed into the tanks, and the U-1000 rose.

"Surfaced!" the chief called.

"Equalize pressure!" Wierdring was at the upper hatch. "Opening upper lid—now!"

Cold, fresh air rushed into the boat, and Wierdring scrambled up to the bridge, closely followed by the watch crew.

"Blow to full buoyancy with diesel!" Wierdring commanded. "Stand by main engines. *Leutnant* Winkler to the bridge!"

Mahler paused. For a moment he allowed himself to bask in remembered excitement. He'd felt keyed up to the point of intoxication when he opened the forward cargo hatch and felt the cold, salt spray hitting his face as the U-1000 bucked into the chop of a stiff westerly.

It was beginning. He, Heinrich Mahler, was about to play a major role in forcing the enemies of the Reich to their knees and wrest from them an unconditional surrender—a victory for the Führer and the Fatherland.

"The Old Man personally took command of the execution of step one of the Führer's Operation Ultimatum," he said. "He left Winkler on the bridge while he took charge of the work at the No. 4 hatch. It was a chancy procedure. In direct violation of the first rule of the submariner—never to break 'rig for dive' while surfaced in the war zone—we had to do just that. We would be a sitting duck for as long as the operation took. It was enough to make your damned oilskins itch. But Wierdring had no choice. The sea was dark and empty, and he was maintaining radar silence, so his radar was inoperative. He had to rely on his lookouts to keep their eyes skinned and detect any enemy presence visually.

"There were six of us working at the hatch on deck. Me, *Korvettenkapitän* Wierdring, *Stabsobermaschinist* Karl Johann Tollmann, two *Matrosen*—two sailors—one named Felix Albers, the other Gerhardt, I think, and *Oberleutnant zur See* Kratzer, the exec. We—"

"Kratzer," Einar interrupted sharply. "He was there?"

"He was."

"Why the hell did he try to kill us?"

Mahler eyed them both.

"Orders."

"Orders? Whose orders?"

Mahler shrugged. "One does not question where orders come from. One carries them out."

"And Kratzer had orders to kill us?" Einar said incredulously. "Why? Dammit! Why?"

"You were nosing around, American," Mahler told him. "Becoming a nuisance. You were getting too close. We had to make certain that you got nowhere with your meddlesome investigation." His eyes grew cold. "We had to make certain that you would not in any way be able to interfere with the Führer's plans that soon will strike his enemies and annihilate them."

Einar stared at the German. Was the man mad? Hitler had been dead forty years. What the hell was the bastard talking about? This was 1985—not 1945, dammit! But an icy lump tensed in the pit of his stomach. The "brown sugar." If Mahler was telling the truth, that terrible, deadly poison was about to be used. Any day, as Thompson—or Tollmann—had said. Any day. How? By whom? Where? And when? He had none of the answers. He glared angrily at the German.

"I think you had better tell me exactly what this Operation Ultimatum is all about," he growled dangerously. "Right now!"

Mahler spread his hands in willing resignation. He was enjoying the game.

"Schon gut," he said. "All right. The U-1000 had orders to proceed to a certain destination in the North Atlantic somewhere west of Ireland," he went on. "The poison contained in the drums was in crystalline form, as you know, looking much like brown sugar. If the crystals came in contact with water, they would quickly dissolve, rise to the surface, and immediately vaporize into an odorless mist. The slightest contact with this mist would be fatal. In a most unpleasant way, we were told."

Obviously pleased with himself, he eyed the stony-faced Einar, who was listening to him, for once not interrupting.

"Coinciding with favorable weather reports, we were to release the poison at the latitude and longitude supplied to us," Mahler continued. "It would form a mist of death—and the prevailing westerly winds would move it eastward to the shores of England and Ireland. No one would know it was there until it was too late. It was no different in appearance than the sea haze the English are so used to. But a few hundred thousands would die!"

He stopped.

Aghast, Einar and Birte stared at him.

"It was then the Führer would give the enemy his ultimatum," the German went on. "The poison released would have been only the contents of *one* drum. Only one. If the *Engländer* and the Americans did not immediately and unconditionally surrender to the Führer—the poison contained in the remaining 678 drums would be released. It would form a gigantic cloud of death that would fan out as the wind drove it toward the British Isles. Ultimately it would cover five hundred thousand square miles. All of Ireland, Scotland, and England. It would blanket the area with a lethal poison against which there was no defense. All life, all, would cease. The *verfluchte Engländer*, the archenemies of the Führer, all of them would have been annihilated forever.

"It was, of course, rather a pity about Ireland. After all, the Irish did not side with the Führer's enemies. *Na ja,*" he shrugged indifferently, "their country happened to lie right in the path of the cloud, but that could not be changed. Too bad—but unavoidable, of course."

He smiled a thin, unpleasant smile. "When the gas exploded all over hell, we would, of course, be long gone. Dozens of kilometers upwind, safely out of the way. And not one inch of German soil would ever be in danger of contamination," he crowed. "The mist would dissipate itself into harmlessness before reaching the shores of the Fatherland. But for the Führer's enemies, there would be no way to jump off the devil's shovel."

Stunned, horrified, Einar and Birte stared at the man. They did not doubt him. It was a plan worthy of a desperate Adolf Hitler. He, who had slaughtered millions of innocent people in his concentration camps; he, who would have burned down the open city of Paris; he, who opened the floodgates to the Berlin subways, drowning hundreds of thousands of his own people to gain a few hours for himself. Poison gas. His V-3. Hitler must have thought it a particularly fitting weapon, Einar thought. A weapon of personal revenge as well as a weapon to annihilate his hated enemies. It made a chilling, twisted kind of sense. Einar remembered reading that in October of 1918, Hitler had been caught in a chlorine gas attack launched by the British. He had collapsed in agony, temporarily blinded, and he had been taken to a hospital in Pasewalk near Stettin in Pommern. In his bitter writings about it, he'd said, "My eyes had turned into glowing coals." Einar shuddered in his mind. Adolf Hitler's vengeance weapon, his V-3, was meant to do much, much more than that.

He stared at the German.

"But . . . it did not come to pass," Einar said. His voice sounded strained to his own ears. He could not get the terrible images out of his mind, of millions of people, men, women, and children, young and old, perishing in horror as had the father of Karla Moser. "What happened? Where are the drums now? Do you know?"

Mahler smiled his thin smile. He sat back in his chair, totally disregarding the Walther PPK still pointed at him.

"I do," he said.

Einar leaned forward. "Well?" He gestured with his gun.

"If you will listen, American," Mahler said insolently, "you will learn." He smiled at him. "My way, remember?"

His cement eyes got a faraway look in them. Once again he stood on the foredeck of the U-1000.

Yesterday . . .

. . . The No. 4 cargo hatch was open. The hatch davit had been rigged, the capstan engaged, and the rubber dinghy had already been brought up and inflated, waiting on deck for its cargo. They were working by the light of the stars and the new moon only, showing no lights.

"Bring the drum to hatch trunk!" Wierdring called down into the cargo hold. "Rig the hoisting line, and fairlead it to the capstan!"

The men on deck, all wearing their cumbersome inflatable life jackets, fed the line down through the hatch.

Below, a crew began to fasten it to the ultimatum drum. He knew the drill to come. The single drum would be brought up to the deck. It would be lashed securely into the rubber dinghy, and the timing device on the explosive charge taped to its side would be activated. The dinghy would be launched, and the U-1000 would submerge and run for a position far to the west before the charge on the drum went off and exploded the lethal crystals over the sea.

They were almost finished below.

"Hoist away!" Wierdring called.

At that precise moment, from the conning tower, came the dreaded call from one of the four lookouts.

"Destroyer! Broad on starboard bow. Range four thousand!"

Wierdring at once shouted his orders.

"Lower the drum! Clear the hoisting line! Rig for dive!"

Feverishly the men heaved to. They all knew. At a range of a mere four thousand yards, it would be only minutes before the enemy destroyer could attack with her five-inch guns; only the few minutes it would take to man the guns, energize the loading, tracking, and firing circuits, and acquire the target by radar or visually, load—and fire. Less time than it would take to rig for dive.

From the bridge Winkler's urgent orders drifted down to them. ". . . all ahead!" Trying to outrun the onrushing enemy destroyer? Little chance. Lower the drum and clear the hatch of the hoisting line. Fall down the ladder and slam the lid. Then dive. Their only hope.

The U-1000, as if sensing the danger, kicked ahead, slicing through the sea. The deep-throated rumble of her diesels shook the boat, and the black water scythed away from her bow and foamed along her saddle tanks as the men worked against time.

Done.

"Gerhardt! *Los!*" Wierdring snapped. "Go!"

The sailor leaped for the hatch.

Wierdring whirled toward the bridge.

"Stand by to dive!" he shouted.

In the same instant a shell from the destroyer hit the aft rudder section of the U-1000. The bone-rattling explosion drowned out part of Wierdring's order. A split second later a second shell crashed into the sea, wide of the boat, spouting a geyser of raging water. It jarred the boat. The open hatch slammed shut, pinning the screaming crewman halfway down.

For the thousandth time Mahler relived the terror of the incident. He never knew what happened after Gerhardt was pinned in the hatch, but it happened instantly. Perhaps Winkler on the bridge panicked when the boat was hit, perhaps he only heard part of the captain's shouted order, "Dive!" As if from miles away, he heard Wierdring shout, "*Tauchretter aufblasen!*—Inflate life jackets!" He'd done so automatically. In a dim blur he saw the lookouts disappear from the conning tower as they tumbled down the tower ladder, followed by Winkler, each man taking one and a half seconds to clear the bridge. He thought he heard the lid slam shut, and in that same instant the deck under him tilted sharply toward the bow.

The U-1000 was crash diving.

With her forward cargo hatch No. 4 open!

He dove into the frothing black water. He plunged below the surface. He had a moment of panic before his life jacket brought him sputtering to the surface.

"The U-1000 was slicing into the deep," he said, "so steeply her damaged rudder section rose out of the churning water. Out of control she plummeted down, water pouring into her holds through the open hatch . . ."

He stopped. For a moment he sat silent.

"We were swept away," he said. "We of the deck party. We survived. Except Gerhardt. We found each other in the water, and we found the dinghy. The rest of the crew, fifty-two good men, died. They did not have a chance. And Felix Albers . . ."

He paused in thought.

Einar kept quiet. The man was obviously not finished yet. And he did not want to deflect his thoughts.

"There were only four of us on the U-1000 who knew the full facts about Operation Ultimatum," Mahler continued. "Wierdring, Tollmann, Kratzer, and me. Felix was just muscle on the deck. He was a *Scheissidiot,*" he said disdainfully. "Always horny as an *Oberprimaner*—a high school senior—and so dumb he thought paper planes were made of fly paper. But he was strong, and good with his hands. So we had included him in the deck party along with Gerhardt—the poor devil. We were all four in the dinghy when Felix came swimming by and tried to climb in with us. We knew we might be spotted by the destroyer bearing down on us, and we knew we could not afford to be taken alive. We knew too much. And we were resigned to the fact. We had our pills. But we could not be sure of that idiot, Felix. And he had seen more than he should. So Karl Johann grabbed the paddle and struck him across the face as hard as he could. He split Felix's face open from the middle of his forehead, across his right eye to the heel of his jaw—and the man slipped beneath the water. We thought him dead."

"He . . . wasn't?" Einar could not contain himself.

Mahler shook his head.

"The destroyer was closing fast," he said. "She passed some distance away. She did not see us in the dark, bobbing in the chops. She dropped a few depth charges. We saw them explode. But it was a perfunctory run rather than a directed attack, and she headed back at full speed toward whatever convoy it was we'd run into. Wierdring had been badly wounded, his leg laid bare to the bone. Two days later we were picked up by a 'milch cow,' a submarine tanker and resupply boat dead-heading for Kiel. The war was over a couple of months later."

He paused. He regarded Einar and Birte.

"We stuck together, the four of us," he said. "Our common secret bound us to one another. We settled here. In Weiden. It was an inconspicuous place. But a few months later Felix showed up, with a scar that split his face in half and a hate that screamed for revenge on Karl Johann. Karl Johann ran, and Felix swore he'd find him and kill him. Preferably very slowly. I don't know what happened to the bastard. The last I heard of Karl Johann, he was killed in an automobile accident in New York."

Einar nodded. "I know."

Mahler gave him a quick look, but he did not comment. Instead he grinned maliciously.

"So, American," he said. "That is where you will find your 679 drums of 'brown sugar.' In the broken hull of the U-1000 at the bottom of the Atlantic Ocean. That's where they are."

He took a deep breath. His face glowed with smug triumph. "But not for long," he said.

Einar stared at him.

"What do you mean?"

"Captain Wierdring is a scientist. A metallurgist. He knows the composition of the metal alloy used to make the drums. He has calculated exactly how long it would take for the sea water to erode them to the point of bursting, to the point of releasing their contents. The crystals will at once dissolve and rise to the surface. And the cloud of death that will be the Führer's final vengeance weapon, his V-3, will begin its inexorable journey toward the destruction of his enemies. A wind-borne journey no man can stop, American. It may already have begun. Or it will happen soon. Any day!"

Appalled, Birte stared at the gloating German. She squeezed her folded hands lying in her lap so hard her knuckles showed white.

"Oh, dear God!" she whispered.

Einar strove to harness his whirling thoughts. Was it possible? With icy certainty he knew it was. He still remembered the headlines. Only a few years before, it had been disclosed that a deadly time bomb had been ticking for three years beneath the waters of the Mediterranean off the village of Otranto on the heel of Italy. More than nine hundred barrels of lead tetraethyl and lead tetramethyl had sunk three hundred feet to the bottom, when two freighters collided two miles offshore; a poisonous substance so lethal that someone had claimed it could kill millions of people if the barrels burst. But the barrels had been salvaged, the threat averted. It would have been a mosquito sting on an elephant's back compared to the effects of the V-3. If what the German ex-U-boat officer had told them was true, the world was faced with the greatest catastrophe ever imagined. Untold millions would perish, die an indescribably horrible death.

With the familiar surge of adrenaline through his system, he knew Mahler had told him the truth. It fit. The empty storage magazines at the Sudeten plant. The few remaining drums—also empty. The train, loaded with the other drums, headed north. Toward Kiel. And the U-1000.

Perhaps. Perhaps there was a chance. The slightest hint of a chance. If the drums could be located and brought up, secured before they burst, the disaster might be averted. He had to know exactly where the U-boat went down.

"Where in the Atlantic does the U-1000 lie?" he asked urgently. "Longitude? Latitude? Where?"

Mahler sat back in his chair. He smiled his thin, mirthless smile. "That," he said with obvious self-satisfaction, "that is the only thing I cannot tell you. I do not know."

"Who does?"

"Only Captain Wierdring."

"Where is he?"

Again Mahler smiled his smug smile.

"I was wrong," he said in mock apology. "That is the second question I cannot answer."

"Can't—or won't?" Einar snapped angrily.

Mahler shrugged. "It is the same, is it not?"

Einar glared at the German. Only with difficulty did he suppress the urge to kill him. Now. As he sat there, safely in his chair, gloating over the imminent death of millions. It was time, he thought, time he took the offensive. Once taken, he could not give the man a chance to think, until he had given him the information he wanted. So be it.

"You are a fool, Mahler," he snapped. "Appearances can sometimes be fatally misleading." His manner abruptly changed. His voice grew harsh, his eyes cold. He sat rigid in his chair—like a coiled spring. "I am a member of the United States military intelligence," he said deliberately. "Under cover. Now—*where is Wierdring?*"

Stubbornly Mahler shook his head. "There is no way you can force me to tell you," he said.

"I think there is," Einar flashed back, his Walther PPK unwaveringly aimed at Mahler's guts.

"You can shoot me," the German said defiantly. "It will not get you your information. I was willing to give my life for my Führer and his beliefs and goals forty years ago. I am today."

"I will give you ten seconds to tell me where Wierdring can be found. Or you will find yourself on the way to England. To the Irish coast. Your death will not be as easy as a bullet between the eyes."

"You can't," Mahler said, but he sounded less certain, less cocky. "You do not have the authority."

"As I said, you are a fool," Einar countered contemptuously. "Don't you realize we are not alone in this?" He nodded at a telephone on a table in the studio. "One phone call from me—and before I hang up, you'll hear the wails of police cars and military vehicles converging on this place!"

His eyes bored into Mahler.

The German sat in obstinate silence. But the smile was gone from his face.

"Birte," Einar snapped. "The telephone."

Birte reached for the phone. She fought to keep from trembling. Einar was bluffing. Would it work? The cord was just long enough to reach. She brought the phone to Einar and held it for him.

Mahler followed the action with his eyes, his face suddenly gray and drawn. Einar, watching him, knew the vision of horror that filled the man's head. He lifted the receiver.

"Wait!" The word almost exploded from Mahler.

Einar stopped. He held the receiver in his hand, off the hook. He did not put it back. The faint buzzing sound of the dial tone was the only sound in the room.

Finally Mahler seemed to collapse within himself. "Captain Wierdring is right here," he said tonelessly. "Still right here in Weiden. But it will do you no good," he rallied. "It is too late."

Einar replaced the receiver.

"Well?" he said curtly.

"Wierdring is a teacher. He teaches physics. At the Realschule. He is now Professor Günther Wierdring."

The sprawling state high school complex was located next to the new Town Hall, where they had been before. The little student receptionist looked brightly up at Einar.

"I am sorry, sir," she said, batting her blue eyes at him. "You just missed him. Professor Wierdring left early today."

"Where did he go?"

"Home, I believe. He got a telephone call. It must have been important. He left right away."

Einar cursed himself. He should have torn the damned phone in Mahler's place from the wall. It was merely a reaction of frustration. He knew it would have made no difference. Mahler would have found somewhere else to call from.

"Mein liebes Fräulein," Einar said earnestly. "I know about the phone call. It is of the utmost importance that I speak with Professor Wierdring. As soon as possible. Could you give me his home address?"

The girl smiled at him. "Sure," she said. She searched through a card file. "It is on Marderweg. That is in the east part of town, across the river. On the road to Vohenstrauss."

Even as Einar and Birte barreled along in their Volkswagen on their way to Marderweg and the home of former *Korvettenkapitän* Günther Wierdring, the captain's wartime shipmate, Heinrich Mahler, was making a second telephone call. This one overseas. To New York.

When his call was answered, he said tautly, "Four. Nine. One. Two."

And the instant answer came back.

"One. Zero. Zero. Zero."

The Wierdring house on Marderweg was a small, pleasant two-story brick house, painted battleship gray. The little garden around it was well kept, and the picket fence newly painted.

The front door stood wide open.

Cautiously Einar peered into the hallway beyond.

It was empty.

He reached for the bell button. He pressed it. A muted ring sounded inside the house. And a man's voice.

"Come in, Herr Munk. I have been expecting you."

Einar motioned Birte to stay behind him. He felt for the comforting presence of his Walther PPK in his belt, but he did not draw it.

Cautiously he walked into the hallway. Birte followed.

The first room he glanced into was empty. Another door down the hall stood open. He walked to it and looked inside.

It was a den. On the walls were pictures of U-boats, plaques, and framed documents. A brass shell casing stood in one corner, a wagon-wheel life preserver with the name of a British ship in another. Shelves held other U-boat memorabilia, and the room was dominated by a large oak desk.

Behind the desk sat *Korvettenkapitän* Günther Wierdring, ramrod straight, clad in his immaculate, midnight blue U-boat officer's dress uniform. On the right side of his jacket, even with the fifth or top pair of ten golden buttons in two rows, the *Hoheitsabzeichen*—the German eagle and the Nazi swastika in gold—gleamed imposingly. Through the right buttonhole of the fourth pair of buttons sat the red, white, and black ribbon of the Iron Cross Second Class; on the left side of his jacket, even with the third and second rows of buttons, the Iron Cross First Class and the golden U-boat *Kriegsabzeichen*—the submarine war badge—were affixed. Around his neck hung the Knight's Cross with Oakleaves and Swords.

Both his hands rested on the desk top before him, displaying the gold stripes that circled his sleeves, topped by a single star.

On the desk lay his cap with its golden emblems and gilt-edged visor, and near his left hand his naval officer's ceremonial dagger with its ivory hilt topped by a golden eagle and swastika.

His right hand rested on a jet-black Luger!

26

Instinctively Einar's hand reached for his gun.

"You will not need that, Herr Munk," Wierdring said calmly.

Einar stayed his hand. The German officer was making no threatening motions.

"Neither will you," he snapped.

"I believe I will," Wierdring said with a quiet little smile. But he removed his hand from the Luger. He indicated two chairs placed before his desk. "Frau Munk," he said politely. "Herr Munk. Please sit down."

They did.

"You know why we are here," Einar said grimly.

Wierdring nodded. "I do." He contemplated Einar. "I congratulate you," he said. "You have shown admirable perseverance and imagination. Admirable."

"This is not a mutual admiration society, Captain Wierdring," Einar said curtly. "I want to know the location where the U-1000 went down. Longitude. Latitude. And I want to know now!"

Wierdring smiled. "And—forceful as well," he said, a hint of mockery in his voice. "What makes you think I will tell you?"

"I think you will."

"Or you will have me taken to England? I do not think that is realistic."

"Then you will tell me here. And now."

"Why should I, Herr Munk? Do you not realize that for years it has been a secret I have jealously guarded?"

"So millions of innocent people would die?" Einar could not keep his bitter disgust from his voice.

"So that the oath I swore to my Führer and the Reich would not be violated."

"The war is lost, Captain. Hitler is dead. The Third Reich no longer exists."

Wierdring nodded solemnly. "When I swore allegiance to Adolf Hitler and his cause, it had no time limit."

"Captain Wierdring," Birte said softly. "Don't you realize what will happen if you withhold your knowledge from us? Millions, Captain, millions of people who are not your enemies, never were, will die in a terrible, terrible way. How can you let that happen? If it is not too late, you must let us stop it."

"Gnädige Frau," Wierdring addressed Birte courteously. "We all believe in something, or we would have little reason to exist. I believe in Adolf Hitler and what he stood for, and still stands for. I know he . . . terminated millions of undesirables: Jews and Gypsies, homosexuals and criminals, the insane and the deformed. It was for the good of mankind, to cleanse our ranks. I realize that what was done then would be a paltry triviality in comparison with the achievements of the Führer's V-3. But it was his will—and it will be carried out, as I swore it would." He spoke with chilling calm. He

turned to Einar. "We seem to have several options, Herr Munk, in bringing this matter to a close."

Einar studied the man. He sensed he was by far the most dangerous of all the adversaries he had faced. The realization kept him tensely alert. Wierdring possessed the knowledge—the *only* knowledge that might prevent an entire nation from being wiped out, and only *he* possessed it.

"Several options?" he said coldly. "Only one is acceptable. You tell me what I want to know."

"Ah, but there are others, *mein lieber* Herr Munk," Wierdring contradicted him with an icy smile. "You could kill me, for instance. You have a gun. But then—you would not have your information, nor any possible way of getting it. Or, I could kill you, of course. But if I did, others would quickly take your place. I would only have verified the importance of your quest. I reject both these options, Herr Munk, as I trust you do."

He fixed Einar with his penetrating eyes.

"It is your duty to get the needed information about the U-1000 from me," he continued. "It is mine to prevent you from getting it. The option, then, also exists that you can have me . . . interrogated. Against today's chemical means—so much more effective than the old Gestapo methods—I should have little chance of resisting such interrogation."

He paused. Soberly he looked at Einar.

"Only one option was not open to me," he said. "I could not . . . run away. Oh, I should have done so, of course, had it been at all possible. Stay hidden for just a short while. Until no power on earth could stop the inevitable." He sighed. "But it was not possible. You see, I already gave one leg to my Fatherland." He patted his left leg. "I could not hope to be successful as a hunted fugitive. So, you have the rest of me. It, too, belongs to the Fatherland."

His eyes grew curiously luminous. Once before, he had been confronted with the possibility of capture and interrogation. When he was bobbing in a rubber dinghy in the North Atlantic. At that time he'd had a pill, a little deadly pill to ensure he would not be forced to talk. That pill was long lost. But he had another.

It was made of lead.

"And this, Herr Munk," he said. "This is my final option."

Quickly he picked up the Luger and raised it to his mouth.

Einar catapulted himself from his chair.

He was too late.

The 9mm Luger bullet exploded through the roof of *Korvettenkapitän* Günther Wierdring's mouth, tore through his brain, disintegrating any knowledge in it, and shot through the crown of his head.

The force of the explosion from the muzzle of the gun in his mouth violently thrust his upper teeth out, to protrude at a grotesque angle through his bloodied lips.

He was dead before his eyes could blink in shock.

Directly behind him the glass on one of the U-boat pictures was suddenly splotched with blood and pale pink brain matter.

Horrified, Einar stood frozen, watching the vital knowledge he had sought ooze down the spattered glass. . . .

They returned at once to their hotel. They had touched nothing in Wierdring's den. They made no report. It was an obvious suicide; the Luger was still clutched in the dead man's hand. By the time they might be connected to the former U-boat commander, through the student receptionist at the Realschule, they would be long gone from Weiden.

There was nothing to keep them there.

Now.

In the lobby, the desk clerk called to Einar as he and Birte hurried through.

"Herr Munk! *Bitte!*"

Einar walked over to him.

"You have a telegram, Herr Munk." The clerk reached back to his pigeonholes and took out a white telegram envelope. "It came in just an hour ago."

Einar took the envelope. *"Danke,"* he said. "Thank you."

It was a wire from Henderson:

> YOUR TELEGRAM ACKNOWLEDGED STOP BE ADVISED YOU ARE IN NO WAY REPEAT IN NO WAY ACTING ON BEHALF U S GOVERNMENT OR MILITARY STOP ADVISE FURTHER DEVELOPMENTS STOP HENDERSON COLONEL CID

"I wish the bastard would make up his damned mind," Einar growled. "In one short telegram he tells us to butt out—and keep him informed. About what? Sightseeing?"

Angrily he crumbled the telegram and threw it at the wastepaper basket. His aim was bad. He missed. He picked up the crumbled paper and was about to toss it into the basket, when he thought better of it.

"Actually," he mused, straightening out the telegram and putting it in his pocket, "he doesn't say to stop our investigation. He's only covering his ass by disclaiming any connection with us. In case we screw up too drastically. That's par for the course. And in a way he does encourage us to keep at it. How else could we report any further developments? Sure is a devious SOB."

"But what can we do?" Birte asked. "Where can we go now? Every second that goes by brings us closer to the point where no one can do anything." She looked at her husband, her eyes haunted. "A whole nation, Einar," she whispered. "A whole nation . . . What if it has already happened?"

"We can't even think that way, Birte. We'll have to go on trying—until we are proven too late. Dammit! There's nothing else to do. You can't evacuate an entire nation. We've got to keep trying."

"But how?"

Einar looked thoughtful. "We're not going to get any more information from anyone here," he said. "We sure as hell aren't going to be told anything by the captain of the U-1000." He looked up, a sudden glint in his eyes. "But—what about U-1000 herself? Perhaps she can give us some answers."

"How?"

"Archives. The German Navy must keep records, archives. We do. There may well be information on the U-1000. Perhaps even the destination of her last voyage. It's sure worth a try."

"Do you know where they are located?"

"No idea. But it should be easy to find out. I know the German federal archives are in Koblenz. They'll be able to tell us where the naval archives are kept."

A telephone call to *Bundesarchiv* in Koblenz disclosed that the military section of the archives was located in Freiburg im Breisgau, a town of some 175,000 inhabitants on the western edge of the Black Forest where the Dreisam River flows into the Rhine Valley. The town, dating back to the twelfth century, enjoys the best of both worlds: as the hub of a thriving timber trade from the forest and as an important wine center for the product of the Rhineland vineyards.

From Weiden it was a trip of 279 miles clear across Germany, through Nürnberg and Stuttgart. The Volkswagen Jetta made it in a little over five hours, and it was just past nine in the evening when Einar and Birte checked into the Schwarzwälder Hof hotel on Herrenstrasse. They had stopped only to send another long wire to Henderson with the "further developments"; an exercise in futility, as Einar put it.

Einar had never been in Freiburg before, but he knew the town had been nearly 50 percent destroyed during the war. Like Weiden, it had undergone a miraculous resurrection.

Bone-tired after their long trip, they had a glass of Rhine wine in the picturesque *Weinstube* at the hotel before they turned in. First thing in the morning, Thursday, May 16, they would descend on the *Militärarchiv* on Wiesenthalstrasse No. 10, in search of the fateful U-1000.

Einar marched up to the reception and information desk in the lobby of the *Militärarchiv,* Birte at his side.

"Guten Morgen," he greeted one of the two receptionists. "I should like to see the head archivist, please."

"You wish to consult our archives?"

"Yes. I—"

"Please fill out this application." The woman placed a printed form in front of Einar. "You will find a pen on the desk over there." She pointed.

Einar glanced at the form:

BENUTZUNGSANTRAG
(bitte deutlich lesbar ausfüllen)
REQUEST FOR USAGE
(please write clearly and legibly)

There were twelve questions to fill out in detail, including name, address, nationality, profession, reason for research, and subject matter, as well as a solemn declaration to respect and follow all regulations and restrictions of the *Bundesarchiv;* an application worthy of the most meticulous Teutonic thoroughness.

Einar disregarded it.

"I don't think that will be necessary," he said. "We merely want to see the head archivist."

"Do you have an appointment?" the woman asked.

"No. But I am Professor Einar Munk from Columbia University in New York." Einar fished out one of his cards while he finished his sentence. "And if it is at all possible, we should like to see him." He handed the receptionist his card. She glanced at it.

"In reference to what, Professor Munk?"

"A special research project," Einar said importantly.

The receptionist looked dubious. "Well . . . I . . ."

"The chief of the *Hauptbundesarchiv*—the main federal archives—in Koblenz suggested that I see him," Einar went on. "But, of course, if you feel that it is not possible, we—"

The woman gave him a quick glance.

"I shall see if Herr *Archivar* is in." She made an interoffice telephone call. She talked briefly. She turned to Einar.

"If you will follow me," she said. "The head archivist will see you."

"Thank you," Einar said. "By the way, what is his name?"

"Pemsel," the woman answered, as she got up. "Herr *Archivar* Leopold Pemsel."

Leopold Pemsel was a short, stocky man in his sixties, who wore thick glasses and who combed a few strands of graying hair over his bald pate, holding them in place with pomade and difficulty. He rose from behind the desk as Einar and Birte were shown into his office. He made a small bow in their direction but did not offer his hand. He indicated a couple of chairs in front of his desk.

"Bitte," he said.

Einar and Birte sat down.

"What may I do for you, Professor Munk?" Pemsel asked, his eyes slightly wary.

"We need some special information for a research project we are doing at the university," Einar said. "Specifically concerning U-boat activities during World War II."

"I see," Pemsel said, his mouth set in a straight line. He looked over his glasses at Einar, not exactly with a hostile mien, but close enough. Einar could read the man's mind: another American out to chronicle the horrible, inhuman acts perpetrated by the German wolf packs against Allied shipping.

"We were told you were the man to see," Einar went on. "We were told that if anyone could help us, it would be you."

"By whom?" Pemsel asked, intrigued.

"Why, the *Bundesarchiv* in Koblenz," Einar answered him.

Pemsel was not quite able to conceal his gratification. So they did recognize the importance and the worth of someone not at the main branch, his attitude seem to say.

"Yes," he said. "Of course. I was in the navy myself."

"In the U-boat service?"

"No. I was *Obersteuermann*—helmsman—on a destroyer. There are not many U-boat veterans in Germany, Herr Professor. Of the forty thousand who served, more than twenty-eight thousand were killed. Of course, most of the survivors are still alive."

Einar nodded. "I know the men in the U-boat service were all very young. Teenagers, many of them, I understand. Except the officers, of course."

"They were very young, too, Herr Professor. A seven-year veteran, a rarity such as *Leutnant* Günther Prien, who was the one who penetrated the British naval anchorage at Scapa Flow with his U-47, back in 1939, and sank the British battleship, *Royal Oak,* he was only thirty-one at the time."

Einar shook his head in wonder. "A hardy lot," he said. "It must have been a very difficult service to have been in."

Pemsel nodded his emphatic agreement. "Now, Herr Professor," he said officiously. "What can I do for you?"

"We are seeking information about a special U-boat, Herr *Archivar.* The U-1000."

Pemsel frowned in concentration. "The U-1000," he mused. "*Ach ja!* An oceangoing transport, I believe."

"Exactly," Einar acknowledged, obviously impressed. "Can you tell me what happened to her?"

"But, of course," Pemsel said expansively. "Our records here are quite complete." He stood up. "If you will excuse me for a moment, I shall personally fetch the appropriate archive volume."

"Certainly, Herr Pemsel."

Pemsel left the office.

Birte looked at her husband, an amused twinkle in her eyes.

"Excuse me, Herr Professor Munk, sir," she said with studied innocence. "Is that what is called buttering up?"

He grinned and gave her a make-believe karate chop.

Presently Pemsel returned, carrying a large, dust-dulled record book. He put it reverently on his desk. He searched through it.

"Ah, yes. Here it is," he said, self-satisfied. "U-1000."

"May I see it?" Einar asked.

Pemsel peered at him over his glasses. "I regret, Herr Professor, but that will not be possible. Regulations, you understand. These records are old. They are to be handled by archive personnel only."

Einar nodded. "I understand."

"But I shall be happy to give you all the information you need about the U-1000."

"That will be fine."

"As you already know, she was a submarine transport. Type XX," Pemsel began, referring to the record. "She was built by Blohm and Voss in Hamburg and launched in 1943. She was primarily intended for carrying rubber and other priority materials from the Far East. There were only sixteen such transports built. The U-1000 had a displacement of 2,962 tons and a cargo deadweight of 800 tons."

Birte was taking notes. Pemsel looked up at her. "Am I going too fast, *gnädige Frau?*"

"Not at all, Herr Pemsel," Birte smiled sweetly. "It is all so fascinating."

Pemsel preened himself. He continued.

"She had eight cargo compartments for either dry or liquid cargo, and she carried a crew of fifty-eight."

"What was her last mission?" Einar asked.

Pemsel consulted the record book.

"She mined the Baltic Sea," he said. "In August of 1944."

"Wasn't there a mission after that?" Einar asked. "Out of Kiel?"

Pemsel frowned at the book. He shook his head. "No. The U-1000 was salved and paid off on September 29, 1944."

"What does that mean?"

"She was retired from service."

"What happened to her?"

Again the archivist studied the record book. He turned a few pages and searched them with increasing dismay. Finally he looked up, an expression of chagrin on his face.

"I do not know," he said. "I can find no reference to the ultimate fate of the U-1000." Defiantly he looked at Einar. "Of the more than fifteen hundred U-boats that saw service in World War II, we know exactly what happened to each and every one of them—except five."

He closed the record book.

"One of them is the U-1000."

Einar drove back to the hotel as if in a funeral procession. Glumly, silently he stared through the windshield, dust-streaked from their long trip.

Birte watched her husband with concern. She knew him well enough to know what he was doing. Fighting his discouragement. He always did. Whenever everything seemed to go completely awry, he got discouraged. It was a kind of catalyst. Somehow—fighting his discouragement—an obstinate streak in him was stimulated, and he'd plow ahead in a new direction, just to get even.

And if ever he'd looked discouragement in the face, this surely was it. All their avenues of investigation had dried up, one after the other. All their leads had turned sour. And never before had the stakes been as high.

And worse, she could see no way for them to prevail.

"Einar," she said quietly. "Are we . . . licked?"

He gave a little start, as if he'd been suddenly awakened. Perhaps, in a way, he had.

"Hell, no!" he growled. "We are not licked until we admit we are."

They parked the Jetta in the hotel lot and walked to the front desk for their key.

"Room 207," Einar said to the clerk. "The name is Munk."

"Yes, Herr Munk," the clerk said, his voice unnecessarily loud. He seemed nervous. He refused to look Einar in the eyes. He reached for the key. "Here is your key, sir." He gave the room key to Einar.

As they turned away, two men blocked their way.

"Professor Munk?" one of them asked. He was obviously American. "Professor Einar Munk?"

Startled, Einar stared at him.

"Yes?"

"We must ask you to come with us," the man said, his face a blank mask.

"Why?" Einar bristled. Dammit! This was getting to be a bad habit. "Who the hell are you?"

"CIC," the man said laconically.

Einar stared at the man. Imperceptibly he pressed his left elbow to his side. The Walther PPK was a reassuring, hard bulk.

"Let me see some identification," he snapped.

Both men took out folded ID cards and flipped them open. "I am Special Agent Davis," the spokesman said. He nodded toward his companion, who hadn't taken his eyes off Einar for a second. "That is Agent Banner."

"What do you want with me?"

"We are here to inform you, Major Munk, that your reserve status has been called. As of now, you are on active duty in the United States Army."

"You're pulling me back just like that?" Einar sounded incredulous.

"That's correct, Major." Davis brought out a document from his pocket. "By special emergency orders," he said. He handed the paper to Einar. "From Washington CID via our Bonn office."

Einar glanced at the document. It was an order placing him on immediate active duty as per order of Colonel Jonathan Henderson, CID. It was signed by a Lieutenant Colonel Baldwin of the Bonn CIC office.

"This is totally irregular," Einar snapped. "What the hell happened to regulations? Going through channels? Proper directives?"

"Sorry, Major."

Grimly Einar handed the paper back to Davis.

"You are under orders to report at once to Bonn, Major," the agent said. "We have a military helicopter standing by."

"That's impossible!" Einar exploded. "We're at a hotel. We've got to check out. We have a rental car. Our luggage—"

"It is all being taken care of, Major," the CIC agent interrupted him. "Your belongings are already on board the helicopter."

"My wife?"

"We have authorization to allow her to accompany you to Bonn."

"Why Bonn?"

For a moment Davis looked at him. "It is the nearest office that has a telephone connection with the Pentagon," he said. "With scrambling capacities." He smiled a cold little smile.

"I have a hunch you'll need it."

27

It took exactly one hour to reach Bonn, and again that long to get to the CIC office and establish a scrambler connection with the Pentagon.

And Colonel Jonathan Henderson.

As Einar sat waiting for the connection to be completed, he grew increasingly irate with every passing minute, and when Henderson finally came on the line, he lit into him.

"What the hell are you trying to pull, Henderson?" he growled angrily. "Use my reserve status to get me under your control? Put a stop to the inquiries I've been making, because they don't coincide with your own narrow view that it's all bullshit? Let me—"

"Munk! Listen!" Henderson tried to break in.

"You listen, Colonel!" Einar plowed on. "I'll—"

"Button up, Major! That's an order!" The authority in the colonel's voice was unmistakable. Einar shut up.

"Now," Henderson said. "Let us talk. You were right. I was wrong."

"What!?" Einar was taken by complete surprise. "What did you say?"

"I think you heard me, Major," Henderson said acidly. "Your reports have been studied here and evaluated. The conclusion is that there *is* a clear and present danger existent, which must be dealt with at once. I agree with that decision. You will report in Washington immediately."

"No, Colonel. I—"

"That is an order, Major Munk!"

"I can't tell you anything I haven't told you already."

"The Combined Chiefs want a complete and detailed briefing. And they want it now."

"Then give it to them. You know as much as I do."

"This is not a matter for argument, Major. If you do not obey your orders and return at once, I will be forced to have you brought back."

"Dammit!" Einar exploded. "What the hell good would I . . . would we be doing back in D.C.? You've seen what we've been able to do here.

We're the best damned bet to hunt up some answers you've got. Why negate us?"

"The government, in collaboration with the British, is taking over all further investigations, Munk. You are to return. At once. Those are your orders. I remind you that you are on active duty now."

"The hell with that!"

Einar thought fast. It was an either-or situation, with both alternatives unacceptable. He could either refuse to obey—and he'd be hauled back by force. Or he could agree, and then renege—and he wouldn't get two blocks before he'd be picked up and shipped back. There had to be a third way. There always was.

"Look," he said. "Orders can be changed. Put me on a special TDY."

"Impossible, Munk," Henderson snapped. "That would be highly unorthodox. You should know that."

"The whole damned mess is unorthodox, Colonel," Einar argued earnestly. "You just told me that I'd been right. I appreciate that. Now—in your honest, bottom-line opinion, where do you think I'd be able to do the most good? In Washington? Or here?"

There was no answer. Einar went on.

"Whatever your answer is, Colonel, the fate of an entire nation may well depend on it," he stated persuasively. "I know it would be . . . unorthodox. So is my being pulled in on special orders. So is the threat that might wipe out all of the British Isles. Place me on TDY. Let me do what I can here. I may very well fail, but at least we'd have tried. Not so, if you drag me back. Dammit! Henderson, you owe me one!"

"I have orders to bring you back to Washington immediately, Major. I have no choice." Henderson's voice was flat and cold.

"The hell you don't. You can change those damned orders."

"You are asking me to stick my neck out a mile."

"So do it. Soon hundreds of millions of people may not *have* a neck to stick out if we can't find and neutralize that blasted U-1000 and its blasted V-3 before it is too late. Let's do our damnedest to stop it, Colonel. Together. You, in your way. We in ours."

Again there was a pause.

"I am here," Einar continued. "On the scene. We're here. We know the situation better than anyone. You cannot afford to take the time to have someone else learn what we already know."

He waited for Henderson's reaction. The colonel was silent.

"Look," Einar went on. "I've got some ideas, some leads I want to follow up." It was only a small lie; he'd have used a big one if he could've thought of it. "You can't afford not to let me go on. Who would take the responsibility for failure—if you do pull me out, and I sit on my ass in Washington—when the poison bursts out of the ocean?"

Silence.

"There is a chance, Colonel, even if it is the tiniest of chances, that I may stumble on something. Can you afford not to take that chance?"

Henderson made no reply. Einar kept quiet. He had said his piece.

"Major Munk." Henderson's voice was clipped and ragged. "As of now and until further notice, you are placed on special TDY, responsible to me personally. I will have orders cut at once and telexed to CIC, Bonn."

"Thank you, sir." Einar took a deep breath. It felt as if it were the first in several minutes.

"I want to be kept fully informed, Major," Henderson went on. "On anything and everything you do and learn. Is that understood?"

"Yes, sir."

"And Munk. If you neglect to include your . . . ah, whereabouts in your reports, it would, of course, be difficult for any countermanding of my orders to reach you. I . . . I hope you will bear that in mind."

"Yes, *sir!*"

"That is all, Major. Do your damnedest! Now, get Special Agent Davis and put him on the line. I'll give my orders verbally to him."

"Yes, sir. And . . . thank you."

"One more thing. Your investigations, in fact all your activities, must be kept top secret. Not even a hint of what is happening must leak to the public. The ensuing panic would be as catastrophic as the results of V-3 itself."

For a moment Einar sat before the scrambler phone. He felt utterly drained. But—he'd won.

And suddenly the full weight of what he'd asked for and had taken on came crashing down on him. . . .

Birte was waiting outside. In that special way that speaks volumes of love and support, she touched his arm as Einar sent Agent Davis into the scrambler room.

Gravely she looked up at him. There was no need for questions; his face told her his conversation had been critical and depleting. But from the set of his jaw, she also knew he had prevailed. In what?

Tersely he told her.

"At least they're taking you seriously now," Birte said. "Maybe now they'll do something."

Einar nodded. "Yeah, but what?" he said soberly. "The machinery of government always creaks slowly into high gear. There'll be opposition to overcome, verifications, further interrogations to conduct, document searches, analyses and discussions ad infinitum, determination of responsibilities, and with two governments involved that ought to be a lulu. There'll be reports, appropriations, and miles of bureaucratic red tape. Do we have that much time? Can we wait?"

"What are you planning to do?" Birte asked. "You said you told Henderson you had some leads you wanted to follow. Do you?"

"Hell, no. Just loading the dice a little. We've exhausted the Sudeten factory crew and the U-1000 survivors. And the German archives. Who else would have any information about where the sub went down?"

"Our government. They have records. The navy. How about the destroyer that fired on the U-1000? Their log might show the location."

"Possibly. But we'd have to know the exact date in March of 1945 when it happened. And we don't. And there must be hundreds of cases where destroyers escorting a convoy in the North Atlantic dropped depth charges on suspected U-boats during that time. It would take months to wade through such reports, if—in fact—they exist at all. And longer to check out each location. Totally impossible, for our purposes." Bleakly he looked at her. "What we need is a whole new approach."

"I don't know what that could be," Birte said discouragedly. "Short of using a crystal ball."

"Believe me," Einar laughed bitterly. "If I had a reliable one, I'd use it. Of course, we could always get us a couple of psychics, like some police departments have done when they've been stumped on a case. I can see them now, sitting around their crystal ball, fishing the depths of the occult for answers to—"

Abruptly he stopped. His eyes lit up. Excitedly he turned to Birte.

"I've got it!" he exclaimed. "Fishing! The Kyll River!"

Puzzled, Birte stared at him.

"What?"

"The Kyll River. You remember? I told you about it?" Einar gestured animatedly. "During the war? In Luxembourg?"

Birte frowned at him.

"Back in February of 1945," he reminded her, "Corps was about to launch an attack across a river called Kyll. It was the initial thrust into Germany. An armored assault. But all the bridges across the river were down, so the tanks would have to ford the river, which was badly swollen. Easier said than done, because no one knew how deep the river was, nor anything about the riverbed. Would it support heavy armor? Or would the tanks bog down and become sitting ducks? PI—photo intelligence—couldn't come up with those kinds of answers, and neither could reconnaissance patrols. So we had an idea. We rounded up as many members of a local hunting and fishing club as we could find. They'd fished in the Kyll. Trudged the banks and waded in the middle of the stream. They knew every damned foot of it for the whole thirty-mile stretch of the corps front. They knew the width and depth, the banks, the current, and the bottom condition of every inch of the river, swollen or not. And they knew every ford that would support armor. We came up with dozens of spots where the corps tanks could cross. And they did. You see? We can do the same here."

"How?"

"Fishermen," Einar said. "Irish commercial fishermen. They fish in the Atlantic." He formulated his attack on the problem as he went on. "From what Wierdring said, we can pretty much figure the approximate area where the U-1000 must lie. He said the prevailing winds would blow the poison gas cloud across Ireland, England, and Scotland as it fanned out. The prevailing winds are westerly there. More correctly, southwesterly. So, the U-1000 will have to lie somewhere in the Atlantic southwest of Ireland. Probably one or two hundred miles out. No more. Most likely still on the continental shelf." He looked at his wife, his eyes bright with renewed excitement. "Once we know the probable speed of the wind and figure the extent of fanning out necessary to cover the whole area Wierdring talked about, we can narrow it down to an area of about a hundred miles square."

"That's . . . ten thousand square miles," Birte interposed.

"Damned sight better than the whole Atlantic," Einar countered. "And it would be an area where the Irish fishing fleets operate. If we can find the ones that have fished there recently, they may be able to come up with something for us."

"About the U-1000?"

"Not about the U-boat," Einar explained, "but those poison drums have been down there a long time. We know that. Wierdring said they're just about ready to crack open. One or two of them may well be more eroded than the others, or lying in a more exposed spot in the wreck; perhaps sprung a leak or something. A tiny one. Perhaps some of the poison has seeped out. Just a minute amount. It might have affected the fish. The fishermen may have noticed something in their catch. Deformed fish? Dead ones? Anything. If we can pinpoint *where*—we'd be a damned sight closer to fixing the exact spot where the U-1000 lies. It's worth a try. Besides—we have no other lead."

"There are a lot of fishermen in Ireland," Birte said. "It's not like a Luxembourg sportsmen's club. How do we go about it?"

"We can disregard most of them," Einar reasoned. "Concentrate on the fleets that set out from the southern part of Ireland. There's got to be some sort of government fishing bureau or department that can help us locate the fleets that have fished in the area. That we can find out. There's bound to be an Irish embassy or consulate in Bonn. They should be able to give us the information. But we've got to move fast."

They used a telephone at the CIC office. The Irish Fishery and Forestry Department was located on Upper Merrion Street in Dublin.

The next flight from Bonn to Dublin was later that afternoon. Einar was placing their reservations when Agent Davis came up to him. Curtly he motioned for Einar to hang up. Scowling, Einar did.

"What the hell now?" he growled. "Didn't Colonel Henderson tell you we are free to go as we please?"

"Sure," Davis said sourly. "But you're not going anywhere. You are both wanted by the police in Freiburg."

Cold-eyed, he looked at Einar and Birte.

"We have orders to bring you back."

28

"Back to Freiburg!" Einar exploded. "What the hell for?"

"The police want to question you," Davis informed him coldly. "It seems they have a body on their hands."

"A body!" Einar exclaimed.

"Found in the car you'd rented. A Volkswagen Jetta, I believe."

"I think you'd better tell us all you know, Davis," Einar said, glaring at the CIC agent.

Davis shrugged. "Why not?" he agreed. "We notified the car rental company you had rented the car from and requested they send someone to pick it up in the lot at the *Militärarchiv* where you'd parked it."

"So?"

"They did. But the man they sent didn't get very far with it. A few blocks away, he plowed into a shop window, scattering broken ceramics all over the place and badly injuring a customer. When they finally pulled the driver from the car, he was dead. Not just—dead. The report is that he was terribly disfigured, shriveled—as if he'd been drained dry—and he was covered with vomit and excrement. There were glass splinters on the floor of the car, apparently from a small vial that had been fastened to the gas pedal and broken when the man stepped on it. They figured it was some sort of poison." He looked narrowly at Einar. "They want to ask you what you know about it."

Birte moved closer to Einar. She put her hand on his arm. He covered it with his. She looked up at him, her eyes bleak.

"Dear God," she whispered. "Mahler?"

Gravely he nodded. "Or—there may be others." He turned to the CIC man.

"It was meant for us," he said quietly. "I . . . I am deeply sorry."

"Sorry isn't enough, Major," Davis rasped. "You'd better have some damned good explanations."

Einar clenched his jaw. "I have," he said. "But this is not the time to give them. We can't possibly return to Freiburg now. We—"

"You not only can, Major, you will!" Davis interrupted doggedly. "I'll personally escort you there."

"We must get to Dublin," Einar said urgently. "As quickly as possible. It is of the utmost importance."

Davis regarded them narrow-eyed. "Don't get any ideas of running out on me," he said ominously. "You wouldn't get far. You'd be picked up at the airport. Or anywhere else you attempted to leave the country. I think you are well aware of that."

For a moment Einar contemplated the determined man. Then he slowly nodded. "I am," he said soberly. "I think I owe it to you to give you the whole story. Then you can decide for yourself if you will haul us back to Freiburg—or help us get to Dublin as fast as possible."

"Shoot."

"I should warn you first," Einar said, "that what you are about to hear is classified top secret. If you discuss it with anyone else, it will be considered a serious security violation drawing the severest consequences."

"I have security clearance, Major," Davis said dryly.

For the next ten minutes, Einar talked. He told the CIC agent about the New York accident; about the Sudeten chemical warfare plant and the "brown sugar"; about the death of Anton Moser; the attempt on his and Birte's lives in the china factory; Wierdring's revelations and suicide; about the fateful U-1000; and the imminent threat of a horrible death to millions of people in the British Isles.

"So you see," he stated, "it is imperative that we get to Dublin at once. You will have to clear it with the Freiburg police."

White-faced, Davis stared at him.

"I suggest," Einar said, "right now, that you check what I have told you with Colonel Jonathan Henderson, CID, the Pentagon. We will wait. You have my word."

Davis turned on his heel and walked into the scrambler room. A few minutes later he came out. He looked shaken.

"When is your plane to Dublin?" he asked, his voice tight. "I'll get you to the airport."

★ ★ ★

It was just past 8:00 P.M. when the taxi took Einar and Birte from the Dublin airport north of the city to the building on Upper Merrion Street, which housed the Fishery and Forestry Department. Agent Davis had pulled a few strings for them and cashed in a few IOUs, and there were still some lights burning in the building.

As Einar and Birte got out of the cab, a young woman came from the building to meet them.

"Professor Munk," she called. "Mrs. Munk. A pleasure it is to welcome ye to Ireland." She offered them her hand. "I am Maureen Hannan, assistant to the director. Ye'r government man, Mr. Davis, made ye'r visit sound so deliciously mysterious, Saint Brendan himself couldn't have kept me from meeting ye!"

As they walked to the building, Birte glanced at the young woman. Sven would have loved her, she thought. Loved her melodious brogue. Just his type. Rich auburn hair, laugh-accustomed eyes, skin as fresh and clear as a Sunday morning, a pert button nose, and a high flush on high cheekbones. She felt the familiar little pang. When would she stop thinking of her son whenever she saw a Sven-type girl?

In her little, pleasant office Maureen offered them chairs.

"Now, then," she said brightly. "Ye'r Mr. Davis said ye would be needing some special information about our deep-sea fishing fleets, for a vital study, he said. And he said ye'd be working toward a deadline."

If she only knew how appropriate her choice of word was, Einar thought. He nodded solemnly.

"That's right, Miss Hannan," he said. "We are interested in fishing activities in the Atlantic off the Irish coast."

"To be sure," Maureen said, pointing to a large map on the wall, "from County Donegal to County Cork, our fleets fish the banks out there. What would ye like to know, Professor Munk?"

"How extensive are your records?" Einar countered with a question. "About the catch brought in?"

"As extensive as the fishermen wish to report it," Maureen answered with a smile. "They are not the most garrulous lot. My own father was the captain of a fishing boat. Out of Ballinskelligs. In County Kerry." She pointed to a picture on her desk of a man, clad in yellow oilskins, his dour, weatherbeaten face peering out from under a large sou'wester. "That's himself." She looked at Einar. "What are ye seeking, then? The catch of cod? Haddock? Flatfish? Or is it herring or Atlantic mackerel? Are ye after knowing about any particular method of fishing? Trawling? Seining? Line or net fishing?"

"Do your records show the . . . the condition of the fish?"

Maureen frowned. "You mean . . . size?"

"That, and other aspects."

Maureen looked prettily puzzled. "Perhaps, if ye would like to tell me what ye are after," she said, "I might be better able to help ye."

Gravely Einar looked at the young woman. "Miss Hannan," he said, "I wish I could. But please understand, I am not at liberty to go into any details. The . . . the study is of a confidential nature. I do hope you'll understand. And we are most grateful for your cooperation."

Maureen nodded. She had grown thoughtful at Einar's and Birte's solemnity. "I do understand, Professor Munk," she said soberly. "How would ye like me to be of help?"

"Perhaps," Einar said. "Perhaps if we could examine your records of the area in question. For the last six months or so?"

Maureen stood up. "It's as good as done," she announced. "If ye'll follow me."

It was in the early morning hours of Friday, May 17, when a bone-weary Einar finally gave up.

The reports, charts, transcripts, and analyses that Maureen had shown to him and Birte were thorough and complete—but nowhere were there any indications that even hinted at anything out of the ordinary as far as the condition of the various fish caught was concerned, from either ground or pelagic fishing, extending a couple of hundred miles into the Atlantic.

While they had been poring over the fishery records, Maureen had booked them into a hotel, the Buswell's on Molesworth Street, just across from Leinster House, the seat of the Irish Parliament, and here, at close to three o'clock in the morning, Einar and Birte collapsed into an oversized bed.

Einar had been quiet, almost withdrawn. And it wasn't merely fatigue. Birte knew the mood. He was worried. Deeply, disturbingly worried. And with good reason.

They were getting nowhere.

A catastrophe was ever closer to happening—and they were getting nowhere in their efforts to stop it.

It had seemed such a good idea to probe the fishery records, but they had learned absolutely nothing. Zero. Eight days had gone by since ex-U-boat crew member Karl Johann Thompson had been run down and killed in New York, and neither she nor Einar had any idea what to do next. They had hit rock bottom—and just kept on sinking.

Aching inside, she watched the worry lines, etched around her husband's mouth, grow deeper.

And she was powerless to smooth them away. . . .

★ ★ ★

"It is easy to see why Ireland is called the Emerald Isle," she said. "It's grand. Just grand."

She was standing on a hilltop overlooking an expanse of meadows and fields shining in different shades of green, patterned like a huge quilt with stone-fence seams and hedgerow borders. In the blue sky above, soft, pale drifts of clouds fled playfully before the sun, their shadows rollercoasting across the hilly land below, and beyond shone the lighter blue of the ocean.

She glanced at her companion. He stood motionless, silent, clad in yellow oilskins, his face hidden in the shadows of his sou'wester. She wondered why she couldn't see his face.

She pointed into the distance.

"What are those big, brown things in the field over there?" she asked.

"Well now," her companion said, his deep voice and thick brogue sepulchral. "If they move, they're cows. If they do not, they're country council workers out collecting a bit of overtime." Solemnly he handed her a big, brass captain's telescope. "See for yourself."

She took it. She put it to her eye. She looked.

The things were not cows. They were not country council workers.

They were fish.

Huge, scaly, round-eyed fish, mouths agape.

Dead.

Startled, she whirled on her companion.

"What are *they* doing there?" she asked.

Slowly her companion turned to her. She gazed up into his face—and screamed.

The hideous sight of his features seared her retinas. His eyes were shriveled, puckered like pale-blue raisins set in shrunken sockets; the skin on his cheeks was brittle and cracked; his lips, parted in an obscene grin, were split open in charcoal gray, exposing a blackened, dried-up tongue.

Slowly, inexorably, his blind eyes imprisoning her, he bent down toward her.

She could not move. She could not breathe.

She felt a relentless, vitiating heat creep over her face, draining it. Her gulps of air were burning hot in her throat.

Desperately she fought against the horror, framed in yellow oilcloth, that threated to engulf her. . . .

"Birte! Birte! Wake up!"

It was Einar's voice—coming from far, far away.

She struggled up from the depth of her terror.

"It's all right, Bo," Einar said, using her little nickname of affection. "It's all right. You had a nightmare."

"I . . . I couldn't breathe," she sobbed.

"No wonder," he comforted her. "You'd pulled that heavy quilt up over your face."

She snuggled up to him, seeking safety. Gradually she calmed down.

Stupid dream.

But—was it?

Einar always said that a dream—an important dream that you remembered—was your subconscious mind trying to tell you something. Visualization on two levels, he had said. One, the surface level, the obvious images taken from recent experiences; the other, the deeper meaning, was the real point of the dream.

What?

Ireland, the fish, that was easy. Surface level. Even the sea captain. And the dumb cows and ineffectual workers. It meant they were getting nowhere. And the terrible face under the sou'wester. That was the ravages of the poison from the deep that might enshroud them at any moment. All surely enough to cause a nightmare.

But—what was the point? The deeper meaning?

And suddenly she knew. With absolute certainty—she knew. She turned to her husband.

"Einar," she said tentatively. "Remember that mustard gas incident in the Baltic Sea? Last year?"

"Remind me."

"Early in 1984. A whole lot of Scandinavian fishermen were severely burned when their nets got caught in a pile of mustard gas containers that had been dumped in the sea by the Germans toward the end of World War II. The metal containers were so badly deteriorated that the poison gas escaped. Several of the men were blinded. They were from a Faeroe Island trawler, I think. It was in all the papers."

"I remember," Einar said. "There were quite a few fishing vessels involved."

"Well, I was thinking, perhaps if a little bit of the . . . the 'brown sugar' had escaped, as you said, might not some fishermen have been poisoned rather than the fish? If the poison rose to the surface and evaporated? Isn't that possible?"

Einar stared at her. "You're right!" he exclaimed. "Dammit! You're right! We have been asking the wrong questions."

"Let's start to ask the right ones."

Einar sat up in bed, wide awake.

"You're damned right!" He looked at his watch lying on the nightstand next to the bed. "Six-twenty," he said. "We've been lolling around here long enough." He swung his feet over the edge of the bed.

"County Cork," he said, determination returning to his voice. "And Kerry. The counties on the southern tip of Ireland. That's our best bet; they're closest to the area in the Atlantic we're concerned with. We'll start there. Ask around. Doctors. Hospitals. Clinics. The fishermen themselves."

He stood up and headed for the bathroom.

"We can fly down to Cork. There's an airport just south of there. Pick up a car and start hounding the fishing villages along the coast."

At the door he stopped and turned toward Birte. "It's our last chance, Bo," he said soberly. "God willing, there'll be time."

"And—if there isn't?"

Einar said nothing.

They both knew the answer.

An answer that might come any minute.

29

The artist's large, tinted rendering dramatically depicting a blazing *Lusitania* going down, bow first, was badly faded. The green hills of Ireland in the background had withered to a dirty gray, and the flames licking up into the air from the sinking ship were pale and lackluster. Flanked by framed and yellowed newspaper clippings recounting the fateful sinking of the huge, four-stacked ocean liner, torpedoed by the German U-boat, U-20, in World War I, and a ghostly, washed-out copy of the Cunard Line poster bearing the ominous warning that the liner would be sailing into a war zone on its voyage from New York to Liverpool, it hung on the wall of the village pub in Courtmacsherry. The tragedy had taken place only ten miles out to sea from the little fishing village seventy years before, but it was still not forgotten; rescue boats from the Courtmacsherry coast guard station had brought in survivors.

But as they sat sipping their "pints of plain"—the strong, dark brown Guinness stout—the minds of Einar and Birte were on another wreck.

The U-1000.

Balefully Einar contemplated the embroidered pub-goer's creed displayed above the bar:

> When things go wrong and will not come right,
> Though you do the best you can,
> When life looks black as the hour of night,

A pint of plain is your only man.
Flann O'Brien

Perhaps. But so far he had found no solace.

It was Saturday night, and the pub was crowded to bursting with patrons banishing their cares with "a good few jars."

All through Friday and Saturday, he and Birte had motored from town to town, from village to village, asking questions of doctors and nurses, at hospitals and clinics, from fishermen and clergymen—in Crosshaven and Robert's Cove, Oysterhaven and Kinsale, Garrettstown and Butlerstown. And in Courtmacsherry.

Everyone had been friendly and courteous.

And tight-lipped when any personal questions were asked.

He and Birte had checked into the delightfully picturesque Courtmacsherry Inn, lucky enough to get one of the five rooms with bath.

Einar looked around the jam-packed place. The pub had a cluttered, homey air. Cut-glass mirrors and wood-paneling; a long shelf overhead holding pewter plates and mugs and running the length of the wall; a wooden bar with brass trimmings and porcelain-handled taps; a busy dart board; and a couple of merry fiddlers, wearing the ever-present visored caps, sawing away in a corner.

Someone, he thought, someone—perhaps in this room—someone has the answer they so desperately needed. How the hell to find him?

He noticed one of the beefy bartenders, shirt sleeves rolled up, threading his way through the good-natured crowd. The man came up to him.

"You are the American, Mr. Munk?" he asked, knowing the answer.

"I am."

The man lowered his voice conspiratorially. "A word with ye, then," he said. He took Einar aside, out of earshot of Birte. Puzzled, Einar frowned at him.

"There's someone ringing ye," the bartender said, his voice low. "On the telephone. She does not say who she is. Are ye here?"

"I am," Einar nodded. "Thank you." He looked around. "Where's the phone?"

"I'll take you to it," the bartender said. With a glance toward Birte, he started to make his way through the crowd. Einar followed in his wake.

The phone was on the wall at one end of the bar. Einar picked up the receiver and put a finger in his other ear to keep out some of the din around him.

"Hello!" he said.

A woman's voice answered. "Mr. Munk, is it?"

"Yes." Scared, he thought. That woman sounds damned scared. Fleetingly he wondered why.

"It is you, then, who is wanting to know about the . . . the sickness?" The last word was a whisper. A frightened whisper, Einar picked up.

"Yes," he said quickly. "You know something about it?"

"Aye," the woman said. "But I cannot tell you over the telephone. You must meet with me, if you've a mind to."

"Of course. When?" Einar felt elated. It was their first break.

"In a half an hour, if you like."

"Where?"

There was a pause; then: "I . . . I don't want anyone from the village to see me talking with you. They would know what I was telling you. Meet me at the old icehouse." She spoke hurriedly as if she wanted to get the conversation over with as quickly as possible. "It is a little mile out of town off the road to Butlerstown. You cannot miss it. It stands on the bluff. It is plain to see, but no one goes there anymore. It will be safe. I'll put a lantern inside so it will be easy for you to see in the dark."

"And you'll be there?"

"Aye."

"Who . . . who are you?"

"My name is Brigid. But that is no matter. Half an hour, then." There was a click.

"Brigid!" Einar called. "Are you still there?"

There was no answer.

He hung up. He began to make his way back to Birte, threading his way through the throng of people enjoying their pints and each other's company, their voices raised in spirited debate or animated storytelling.

They didn't know, he thought. They didn't know . . .

He could see Birte waiting for him. She looked curious as she saw him coming toward her.

At last, he thought. Perhaps they'd finally get some information. The woman *had* referred to—the sickness. The effects of the "brown sugar"? It sure as hell wouldn't be the common cold. At last. But his excitement was darkened by the shadow of a nagging feeling—a hunch, reawakened from days long past—a feeling that the woman who called herself Brigid was hiding something. What? He tried to rationalize the feeling away; it was merely a natural nervousness over breaking what seemed to be a local taboo that colored her voice. That was it. He dismissed his hunch. He had no choice. He would have to meet with the woman, Brigid.

On her terms.

Sheltered by a stand of beech trees, the old icehouse stood on a sea-battered cliff at the mouth of the rocky Courtmacsherry Bay opposite Old Head of Kinsale, a relic of the days before refrigeration when blocks of ice weighing a hundred pounds or more were cut from inland frozen lakes and ponds in midwinter and stored for use in keeping the fish catch fresh during the summer months.

A rectangle of dim light relieved the night-black bulk of the squat building: the open door. And the lantern inside, promised by Brigid.

As Einar and Birte walked down the little-used path to the abandoned icehouse, Einar felt himself grow tense. It was a feeling he remembered well. He peered ahead into the darkness. Nothing moved. There was no sound except the distant bluster of the waves crashing against the rocks below. But he felt a presence of—danger. Automatically he felt for his Walther PPK, reassured by its solid feel at his waist, and he sent a silent thought of thanks to Agent Davis for having arranged for him to retain the gun.

The icehouse had been built perhaps a century before, with local shale and sandstone rocks. Massive walls arched together to form the roof, creating a building in the shape of a can cut in half lengthwise. There were double doors at one end, leading to the spacious interior, the outer door rusty iron, the inner one seasoned wood. Both had solid iron bolts. Both stood open.

"Spooky place to pick for a rendezvous," Birte said with a little shudder. "Look at those walls. Two feet thick if they're an inch."

Einar nodded. Cautiously he peered inside. The walls of the rock structure were lined with wooden boards, and the floor was covered with heavy planks. He noted the thick layer of sawdust. From packing the stored ice blocks, he thought, to keep the melting loss at a minimum. The place was empty.

"Brigid?" he called softly, although it was obvious that the woman was not there. "Brigid?"

There was no answer.

He looked toward the lantern standing on the floor in a far corner. Its wick had been turned way down; the light was dim. A piece of folded white paper lay next to it.

A note?

Together they walked over to the lantern. Cautiously Einar bent down and looked at the paper and the area around it. It seemed clean. He picked up the paper and unfolded it. He frowned at it. He showed it to Birte.

It was blank!

Suddenly, with a piercing surge of alarm, he knew. Cheese! They were in a trap. A giant stone trap. The paper was the bait. Whoever had laid the trap for them knew they had to enter the place to take a look at it. Even as he whirled toward the entrance, a crash shattered the silence as the solid wooden door was slammed shut violently. He ran toward it and heard the sound of the heavy bolt being rammed home.

"Hey!" he shouted. "Hold it!"

He threw his weight against the massive door—and heard the outer iron door clang shut, the bolt ram home.

They were trapped.

Instinctively his eyes searched around the room for another way out. There was none. No other doorway. No window. Not even a ventilation slit. They were imprisoned by solid, two-feet-thick rock walls, and barred by massive, bolted double doors.

Birte, looking pale even in the warm, live light from the kerosene lantern, came up to him. He put his arms around her.

"I should have known," he said bitterly. "Dammit! I should have known."

"Or—I should."

"There was no way for you to know, Bo," Einar objected.

"You are right," Birte agreed quietly. "Just as there was no way for you."

"You're wrong," Einar said. "I had that damned feeling. I knew something was out of kilter. I let my eagerness kill caution. But, dammit!" he flared. "I didn't have to walk blithely into a blasted trap!"

"What else could you have done? You had to find out."

"I could have stayed at the damned door," he said. "Kept my eyes open, that's what I could have done. And let you go get that damned paper."

"Perfect hindsight, love," Birte said. "But would you really? Would you have sent me in here not knowing what? With your hunch telling you something might be . . . wrong?"

"Oh, hell, Bo," Einar said miserably. "I don't know what I'd have done." Again he looked around. "All I know is, we're trapped. And we've got to find a way to get out."

"Who?" Birte asked. "Who would want to trap us here?" Dismayed, she looked up at her husband. "Mahler?"

Einar shook his head. "Not him personally. He wouldn't set foot here for anything. Remember how frightened he was when we threatened to have him brought to England?"

Birte nodded.

"Not Mahler," Einar went on. "Someone he ordered to do it. Someone who doesn't know what is about to happen. Someone who sympathizes with his twisted ideas. Neo-Nazis, perhaps. There are groups of them all over Europe." He looked soberly at Birte. "Or perhaps Mahler and his gang had other accomplices he didn't tell us about. Who the hell knows?"

He walked over to the lantern. He picked it up and sloshed the kerosene in the base.

"Not much fuel left," he said. "We'd better get cracking if we want to get out of here. It's up to us. Apparently no one ever comes to this place. We could shoot off a cannon in here, and no one outside would hear it. We can't expect any help. We're on our own."

He held up the lantern.

"Let's take a good look around," he suggested. "See what we're up against. If we can't get out through the door, we'll have to find another way."

He walked over to the door. He pushed against it. He rattled it. Kicked it. It did not budge. Together they slowly walked around the room, thoroughly examining every inch of the walls. There was no break in the heavy, solid planks that tightly lined the two-feet-thick rock walls. There was no other way out. It was either the impassable door or the solid walls.

An either-or situation, Einar thought, with neither alternative acceptable. But there was always a third way out, if you looked for it. It was his credo. He lived by it.

Or—he might die by it.

For this time, he thought bleakly, there might not be a third way out.

30

Einar put the lantern on the floor.

"Let's see what we have to work with," he said. "Empty your purse, and your pockets, if you have any."

He began emptying his own pockets, putting the contents in a pile on the floor. Birte added whatever she had.

He sifted through the items. Keys, his with a key ring from Niagara Falls he'd saved. Handkerchiefs. Both their wallets with credit cards, IDs, and currency. A few coins. A matchbook cover from Freiburg, optimistically saved for the US book. A roll of Life Savers, half gone; two ballpoint pens and a little notebook, and Birte's toiletries, including a lipstick and a comb.

And Einar's Walther PPK.

Grimly he looked it over. "Not much," he said. "Nothing of any use."

"Could you . . . shoot off the bolt?" Birte asked.

He shook his head. "Works only in the movies," he said. "That bolt—I took a look at it when we came in, and it's a sturdy bastard--it's on the other side of a thick wooden door. I wouldn't scratch the damned thing even if I emptied the clip at it. And there's a second bolt on the outside of the iron door. No way."

He picked up the key ring. It was a souvenir from their honeymoon, a flat metal handle with a picture of the falls. Most of the paint had been rubbed off through the years of use. It had a little bottle opener folded into it on one side, a penknife with a one-inch blade on the other.

"As I said," Einar observed. "Nothing of any use."

He took a deep breath.

"All right," he said. He sat down on the floor. "Let's brainstorm this thing. We are in an old icehouse. What do we know about it?"

"The obvious, of course," Birte said, sitting down beside him. "They stored ice in it. So the walls were made extra thick to act as insulation. And they built double doors to create an air shield at the entrance."

Einar nodded. "And no windows or openings of any kind. I read somewhere, in that funny little magazine you once subscribed to, *Old Stuff* was it?"

"That's right."

"I read that they stored the ice blocks in rows with wide cracks between them, stuffed with straw or sawdust, and they left a twelve-inch gap around the walls, packed tight with straw."

"I remember the article. It had a picture of an icehouse in Maryland. Looked like this, except it had a peaked roof. It said the ice lasted for months and months. All through the summer. And the melting loss was only between ten and twenty-five percent."

"Up to fifty at times," Einar said. "They used to score the blocks to—"

He sat bolt upright.

"Drainage!" he exclaimed. He leaped to his feet. "Somewhere under the planks there's got to be a drain. A large drain. Or the damned place would have been flooded with ice water."

He looked around the place. "Logically it should be right in the center," he said. "For best runoff. Give me a hand."

With his hands he began to sweep the old sawdust away. Birte joined in. Presently the center of the wooden floor was swept clean. The exposed planks were heavy but partly rotted. There were gaps between them, but they were firmly lodged.

"If I can get a good grip on one of them," Einar said, "I can pry it up."

"Can you cut a handhold?" Birte suggested. "With your penknife?"

The tiny blade bit into the wood. Birte watched. She had a fleeting thought. When she bought Einar that kitschy little souvenir, she'd never dreamed that some day it would be used in an attempt to save their lives. She prayed it would.

Soon Einar had cut out a crudely semicircular hole at the end of one of the timbers. He took a firm grip on the board and strained to pry it from the floor. Creaking in protest, it suddenly snapped loose. He wrenched it away.

The others were easier, and quickly a large area of the ground floor was exposed. Dirt and solid rock, and in the center a massive, square iron grate, crusted and rough with rust.

Einar brushed it clean. Below it gaped a black hole. He tried to lift the grate. He strained. He stomped on it to loosen it. He could not dislodge it.

He scraped more of the crusted dirt from the grate—and he saw why he could not lift it up. A heavy, two-inch-wide iron bolt locked it firmly in place.

He tried to free the bolt. He pulled at it. He kicked it. He scraped at it with his tiny souvenir penknife. The bolt moved not a fraction of an inch. It was rusted solidly in place.

Einar stared at it. There had to be a way to get the damned thing loose.

There was.

"Your lipstick," he said to Birte. "Pry the smear stuff out of it and give me the empty tube."

Birte asked no questions. At once she began to work on her lipstick.

Einar took his Walther PPK. He emptied it of rounds. With his bottle opener and penknife, he pried the bullet from the casings.

Birte handed him her empty lipstick. As he poured the powder from the cartridges into the tube, he said, "Take one of the handkerchiefs. Use something—your comb—to scrape a couple of handfuls of dirt from the ground. Put it in the handkerchief and wet it. Make a thick mud. Like clay."

"Wet it? With what?" Birte asked.

"Use your imagination."

"Oh."

Einar took his own handkerchief. Using his little penknife, he tore it in thin strips and tied them all together, end to end, except one.

Birte handed him her handkerchief with a large clump of heavy mud.

"Will this do?"

"Great!" He took it.

He tore a piece from the blank paper left for them and stuffed it into the top of the lipstick tube to keep the powder from spilling out. With his leftover handkerchief strip, he tied it on top of the solid grate bolt.

"I need something to keep the fuse dry when I tamp the wet mud around it," he said.

"I know," Birte said. "Your wallet. Those little plastic sleeves that hold your credit cards."

"Right." Einar quickly ripped two of the sleeves out of his wallet. He opened the fill hole on the kerosene lamp base and dipped his handkerchief fuse into it. He threaded the plastic envelopes around one end of the fuse, removed the paper from the lipstick tube, and inserted the fuse. He took the mud Birte had made and tamped it securely around the charge to channel it at the bolt, careful that the plastic protectors insulated the fuse from the moist clay.

He was ready.

He placed the heavy floorboards back over the grate.

"Go to the far corner, Bo," he said to Birte. "Face away from the explosion. Cover the back of your neck with your hands."

As Birte followed his instructions, Einar cut a splinter from one of the boards. He strung the handkerchief fuse along the floor, and using the splinter as a match, lighting it from the lantern, he lit the fuse. At once the flame sped along its length.

He ran to join Birte.

The explosion was ear-shattering in the confined space. Wood splinters and dirt rained down on Einar and Birte, crouching in the corner. Sawdust flew through the air, filling the place with a cloying haze.

Einar ran to the grate. On his knees he examined the bolt.

It was still there.

He stood up. In angry frustration he stomped on the grate—and the bolt broke in two.

At once he swung the grate aside. Below gaped a crude circular hole drilled into the rock and seeming to slant toward the sea.

"It's a drain hole," he said excitedly. "And it can't be just a sump hole. Not in solid rock. It's got to come out someplace. Probably on the side of the cliff below. Give me the lantern."

Birte handed it to him. He held it over the drain hole.

"Can't see much. But it's got to open out somewhere to drain."

"Are you sure?"

"There's one way we can make sure," he said. He looked at his watch. "It's almost five-thirty in the morning. In another half hour it'll be dawn. We should be able to see daylight down there. If it leads to the outside."

The thirty minutes seemed to last a lifetime. Finally Einar stood up. "Shield the light, Bo," he instructed her. "As much as you can without smothering it. I want to be able to see down there."

He went over to the drain. He knelt on the floor and poked his head down into the hole. For a few moments he closed his eyes to improve his night vision. Then he strained to see.

"I see it!" he shouted. "Light! I see light. The drain hole does go through to the outside down there!"

Birte joined him at the opening.

"I'm going down," Einar said resolutely.

"Wait, Einar. What if it gets narrower?" Birte asked, concerned. "You could get stuck."

"It won't," Einar reassured her confidently. "The hole was made before there was any drilling equipment. Chiseled out by hand. Someone had to get down into it to dig the hole."

He swung his legs into the hole. He let himself down. He barely got his buttocks through the opening in the floor. He stopped. "Dammit to hell!" he swore. "I'll never get my shoulders through. The damned hole is no more than twenty inches in diameter. I'll never fit."

"I will," Birte said soberly. "I'll go down."

"No," Einar said. He wriggled out.

"Don't be a boring chauvinist, love," Birte said tersely. "You know as well as I that I can do it. One of us will have to. And unless we wait till you've starved yourself thin enough to slip through, which I'd rather not, I'm the one."

Einar clenched his jaw. She was, of course, right.

"All right," he said. "But we do it my way."

"And what way's that?"

"We'll put a rope around you. That way, if you get in trouble, I can haul you back up."

"We don't have a rope," Birte pointed out.

"We'll make one. Give me all your clothes, except your skirt and blouse."

He began to strip himself. All he put back on were his pants and his jacket.

He looked at the pile of clothing on the floor: socks, underpants and undershirt, and shirt were his contribution; slip, panty hose, and a sweater were Birte's. And the handkerchiefs.

"Okay," Einar said. "Now we cut everything into strips."

With the aid of the souvenir penknife, they did.

"What now?" Birte asked. "Those strips will never be strong enough to hold anything."

"They will when we braid them," Einar explained. "And tie them together."

They set to work.

The resulting "rope" was almost eleven feet long. Einar tied one end around Birte's chest, just under her arms. The other he fastened securely to his right wrist.

He looked gravely at Birte. "Go slow," he said. "And be careful. It'll be like chimneying. As in mountain climbing. But tight. You know what I mean?"

Birte nodded solemnly.

"If you get in any trouble, sing out. I'll be able to hear you. And I'll get you back up. Remember—don't take any chances."

"I won't."

"Go to it, then."

Birte sat down at the rim of the hole. She swung her legs over the edge and began to lower herself slowly.

Einar kept the rope taut as she slid down. He watched her head disappear into the drain hole. He was suddenly very much aware of how much he loved her.

Slowly, inch by inch, he played out the rope.

"You okay?" he called.

"Fine!" Birte's voice sounded hollow coming from the hole.

Suddenly the rope yanked tight, almost tearing from Einar's grip. Alarmed, he called, "Birte!"

"Sorry!" she called up to him. "I slipped. The hole widens at the bend. I'm fine."

Relieved, Einar resumed playing out the rope. He looked at it. Only two or three feet left. Would it be long enough?

Birte's rate of descent slowed down perceptibly. Einar'd fed her less than a foot in several minutes.

"You okay?" he called again, worried. "What's happening?"

"I'm . . . okay." Birte's voice sounded strained. "It's . . . it's getting awfully . . . tight. I . . . I—Wait! I'm through! I think I'm through. My feet are kicking nothing but air!"

"Be careful!"

Another foot of rope.

And—the last one.

Einar knelt at the opening, his right hand gripping the end of the rope tied to his wrist.

And the rope went slack.

For a split second his heart stopped. Had it broken? Then Birte's voice reached him.

"I'm through!" she shouted. "The hole comes out on the side of the cliff. There's a ledge right below it. Broad enough to be safe. And I'm pretty sure I can get up to the top. It's not too far above."

Einar let the relief flood over him.

"I'm untying the rope!" Birte's voice drifted up from the hole, fainter than before. "I'll be right up. Don't go anywhere!"

Einar hauled up the rope. He untied it from his wrist and discarded it. He walked over to the door—and waited.

In his mind he followed Birte's progress as she made her way up the cliff. He tried to visualize it as a gradual slope with ample handholds and broad ledges. But it came out forbidding, dangerous, and precipitous.

She should be at the rim now. Just crawling over the edge. She should be standing up now—and taking her bearings. She should be running down toward the icehouse—and she should be at the outer door now. Now!

He listened tensely.

There was nothing to be heard.

He waited. She may have been too tired to run, he rationalized. Give her a couple more minutes.

They seemed to take hours to pass.

Now?

Still no sound.

He began to get worried. He refused to acknowledge the image that was trying to invade his mind, the image of Birte lying in a broken, crumpled heap on the jagged rocks at the bottom of the cliff.

It did not happen.

It could not happen.

But there was no sound of her.

He was conscious of his palms getting moist, and the sweat trickling coldly down his sides from his armpits.

Where was she? Where the hell was she?

He looked at his watch.

Dammit! He'd forgotten to look when he started to wait. How much time *had* gone by?

It seemed like forever.

And the blessed sound of the outer bolt sliding free filled his world.

The door opened—and a smiling, grimy Birte, a scrape on her forehead and nursing a broken fingernail, beamed at him.

"Come on out," she said. "The weather's fine!"

Hand in hand, they walked back to the Courtmacsherry Inn. At the pillared gate in the stone wall around the grounds of the inn, the caretaker was sweeping the walk. He tipped his cap to them.

"Top of the mornin' to ye," he said pleasantly. "Did ye have ye'rself a good night's rest, then? I hope ye enjoyed ye'r morning walk. A fine, blessed Sunday mornin' it is."

"Good morning," Einar said. "And I agree with you. It *is* a blessed day!"

As they walked through the high-ceilinged lounge decorated with numerous watercolors of local scenes, the desk clerk called to them.

"Mr. Munk. A word with you, please."

They walked over to the desk.

"Yes?" Einar said.

The clerk seemed unaware of their strange attire. He lowered his voice to a confidential half-whisper.

"There is a woman waiting to see ye, Mr. Munk," he confided. He glanced toward a group of comfortable velvet chairs that joined a sofa rest and a low table on a large Aubusson-type rug. " 'Tis her, sitting over there. A Mrs. Mahoney, she says." He looked slightly disapproving. "She is not local, Mr. Munk. She says she comes from Barryroe, a small village across the head. A good four miles it is."

"Thank you," Einar said. "We'll talk with her."

The woman sitting stiffly and uncomfortably on the edge of one of the chairs looked to be in her fifties. She wore all black and had a large knitted shawl draped over her head. Her work-worn hands rested uneasily in her lap.

"Mrs. Mahoney?" Einar said. "I am Einar Munk." He indicated Birte. "And this is my wife. You wish to speak with us?"

The woman raised her eyes to him, eyes that spoke of grief and bitterness.

"Aye, that I do," she said solemnly. "Why are ye wanting to know about the sickness that comes from the sea?"

Einar stared at her.

"We want to help," he said simply.

For a moment the woman regarded him with her mournful eyes. Slowly she nodded.

"I'll be telling ye, then," she whispered.

31

For a moment the dark, somber woman sat silent, looking down at her hands in her lap. Birte sensed her distress.

"Can we get you anything, Mrs. Mahoney?" she asked. "A cup of coffee, perhaps?"

She glanced toward the dining room. Immediately she regretted her offer. The tables glimpsed through the open door, their bright red linen tablecloths overlaid with gleaming white napkins, seemed much too festive for the moment.

The woman shook her head. "I thank you, no," she said.

"Would you like to come up to the room?" Einar suggested. "We can talk undisturbed."

Again the woman shook her head. "Here will be fine."

Einar pulled up a chair for Birte and one for himself. They sat down facing the doleful woman.

"What can you tell me, Mrs. Mahoney?" Einar asked quietly.

She looked up at him, her eyes tormented.

"About Liam," she whispered.

"Liam?"

"My son." She sighed deeply. "Dead from the sickness, he is."

Gently Birte touched her arm. "I'm so sorry," she said.

"Your son," Einar asked, "was he a fisherman?"

"Aye, that he was and one of the best," the woman said with obvious pride. "He had his own boat, he did. *Manannan* he called it, and one of the finest it was, with a crew the best in Barryroe."

"What . . . happened?"

"They came home," the Mahoney woman told them, her voice strangely flat and lackluster. "Early last month, it was. All the men were with the sickness, but Liam the worst. More dead than alive he was." There was a small catch in her voice, but she went on. "He was dead before the night was out."

Gravely Einar looked at her. "Mrs. Mahoney," he said softly, "I do not want to add to your grief, but what I am about to ask you is of the greatest importance. It may be helpful in saving many lives. You understand?"

Solemnly the woman nodded. "That is the only reason I'm after talking with you," she said simply.

"How did your son die?" Einar asked. "What were his . . . his symptoms?"

The woman sat very still. Her tension showed only in the clenched hands in her lap, their knuckles white. She did not look at them as she spoke.

"I am not a *seanachie,*" she said, using the Irish word for storyteller. "I will not tell you so many tales ye'r head will be so crowded with them they'll be pressing against ye'r ears hard enough to make ye deaf. But this I'll be telling ye. My Liam caught the ocean sickness. He was all trembling when they carried him to his own door. He could not see with his eyes, and he had no mastery over his own functions at all, at all." She swallowed hard and doggedly went on. "It was little he could tell me, his breathing so hard and his mouth so dry he could not speak. So weak he was he could not crawl—and him all man with the strength of two."

She fell silent, lost for a moment in her grief and incomprehension.

"What about . . . the others?" Einar asked.

The woman shook her head slowly. "It was turrible, that it was, all being sick the same as Liam, but not to the dying of it. They all stayed at home, they did. And no man of them has gone near the ocean after."

"Did you ever talk to any of them?"

"Aye, I did. To Liam's best friend, sick as the others. He told me Liam had been on deck early in the morning with everyone else asleep below. They had just come to a new bank for the fishing, he said. Liam woke them up, feeling the sickness come over him. And soon they all felt as bad as he."

"One more question, Mrs. Mahoney. Do you know where in the Atlantic Ocean your son's boat was, when he became ill?"

"Liam was in the navy," the woman said proudly. "And he always kept a log."

She put her hand under her shawl and produced a worn, black-covered logbook. "Ye are welcome to see for yer'self where the *Manannan* was when the sickness came upon her." She looked bitterly at Einar. "Liam'd thought the ocean waters would smile on him if he named his boat after the ancient Celtic god of the sea. They did not."

She gave the logbook to Einar. "It is his last writing in it that will tell ye."

Quickly Einar looked for the final entry in the log. He found it:

> April 7, 1985. 1920 hours. Hailed the Invernia out of Schull. Capt. Sean MacManus on board. Their catch better than ours. Heading for new and better grounds farther out.
> April 8, 1985. 0520 hours. Destination reached. Latitude 49 degrees, 17 minutes north, Longitude 12 degrees, 29 minutes west. There is a sickness coming over me. I—

Einar frowned to visualize the map of Ireland and the surrounding waters: 49 north, 12 west would be about 150 miles southwest of the southern tip of the island.

It fit!

Einar was getting used to driving on the left side of the road. Birte had refused even to try. It was some fifty miles from Courtmacsherry to Schull, driving west along the lovely country roads over Clonakilty and Skibbereen, and he expected to make it in an hour and a half and be in Schull well before noon.

He had to struggle with himself not to get too excited at what he'd found out. There were still questions that remained, puzzling and unanswered. The crew of an Irish fishing boat had all become ill with what certainly appeared to be the effects of a minute, highly dissipated amount of the "brown sugar." And the exact spot in the ocean where contamination apparently had occurred was known.

Latitude 49 degrees, 17 minutes north, longitude 12 degrees, 29 minutes west.

Was that where the U-1000 had gone down?

It was logical to assume that one or more of the drums, perhaps damaged in the attack on the sub, had corroded faster than the others and might have developed a small leak from which minute amounts of the exsiccating poison had escaped.

But if so, why hadn't there been a rash of contamination cases since March? Other fishing boats must have been working the area. Was it simply that the Irish fishermen were that damned closemouthed? Or was there another explanation? If so—what?

He had decided that before he apprised Henderson of his discovery, he'd follow up the one additional lead he had: the captain of the fishing vessel that, according to Liam's log, had been in the same waters and might have proceeded to latitude 49 north and longitude 12 west.

Captain Sean MacManus of the *Invernia* out of Schull.

Schull was a small fishing village of some four hundred townspeople, lying sheltered from the north winds by Mount Gabriel. From its excellent little harbor, home port of several trawlers and other fishing vessels, the group of windswept, green-carpeted islands known as the Carbery's Hundred Islands could be seen.

Einar stopped at a fish-processing plant at the pier to ask directions to the house of Captain MacManus from a few men spending their Sunday spinning tall tales for one another. With some reluctance they referred him to the local pub frequented by the Schull fishermen, Tom Newman's Corner House on Main Street.

The pub, which doubled as a grocery store, was already alive with people "having a Sunday jar."

Einar and Birte struck up a conversation with a weather-beaten old fisherman sporting a shock of white hair and eyebrows to match, who told them his name was Paddy and who looked as if he'd know everyone in Schull. The man was jovial and gossipy, his broad Irish brogue beguiling and melodious. But when it came to Captain Sean MacManus, he was totally uninformative, telling them only that he did not know where MacManus could be found, and that they'd be fools if they be seeking out the company of a dour captain when they could have his, Paddy's, for the asking.

There was one other pub on Main Street, The Black Sheep Inn, a quaint, rambling old inn entered through an alley and a cheery back garden.

The bartender who served them their stout was intrigued at having American visitors. He listened attentively to Einar's urgent request for information.

"Ye'll best be going to Tom Newman's," he advised them. "It is the fishermen ye'll be finding there to tell you what ye want to know."

"Thanks," Einar said dryly. "We were there. Talking to a man named Paddy. Didn't get to first base." And he told the bartender what Paddy had said.

The man nodded sagely. "There's a lot of truth in the lies old Paddy was telling ye," he observed. For a moment he contemplated them.

"If it is as important as ye say it is, ye can find MacManus in the next to last house on the road to Ballydehob. Bright yellow it is."

He looked straight at Einar.

"But if it is not important—I never told ye."

The woman who answered their knock on the door of the bright yellow house on the road to Ballydehob watched them with a glare of suspicion that bordered on hostility, while she remained safely ensconsed behind the only half-open door.

"What do ye want, then?" she asked curtly.

"I'm Einar Munk," Einar said. He nodded toward Birte. "That's my wife. We are looking for Captain Sean MacManus."

"Are ye, now? Well, ye won't find him here."

"This is his house, isn't it?"

"Aye. Ye're right in that. But I told ye—ye'll not be finding him here."

"Is he away? At sea?"

"Aye." The hesitation was ever so slight.

"When are you expecting him back?"

"There's no saying."

"Look, Mrs. . . . you are Mrs. MacManus?"

The woman nodded.

"Look, Mrs. MacManus. It is extremely important that we see your husband. You're certain he's not home?"

"Ah, sure, what's the matter with ye?" the woman snapped angrily. "I told ye he is not!" And she slammed the door in their faces.

As they walked to their car, Einar glanced back toward the house—in time to see the curtain move at one of the white-framed windows. They were being watched.

By Mrs. MacManus? Or Sean?

"She's lying," Einar said.

"Even without the benefit of a hunch," Birte agreed, "I could tell that."

"Question is, why?" Einar went on. "Look. You drive. Take us around the bend. I'll hop out. You drive on until you're out of earshot. Leave the car and come back. Stay out of sight and wait for me."

Birte nodded. She did not have to ask any questions. She didn't even object to having to drive on the left side of the road. She knew what her husband was up to.

The garden around the MacManus home apparently had been untended for a while. Under cover of the shrubbery, Einar made his way to the rear of the house. There were four double windows and one smaller one. At least one of them would open on the bedroom.

The first window was the kitchen. Clean, simple, with several gleaming copper pots and pans hanging on one wall. The small window was the bathroom. The third one, the bedroom.

There were two beds. On one lay a man, covered to his chin with a colorful quilt. The face that showed above it was sallow and drawn and shriveled; the lips were thin and blue and cracked, the sunken eyes were closed.

Sean MacManus, skipper of the *Invernia,* had come home from his last fishing trip with the ocean sickness.

Einar doubled back to the waiting Birte.

"He's there," he said grimly. "And he's got it. Been exposed to the damned gas." He looked soberly at Birte. "We've got to talk to him. We've got to find out where it happened." He started to walk back toward the house. "Play along with me," he said resolutely.

Once again Einar knocked at the door of the bright yellow house.

The MacManus woman opened it. When she saw who it was, she at once started to close the door. Einar stepped into the doorway.

"Just a moment, Mrs. MacManus," he said sternly. "You are, I'm sure, aware of the serious consequences of obstructing a government investigation?"

The woman stared at him.

"We are conducting an international investigation, Mrs. MacManus," Einar went on importantly. "In close collaboration with Upper Merrion Street. The Fishery and Forestry Department." He let it sink in. The woman looked troubled. "You informed us that Captain MacManus was not here." He looked at her, flinty eyed. "However, I believe he is lying in bed in the bedroom in the rear of the house. I strongly suggest that you let us talk with him, or I will be forced to call in the constable!"

Without a word the woman held open the door. Einar and Birte stepped inside. With a quick, worried look out the door, the woman closed it behind them. Mutely she turned to them, her face taut and white.

"May we speak to your husband, now, please?" Einar asked.

Slowly the woman nodded. She sighed.

"I was not lying to ye, ye know." Her voice was tired and worn. "My husband is not really here, ye might say. He cannot talk and he cannot hear. He cannot see. It is soon he will be dead." She swallowed to stifle a sob. "And I'll miss him for not being here."

Birte looked at the woman, compassion softening her eyes. "Shouldn't your husband be in the hospital, Mrs. MacManus?" she asked softly. "Where they can take care of him?"

"And for what reason, I ask ye?" the woman flared. "He'll die there as quick as here. The O'Neil lad did, and him only twenty. Best that himself pass over in his own bed under his own cover."

"Mrs. MacManus," Einar said quietly, "perhaps it would be best if you told us what happened."

The woman nodded.

"Come into the parlor," she said.

Unsteadily she led the way. She sat down. They joined her.

"They come home, they did. They brought her home, the *Invernia*, and all of them sick. Sean as sick as the next man. A month ago, it was, and eleven days." Miserably she sat stiffly on the straight-backed chair, staring unseeingly into space, not looking at her unwelcome visitors. "The O'Neil lad died, Monday last. Sean will soon be following. The other lads are home. Sick. They may all go."

"Mrs. MacManus," Einar asked, "do you know from where your husband brought his boat back? Do you know where in the Atlantic he was fishing when he . . . when he got the sickness?"

The woman shook her head. "It was hard for Sean to talk even when he came home," she said. "He was angry at the sea, he was."

"Can you remember what he said?" Einar asked. "It is very important. Did he mention any location?"

Again the woman shook her head.

"I cannot say. It was no sensible thing, he said. He was only talking about the sickness, he was. The curse that hit them all. The curse, he said, of forty-nine and twelve . . ."

Colonel Jonathan Henderson shot out of a deep, dreamless sleep. His bedside telephone rang again, loud in the quiet room. He fumbled the receiver to his ear.

The luminous numbers on his digital clock showed 6:17. Sunday morning—the only morning of the week he allowed himself an extra hour's sleep—was well under way.

"Hello!" he grated into the phone. He knew who the caller would be before he heard Einar's voice.

"Colonel! I have it!" Henderson was instantly totally alert. "I know where the—"

"Munk!" the colonel exploded into the phone. "This is an open line!"

There was a minute pause.

"Yes, sir."

"Where the hell are you?"

"In Ireland, sir."

"Listen, Major. You and your wife are both to return to Washington at once. And Major, this is an order. It is not to be negotiated."

"I understand, sir."

"Where in Ireland are you?"

"In a small fishing village on the south coast." Einar hoped the information would not be lost on the Pentagon officer.

"How far from Shannon?"

"About ninety miles."

"Go there at once. I'll have transportation waiting for you at the airport there."

"Yes, sir."

"Now, Munk, give me your information. Essentials only."

"Forty-nine, north," Einar said. "Twelve, west."

Transatlantic Telephone Cable, TAT #7, runs from Tuckerton, New Jersey, to Land's End, County Cornwall, the westernmost point of England. Three thousand ninety-five nautical miles long, it can handle forty-two hundred calls simultaneously.

This Sunday morning, May 19, it was humming nowhere near capacity, but at the exact same moment the tense conversation between Einar and Colonel Henderson surged along the cable, another conversation fully as taut whirred through side by side with it.

"One. Zero. Zero. Zero," a man's voice said in New York.

"Four. Nine. One. Two," responded the caller in Freiburg, West Germany.

"Is it done?"

"No. The Irish operation failed."

"*Verdammt nochmal!* You bungled it!"

"The . . . the subject is very resourceful, Herr *Doktor.* I—"

"How much does he know?"

"That . . . is not certain. Perhaps . . . everything."

"We cannot fail. Not now. So close."

"What . . . can we do, Herr *Doktor?*"

"You—nothing," the man in New York snapped, cold disdain in his voice. "Return to your home and wait. I will take over. Personally." There was a slight pause. "Even if they have all the information, time is on our side. There is still a massive operation to be mounted and carried out before the Führer's V-3 can be rendered harmless. They are still confronted with a monumental task, my dear Mahler."

There was silence for a brief moment. When the man in New York spoke again, his voice was harsh and determined.

"I promise you—they will not succeed!"

PART

May 1985

32

Einar watched Colonel Jonathan Henderson steeple his fingers. It was a gesture he'd come to associate with the man. He hated it. It was a gesture devoid of urgency and drive. Instead it bespoke passiveness and inactivity. Exactly what was not needed now.

It was less than eight hours since he had talked to the colonel on the phone from Schull. He and Birte had landed at Andrews Air Force Base in the KC 135 jet that had flown them from Shannon. They had at once been beelined through the light Sunday traffic to the river entrance of the Pentagon and whisked into Henderson's office.

The colonel had listened to their report. Every detail of it. He looked grim.

"You did a hell of a job, Major," he said. As an afterthought he nodded at Birte. "And you, ma'am. And you are right. We'll have to move with all possible speed. We'll take it from here." He took down his hands. "I'll set up your debriefing by the DIA—" He looked at Birte. "That's the Defense Intelligence Agency, ma'am," he explained. "This office is part of it. I'll set up your debriefing at once."

Einar bristled. "Debriefing!" he exclaimed. "Again? We've just debriefed ourselves to hell and back."

"Your initial debriefing only, Major," Henderson snapped testily. "You will have to go through your high-level debriefing by the DIA. The agency is now headed by Admiral Roberts. Wilbur Roberts. A three-star admiral. And then you'll be questioned by the JCS—" Again the look to Birte. "—the Joint Chiefs of Staff, ma'am. If the chairman, at the moment Admiral Paul A. Peck, a four-star admiral, if he thinks there is enough substance and urgency to the matter, he'll take it to the National Security Council at the White House—and the President." Automatically his mind ticked off the team. Taylor, the air force chief of staff; Sinclair, the army chief of staff; Potter, the chief of naval operations; Mitchell, the commandant of marines, and, of course, Peck, the chairman. The top military minds in the country. He wondered what the final recommendations of these officers would be. Under the circumstances.

"That'll take hours!" Einar protested.

Henderson nodded.

"But dammit!" Einar exploded. "We may not have those hours! Cut through all that red tape, Colonel. Get to the White House. Right now!"

"That is not possible. I can't do that."

"Can't—or won't?" Einar glared at the officer.

Henderson returned his look steadily.

"I understand your zealousness, Major," he said quietly. "But consider my position. I have only your and your wife's report to go on."

Say it, Einar thought bitterly. An over-the-hill reserve officer and a civilian broad.

"That," Henderson went on, "and some local events that could well be coincidental. I can't cut through the normal, prescribed emergency procedures on the strength of that." He looked at Einar. "Though, believe me, I wish I could. But when you cool down under that collar of yours, you'll see I'm right."

Einar shut up. He saw the point.

"Perhaps it will ease your misgivings if I tell you that I do now believe there is a clear and present danger. An urgent danger, Munk." Again he steepled his fingers. "I have not sat on my hands. I have already given the JCS a preliminary report, based on your wires and calls. They can convene within an hour after recommendation by the DIA. And I have mobilized every man jack I could find to go through the World War II naval records to see if they can find anything. Anything at all that will corroborate your report. Until then—"

A knock on the door interrupted him. With a frown of irritation, he called, "Come in!"

An aide entered.

"Sorry to disturb you, sir," he said. "But you wanted to see at once anything we could find about that destroyer attack." He held out a piece of paper.

Henderson literally tore it from his hand. He read aloud:

"07 March 45. 2330 hours. Convoy 34 E. Destroyer escort fired on surfaced U-boat, which then executed emergency dive. Depth charge run executed. Inconclusive. Position, latitude 49° 17′ north, longitude 12° 29′ west."

Without a word Henderson stabbed the button on his intercom. "Get me Admiral Roberts!" he barked.

"Roberts," the box squawked.

"Admiral. John," Henderson snapped. "This is top priority. I want to see the chairman as soon as possible. Can you get him on the scrambler?"

The voice box on the desk squawked again.

"Don't have to. He's in his office."

"Good. Bill—this can't wait!"

"What is it?"

"The U-1000 case. It's blown wide open."

"See you there in ten minutes." The sound over the intercom cut out.

Henderson turned to Einar.

"Now," he said. "Now we've got something!"

Admiral Paul A. Peck, chairman of the Joint Chiefs of Staff, listened without interruption to Colonel Henderson's report covering Einar's and Birte's encounters and discoveries in Europe. Henderson spoke concisely and authoritatively, and Einar was grudgingly impressed with his succinct presentation, which didn't miss a point.

When the colonel was finished, Peck turned to Einar.

"Professor Munk," he said, "did your informers in Germany—Mahler and Wierdring, was it?"

"Yes, sir."

"Did they give you a location where the U-1000 went down?"

"No, sir. But from what they said about the dispersal of the gas cloud by prevailing westerly winds, it would have to be somewhere southwest of Ireland. From one to two hundred miles offshore."

Peck nodded. "And the Irish fishermen you spoke to, they both indicated that they'd been at latitude 49 north and longitude 12 west?"

"That position was logged by one of them, sir. The other one indicated that he'd been there, too."

"And that was the location of the inconclusive destroyer attack on 7 May 1945, according to naval records? Correct?" He looked at Henderson.

"Correct, sir."

"Did your German informers mention any specific date?" Peck asked Einar.

"Nothing specific, sir. Only early March."

"Significant, I think, is also the fact that the Germans don't know the fate of the U-1000," Admiral Roberts interjected. "Quite surprising. They usually have every fact at their fingertips."

Peck nodded. He pushed the button on his intercom.

"Call the President," he said crisply. "I'm coming right over. On a top-priority matter."

He looked up at Roberts. "Bill, get the team together," he said. "I want to be able to get the ball rolling the minute I get back."

"Right."

Peck turned to Einar and Birte.

"Professor Munk, Mrs. Munk," he said. "I want you to accompany me. The President may want to put some questions to you personally."

It was 1609 hours when Admiral Peck, Einar, and Birte drove up to the White House entrance. They were at once ushered to the Oval Office. Peck was shown in immediately; Einar and Birte were asked to wait in the corridor.

They sat down on a sofa.

Birte looked around, at the plush furniture and the high ceiling. She let her senses soak up the historical atmosphere. It suddenly struck her. They were actually sitting in the White House, waiting to see the President of the United States!

During the nine days since their quiet, uneventful academic lives had been interrupted by two strangers coming to their door, they had traveled to two foreign countries; they had been in danger of losing their lives twice; they had seen two men die a violent death; and they had unearthed perhaps the greatest threat the world had ever faced. And now they were sitting in the corridor outside the Oval Office in the White House waiting to see the President.

And it might all still be in vain.

Quietly she stole her hand into Einar's. She glanced at him. She knew he felt as she did.

It was twenty minutes before they were asked to enter—the longest twenty minutes in their lives.

Einar at once recognized the two men sitting with Peck before the President's desk: David Rosenfeld, the secretary of defense, and George Pelham, the secretary of state.

Birte took in the famous room with delighted interest. It was bright and airy; the President's desk at the southern tip of the office dominated it. Comfortable, leather-upholstered chairs, and opposite the desk, the fireplace and the white marble mantelpiece with the big Swedish ivy plant right in the middle under the Peale painting of George Washington. She knew about that ivy plant. She'd read about it. Been on the mantelpiece through four presidents. Not the same one, of course, but a succession of exact look-alikes. Like horticultural Lassies.

The men all rose.

The President, looking grave, came around his desk. He offered his hand, first to Birte, then to Einar.

"Mrs. Munk," he said, a quick smile lighting his face. "Professor Munk. Thank you for coming."

He looked closely at them.

"I wanted to meet you before making a final decision," he said. "And to ask you just one question."

Soberly he looked from one to the other.

"What it boils down to is really this. You were there. You talked to . . . those people. In your hearts—do you believe this terrible menace does exist?"

Without a second's hesitation Einar answered, "Yes, Mr. President. With no reservations at all."

"I agree with my husband," Birte said.

The President took a deep breath. Resolutely he turned to the other men.

"We go!" he said firmly. He looked at Peck. "Paul. What's our first step?"

"We do have the necessary salvage capabilities," Peck said. "Best available. Provided the wreck lies at a depth that is at all accessible, which—considering the indicated area—is probable." He thought for a moment. "I suggest we bring in Brannigan. Jason is a good man. It's a job for CINCLANT."

CINCLANT? Einar thought. Pentagonese. Commander in chief, Atlantic.

"Better yet, SACLANT," the secretary of defense interjected. "We need international cooperation. Certainly the British must be involved. SACLANT has participants from all the NATO countries."

"I agree," Peck said. "Brannigan is, of course, also SACLANT."

SACLANT, Einar thought. Supreme Allied Commander, Atlantic. The top NATO command in the Atlantic.

The President turned to the secretary of state.

"George. We're going to pull all stops on this one. Inform Her Majesty's Government right away. Give them a full briefing."

Purposefully he walked to his desk. He picked up a phone.

"Get me Admiral Jason Brannigan in Norfolk," he said crisply.

It was Sunday, 1729 hours, 19 May 1985. Ten days, two hours, and twelve minutes from the time one Karl Johann Thompson had been run down on Second Avenue in New York City . . .

CINCLANT/SACLANT, Admiral Jason Brannigan, considered himself lucky to have his quarters in Virginia House, generally thought to be the most desirable on the row of grand homes on Dillingham Boulevard, built for the Centennial Exposition of 1907, when each state put up its own mansion.

It was 1731 hours, EST, Sunday evening when the scrambler phone in his den rang.

Brannigan had just returned home—early for a change. He'd shrugged off his shoes and settled down with a dry martini before dinner at 2000 hours. To relax his mind he'd turned on his Fisher VCR to watch one of his favorite old films. Brannigan was a secret science fiction fan—the good, imaginative kind of sci-fi, he'd say, which takes a plausible idea and runs with it, not the BEM stuff, the bug-eyed monster crap. He'd selected a twenty-year-old film called *Robinson Crusoe on Mars,* one of his favorites. Man's-survival-against-impossible-odds sort of thing.

He pushed the PAUSE button on his remote control and—slightly annoyed—picked up the phone.

"Brannigan!" he barked. He listened for a few seconds, then jerked bolt upright. "Yes, Mr. President," he said.

For the next twenty minutes he listened. When he finally hung up, his face was white, his eyes bleak.

For a few seconds he sat immobile, staring at the frozen picture on his set—not seeing it at all. Then he picked up the phone.

When his call was acknowledged, he said, "This is Admiral Brannigan. I want so speak to the command center duty officer. At once!"

Impatiently he waited.

"Commander Fenwick, sir," a voice came over the receiver.

"Commander," Brannigan snapped. "This is top priority. Get hold of Admiral Handel and Admiral Mertens and the other members of the Crisis Response Team. Get on it at once. I want them in the command center in one half hour!"

The hub of the CINCLANT command center was a huge room, approximately sixty by one hundred feet. The floor was tightly dotted with computer desks, instrument consoles, and control panels. One wall was completely covered with large data display panels, and facing these panels, high above the main floor, a glassed-in balcony ran the length of the room.

Sixteen officers were present on the balcony—the normal watch as well as the full Crisis Response Team: Admiral Jason Brannigan; his operations officer, Real Admiral Dirk A. Baldon; the fleet material readiness officer, Rear Admiral Jack Caulfield; the intelligence officer, Captain J. Harnum; the commander naval surface force, Atlantic, COMSURFLANT, Vice Admiral L. Handel; and the commander naval air force, Atlantic, COMNAVAIRLANT, Vice Admiral P. Mertens.

In grim silence they all stared at the commander in chief, Atlantic, Admiral Brannigan. This was no drill. This was the real thing. A crisis of almost unimaginable magnitude.

"You got the picture," Brannigan finished briskly. "We've got a salvage operation to beat them all on our hands. They've thrown the ball to us. It's up to us to run with it. Recommendations?"

"Let's see what we've got," Baldon, the operations officer said. He flipped a switch.

"Display all salvage assets, Atlantic Fleet, on board one," he ordered.

The men all turned to look at the display panel. Within a few seconds a list of salvage vessels, between thirty and forty of them, appeared on the big screen.

Baldon pointed to the display.

"The ASR-23, the USS *Cormorant*, is at Holylock," he said. "On the western coast of Scotland. It's the most sophisticated submarine rescue ship in the navy. I can have her in the operations area within thirty-six hours if I give her her orders now."

"Get her under way," Brannigan nodded.

Baldon went at once to a phone.

"We'll need a code name for the datum point," Harnum said. "Latitude 49° 17′ north, longitude 12° 29′ west."

Brannigan turned to COMSURFLANT. "Leo, any ideas?"

Admiral Handel thought for a moment. "This promises to be the biggest damned operation we've ever undertaken," he said. "Why not Operation Giant? Point Golf for the datum point?"

"Sold," Brannigan agreed. He turned to one of the officers present. "Follow through. Including the White House."

Baldon, on the phone, could be heard giving his orders: "I want the ASR-23 to proceed to that location immediately and await further instructions."

"The ASR-23 won't be any damned use until we find the U-1000," Brannigan said. "What kind of assets do we have available?"

"We'll need several minesweepers with top mine-hunting sonar," Admiral Caulfield said. "The nearest ones are in Charleston. That's a good eight days from Point Golf. With no glitches."

"We don't have eight days!"

"How about the Brits?" Harnum asked. "Are we cleared?"

"Yes. We'll put it to them when we convene SACLANT." He consulted his watch. "In one hour."

"We're going to have a lot of people out there," COMNAVAIRLANT Mertens said. "We'll need plenty of secure communication. A lot of space and advanced technical facilities. I suggest a carrier."

"Isn't the *Coral Sea* just finishing Operation Morningstar off Norway?" Brannigan asked.

"Yes," Mertens acknowledged. "She's scheduled for a port call at Plymouth, 1400 hours tomorrow. Admiral Benjamin Reed is on board."

"Excellent! Couldn't ask for a better man. Have him take on-the-spot charge of Operation Giant. Cancel that port call. Divert the *Coral Sea* to Point Golf." Brannigan turned to his Operations officer. "Dirk," he said. "Have them set up a secure voice communication circuit with the *Coral Sea.* Admiral Reed. I want him on the way before we convene SACLANT."

Brigadier Howard Burley-Winningham scowled at Brannigan.

"Why were we not informed before now?" he demanded to know.

"I only received word myself less than two hours ago, Howard," Brannigan said. "From the President personally. He assured me your government had been informed at once. You'll probably get your instructions any moment."

Burley-Winningham grumbled an inaudible reply.

The representatives from the sixteen NATO countries that constituted SACLANT, looking shaken, tensely watched Brannigan as he finished his briefing.

"As I was saying, a task force of U.S. and British ships is even now being assembled. It will be TF-49. Admiral Reed aboard the carrier *Coral Sea* will be in charge. I have been informed that Her Majesty's Royal Navy is collaborating fully with us. Operation Giant will be a joint British-U.S. effort all the way."

"Are any evacuation measures being planned?" the Canadian SACLANT member asked.

"None," Brannigan said grimly. "It would be a total impossibility. At best, only a tiny fraction of the people threatened could be evacuated. But the panic, the chaos, that would ensue, should the situation become generally known, would undoubtedly kill many times that. And to no avail—if we succeed."

"If anything is needed that we can supply," the Danish member officer said, "I know I speak for my government when I say we stand ready to do anything we can."

"Thank you, Major Nielsen," Brannigan nodded. "Your offer is appreciated."

"That goes, of course, for my government as well," the West German said.

"I'm sure everyone here feels the same way. We shall not hesitate to call on any of you if necessary. However, our only real chance is to locate the U-1000—and fast! Bring the damned drums up and neutralize the poison. It won't be easy. More like trying to find a pine needle on the bottom of a dark swimming pool at midnight."

"You'll need those mine sweepers," Admiral Burley-Winningham spoke up. "We've got them. With top mine-hunting capabilities."

"How many can you get there, Howard? Right now?"

"At least . . . six. I'll give it a go at once."

He rose and headed for the communication spaces.

Gravely Brannigan looked at the assembled officers.

"Any suggestions, any help that you can give, will—of course—be appreciated. I am available at any time."

He paused.

"Gentlemen," he said soberly. "The life of a nation depends on what we do here—and what Ben Reed does out there."

It was melodramatic, but—dammit! The truth often was.

33

The USS *Coral Sea*, CV-43, plowed steadily and majestically through the dark North Atlantic waters.

Alone on the admiral's bridge, Rear Admiral Benjamin Reed sat in the big admiral's chair with the two white stars on the back, staring into the night. The night-view television screen to his left was dark. There would be no takeoffs, no landings to observe. This was a different mission.

Once again he let his mind review the conversation he'd had with SACLANT, the responsibilities placed upon him—and the decisions he had to make.

First—the task force itself. TF-49. Rendezvous would be at Point Golf. The *Coral Sea* would be the flagship; the USS *Cormorant*, ASR-23—already en route—the main recovery vessel. He'd ordered a U.S. destroyer and a frigate to the area as well, as carrier and sonar support. Seven British minesweepers were already on station, scanning the search area grid; two French minesweepers would be joining them within hours. A British frigate with the British task force commander on board, Rear Admiral Everett Stirling, would link up with the task force, as well as a deep submergence rescue vessel of advanced design. When the U-1000 was located and the salvage job evaluated, an amphibious landing platform dock would join the force, if needed. There was an LPD of the Raleigh class already standing by at Plymouth.

And special personnel. He'd need expert toxicologists at the scene. No way of knowing what kind of damned poison they'd run into. He'd request three specialists. They'd probably come from the private sector. He'd let SACLANT deal with that and the selection of the scientists. And Chemical Warfare Service. Two officers. There was that Colonel Pauling. Or Pauley. That was it, David Pauley. He'd run into him in Washington. Bright, knowledgeable officer. He'd ask for him. And one more. He'd let them tackle the task of providing the best possible protection for every crew member of the task force. Just in case. TF-49 would comprise between fifteen and seventeen ships. He hoped to heaven that someone at SACLANT had thought of informing the Russians of the operation, or they might well panic and put their whole damned fleet to sea.

Salvage personnel. The USS *Cormorant*, ASR-23, the latest submarine rescue ship in the navy, differed slightly in configuration and salvage gear from other ASRs, such as the USS *Pigeon* and the USS *Ortolan*. She had a first-class team, he needn't concern himself with that, but he would want as much information about the U-1000 herself as he could get. All configurations and specifications. Someone who had firsthand knowledge of her, preferably someone who'd served on her—or on a similar transport sub. He'd request SACLANT to get the member from the *Bundesrepublik* on that.

And then there was the matter of Professor Munk and his wife. What he was about to request was unorthodox. But—dammit! The whole blasted situation was unorthodox. As unorthodox as they come. He'd want to debrief Munk and his wife himself, and not rely on secondhand information. He had, of course, been thoroughly informed of the knowledge obtained during the preliminary debriefings in the States, but that wasn't good enough for him. No matter how well you try to reconstruct matters, it can never be done as well as by personal observation. He'd learned that long ago—the hard way. And Munk and his wife had that personally obtained information. He wanted to know what they had to say firsthand—even if it did mean bringing a civilian woman on board at sea.

Resolutely he picked up the phone.

"This is Admiral Reed," he said briskly. "Get out a message, operational immediate. To CINCLANT info SACLANT. Request following personnel to rendevous with the *Coral Sea*—give the time of arrival—at Point Golf. Item One . . ."

Everyone had eyed her. She had enjoyed it, even preened a little. She chose to believe it was because she was a woman, a good-looking woman. But deep down she knew it was really because she was the *only* woman—a woman out of place. It didn't diminish her pleasure. Everyone is entitled to a little self-deception. Especially if it could be true.

She looked at the other passengers on the plane. An A3D Skywarrior, they called it. A sleek navy jet with two engines, equipped for carrier landing. Einar'd told her that some of the planes had been assigned the mission to deliver passengers to carriers under urgent circumstances such as this one.

Besides Einar, there were five passengers on board with her. All men. Two of them were army officers, a colonel and a lieutenant colonel; the other three were civilians. Toxicologists. A Dr. Clarence F. Ramsey, a Dr. Walter L. Hart, and a Dr. Steven Erlanger. Top men in their field, Einar had told her, impressed when he'd met them. He'd known the reputations of them all. One was even a Nobel Prize winner.

It had been a hectic time since their visit to the White House, and she'd welcomed the rest during the five-hour flight.

Sunday night, after returning to the Pentagon from the White House, they'd spent endless hours answering questions put to them by Admiral Peck and the Joint Chiefs of Staff, before they were whisked to Norfolk Naval Base in Virginia. Here they'd been put up for the night at the visitors' quarters and gone through yet another day of debriefing by an Admiral Brannigan and a group of other officers from both the United States and several European countries. Einar'd been anxious to "get the show on the road," as he said, but it hadn't been until 9:00 P.M. that all the scientists had been gathered together as well as the two officers, who were from the Chemical Warfare Service, and they could finally take off from Andrews Air Force Base.

And now it was early Tuesday morning, May 21.

Einar poked her out of her reveries. He pointed out the window.

She looked down.

Far below she could see a tiny ship on the vast expanse of water—like a match floating in a bathtub, she thought. She turned to Einar.

"We're supposed to land on *that?*" she exclaimed in horrified disbelief.

"It gets bigger as we go down," he grinned. "Just sit still and don't rock the plane, and we'll make it all right."

She wrinkled her nose at him. She'd been excited at the prospect of landing on a carrier. But she'd had no idea it was that small . . .

Einar, too, looked down at the carrier below. He'd never landed on one before. It did look damned small, but he knew it wasn't. After all, a ship the length of three football fields is hardly small. His thoughts, however, were not on the *Coral Sea,* but on the expanse of dark water around her—and the horror that lay waiting somewhere beneath the surface.

He was suddenly conscious of the plane dropping as it descended along the glide path toward the carrier deck and the hook aim-point at the center of a set of four steel arresting cables strung across the deck at forty-foot intervals one third down the seven-hundred-foot-long angle deck. Involuntarily he tensed. He glanced at Birte. She sat stiffly, staring straight ahead. There was a sudden, brief scraping sound of metal against metal and the jolt of the hook engaging the arresting cable. The plane dropped jarringly to the deck—and Einar's back teeth seemed to crowd to the front as the A3D was successfully trapped and came to a stop.

He looked at Birte. Nothing to it. He winked and wondered why the wink twitched.

Quickly they all deplaned and were at once ushered toward the "island," the superstructure towering eight stories above them on the starboard side of the flight deck, which now impressed Birte with its huge expanse. In single file they followed their guide down into the iron innards of the mammoth carrier, down steep companionways, through a steel labyrinth of narrow corridors to their quarters. They were informed that they would be fetched in thirty minutes and conducted to the wardroom for a conference with Admiral Reed and his staff.

Each of them was given a little pamphlet, "Welcome Aboard! USS *Coral Sea,* CV-43," with a brief history of the ship; what to do and not to do while on board; how to get around; and some facts of interest about the carrier: 2,500 miles of insulated copper wiring; 150 miles of piping, and 2,450 separate compartments. No little pamphlet would ever be guide enough through that kind of maze, Birte thought, as she glanced through the pamphlet. She hadn't expected anything like it. It was just like a brochure put out by a small-town chamber of commerce, she thought. But then—why not? The *Coral Sea* was a small town, a self-sufficient town of some forty-five hundred inhabitants supporting an airfield. With interest she noted that they'd come aboard her ten years almost to the day from the time the

Coral Sea had provided air support during the action that followed the notorious seizure of the American ship, SS *Mayaguez*, by Cambodian forces. She was also interested in learning that she and Einar could buy junk food in a special store aboard called the Gedunk!

Admiral Reed, flanked by his aide, Lieutenant Commander Raymond Nelson, and the rest of his staff, looked solemnly at the assembled visitors.

"Thank you for coming," he said. "I shall be brief and to the point. You are all familiar with the situation that confronts us."

He paused. He looked at each one in turn.

"And you know the importance of what we must accomplish," he added. "Operation Giant will be conducted in three separate phases. Each phase will specifically involve some of you. Phase One: discovery. The location of the U-1000. This phase is already under way. The search area as of 0600 has been closed to all shipping. NATO maneuvers," he said dryly. "Phase Two: the salvage and retrieval of the poison drums. A naval salvage vessel will rendezvous with us at 1220 hours today. Phase Three: neutralization and disposal of the poison agent. Phase Two will—"

He stopped as the door to the wardroom was opened. A civilian, a man around sixty years of age, was ushered in and escorted to the admiral. There was a brief exchange of words. Reed looked up.

"Gentlemen," he said. "I want to—" He caught himself. With a disarming little smile, he nodded to Birte. "And lady," he said. "I'm afraid we're not used to having ladies among us. Forgive me. But from now on—in the interest of expediency—it is perhaps best if you become . . . eh . . . 'one of the boys'!"

Birte smiled back at him. "That's fine with me, Admiral," she said. "It won't be the first time."

"Gentlemen," Reed repeated. "I want you to meet Herr Werner Dietrich. He just arrived by helicopter from Bremerhaven. Herr Dietrich served on a sister sub of the U-1000 during the war, the U-992, as a chief engineer. The U-992 surrendered at Narvik in Norway on 19 May 1945, and was subsequently scuttled in the North Atlantic. Herr Dietrich is thoroughly familiar with the configurations of the U-1000 and can be of immeasurable help to us."

Dietrich made a short, stiff bow. He all but clicked his heels.

Einar watched him. An ex-U-boat officer, he thought warily. Another Wierdring?

He was not charmed.

* * *

Birte was wide awake. The night before she'd been dead tired, but now, the events of the day aboard the *Coral Sea* made it impossible for her to sleep. She looked at her watch, barely visible in a thin ray of light that sliced into the dark, cramped little cabin from a crack in the door. Twelve minutes past five o'clock in the morning. Wednesday morning.

For a while she lay still, listening to the deep breathing of sleep of her husband in the bunk above her. She envied him his ability to sleep. Anywhere. Any time. She was aware of the soft hiss of the air conditioning and a myriad of faint noises coming from the vastness of the ship, all of them unidentifiable.

She had been overwhelmed by the size of the carrier, remembering with amusement how small it had looked from the air. The gigantic elevators at the edge of the flight deck that could whisk a couple of great aircraft from the flight deck to the hangar deck four decks below in seconds. Down there the planes were stored, parked in rows so tightly you could hardly get a hand between them. More planes, in addition to those that lined the flight deck above. The 04 level, they called it. With the hangar level being 01.

She'd never walked as much in her life. The passageways seemed endless. Every thirty feet or so, an iron partition, a bulkhead, was built across the passage, each with an oval opening with a foot-high threshold. She'd learned that the men called them kneeknockers. With good reason, she thought. Walking along the flatly lit passageways of the steel warren had become a curious kind of nautical dance routine: stride, stride-stride, stride-*step* . . . stride, stride-stride, stride-*step*. But the worst leg-killers were the stairways, ladders they were called. And they certainly were steep enough to live up to their name. And most of them with only an oily metal chain for a banister. The ache in her calf muscles attested to the number of ladders she'd climbed. Up and down.

And there'd been another painstaking debriefing. This time by Admiral Reed.

But it had all been worth it. She'd watched the British admiral arrive in a helicopter from his ship, which was one of the vessels she could see from the deck of the *Coral Sea*. And she'd watched the planes of the entire air wing take off. They were not needed, and Admiral Reed wanted no nonessential personnel in the area. They would head for an airfield on land. A bingo field, they called it. She had no idea why.

It had been an awesome sight. Hooked up to the steam-powered catapults at the bow of the flight deck, the planes were hurled into the sky, plumes of steam racing after them as they were slammed away by the giant-fisted force of the "cats" in two seconds of unbridled power, to soar on circles of fire; the jet blasts going to takeoff power rose to an ear-penetrating crescendo that knifed through even the rubber-and-foam bowls of the protectors they'd given her, which tightly cupped her ears. Above, a watchful helicopter circled throughout the whole operation, and behind, an escort destroyer dogged the carrier, both serving as safeguards against any mishaps. There hadn't been any. They told her that the width of the carrier was so great that you could place the whole destroyer on deck crosswise—and she'd barely reach from side to side. Some matchstick.

Only a few planes had remained on board. Birte'd been most charmed with watching the landing of a strange, twin-engined plane they called an E-2 Hawkeye; a turboprop aircraft with a huge, saucer-shaped structure riding on its back. It was actually a radar dome, and the plane was used to see to it that the sanctity of the search area wasn't violated. There were two of them in the air all the time. She'd watched one of them land, pulling the arresting wire taut and coming to a stop only a few feet from the end of the angle deck. With oddly clumsy grace, looking startlingly like a colossal exotic insect preening itself, she'd thought, the plane actually folded its long wings back along its gleaming white body and moved haughtily to a parking area to wait for its next tour of duty. She'd loved it.

She looked at her watch again. Five-sixteen. A watched watch always seems to have stopped.

A sudden knock on the door startled her. Before she could answer, she heard Einar's voice.

"Yes?"

"Sir!" a young voice called from the passageway outside. "The admiral's compliments. And would you and Mrs. Munk please get your gear together and come to the wardroom right away. I'll wait here for you."

Einar swung his legs over the edge of the bunk.

"Be with you in a minute," he called.

"There'll be coffee and Danish, sir."

"Thanks. Be right there."

The three civilian toxicologists and the two Chemical Warfare officers were already in the wardroom when Einar and Birte were shown in. They all looked toward them as they entered. On a table lay a pile of gas masks and chemical warfare survival gear.

One of the toxicologists, Dr. Hart, came up to them.

"Good morning, Professor Munk. Mrs. Munk," he said. "Do *you* know why we were summoned here so abruptly?"

"Good morning, Dr. Hart," Einar replied. "No, I've no idea."

Hart looked around the wardroom. "We're all here," he observed. "Except our German friend, Herr Dietrich."

"So I see."

"I wonder what's up."

"I'm sure we'll find out soon enough," Einar said.

Hart eyed the table with the gas masks.

"You . . . you don't suppose the poison has . . . eh . . . escaped?" he asked apprehensively.

"I doubt it," Einar said. "There'd have been a more urgent alarm."

"I suppose you're right."

"How about some coffee?" Birte asked her husband. "I'll get it for you."

"I'll join you," Einar said. He turned to the toxicologist. "Please excuse us."

They started toward the coffee urn when the door to the wardroom opened. Admiral Reed strode in, followed by his aide, Lieutenant Commander Nelson, and the German ex-U-boat officer, Werner Dietrich.

All eyes were riveted on Reed.

"Gentlemen," he said. "The U-1000 has been found!"

34

For a moment there was silence; then everyone spoke at once. Reed held up his hand.

"Gentlemen, please," he said soberly. "So far we have lucked out, but the main body of our mission is still ahead of us."

"Any information on the condition of the drums?" Dr. Erlanger asked, his voice tense.

"No," Reed answered. "That will not be known until our divers get down to the wreck. The first dive is scheduled for 0700 hours. Two diving crews are already undergoing compression in both DDCs." He looked around at the raptly listening people in the wardroom.

"Here is the situation," he continued briskly. "After a forty-three-hour seabed search of the high probability area by nine minesweepers using ocean-bottom-scanning sonar, or the British asdic, as well as side-scan sonar, one of the British sweepers located the sub. Numerous contacts were found, investigated, and eliminated. Contact #179 was the U-1000. She is lying at the edge of a hundred-fathom curve at 49° 09′ 27″ latitude, north, 12° 32′ 16″ longitude, west. The bottom is extremely rocky. Fathometer readings indicate the depth to be 652 feet. Mass identification indicates the sub is broken in two, the parts lying at a 120° angle to one another. Apparently the U-1000 hit a rock outcropping on the bottom, and the uncontrolled descent was rapid enough to produce an impact that broke her back.'' He nodded at the German ex-U-boat officer who stood, stony-faced, beside him. ''Herr Dietrich informs me that he is 90 percent certain the drums will be contained in the forward holds. There is no preliminary indication that there is any damage to these holds.''

He looked at his watch.

''As you know, the submarine rescue vessel, the USS *Cormorant*, ASR-23, joined the task force yesterday. She is now mooring over the diving site. I am transferring my flag to the *Cormorant* and request that you make yourselves ready to leave in fifteen minutes. 0600 hours. There will be an SH3 Sea King helicopter ready to take us over. Thank you.''

With his aide he strode from the wardroom.

The Chemical Warfare colonel, Colonel Pauley, walked over to the table with the gas masks.

''Please pick up a gas mask and protective gear before you leave,'' he said. ''From now on you will be required to carry them on your person at all times. Those of you who may not be familiar with their use, please see me or Lieutenant Colonel Bouvier.''

Einar and Birte walked over to the table. One of the toxicologists, Dr. Ramsey, was picking out a mask.

''Tell me, Doctor,'' Einar asked. ''Do you think those things will work? When we don't know what we're up against?''

Ramsey gave a wry little smile. ''Who knows?'' he shrugged. ''I think they'll work to the extent of setting people's minds at ease.''

Einar picked up a mask. He turned it over in his hands. As far as he was concerned, it was already a failure, according to Ramsey's theory. He fervently hoped he wouldn't have to test it any further.

The flight to the *Cormorant* took only a couple of minutes. Once again Birte had been fascinated by watching the SH3 Sea King getting ready for the trip, stretching out its five great rotor blades that had all been folded like complicated jackknives. A robotlike unraveling of a mechanical Gordian knot, she thought.

The *Cormorant* was moored with heavy hausers to four large cylindrical buoys, anchored by eight-thousand-pound bottom anchors. From the air, the salvage vessel and the precision four-point moor looked exactly like a pond skater, that long-legged insect that can scoot around on the surface of the water without falling through.

As the helicopter descended toward the helo pad over the fantail of the ship, she and Einar got a quick look at the submarine rescue vessel. She was a catamaran, much like two ships, joined together by a bridge and a massive, electrohydraulic crane gantry, with a well of open water between the twin hulls. Her mission being one of salvage and rescue, she bristled with special equipment and gear.

Six hundred and fifty feet directly below her lay another vessel whose mission was the exact opposite.

It would be a battle between the two, Einar thought, to see which one would prevail, a battle about to be joined . . .

Senior Chief Petty Officer Leroy Jackson's face was rigid with resentment. In fact, he was damned pissed off. The *Cormorant* was about to begin the most important mission of her existence—he wasn't quite sure what the hell it was all about, but he knew it was supposed to be all-fired important, a damned vital operation—and *he* was saddled with playing nursemaid to a bunch of civilians, including a broad, for God's sake. So they were VIPs, arrived from the *Coral Sea* only minutes before along with Admiral Reed. So what? The admiral was in conference with the skipper, and he, Senior Chief Petty Officer Leroy Jackson, was about to run off at the mouth with a lousy orientation briefing for a lousy pack of citizen dudes.

Standing before them on the main deck at a peeved parade rest, he began. "The mission of the USS *Cormorant*, ASR-23, and her crew of 196 officers and men," he intoned stiffly, "is to locate and rescue entrapped personnel in a sunken submarine and to recover equipment. The ship is equipped with a deep-diving system, the DDS MK 2 MOD 1, which has open-sea diving capabilities to depths in excess of 850 feet. The MK 2 MOD 1 is a double complex saturation diving system that maximizes effective diver work hours while eliminating the need to decompress between each working dive."

He paused. To his surprise, he could feel their interest in the way they watched him with silent attention. He mellowed.

"The system consists of two deck decompression chambers called DDCs," he continued less distantly, "built into the hull of the ship just below the deck we're standing on. Each is capable of completely supporting and providing living quarters for a six-man diver team during a fourteen-day diving operation, thereby eliminating the necessity for decompression between working dives, which in the case of a 650-foot dive would require seven days."

He cleverly chose that depth because he'd learned that this was the depth at which the present target lay. He pointed to two large, round diving chambers ringed on the outside with big cylindrical tanks marked Helium-Oxygen, each sitting on four massive jacks next to each other on the deck, one topped with a red, the other with a green open metal cap. Just like two colored wire cages over the corks on a couple of giant champagne bottles, Einar thought.

"On deck, above each of the DDCs is a personnel transport capsule called a PTC, mated through a transfer trunk to the DDC below," Jackson went on, warming to his task. "Each PTC can be released from the DDC and transported by that crane—" He pointed to the massive crane gantry that straddled the open water between the two hulls of the catamaran vessel. "—to the center well, where it can be lowered to the required depth. We like to think of it as a pressurized elevator," he added, in a feeble attempt at sounding jaunty. He debated with himself if he should explain the entire hookup procedure to them; the purpose of the stabilizer beam; the stainless steel SPC cable, two and a half inches in diameter through the center of which ran the power and communications cables; and the umbilical cable that carried the hoses with breathing gas, the hot water for heating, and the depth gauge conductors. He decided against it. No use tangling their civilian minds too hopelessly in mental hula hoops.

Instead he said simply, "Those red and green baskets on top of the PTCs are also the color codes of the divers—red divers and green divers. They stay on the crane when the capsule is lowered into the water."

He looked at his watch. 0654 hours.

"The first dive will get under way in six minutes. If you'll follow me, please, I'll take you to a place where you can watch in safety." And out of the damned way, he thought.

From the helo deck they watched several men working on the huge crane gantry that rested on heavy tracks on either side of the center well at the opposite end from the PTCs.

Senior Chief Petty Officer Jackson kept up his orientation lecture.

"Amidships, on each side, you will see two triangular booms," he intoned. "They are the DSRV—that's deep submergence rescue vehicle—the DSRV loading arms. They can be swung out over the water and are operated by deck-mounted winches. They will be used to retrieve any objects from the ocean bottom."

He paused. He was actually beginning to enjoy himself.

"Velocity and direction of currents below, bottom topography, and possible obstacles must all be assessed and taken into account prior to any dive," he recited importantly. "And weather is, of course, an important factor. In addition—"

"Excuse, please." It was Dietrich, the German ex-submariner. "I think we would all learn much more about the actual problem facing us if you would take us to a place where we can follow the entire operation, see and hear what is going on, *ja?* There must be some sort of . . . of control center, *ja?*"

"Of course there is, sir," Jackson said, tight-lipped. "But during a dive, unauthorized personnel are not—"

"Young man," Dietrich interrupted him. He drew himself up. "We are all here for a very specific purpose, *ja?*" His guttural, Teutonic accent obviously grated on Jackson's ears. "We can be of no value by being kept uninformed, *ja?* Now, please be good enough to take us to whatever control center will give us a complete picture of what is going on, *ja?*"

"Sir, I have no authority to—"

"Then, young man, I suggest you contact someone who has, *ja?*"

For a brief moment Jackson glared at the German. I knew it, he thought. Foreign bastard. Nothing but stinking trouble. The whole damned bunch.

"Aye, aye, sir," he said stiffly.

He stalked to a nearby telephone on the wall of a small housing on the deck. For a while he talked and listened. Then he returned to the group.

"Follow me," he said, obviously filled with resentment. "I have orders to take you to the Main Control Console number one below."

The President stirred.

"Yes?" he murmured groggily. "What is it?"

"I'm sorry to wake you, sir," the White House chief of staff said. "But you wanted to be informed as soon as there was word from Point G."

The President sat up in his bed, immediately alert.

"What is it?"

"The U-1000 has been found. The first dive is under way. Admiral Peck is waiting in the sitting room."

"Excellent. What time is it?"

"Two-nineteen in the morning. Seven-nineteen at Point G."

The President was out of bed, struggling into a robe. He walked to the door to the sitting room and entered. Admiral Paul A. Peck, chairman of the Joint Chiefs of Staff, rose from a chair as he came in.

"Good morning, Mr. President," he said.

"Seems too damned early to say good morning," the President grinned. "But I suppose it is. What's the story, Paul?"

"The sub has been located."

"What about the drums? And the poison gas?"

"We have no information about that, yet. The first dive was scheduled for 0700, their time."

"When did they find the U-1000?"

"At 0200, their time. A British sweeper located her."

"0200? Five hours ago? Why was I not notified earlier?"

"Ben Reed notified SACLANT, Mr. President. As soon as he had verified the contact, Brannigan called me."

The President frowned. "Reed to Brannigan to Peck to me. Not good enough, Paul. I don't like the delays." He looked up. "I want you to assign a man to Operation Giant. To Point G. He is to report directly to the White House. To me. I want to be on top of this thing all the way."

"Will do, sir."

"Any recommendation?"

Peck thought for a while. "Yes, sir," he said. "Colonel Jonathan Henderson. Assistant chief of staff, intelligence. Chief of the Counter Intelligence Directorate."

The President smiled.

"An *army* man, Admiral?"

"Yes, sir," Peck replied. "Henderson has been in on everything since the word go. Already knows as much about the situation as anybody. There'd be no need to take the time to deep brief anyone else." He frowned. "Of course, it could create chain-of-command problems. But I think I can get around that. Henderson can join the task force as a civilian representative of CID. That way, there will be no breach of protocol. And Henderson's status would not be dependent on rank. He will simply be Mr. Henderson."

"Excellent. I'm sure the colonel will go along with that. How soon can you have him at Point G?"

"Within seven hours, Mr. President."

"Done!"

On their way down to the Main Control Console #1 located amidships, Einar was curious at the fact that Dietrich kept up an animated stream of questions directed at the senior chief petty officer about everything they saw on their way. Einar was puzzled. Was the German—realizing that he had humiliated the young man—trying to restore some of the dignity the man had lost by making him appear knowledgeable? Or was he genuinely interested?

They passed the SPC winchroom and the two DDCs. As they walked by a small compartment, where a man sat in front of a console that displayed a bewildering array of dials and meters, gauges and lights, switches and scales, Dietrich asked, "And what is that instrument panel, Chief?"

"That's the mixmaker, sir."

"Mixmaker?" Birte asked, the word conjuring up a kitchen appliance. "What's that?"

"It's where the mixing of the gas the divers breathe is being controlled, ma'am," Jackson answered her. "The divers don't breathe just ordinary air on a dive. They breathe a mixture of helium and oxygen. The EN1(DV)—that's engineman first class, diver, ma'am, we call him the Gas King—he dials the correct mix of gas for the depth the divers are at. At 650 feet they'd breathe 95 percent helium and 5 percent oxygen."

"That little oxygen?"

"Yes, ma'am. Oxygen becomes toxic at great depths. Green gas, that's too much oxygen, it can be real bad. You get tunnel vision. Nausea. Tremors and seizures, ma'am. It can even kill you."

The man at the console pushed an intercom button.

"Control. Gas King," he said. "I have an oxygen analyzer go."

"Okay, Hank. Stay with it," a voice came over a speaker.

"That was the dive supervisor," Jackson said. "He's at the Main Control Console."

The Main Control Console was really a room, dominated by instrument panels and scopes and screens. Two closed-circuit television screens glowed busily on the right. Several men were reading meters and checking scopes. The dive supervisor—a BMC(DV), boatswain's mate chief, diver—was stationed near the intercom. There was a steady stream of communication between the control center and the various stations involved in the dive.

"Control. Capsule," the speaker squawked. "Divers are in PTC."

"Capsule. Control," the dive supervisor acknowledged. "Understand." He checked a couple of dials. "Shut and dog the hatch."

"Control. Capsule. Hatch is shut and dogged."

"MCC. Control. Open TT-7 slowly. Check for seal."

"Control. MCC. We have a seal."

"MCC. Control. Vent the trunk."

"Control. MCC. Transfer trunks on the surface."

"Topside. Control. Commence operating procedure six."

"Topside, aye."

Suddenly the raucous shriek of a Klaxon alarm knifed through the buzz of activity in the room, assaulting their ears. A bright red warning light began to blink insistently.

The dive supervisor instantly pushed a button. "Emergency!" he shouted at the intercom. "All personnel, emergency stations! This is no drill! Emergency! Emergency!"

35

The activity at the console was suddenly tense and urgent. It was evidenced in the men's voices, although their actions remained controlled and contained.

"Control. Gas King," the speaker squawked. "I have a high PO-2 mixmaker shutdown."

"Gas King. Control. Check it out. Get back to me." The dive supervisor grabbed a phone. "Dive Officer!" he called.

"What the hell is happening?" Einar asked Jackson.

"The breathing gas has been contaminated," the chief answered him. "A dangerous increase in oxygen percentage, I'll bet my ass."

"What'll happen?"

"They'll have to abort the damned dive."

"Then what?"

"Shit, man!" In his excitement Jackson forgot his forced decorum with the VIPs. "They've got to dump the whole stinking mix in the volume tank. And analyze all the other tanks for oxygen percentage. It'll mean the dive will be delayed for at least three hours."

"How?" Einar asked. "How could that happen so—all of a sudden?"

Jackson looked at him.

"Hell, it's only a turn of a damned dial on the mixmaker panel. Shouldn't happen. But it damned well did."

Einar felt a sudden chill. The turn of a dial. By anyone passing by the mixmaker. Anyone.

Like—Dietrich.

Out of the corner of his eye, he looked at the German. And at the three scientists, all tensely watching the activity at the console.

Or—for that matter—any one of *them*, Einar thought bleakly.

Did the glitch happen accidentally? Or did the malignancy of *Korvettenkapitän* Günther Wierdring reach even to the USS *Cormorant?*

Einar and Birte were standing aft on the fantail helo deck, leaning on the railing. It was 0849 hours, Wednesday, May 22. Almost twelve days had gone by since the two CIC officers had come to their door on West 119th Street in New York. Time was running out, Einar though bleakly, and the first dive would not be ready to get under way for another two hours.

He stared out over the calm, black-blue expanse of the ocean. The young morning sun was reflected in the wavelets in a shimmer of pale gold, and it was a scene of beauty and serenity. But he knew that at any moment the placid surface of the water might roil and churn with an alien liquid rising from the deep to turn into a poisonous, uncontainable cloud of death. Involuntarily he shivered.

Birte placed her hand on his arm.

"You don't think that . . . that mishap was accidental either, do you?" she said quietly.

He looked soberly at her.

"No, I don't," he said. "But I also know that it *could* have been." For a moment he was thoughtfully silent. "But, dammit! You're right. My gut feeling keeps growling that it was a deliberate attempt to delay the operation. Or worse." He frowned. "Just a turn of a damned dial, the chief said. Any one of us trooping through the mixmaker compartment could have done it. With no one noticing. You—or I; any one of those three toxicologists, or that German ex-submariner. But why, dammit?" He pounded the railing. "Why?"

He turned away from the sea.

"What earthly reason could any of *them* have to . . . to sabotage the operation? Perhaps . . . perhaps I'm just being paranoid."

"Well, you know what they say," Birte smiled at him. "Even if you *are* paranoid, it doesn't mean they're not out to get you!"

He grinned at her.

"Big with the clichés, aren't you?" he commented.

"Only when it so happens that they might be true," she countered.

A man came walking toward them across the deck, his collar up against the breeze. It was one of the toxicologists, Dr. Steven Erlanger. They'd learned he was from California. UCLA. His accent sounded a little strange to their New York ears.

"Mr. Munk," the man said. He nodded to Birte. "Mrs. Munk. I wonder if I could have a word with you? Ask you a few questions?"

"Of course, Dr. Erlanger," Einar said. "Fire away."

"I understand that you have firsthand knowledge of the effects of the toxin down there." He looked out over the water. "I wonder if you would describe to me, in detail, what you know."

"What we were told," Einar said. "We never actually saw any of the victims."

"What you were told, then, please."

For a moment Einar contemplated the scientist. Then he told him. In detail.

Erlanger nodded gravely. "I agree with you," he said. "It does sound like some kind of nerve gas—with the effects of an exsiccator."

"Let me pick your brain for a moment, Doctor," Einar said. "Could such a poison have been developed? In 1945? And could it be as powerful and deadly as claimed?"

Erlanger nodded slowly. "Yes. On both counts," he said. "It is not at all inconceivable."

"Could you elaborate?"

"Certainly. The effects of a toxin depend on dosage, or in the case of a gas, concentration; and in the present situation, certainly persistence.

"The mobility of a toxic gas cloud in World War I, under favorable circumstances, might be more than twenty-five times as large as the area of release. Thus—if the gas was exploded over a ten-mile area, for instance, it could expand to 250 miles. That was sixty-five years ago, mind you. There is no telling what the Germans were able to perfect forty years ago. Perhaps a mobility ten times that. Enough to blanket the British Isles, before being diffused to noneffectiveness. The annihilation of life might not be as total as they wanted to believe, but many millions most certainly would die.

"As for concentration, the lethal laboratory dose of, for example, palytoxin, a poison derived from a plant that grows on coral, is a mere 0.00015 milligram per kilogram. The death rate resulting from the release of the U-1000 poison cloud could well be enormous, since lifesaving treatment depends primarily on knowing what kind of toxin is to be overcome, which—in this case—we still do not know. And treatment cannot be generalized. What might be effective in the treatment of one case of poisoning, might kill in another."

"You are not painting a very comforting picture, Dr. Erlanger," Birte said.

"I did not mean to, Mrs. Munk," the toxicologist said quietly.

"What you *are* saying," Einar observed, "is that if any of the V-3 poison does escape, there's nothing anyone can do to keep it from killing."

Erlanger looked directly at him.

"That, Mr. Munk, is exactly what I am saying," he nodded.

"Control. Topside. I have a release. Capsule dangling on the string."

Einar and Birte were standing in back of the Main Control Console area. The dive was getting under way. Finally. Einar by now knew that "dangling on the string" meant that the personnel transfer capsule with the divers was suspended on the strength, power, and communications cable over the center well, ready to be lowered into the deep. The descent to the bottom, 652 feet below, would take one hour.

"Topside. Control. Stand easy on station. Winch, stand by to lower away."

"Winch. Ready to lower away," the speaker rasped.

"Winch. Control. Lower away. Give me depth every twenty feet."

"Winch, aye."

Senior Chief Petty Officer Jackson came up to Einar and Birte.

"Sir," he said to Einar. "The admiral's compliments, and would you please report to the stateroom in one hour? 1130. You and your wife, please."

"Aye, aye," Einar said. "We'll be there."

There were five other officers in the stateroom with Admiral Reed: his aide, Lieutenant Commander Barney Nelson; the skipper of the *Cormorant*, Commander Frank Cannon; the British Rear Admiral, Everett Stirling; the dive officer, Lieutenant Pete Avellino; and the salvage master, Lieutenant Commander Patrick Dedham.

Reed introduced Einar and Birte around.

"Major Munk, Mrs. Munk," he said. "I want you to know how grateful we all are for your unstinting cooperation. What you have accomplished has been of immeasurable value."

"I only hope we are in time," Einar said.

"So do we, Major. So do we." Reed walked up to them. "I asked you here, first of all, to thank you and second to say farewell to you. We—"

"I beg your pardon?" Einar interrupted.

"Within the hour, before the actual salvage operation becomes operative, you will be taken by Sea King to the *Coral Sea*. From there you will be airlifted to Brawdy and then on to the States."

"Why?" Einar asked. "I thought you requested our presence here?"

"I did," Reed said solemnly. "I wanted to talk with you in person. And I felt that if there was even the slightest chance you would be able to contribute to the operation, it was something we could not afford to overlook."

"What has changed?"

"The retrieval of the drums from here on is strictly a navy salvage operation," Reed said. He nodded toward Commander Cannon. "The skipper of the *Cormorant* feels his crew can handle that aspect of the mission adequately. I agree. All unnecessary personnel have been, or will be, evacuated from the danger area. For obvious safety reasons. Already most of the ships of TF-49 have left. All the sweepers and tenders. Commander Cannon feels he cannot take the responsibility of having civilians on board, unless they are absolutely essential to the operation, as are the toxicologists."

"Sir," Einar said. "We will take responsibility for ourselves. We have been in on this crisis from the beginning. Please allow us to see it brought to a finish."

"The decision is Commander Cannon's to make," Reed said. "He is in command of this vessel."

Einar turned to Cannon.

"Commander," he said earnestly. "Allow us to remain. On our own responsibility. There may still be something we can contribute."

"Major Munk," the commander said soberly. "I understand your desire to see this thing through. But since the—"

Lieutenant Commander Nelson, holding a telephone in his hand, interrupted.

"Admiral. The divers are reporting, sir. The marker buoy has been deployed. The tag line tie-off to the buoy line has been completed; the PTC is stabilized. The divers have entered the wreck. They have the drums in sight."

All eyes were at once upon him.

"Where are they located?"

"In the forward holds."

"Put it on the PA," Reed ordered.

Nelson flipped a switch.

"—in rows securely lashed to deck anchors," the speaker squeaked, the voice curiously high, the speech unusually deliberate. Puzzled, Birte glanced at Einar.

"The helium in the breathing gas," he whispered to her. "Makes your voice sound funny."

"That's quite right," said Lieutenant Avellino, who stood next to them. "The helium environment in which the divers work makes it necessary that all speech is very distinct and slow. It is transmitted through a special electronic unscrambler."

"Thank you," Birte whispered.

"Describe the drums." It was the voice over the speaker.

"They are unusually big," the answer came tinnily. "Estimate forty inches high, thirty inches diameter. Two stabilizer bands run around the circumference. Two more lengthwise. Never seen that before. They are painted red. The bands, that is."

"What is the condition?"

"Stand by."

There was a pause. No one in the stateroom spoke. The very air was tense. Then—

"They look badly corroded. Crusted. I will try to move one of them."

"Easy!"

Again a pause, as the divers below loosened the tie-downs of a drum. Then—

"I will not try, repeat *not* try," the speaker squeaked in its high-pitched voice. "Those damned drums are ready to come apart. Very badly deteriorated. We will never be able to manhandle them without cracking them apart. No way."

"Understand. Stand by . . . Topside. PTC. Standing by for orders."

"PTC. Control. Understand."

The dive officer, Lieutenant Avellino, turned to the salvage master. "What the hell do we do now, Pat? If those damned drums are that brittle, how *do* we handle them—without rupturing them?"

Dedham frowned with worry. "There's got to be a way," he said uncertainly.

"Ziploc," Birte said quietly.

They stared at her.

"What?" asked the salvage master.

"Ziploc," Birte repeated. "You know. Those little plastic bags for leftovers that can be sealed. If you had anything like that, big enough, you could slip them over the drums, and it wouldn't matter if they leaked a little. I bet that—"

"Please, Mrs. Munk," the dive officer interrupted. "Not now. We—"

"Hold it, Pete," the salvage master broke in quickly. "She may have something. Principle is right. Would work. What kind of . . . of bags do we have available that could do the job? Or that we could get? Any kind of covers? Airtight? Storage bags?" He looked around.

"Balloons!" Pete burst out.

"Balloons?"

"Weather balloons!"

Salvage Master Dedham at once turned to Admiral Reed. "Sir," he said urgently. "Who's the senior meteorologist on the *Coral Sea?*"

"Craig," Reed answered at once. "Commander Ernie Craig." He spun around to face his aide. "Ray!" he snapped. "Get Craig over here. Now!"

"Aye, aye, sir!" Nelson hurried from the room.

Reed turned to the *Cormorant* skipper. "Frank," he said. "I suggest we set up a special command center. Right here. Round-robin communications. A TV monitor. I suggest representatives of the civilian specialists be present here during crucial steps of the salvage operation, including the toxicologists."

"I agree, sir," Cannon said. "I'll get it done immediately."

There was suddenly no talk of shipping Einar and Birte out.

* * *

It was less than fifteen minutes later when Commander Ernest Craig entered the room with Lieutenant Commander Nelson. Reed at once motioned them over to where he stood with Avellino and Dedham.

"Lieutenant," he said without any preamble, knowing his aide would have briefed the meteorologist. "How many weather balloons do we have on the *Coral Sea?*"

Craig looked startled, but he answered at once.

"Several hundred, sir. I don't know the exact number."

"How big are they?"

"Out of the box, sir, five to six feet long. They expand to about thirty feet aloft."

Reed turned to the salvage master. "Will they do, Commander? Explain to the lieutenant what we have in mind."

Crisply, concisely, Dedham filled the meteorologist in. The command center communications system was nearly completely installed, and Nelson joined the group. Craig looked dubious, as Dedham finished his summary.

"The balloons would be big enough to fit around a drum that size," he said, "and long enough to gather and double up at the end so they can be tightly sealed. We'll be using them in their uninflated state; they'll be airtight. But—it's a matter of strength."

"What do you mean?" Dedham asked sharply.

"They're pretty delicate, Commander," Craig explained. "Even if they do expand. Any sharp or rough object might easily tear them. And from what you have told me, those drums have a pretty abrasive surface."

"How are you planning on bringing up the drums, Pat?" Commander Cannon asked.

"Cargo netting."

"I doubt if the balloons would survive the ascent intact," Craig said.

"Damn!" the salvage master swore. "Damned balloons! Shot down before we can even deploy them."

"They don't make weather balloons out of cast iron," Craig said testily.

"Then—why not use cast-iron balloons?" Nelson said quietly.

They all stared at him.

"Containers," he explained. "Aircraft jet engine shipping containers. For replacement engines. They're made of metal. They're reinforced. They can be pressurized with nitrogen to prevent corrosion, so they'd be airtight. And they're big enough. Probably hold five or six drums at a time. And they're already fitted with crane points."

"How big?" Dedham shot at him.

"Two sizes. One twelve feet long, one fifteen. Both with a six-foot diameter."

"How many have we on board the *Coral Sea?*" Reed asked.

"At least thirty of the smaller ones. Maybe ten of the larger. It would be a start, sir. We can get more flown out from Holylock." He looked at the admiral. "Of course, most of them are not empty."

"Empty them!" Reed snapped. "Take the engines out and remove the inside mounts. Get on it, Ray. Right now!"

"Aye, aye, sir."

"Have the first half dozen flown over here at once. If the Sea Kings can't handle it, try the Ch-53E Super Stallions." He thought for a moment. "Those containers will weigh tons coming up loaded," he mused, "filled with water. If worst comes to worst, we'll have to borrow a few Sikorsky S-64 Sky Cranes from the army. Those babies can lift the Brooklyn Bridge. See what you can arrange on standby."

"Aye, aye, sir."

Nelson hurried off.

Reed turned to Cannon.

"Can you handle those containers?" he asked.

"We can handle them okay," the commander answered. "Storing them is another matter."

"There is an amphibious transport dock of the Raleigh class on the way from Plymouth," Reed said. "I ordered her to proceed to Point Golf. She will join us in a few hours. That should take care of any storage problem."

"It will."

"Would another ASR be of any help, Frank?"

"No, sir. We'd get in each other's way. It's bound to be pretty damned cramped down there. We're capable of working around the clock. Two shifts."

"I'd like those weather balloons flown over as quickly as possible, Lieutenant," the salvage master said to Craig. He turned to Cannon. "I want to get them down to the divers as soon as I can. I propose to use both the balloons and the containers. That way we'll provide protection both ways. While loading and transporting to the surface."

"Agreed," Cannon said.

It was 1434 hours when the weather balloons reached the U-1000 diving site. In the command center aboard the *Cormorant,* 650 feet above, the assembled officers and specialists followed the communication between the divers, trying to get a balloon around the first drum, and the capsule operator in the PTC, their voices high and tinny over the speaker, the pictures on the two monitor screens transmitted by the TV cameras mounted on the helmets of the divers, murky and unsteady.

"Have you reached the holds?"

"Affirmative."

"Can you see the drums?"

"Affirmative. There they are!"

The camera jerked, moved forward, and steadied. In the beam from the hand-held work light could be seen several large drums, standing upright, packed tightly together, their red stabilizer bands barely standing out on the crusted, corroded surfaces.

Einar stared at the screens. A rush of icy cold surged through him.

There they were. The drums. The "brown sugar," capable of annihilating a nation. Adolf Hitler's V-3 . . .

He felt Birte's hand tighten on his arm. They were seeing the enemy. For the first time.

The pictures on the monitors moved, grew fuzzy as the divers bent over the drums to examine them.

"Go easy."

"You better believe it."

"Tie-downs all freed on drum number one."

"Understand."

"Get on the other side, Fred . . . Hold it! . . . Go easy . . ."

"Try getting behind."

"No way."

"Red Diver, Capsule. You need any help?"

"Hell, no, Capsule. There's barely enough room for the two of us to work."

"Understand."

For a while there was silence, both from the speaker and the listeners in the command center. The pictures on the monitor screens became blurry and moved dizzily as the divers strained to move the freed drum. Then—

"Capsule. Red Diver. There's no fucking way anyone is going to move those drums!" Even over the speaker, the man's voice sounded frustrated and angry. "No way!"

"Red Diver. Capsule. What do you mean? What is wrong?"

"What is wrong? The damned drum weighs a damned ton! We can hardly budge it. There is no way to get any equipment in here, and any attempt to haul the damned things out with a cable would tear them apart long before any damned balloon can be tucked around it! Those drums are there to stay till they rot—unless you can get Superman himself down here!"

36

The men sat in stunned silence, staring at the television monitors, each haunted by his own desolate thoughts and the grim realization that the decomposing drums, ready to rupture, were too heavy to be manhandled by the divers, much less be wrested from their watery coffin, and too fragile to withstand the stress of mechanical means. They were buried in the metal bowels of the U-1000 until they disintegrated. Those were the chilling facts.

The lethal poison contained in them, Adolf Hitler's V-3, would carry out his final, abominable deed of vengeance.

And no one could stop it.

Admiral Reed was the first to speak.

"Alternatives," he said resolutely. "If we cannot get the drums safely out of the sub and up to the surface, what are our alternatives?"

"Do we have any?" Lieutenant Avellino asked.

"There are always alternatives," Reed snapped.

"If . . . if we can't get the drums out because the space is too cramped the way the sub is lying," the salvage master said tentatively, "could we . . . could we provide better access? More room for the divers to work more efficiently? As many as two or three to a drum? Cut through to the holds?"

Reed looked at the German ex-submariner. "Herr Dietrich?" he said.

The German slowly shook his head. "You would have to cut through the hull of the sub herself, the way she lies. And then the interior bulkheads. It . . . it might be done, but it would take a very long time."

"Which we do not have," Reed snapped. "Any other suggestions?"

"If we could get just one drum safely to the surface," Colonel Pauley from Chemical Warfare ventured, "perhaps the poisonous agent could be analyzed, and possible measures against it devised."

Reed looked to the three toxicologists.

"Gentlemen?"

The three scientists glanced at one another. Dr. Ramsey coughed self-consciously. "There is no . . . no definite answer to that question, Colonel," he said. "Under normal circumstances, it would take a long time to analyze the substance, and even longer to come up with a possible antidote or neutralizer, to say nothing of implementation. And Admiral Reed has pointed out that we have virtually no time. I am afraid the rest of the drums left in the submarine would deteriorate to the point of rupturing long before we could arrive at any answers." He looked to his colleagues for confirmation. Dr. Erlanger nodded.

"I agree," said Dr. Hart. "And at two hundred and fifty kilograms of crystals per drum, the toxic agent in liquid form would make an ocean of its own. We cannot let that happen."

"We might be able to seal off the holds with the drums," Commander Cannon suggested. "Plug the break and all possible leaks. Contain the poison in the wreck."

"Rather like sweeping your dirt under the carpet, I'm afraid," the British admiral objected. "It would merely postpone the inevitable, would it not?"

"Admiral Stirling is right," Reed said. "We have to deal with the problem here. And now."

"It would buy us some time," Cannon argued. "Better than nothing."

"Granted. But not good enough."

Einar had been listening to the various suggestions. An idea was forming in his mind. Something he remembered reading about in a journal at Columbia. Years ago.

"Admiral," he said. "May I make a suggestion?"

"Of course."

"The diver said Superman himself would be needed to move those drums. And I remember—it *is* possible to make a man into a Superman. I—"

"Major Munk. We—"

"Please, Admiral, hear me out," Einar pleaded. "I'm talking about the Man-Amplifier." No one reacted. "Twenty years ago?"

The men stared at him with expressions that ranged from puzzlement to exasperation.

"Man-Amplifier?" Reed asked.

"Yes, sir. It was a project, a research project, carried out at the Cornell Aeronautical Laboratory in Buffalo, New York. In the early 1960s. The Office of Naval Research was involved."

"I think we should get back to the problem at hand," Lieutenant Avellino said caustically. "A twenty-year-old research project doesn't seem relevant."

"If you'll let me finish, Lieutenant," Einar bristled. "You might just—"

"Please, Major. I think the salvage operation is best left to—"

"Lieutenant," Reed broke in. "Let Major Munk continue. After he has finished, you can voice your objections. If any. But I do seem to remember something along the lines Major Munk is talking about." He nodded at Einar. "Major."

"It was a sort of elaborate steel harness," Einar went on. "The operator was strapped into it. They called it an exoskeleton, I think, and it really was like a skeleton worn on the outside. Like a full-body brace. It had sensor instruments that could detect any muscular exertion by the operator, and there were small, powerful, electrically driven booster engines located at his joints that would amplify his efforts."

He paused. He looked around at the men. They were listening attentively.

"For instance," he went on, "if the man flexed his knees and elbows to lift a heavy object, the Man-Amplifier would detect the effort and would automatically activate its own power to do the job. That way, heavy loads could be handled that otherwise might snap a man's bones."

"Where did the power come from?" Reed asked.

"The power supply was supposed to be worn as a backpack. I guess it could also be fed through a power cable."

"I remember it," the salvage master broke in. "When I was at the Naval Ocean Systems Center in Panama City in Florida. The Naval Experimental Diving Unit was working on a couple of contraptions like that. We called it the Iron Midwife because it made labor so easy. They were trying to marinize them. Waterproof them. Like underwater cameras. They were looking for some sort of gizmo that could perform in tight and inaccessible working situations during special salvage operations. Where machinery couldn't be used."

He turned to Admiral Reed.

"Sir," he said. "Major Munk really has something there. Those . . . eh . . . Man-Amplifiers could give a man the strength of ten. Make it possible for him to lift twelve, fifteen hundred pounds! That's pretty damned close to being Superman!"

"Were they successful in marinizing them?" Reed asked.

"I don't know, sir. I think there were only about half a dozen prototypes built." He frowned. "I don't know if they even still exist. All I know is, they're not part of any standard diving equipment in the navy."

Reed turned to the dive officer. "Lieutenant?" he said.

"Sir. If those . . . amplifiers are as described, they're just what we need," Avellino said. He grinned at Einar. "Right on!" he said.

Reed turned to his aide. "Ray," he said. "Contact SACLANT. Make an urgent request that they look into the status of the Man-Amplifier project."

"Aye, aye, sir."

"If they locate any of the devices, I want them flown here at once. Along with an expert in their use. And request that they advise me as soon as they know."

★ ★ ★

It was twenty-seven minutes later when Nelson reported back to the admiral. Satellite communication and computerized records had done the job.

SACLANT had located three experimental models of the Man-Amplifier, marinized at the Naval Ocean Systems Center, and one more at the Naval Air Test Facility at Johnsville, Pennsylvania. They were all on their way to Point Golf—ETA 2030 hours. And along with the MAMs would come one senior chief petty officer, Stanislaus Kowalski, Retired, who had worked on the exoskeletons at Panama City.

"Gentlemen," Admiral Reed said. "I suggest you get some rest. When the Man-Amplifiers arrive, we will be working nonstop until the job is finished. You will have to grab whatever sleep you can, whenever you can. You will all be on twenty-four-hour duty. Any questions?"

There were none.

"And I suggest you all give some further thought to other means of retrieving the drums safely. Let us be certain to have a viable alternative to the Man-Amplifier."

The men nodded.

"I want to use some of the time below," the salvage master said, "to clear away any obstacles that may hinder the retrieval of the drums from the wreck."

Reed nodded.

"After that, I'll bring the men up," the salvage master continued, "so they can get some rest. The Iron Mid . . . eh . . . the Man-Amplifiers should be here by then."

He started to leave, when something he heard on the TV monitor stopped him cold.

"—Watch it! Fred! Watch that sharp edge behind you. You are—"

There was a choked gasp, tinny and raspy over the speaker. Then—a strained voice:

"Shit!—Capsule. Red Diver. My suit is ripped!"

37

Salvage Master Dedham and Dive Officer Avellino at once hurried from the room. The others stood staring in frozen tension at the monitor and the molasses movements of the shadowy figures struggling across them.

"Green Diver. Capsule. Assist Red Diver back to capsule. Move, Bob!" Even over the speaker, the voice sounded taut and urgent.

"Green Diver. Understand . . . On my way, Fred. How bad is it?"

"I . . . I don't know. I'm trying to hold it."

"Hang in there."

"Man—that damned water is cold . . ."

"Capsule. Topside." It was the main deck supervisor. "Inform when both divers return and condition."

"Capsule. Understand."

"Capsule. Topside. We'll have medical supplies in the ML."

"Capsule. Understand."

"Capsule. Topside. Let me know when you are ready to leave bottom."

"Capsule. Understand."

For a while the monitor speakers were silent. The divers below were not wasting their energy speaking. Topside did not interfere. No one in the command center moved. Then—after what to Einar and Birte seemed an eternity—the monitor sputtered to life.

"Topside. Capsule. All divers in capsule. Red Diver suffers from exposure. No major injuries."

"Capsule. Topside. Understand. We'll get you up as quickly as possible."

The men in the command center drew a collective sigh of relief. They all knew that even the smallest mishap that far down could easily prove fatal.

There was a short, shrill ring on one of the newly installed telephones. Lieutenant Commander Nelson answered it. He listened. He turned to Commander Cannon.

"Commander," he said. "Mr. Henderson, the White House liaison representative, has arrived on the *Coral Sea.* He requests permission to come aboard."

"Permission granted," Cannon grumbled.

That's all I need, he thought peevishly. A busybody civilian poking his uneducated nose into a complicated dive already beset with glitches. . . .

It was 2043 hours when the crated Man-Amplifiers aboard a Sea King settled down out of the darkness on the helo deck of the *Cormorant.* And with them a bear of a man in his late forties, sporting a soiled old navy pea coat that definitely had seen better days.

"Kowalski, ma'am," he boomed when he shook Birte's hand in his ham-size fist. "Owner, operator, and chief bottlewasher of Kowalski's Kar Klinic, corner of Kenmore and Cornell, Fredericksburg, Virginia." Somehow the man exuded confidence and strength.

When Henderson had arrived a few hours before, Einar had felt as if he were welcoming an old friend when he greeted the officer—until he'd remembered how he'd cursed the man's supercilious obtuseness on too many prior occasions. He fervently hoped the colonel's presence aboard the *Cormorant* would not in any way make an already critical operation more critical. The man had already shot off his first hot flash to the White House. God only knew what he'd reported—after finding out that the operation already had suffered two mishaps during the first dive.

He'd debated with himself if he should share his suspicions of possible sabotage with the officer—but recalling past run-ins with the man, he'd decided against it. Besides, he had little to go on. But something was nagging him. Something he'd missed? What? He couldn't pin it down. It bothered him.

The marinized Man-Amplifier was actually a modified regulation diving suit equipped with fittings to receive the standard Mark 1 Mod S diving helmet with its built-in communications capabilities. The neoprene rubber suit completely covered the diver and the exoskeleton in which he was encased. There was no power backpack. Power would be supplied through a 150-foot-long special power cable, the exact length of the diver's umbilical to which it would be bonded. As in the regular diving system, the umbilical consisted of the diver's gas hose, which fed him his breathing gas; the hot water hose, which delivered hot water to the heating tubes in the suit and warmed the breathing gas; and the strength member, a sturdy nylon rope, all bonded together every eighteen inches. A miniature SPC.

The three marinized devices were introduced into the DDCs through the outer locks, but since none of the divers were familiar with the Man-Amplifiers, a display area had been rigged from which Kowalski's demonstrations and instructions—using the fourth, nonmarinized device—could be fed to the divers via closed circuit television.

Fascinated, Einar and Birte watched the big man begin to strap himself into the complicated-looking device, clearly showing each step.

"It's simple," he boomed at the TV camera. "So simple a child of five can do it." He peered directly into the camera lens. "Anyone that age in there?" he asked. He grinned hugely. "Guess not." He shrugged elaborately. "Well—you'll have to do the best you can!"

Step by step he guided the divers through the intricate procedure of donning the device.

Looking like a bear trapped in an erector set, Kowalski stood before the camera, steel-soled feet firmly planted on the deck.

"Demonstration time," he boomed. "A little taste of what you'll be able to do. Give your self-confidence a boost."

He motioned off screen.

"Okay," he called. "Bring her in!"

A seaman pulled a small yellow cargo trailer onto the set, part of the ship's yellow gear. Kowalski patted it affectionately.

"That's a twelve-hundred-pound baby," he said. "Just my size."

The seaman started to leave.

"Where're you going, sailor?" Kowalski asked.

"I thought—"

"Stay," Kowalski said. He pointed at the trailer. "Climb in. Don't want to be here all by my lonesome."

Bewildered, the seaman climbed up onto the cargo bed. Kowalski bent his knees and put his arms around the steel, rubber-wheeled trailer. With his exoskeleton-encased hands, he took a firm grip on it.

Slowly, seemingly without effort he straightened up—and lifted the trailer, sailor and all, clear off the floor.

He put it down. He turned to the camera and winked broadly. "Nothing to it!" he boomed.

"He makes it look as easy as falling off a piece of cake," Birte muttered, mangling her metaphors again.

Mouth open and eyes wide, the seaman dismounted from the trailer and pushed it off.

Kowalski had the divers in the DDCs remove the exoskeletons, again following his lead. And put them back on again.

"All set?" He boomed the question at the camera. "You guys ready to go without screwing up?"

Via the control console he was assured the divers were ready.

He held up a big, grease-mottled thumb toward the camera lens.

"Hop to it!" he boomed heartily. "And don't go clog no engines!"

One hour and thirteen minutes later, at 2353 hours, seven minutes short of a new day, the fourteenth since the death of ex-*Stabsobermachinist* Karl Johann Thompson, the first team of divers engirded in MAMs reached the poison drums in the wreck of the U-1000.

It was, of course, impossible for Einar and Birte to heed Admiral Reed's admonition to get as much sleep as possible. Too much was happening; the culmination of two grueling weeks. The salvage operation of the V-3 poison drums was finally under way.

The LPD, a sleek, shiny vessel over five hundred feet long, had joined the task force hours before and lay moored close to the *Cormorant*, bathed in work lights. The first aircraft jet engine shipping containers had been ferried by helicopter from the *Coral Sea* to the deck of the ASR, and the first one had been lowered to the bottom by the massive DSRV loading arm. The

A-team divers from the *Cormorant* had been relieved, and the B-team, engirded in the MAMs, was working below.

Already several drums had been removed from the first hold of the U-1000 and secured within the heavy weather balloons.

Einar and Birte had watched it on the television screens on the Main Control Console. The pictures transmitted by the underwater TV cameras were murky and unsteady, but adequate.

It had quickly become routine for the experienced divers. Before they were taken down, the balloons had been cut open at the bottom so they would fit over the big drums. Carefully a balloon would be pulled down over the corroded barrel. One of the divers, utilizing the power of his Man-Amplifier in the cramped space, would lift the drum up while another gathered the balloon at the bottom, doubled it up and securely tied it off. Should any small leak develop, the rising poison would be trapped inside the balloon. So far that had not happened.

It was 0448 hours, a couple of hours before dawn, and already the first three balloon-sheathed drums had been transported from the wreck and placed in an engine container, ready to be hoisted on board the ASR.

From the helo deck where he stood with Birte, Einar looked out over the main deck of the *Cormorant.*

The center well area, where several men were to be seen, was flooded by powerful lights that created a checkerboard world of brightly lit sections and pockets of pitch black shadows; an eerie world of brightness and gloom, lorded over by the looming hulk of the giant crane gantry squatting on its massive rails at the far end of the well.

Senior Chief Petty Officer Leroy Jackson was another of the *Cormorant* crew who couldn't sleep. He was going on duty in less than an hour and felt the need to grab some fresh ocean air before having himself a good breakfast.

He stood at the railing on deck near the towering crane gantry, looking out over the black water, watching the floodlit LPD rolling gently on the swells a short distance away. He was alone. And enjoying it.

Suddenly he heard a small scraping sound. It came from the gantry. He turned.

The sound was not repeated, and he could see nothing in the darkness.

Just as he was turning away again, one of the deep black shadows seemed to move. An almost imperceptible shift of density. He'd seen the movement out of the corners of his eyes and could not be sure. He turned toward the spot. He peered into the gloom. Who the hell would be working on the gantry without a light? he thought. As he was watching, he saw it again. A quick, furtive movement.

What the hell?

It was near the ladder to the port-side service platform up on the gantry. Quietly he walked toward it.

The figure of a man detached itself from the shadow and silently started toward the ladder.

"Hey!" Jackson called.

Startled, the man turned toward him.

Jackson recognized him at once. He was one of those damned VIPs. That bunch of self-important pricks who'd given him a hard time when he was chaperoning them around. He didn't remember the man's name.

"Sir," he said. "What are you doing here? No one is supposed to be on the gantry."

"Oh? Sorry," the man shrugged unconcernedly. "I couldn't sleep. I . . . I was merely looking around."

"Sir," Jackson said. "You are in a restricted area. I must ask you to come with me. I'll have to report you to the duty officer."

Again the man shrugged. With a much-put-upon sigh, he turned and started to walk away. Jackson followed him.

Suddenly he heard a faint sound. A sound that sent an icy chill through him. A sound he'd heard before. On the streets of upper Harlem. A soft swish—and a faint, metallic click. The sound of a switchblade springing to life in the span of a heartbeat.

"What the hell are—" he exclaimed.

They were the last words he was ever to utter. The stiletto's sharp blade buried itself to the hilt in his flesh. He went rigid. His back arched. His scream never reached his lips; it gurgled in a pink froth around the blade of the knife in his throat. . . .

Birte shivered.

"It's getting a little cold," she said. "I think I'd like to go down."

"I'm with you," Einar said. "Let's stop by at the control console. See how they're doing down there. Then maybe we should turn in."

They started toward the companionway.

The man at the gantry stood stock-still, staring down at at his lifeless victim. Silently he cursed. His task would have to wait. He'd have to get rid of the damned body. That was now the most pressing job.

Throw it overboard? Too risky. Someone might see. Or hear. The body might not sink and be discovered. Hide it. Somewhere it would not be found quickly. That was it.

At once he grabbed hold of the body—surprised at both the dead weight and the small amount of blood from the knife wound.

Death had come too quickly to bleed.

He hefted the heavy body up on his shoulder. He looked up toward the crane service platform.

Dammit!

But there would be another time. . . .

The dive supervisor was watching the murky pictures from the dive below on the closed-circuit television screens. He nodded as Einar and Birte entered. The monitor speaker was on.

". . . give me a little more slack, Brad. There are some pretty treacherous currents down here."

"You got it."

On the screens they could see one of the divers slowly moving toward a drum still lashed with the others to the deck of the hold. He began to free it.

"Hey, I can make out some writing on this one."

"They all got it. Too crusted over to read."

"Not this one."

"What's it say?"

"Green Diver. Control. Give me a picture of that writing."

"Control. Green Diver. Understand."

On one of the monitor screens the picture swam unsteadily to a close shot of the writing on the drum. Stenciled on it could be seen:

Nr. 646
250 Kg.

"No wonder those damned things are so heavy," the dive supervisor commented. He suddenly looked impressed. "Man alive! That's better than three hundred and seventy-three thousand pounds of toxic crystals in all!"

Another man joined Einar and Birte at the control console. It was the toxicologist, Dr. Erlanger. He nodded pleasantly to them.

"Disobeying the admiral's edict?" he smiled. "I don't blame you. So am I. It is too exciting to miss."

"This contraption is really something else," the speaker squawked.

"Got the hang of it?" It was the capsule operator.

"No sweat. Want me to carry the whole damned sub over?"

"I'd be satisfied with just the drums—without any screwing up."

"You got it."

"Ready for the king-size condom?" It was the other diver.

"Hey! Does that Superman bit go that far?"

"You wish!"

There was a moment's silence. Then—

"Can you get that thing a little further this way?"

"Yeah. Just—"

The diver who was moving the drum from its storage place to be enveloped in a weather balloon suddenly gave a sharp cry.

"Damn!" he exclaimed. "There is a leak. The drum is leaking! There is a string of bubbles rising from it! I've got to—"

Abruptly the television screens collapsed into static noise, and the monitor speaker went dead.

38

The men in the control room galvanized into action.

"Light off the UQC!" the supervisor shouted. "Move!"

An operator at once threw a series of switches in rapid succession, cutting in the underwater telephone system, a series of underwater transceivers already installed on board the *Cormorant* and in the PTC as an emergency backup communications system.

"Get to the com panel," the dive supervisor barked at a seaman. "See what the hell is going on!"

The sailor rushed off.

"Control! Control! Capsule. We have a leak! We have a leak! Air bubbles are coming from a drum!"

White-faced, the supervisor reached for the alarm switch.

The V-3 poison had escaped its confines!

Suddenly Erlanger stayed the man's hand.

"Wait!" he shouted.

Startled, the man stopped.

"Air bubbles!" Erlanger said urgently. "*Air!* The poison is not yet dissolving. Only air is escaping." He fixed the supervisor with his eyes. "Don't let any water get to the crystals. You must stop it. Put a hand over the leak. Stop it!"

For only a split second the supervisor stared at the toxicologist. Then he made up his mind.

"Capsule! Control!" he said resolutely. "Urgent! Instruct diver to stop leak with his hand. Do not let water into the drum! Advise."

"Control. Capsule. Understand."

It seemed an eternity before the capsule operator came back on the speaker.

"Capsule. Control. Diver has stopped bubbles. Cannot hold on for long. Standing by for instructions."

"Capsule. Control. Understand."

The supervisor turned to Erlanger. "Sir?"

The scientist knit his brow. "Have you . . . have you anything like . . . like caulking? Or putty, down there? Any kind of adhesive material that would stick to the drum? Even for a short while?"

At once the supervisor spoke.

"Capsule. Control. Have you any caulking tubes in capsule? Or any other adhesive material?"

"Control. Capsule. Stand by."

Again the nerve-wracking wait. Then—

"Control. Capsule. Negative on caulking. We have a roll of self-adhesive tape. For umbilical bonding."

The supervisor glanced at Erlanger. The scientist nodded.

"Capsule. Control. Listen, Brad. Get that tape over there. As fast as you can. Have them seal the leak, and then at once, repeat—*at once*—place a balloon over the drum."

"Control. Capsule. Tape is on its way. Will advise."

The seaman the supervisor had sent to check on the main communications panel came back.

"Chief," he said. "I don't know what the hell is going on. The wires are burned through. Shorted out. It looks like . . . like someone spilled some acid on them! I swear!" He shook his head. "The damned stuff ate right through 'em. But what gets me, who the hell would be playing with acid at the com panel?"

"How bad is it?"

"It's only at one spot," the sailor said. "We'll have it fixed in twenty minutes."

The speaker crackled to life.

"Control. Capsule. Drum secured."

The supervisor gave Erlanger a long look.

"Capsule. Control. Understand," he said. "Carry on."

He mopped his brow and looked with surprise at the sweat that he wiped off on his hand.

"There can be no doubt," Admiral Reed stated. He sounded angry. He glared around at the officers gathered in the wardroom. Gravely they returned his gaze. "The first mishap, the mixmaker shutdown, could—and mind you, I say *could*—could have been accidental. But the disablement of the communications wiring was definitely a deliberate action. There is no doubt. We have a saboteur on board."

He looked at Commander Cannon. "Commander," he said. "What safety measures have been taken?"

"I've placed guards at all critical points, sir," Cannon answered crisply. "And two armed guards on each of the four main system valves. A shutdown of any one of them could disable everyone in the DDCs and the capsules. Ultimately kill them."

Reed nodded. "I have asked Mr. Henderson to take charge of an onboard investigation," he said. He turned to Cannon. "With your permission, Commander?"

"Of course, sir."

"Mr. Henderson is here in the capacity of civilian representative of the Counter Intelligence Directorate," Reed went on. "And as liaison with the White House." He turned to Henderson. "Mr. Henderson."

"Thank you, sir." Henderson steepled his fingers in front of him. "Let's examine what we have," he said solemnly. "Based on the obvious act of sabotage against the communications panel." He thought for a moment.

"The subject we're dealing with had to be someone familiar with the properties of a strong acid, which was obviously used instead of simply cutting the wires, so that the perpetrator could be away from the panel when the actual short occurred. Establishing an alibi, as it were."

He looked around at the officers listening to him. He was rather enjoying himself.

"But," he said portentously, "whoever did it obviously did not know of the backup communications system that could instantly be activated. The disruption he caused actually meant very little." Again he steepled his fingers. "That," he said, "it seems to me, speaks against the saboteur being a member of the *Cormorant* crew, who are all familiar with that system, and who would have known his act would have no significance whatsoever."

He leaned back in his chair.

"We do have several noncrew members on board," Commander Cannon pointed out. "Including several civilians."

Henderson nodded. "I am aware of that, Commander. And while I am ruling no one out, that is quite likely where we'll find our man."

He sat up.

"But," he asked, "did you augment your crew or receive any replacements just prior to joining TF-49?"

"At Holylock?" Cannon turned to his executive officer. "Did we?"

"Yes," the exec said. "Three men. I would have to look up their names and assignments."

"Do so," Cannon snapped. "And give Mr. Henderson the information."

"Aye, aye, sir."

The officer hurried from the wardroom.

"That brings us to motive," Henderson said. "Whoever is behind the sabotage obviously wants the salvage of the poison drums to fail. Through delay. Or total shutdown. And—also quite obviously—at the price of his own life. A fanatic, gentlemen, in this case, a diehard Nazi zealot." He frowned. "And that is quite in keeping with events prior to Operation Giant."

Commander Cannon turned to him.

"We seem to have a dozen possible suspects, then," he said. "The three civilian toxicologists; the two army officers from Chemical Warfare; the German ex-U-boat officer; two or three recent crew members; Major Munk and his wife; perhaps even the ex-senior chief petty officer who came with the Man-Amplifiers."

"You can strike two names from that list right away, Commander," Henderson said firmly. "If you knew what the Munks went through to get this operation activated, you'd know they could not possibly be involved in anything that would sabotage the effort. In fact, I plan to have Major Munk assist me. He's had extensive experience in investigation. And as for Chief Kowalski, it seems unlikely. He was not even on board when the first mishap took place."

He looked around the table.

"Actually," he said, "it seems to me that we must look for someone who had prior knowledge of the U-1000 and her cargo, and who in some way could have influenced his getting aboard the *Cormorant* once he discovered her mission. Find him—and we'll have found our saboteur."

He turned to Reed.

"Sir," he said. "I need the full names of the three toxicologists, the German U-boat specialist, and the two Chemical Warfare officers. I want to forward them to CID at the Pentagon with a request for an urgent and thorough investigation of each individual."

Reed nodded agreement. His aide, Lieutenant Commander Nelson, made a note. Henderson turned to Commander Cannon.

"And I also want the navy to give me a complete rundown on the men taken aboard at Holylock."

"We'll get on it at once."

Salvage Master Dedham spoke up.

"Sir," he said. "There is one other matter I'd like to bring up. I don't know if there is any connection—but, I have a man missing."

Cannon stared at him.

"Missing?" he exclaimed.

"He did not report to his duty station, sir, an hour ago. And no one seems to know where he is."

"Who is he?"

"Senior Chief Petty Officer Leroy Jackson."

"I suggest you mount a search for him. If there *is* a connection, the sooner we find out, the better."

"Aye, aye, sir."

Henderson stood up.

"With your permission, sir," he addressed Admiral Reed, "I want to get on with my investigation. I want to talk with Major Munk. Will you excuse me?"

"Of course. Keep me informed."

"Yes, sir."

Einar and Birte listened attentively as Henderson briefed them on what had gone on at the conference. Einar frowned.

"There's something I want to tell you," he said.

"Shoot."

"When that mixmaker shutdown occurred, we had all just trooped through the control room where the valve that malfunctioned—accidentally or not—was located. We were all there. The scientists, the Chemical Warfare officers, Dietrich, the German. I . . . I suspected that something, some tampering had taken place, but I had, of course, no proof. Only a . . . hunch. A suspicion."

Henderson glared at him, his face stiff with anger.

"Why the hell didn't you tell me when I got here?" he exploded. "We could have placed the guards at once. Prevented any further sabotage."

"Dammit, Colonel!"

"Mister!" Henderson shot at him.

"Dammit!" Einar bristled. "Don't try to lay that on me! Would you have believed me? You had to have everything else proven to you, in spades. Would you have believed me if I'd marched up to you the minute you came aboard and told you I had a hunch there was a damned Nazi saboteur on board?"

For a moment Henderson glared at him.

"No!" he snapped.

A seaman came hurrying up to them. He looked frightened.

"Sir," he said to Henderson. "You are wanted in the ship's laundry. Right away. Will you please follow me?"

Henderson frowned at him. "The . . . laundry?"

"Yes, sir."

"Why?"

"Sir." The seaman swallowed. "They . . . they found Leroy Jackson."

Senior Chief Petty Officer Leroy Jackson lay crumpled grotesquely at the bottom of a large laundry hamper. His eyes were open, glassy in death, staring unseeing from an ash-gray face frozen in fear.

The hilt of the switchblade knife still protruded from his throat, discolored by black-brown, clotted blood.

Einar and Birte gazed at the young man. The bile rose in Birte's throat. So—young. Not much more than Sven's age, when . . . She could feel the tears burning in her eyes. Only two days before, they had listened to the young man's self-conscious yet proud briefing on the capabilities of his ship.

Einar felt the surge of impotent anger rise in him. He looked away and met Henderson's troubled eyes.

Whoever was behind the disruptions on board the *Cormorant* was not just a saboteur.

He was a killer.

39

"Mr. President! Mr. President!"

The President struggled up from a deep, dreamless sleep.

"Yes?" He sat up on one elbow. He peered with sleep-gritty eyes at the White House chief of staff who stood next to his bed. "Jerry. What is it?"

"A communication from Colonel Henderson," the chief of staff, Gerald Morgan, replied. "There have been some . . . disturbing developments on board the USS *Cormorant* at Point G."

The President was at once fully awake.

"What time is it?" he asked.

"A quarter past four in the morning, sir."

The President swung his legs over the edge of the bed and sat up; he worried his feet into a pair of slippers.

"What has happened?" he asked, deep concern coloring his voice.

"It seems there is a saboteur on board the salvage vessel, sir."

"A saboteur?"

"Yes, sir. There has been a killing."

"Who?"

"One of the crew, sir. Colonel Henderson has asked CID for full investigations of all the civilian and military specialists on the scene. He sent a telex copy of the request for your information."

The President pointed to a paper in Morgan's hand.

"Is that it?"

"Yes, sir."

"Let me see it."

Morgan handed the message over. The President quickly read it. He looked up at Morgan.

"The CID will handle the matter of the military personnel," he said crisply. "But I want you to get hold of the director. Right now. I want the FBI to conduct a thorough, top-priority investigation of all the three civilian scientists. Independent of any investigations carried out by the CID. And I want Brannigan to get a full report on the German—Herr Dietrich, is it?"

Morgan nodded.

"And I want the reports on my desk within twenty-four hours, with copies to Colonel Henderson, immediately they are available."

"Yes, Mr. President."

For a brief moment the President sat quietly on the edge of his bed. Slowly he rubbed his temples.

"Jerry," he said softly, "I think we both should offer up a little prayer for the success of Operation Giant. Now that they are facing an enemy both below—and above . . ."

"The answer is categorically *no!*" Admiral Reed's voice had a brittle edge of anger to it. "There will be no further discussion!"

"Sir. May I—"

"You may not, mister!"

"Sir. You yourself put me in charge of—"

"You are exceeding that authority!" Reed snapped. "I will under no circumstances be subjected to having a bodyguard aboard my own flagship! It is—preposterous!"

"Sir," Henderson went on doggedly. "This is not a courtesy call to a friendly port. We are dealing with a diehard Nazi. A fanatic. We are dealing with the Nazi mentality. I *know* that mentality, Admiral. From bitter, personal experience during the war. They believe that the way to subvert a project, to crush it, is to eliminate the leadership, cut off the head. A belief they demonstrated often enough. Your life may very well be threatened. I strongly suggest—"

"Mr. Henderson," Reed interrupted him, his voice under deliberate control. "I presume you are acting in what you believe is my best interest—"

"And that of the entire operation—"

"—but this discussion is terminated!" Reed overrode him. *"That is all!"*

For a moment Henderson stood silent, glowering at the naval officer.

"Yes, sir!" he snapped bitingly.

He turned on his heel and stalked off.

The mood aboard the USS *Cormorant* had changed. Einar and Birte could feel it in the way they and the other non-navy outsiders were eyed by the grim crew members.

When the *Cormorant* had lost one crew member, two others had taken his place.

Fear and Suspicion.

And they, in turn, had spawned a bleak atmosphere of testiness and short tempers that only led to further tension on board.

But the salvage operation had progressed without any further mishaps. Already several jet engine containers, filled with the lethal drums from the U-1000, had been brought up by the *Cormorant* and ferried to the LPD on board special barges to be stored in the holds.

It was an awesome and somehow frightening experience to see the huge cylindrical engine shipping containers like some mythical sea monsters slowly and ponderously rise up out of the dark ocean, the water running off their glistening iron sides, pulled up by the cable on the *Cormorant's* loading arm, and know that each one of them contained enough poison sealed in it to inflict a horrible death on thousands and thousands of people.

Birte had been awed watching the operation. The LPD was an astounding vessel. More than 520 feet long, it was riding low in the water, its void holds flooded and its stern gate gaping open so that the water level in the well deck was raised enough to allow the barges loaded with the engine containers to be driven right into the ship.

One by one, the barges transferred their deadly cargo from the *Cormorant* to the storage holds of the LPD.

And time ticked inexorably by.

Henderson had received a preliminary report from the CID.

Both of the Chemical Warfare officers were career officers whose records were known in detail. Both were considered above suspicion.

The German SACLANT member had submitted an initiatory report on the ex-chief engineer of the U-992, Werner Dietrich. The man's records showed him to be exactly what he said he was. He had been in a British prisoner-of-war camp for thirteen months, and had returned to his native town of Göttingen upon his release in June 1946. He had been a member of the Nazi party. So had millions of his compatriots. But he had not held any office nor been active in the party. As far as was known. Nor had any ties to known neo-Nazi groups been discovered. He owned and operated a small camera shop in his hometown, and he had a reputation of being a quiet man, one beyond reproach. An investigation in depth was being undertaken.

The three toxicologists were prominent, internationally known scientists. Each had a copious biography in every *Who's Who* of importance—all quoted in the report. Erlanger came from Stanford, Hart from MIT, and Ramsey from Harvard. Each of them had volunteered their services and had been chosen from a larger group of volunteers who had responded to an urgent appeal by the Pentagon. Each had been selected by SACLANT because he was considered tops in his field. Because each of the men was an individual, mature in years, it would take some time to conduct a painstakingly detailed investigation of his past. Such investigations were ongoing.

It was a wordy report with nothing to say.

To Henderson it was completely useless.

He could only wait, impatiently, and hope for further information.

Dusk was turning to darkness. It was 1819 hours, Thursday, May 23—fourteen days after *Stabsobermachinist* Karl Johann Thompson had first called his fateful "You! One thousand!" to a little student nurse in New York. . . .

From their favorite observation spot on the helo deck, Einar and Birte watched as a new shift of divers was preparing to be lowered to the bottom.

Once again the center well area was brilliantly illuminated.

Below, at the control console, the dive supervisor was going through his checklist. The divers were in the PTC, the hatch had been closed and dogged, and the transfer trunk vented.

And it was time to perform operating procedure six, the unmating of the PTC from the DDC.

"Topside. Control," the supervisor called. "Commence OP-6. Keep me informed."

"Control. Topside. Understand."

On deck Einar and Birte watched the PTC being raised on its four leveling jacks. Ponderously the gantry crane lumbered forward to hook up by cable to the capsule. Lifting it from its stand, the crane slowly moved the PTC aft, out over the center well.

The capsule, suspended in the well from the crane stabilizer beam, was almost in position for the transfer of its weight from the handling system to the SPC cable hydraulic system, when the steady, deep-throated drone of the gantry crane motor suddenly sputtered, coughed, and died. The ponderous movement of the crane jerked—and stopped.

The speaker on the control console below urgently rasped, "Control. Topside. We have a gantry motor malfunction. The PTC is dangling on the string!"

Tensely Einar and Birte watched the men scurrying about on the main deck below them.

The capsule, hanging on the crane cable over the water in the well, gradually began to swing from side to side as the ship rolled gently with the swells.

On the deck the main deck supervisor shouted, "Get some guylines on that thing! Or it'll slam into the wall. Move!"

Einar looked at Birte.

"Trouble," he said. "We'd better get down to the command center."

The wardroom command center was already awash with controlled commotion. Men were hurrying in and out of the room. Admiral Reed was talking urgently on a phone, his aide standing by; Henderson was in animated conversation with Dive Officer Avellino.

Einar and Birte quickly started toward them. They were stopped by Erlanger and Hart.

"What's happening?" Erlanger asked anxiously.

"The PTC is stuck," Einar answered, trying to get past.

"Another—sabotage job?" Hart frowned.

"I don't know." Einar pushed past the two men. "That's what I'm trying to find out."

"—air/sea interface," Avellino was saying to Henderson as Einar and Birte joined them.

"What the hell happened?" Henderson demanded.

"I don't know," Avellino replied sharply. "The gantry motor malfunctioned. It stopped. Leaving the PTC dangling over the water."

"Meaning?"

"It's a potentially dangerous situation," Avellino said, obviously distraught, "if we can't get that motor started quickly. The PTC weighs close to thirty thousand pounds. Oscillation caused by water turbulence could snap the cable. Or the brake could give out. The capsule would plunge to the bottom. We'd lose the whole diving crew."

Birte put her hand to her mouth.

"Oh, dear God," she whispered.

An operator at a phone called to Avellino. "Lieutenant!" He held up the receiver.

At once Avellino hurried over. For a moment he talked and listened. They watched him scowl with worry as he rejoined them. Darkly he looked at Henderson.

"Did you find out what happened?" Henderson snapped.

Avellino nodded.

"Well!"

"The gantry crane has its own motor," Avellino said, his voice flat. "It runs on diesel. It has its own fuel tanks. Two of them. The operator can switch from number one tank to number two tank. That is what happened."

He looked almost accusingly at Henderson.

"The fuel in number two tank had been contaminated. With water!"

There was a stunned silence. They stared at Avellino. What was in their minds need not be spoken.

Sabotage!

"And the emergency air regulator is missing. The mounting damaged."

"What's—?"

"It's a backup system, Major. It would have enabled us to run the crane for one revolution, enough to retrieve the capsule. As it is, we're dependent on number two tank."

"Will the men in the capsule be all right?" Birte asked, concern pinching her face.

Avellino nodded. "I believe so, ma'am," he said. "If we can get the capsule stabilized." He turned to Henderson. "But it means we'll have to empty both tanks, purify them, and refill them. It will mean a delay of hours," he said bitterly.

"But how?" Einar asked. "How can it have happened? Wasn't there a guard on those tanks?"

Avellino nodded. "There was," he said. "But the contamination could have been done before we knew there was a saboteur on board. Before the guards were posted."

Soberly they looked at one another.

What other deadly time bombs lay in wait for them?

It was just under six hours when the personal transfer capsule finally was transferred from the crane cable to the strength, power, and communications cable, and lowered into the black water. It was seven minutes past midnight.

The fifteenth day had just begun.

40

The seventeenth day, Sunday, May 2, dawned reluctantly under a gray, leaden sky. The *Coral Sea*'s meteorologist reported weather building to the southwest. The dark water was speckled with brisk little whitecaps. It was not a good sign.

The drums had been stored by the U-boat crew in four of the eight cargo compartments of the U-1000. All the drums from three of those holds had already been sealed in jet engine containers, brought to the surface and stored on the LPD, as well as most of the drums in hold number four.

Despite the overcast sky and the pessimistic weather report, there was an air of optimism on board the *Cormorant.*

They'd make it!

For a grueling sixty-three hours, the salvage crew of the USS *Cormorant,* ASR-23, had been laboring nonstop, once the glitches had stopped. Security on board ship had bordered on paranoia, but as a result no further attempts to sabotage the operation had occurred.

Henderson still had received no additional reports concerning the toxicologists under investigation in the States, and to his urgent inquiries the terse answer had been that telescoping an investigation that normally would take months into a few days would take, well—a few days.

There had been no further glitches, as the salvage work had settled down to a routine. Even the riskiest, most hazardous task can become routine. Just ask any member of a bomb disposal squad. And the crises that had developed had been handled quickly and efficiently. Two more of the corroded drums had started to leak air when they were handled by the divers in their Man-Amplifier devices, but they had been safely and promptly contained. However, it was becoming obvious that the corrosion was rapidly reaching the state of disintegration. It was still a race against time, which Admiral Reed had pointed out with a singular lack of originality.

Einar and Birte were sitting with Dr. Ramsey and Dr. Hart in the wardroom command center, speculating on the chemical composition of the "brown sugar" poison and keeping half an eye on the TV monitor screens that showed the murky pictures of the salvage work below and listening with half an ear to the occasional communications.

Suddenly Einar sat bolt upright. He raised his hand for silence. Intently he listened to the voice coming over the monitor speaker.

"—missing. We have counted twice. I repeat. One drum is definitely missing."

"Capsule. Control. Are you certain all the remaining drums can now be seen?"

"Control. Capsule. Affirmative. The count is 678, including the drums already retrieved."

"Capsule. Control. Understand. Stand by."

Einar bolted from the room. He dove down the ladders to the Main Control Console two decks below. He arrived just as Salvage Master Dedham entered.

"Commander," he said. "Is there one drum missing?"

Dedham nodded grimly. "There is. The count has been verified."

"Then I know where it is!" Einar exclaimed.

Dedham looked at him.

"Huh?"

"The ultimatum drum!" Einar said urgently. "The one drum that was supposed to have been released before the others."

Dedham immediately understood. "Right," he said. "It would not be with the others."

"It wouldn't. There'd have been no time to get it back to the hold, much less tie it down, once the U-1000 was under attack."

"It would still be somewhere between the hold and cargo hatch trunk number four. Where the bastards were in the process of releasing it. You got it!"

"And it would be loose," Einar said soberly.

Dedham at once turned to the dive supervisor. "Dave," he snapped. "Get the divers to work back from the cargo compartments. They should be able to locate the missing drum somewhere between the holds and a forward hatch trunk. When they do, do not touch the drum. Advise."

"Aye, aye, sir!"

The man at once began to issue his orders to the divers.

"It's something that has been nagging the hell out of me for days," Einar said. "Some poison did leak out. Several Irish fishermen can attest to that. But not the whole drum. Or many thousands of people would have been affected. And that did not happen."

"The—ultimatum drum? But—"

"Exactly. It was loose. It may well have been damaged during the crash dive. Weakened somehow and become more susceptible to the corrosion. It may have sprung a leak before the rest of the damned things."

"But—why did it stop? Before emptying itself?"

"Beats the hell out of me, Commander. We'll find out when the divers reach the drum."

The divers found the missing drum in the narrow walkway almost directly under the trunk to hatch number four. It stood on end next to a loading trolley.

"Control. Green Diver. We have the missing drum."

"Green Diver. Control. Understand. Stand by." The dive supervisor looked at Dedham.

"Tell him to give us as steady a picture of the thing as he can," the salvage master told him.

The supervisor did.

The drum shown on the monitor screen looked quite like the others. It did not seem damaged, except for a dent at the bottom end on which it stood. For a while the men stared at it.

"Could we take a look at that . . . that cart next to it?" Einar asked.

"The loading trolley? Sure." Dedham nodded to the supervisor.

The picture showed a wheeled metal conveyance, squat and sturdy. Like the drum, it was rusty and caked with crusty deposit. The picture slowly moved across it.

"Hold it!" Einar suddenly cried. "Hold it right there!"

Quickly the supervisor had the diver hold his television picture. Einar looked at Dedham.

"See it?" he asked. "Right there." He pointed to the monitor. "There is an area on the top of the trolley, toward the end of it, where it is almost clean. Very little deposit."

"I see it," Dedham frowned.

"Let me give you a possible scenario," Einar said. "Suppose the drum *was* damaged. In the crash dive and breakup. Probably near that dent we could see. Suppose it came to rest on top of the trolley when the U-1000 finally settled down, and suppose the damage had caused a weak spot on the bottom of the drum. Like a . . . a wrinkle in the metal from being bashed in. You with me?"

"Sure am. Go on."

"Isn't it then possible that, what?—around four or five weeks ago, a leak developed at that weak spot? The drum was still lying perched on the trolley, the damaged part hanging over one end of it. First the air would leak out, as it did in the drums that were damaged during the salvage operation, and then water would seep into the drum. As this happened, the end that hung over the trolley got heavier—and the damned drum toppled off to stand on end. That accounts for the clean area on the trolley. A small amount of the dissolved toxic substance would have been seeping out—that would account for the poisoned Irishmen. But when the drum toppled off, the leak was under it, sealed off by the weight of the drum itself. That would explain why the rest of the poison didn't dissolve and rise to the surface."

"Dammit! You could be right." Dedham turned to the dive supervisor. "Dave," he said. "Have the diver give us a look at that drum from the other side—the side that's toward the loading trolley."

As the picture on the monitor slowly moved around the drum, they saw it. An area toward the top of the drum was quite clear of crusty deposit. An area corresponding exactly in size to the clear area on the trolley.

"I'll be damned," Dedham breathed.

"You realize what this means?" Einar said soberly. "There *is* an open leak on the bottom of that drum. How much of the dissolved poison has collected beneath it, waiting to rise to the surface the minute the drum is moved? Even a thimbleful could kill the entire task force!"

Dedham stared at him. At once he picked up a phone. "Commander Cannon!" he snapped tautly.

Briefly he spoke on the phone.

It was only seconds later when the PA system all over the USS *Cormorant*—and shortly thereafter all over every ship of TF-49—sprang to life.

"This is the captain speaking," the PA droned. "This is not a drill. Antitoxic protective gear is to be put on at once! It will be worn until further instructions. This is not a drill!"

Einar started to put his gas mask on. Dedham stopped him.

"Wait," he said. "You and I," he nodded toward the dive supervisor, "and Dave, here, we'll hold off a bit. We'll know immediately if anything happens. And it's a lot easier to communicate without those damned things."

Einar looked at the salvage master. "How are you going to secure that drum?" he asked. "The moment they touch it, it may release any accumulated poison—or rupture."

"There is only one way," Dedham said tightly. He turned to a seaman. "Get one of the toxicologists down here. You'll find one in the wardroom command center. On the double!"

The seaman took off.

Dedham turned to the dive supervisor. "Let me talk to the divers, Dave," he said.

The supervisor nodded.

"Green Diver," Dedham said. "Control. This is Dedham. Listen closely. We believe an accumulation of dissolved toxic substance is trapped beneath the drum. It cannot—repeat *cannot*—be allowed to escape."

The speaker rasped its high-pitched reply.

"This is Andy, Pat." The SOP communications procedure was tacitly dropped. It had become a one-on-one concern.

"To prevent it," Dedham continued, "we must seal off the passageway area where the drum is located, before you even touch the damned thing. Just—in case."

"I understand."

"I want you and your teammate—who is it?"

"Gus."

"I want you and Gus to take a look around. See how it can be done. And report."

"Understand."

Dr. Erlanger and Dr. Hart came hurrying into the control room. Quickly Dedham put them in the picture.

"My question to you is," he said gravely, "*if* there is an accumulation of liquid poison under that drum, and *if* it is released, how will we know it has happened? Can it be seen?"

The two scientists looked at one another.

"I mean, before anything happens," Dedham went on. "How would it look? Does it have a color? Is it like . . . like oil, for instance? Or what?"

"We don't really know," Hart said with a frown.

"If there is a trapped deposit of liquid toxin under that drum," Erlanger said slowly, "it would be of a high concentration. It *might* look . . . eh, different from the surrounding water when released. Before it could be further diluted."

"How?"

"That is, of course, conjecture," Hart pointed out.

Dedham nodded curtly. "How?"

"The crystals have been described as being brown," Erlanger explained. "In liquid form of high concentration, it might retain a . . . a brownish color. For a short while, at least."

Hart nodded pensively. "Perhaps—a little oily. Globular, as it were."

"Exactly," Erlanger agreed. "A little like . . . like drops of colored glycerine in water. The liquid poison will have a lesser specific gravity than the water, or it wouldn't rise toward the surface as it is supposed to do. So tell your men to watch out for any drops of a possibly oily, brownish liquid seeping out and floating up."

The monitor speaker suddenly squawked.

"Control. Red Diver. Pat—the cargo hatch above is intact, and there is a small, circular hatchway in a bulkhead a few feet further on. Both are rusted in place, but with these contraptions on, we can close and dog them with no sweat. They should make a pretty solid seal."

"What about the other end of the walkway?"

"The hatch there has been wrested off its hinges," the diver reported.

"Chuck will have to send someone out from the capsule to put it back on. It will have to be welded in place."

"Understand." There was a pause. Dedham was staring bleakly at the monitor. He knew what he had to do, and it was tearing him apart. "Andy," he said finally. "You . . . you understand what has to be done?"

"Sure do, Pat. We'll have to seal off this section while Gus and I try to secure the leaking drum—without spilling any poison into the water."

"I'm sure you can do it," Dedham said. He wished the conviction in his voice had been greater. He'd tried. "But if . . . Look, I'm not going to order you to—"

"Save it, Pat. Gus and I are volunteering. Would you believe it? I've never volunteered for any damned job in my life. But—what the hell. Seems like as good a time as any to start."

"Andy," Dedham said, his voice heavy. "I've got to spell it out for you. If you do spill the leak, or if the drum ruptures, we will have to make the seal permanent."

There was a pause.

"Control. We understand, Pat."

"Okay, Andy. Close and dog the forward hatches. Chuck'll have someone bring you a few balloons, and he'll seal off the other end. We'll leave an opening for your umbilical. I'm sure they can seal around it."

"Understand."

"Report when you are ready."

He picked up the phone. "Commander Cannon," he said, his jaw set in grim resolution.

Cannon came on the line.

"Sir," Dedham said. "We're faced—"

"We have been following your complication up here," Cannon broke in briskly. "We agree with the way you are handling the situation."

"Thank you, sir."

"Carry on."

It was twenty-nine minutes later when the two divers had been sealed in the walkway beneath cargo hatch number four in the U-1000.

They—and the leaking ultimatum drum.

"Control. Red Diver," the speaker squawked. "We are ready to secure drum."

"Understand, Andy. Now—listen. I suggest you use a double balloon. Can do?"

"Can do."

"Slip them over the drum and try not even to jiggle it when you do. Get it all the way down to the deck before you lift the drum. Understand?"

"Understand."

"Now. Keep an eye out for any small oily globules of a brownish color that may escape from beneath the drum. If they are caught inside the balloon, okay. If not—"

"Understand."

"Be damned careful, Andy."

"You better believe it. This bit of real estate is not exactly my idea of a place to settle down permanently. Okay, here goes."

The control room was charged with tension as everyone watched the pictures on the TV monitors, transmitted by the divers in the sealed-off section of the U-1000 six hundred and fifty feet below, and listened to their strained, high-pitched voices.

"Easy, Gus, easy . . . All the way down . . . Careful. Don't touch the damned drum."

"Okay. That's it."

"Yeah . . . I'll take hold of it from here. Get a better purchase . . . Pull the skirt out . . . That way . . . More . . . As much as you can without pulling on the drum . . . That's it . . . When I lift the drum, I'll tilt it slightly your way. Anything trapped under it will come out at that end. You catch it in the balloon."

"Sure as hell try."

"Ready?"

"Ready."

There was a sharp grunt.

"Hold it! I see it! Dammit! I see it! Hold the fucking thing steady . . . It's, it's oozing out from underneath . . . My God! It's as big as my fist! And expanding—"

"Can you . . . get it?"

"Yeah . . . Wait . . . I've . . . I've got it . . . It's floating up into the balloon . . . Wait! There's more . . . Tilt the drum a little more . . . That's it . . . Hold it there . . . Two more small globules coming out . . . Looks like liquid amber . . . Okay, they're caught in the balloon . . . Now. Lift it all the way up. I'll close it off."

There was silence. Then—

"Control. Red Diver. Drum secured. No spill . . . Pat—get us the hell out of here!"

It was getting close to 1500 hours on day seventeen, but the sun was unable to break through the dark clouds gathering overhead. Admiral Reed's race against time had been escalated to encompass a race against the approaching weather as well.

The ultimatum drum had been securely sealed in an engine container and was stored safely on board the LPD, and the cumbersome gas masks were back in their canisters. Another diver team was in the process of "ballooning"—as it was now called—the remaining half-dozen drums, and all indications were that Operation Giant would be concluded successfully.

The mood was relaxed in the wardroom command center, where Admiral Reed and his British counterpart, Admiral Stirling, along with the civilian advisors, were gathered, everyone wanting to be in on the finish.

They were watching the final steps of the operation below on the monitors.

One more aircraft jet engine container to be filled, sealed, brought to the surface, and ferried to the LPD to be stored on board.

And Operation Giant would be over.

Adolf Hitler's V-3 would have been rendered impotent.

The banter from below was almost jovial as the divers "ballooned" a drum, when one of them said, "Hey, Art. Take a look at this."

"What is it?"

"No idea. Looks like a heavy cable. Insulated."

"Where does it go?"

"Let's take a look."

The men in the command center stopped talking. They strained to watch the monitors.

"Here it is. Going right through an opening in the bulkhead. Into the next compartment."

"Which one?"

"Don't know . . . Haven't been there yet . . . Hey, Chris. Are you reading me?"

"Go ahead, Green Diver," the capsule operator answered.

"I'm going into the adjoining hold. Give me a little more slack."

"You got it."

For a while there was silence as the diver made his way to the hold on the other side of the bulkhead. The picture transmitted from the camera mounted on his helmet shifted and blurred. Suddenly it steadied.

"Holy shit!" the man exclaimed. The shock in his voice was unmistakable over the tinny speaker. "Will you look at that?"

The blurry picture on the monitor screen showed stack upon stack of crates. As the diver slowly moved toward the wall where the cable came in from the cargo compartment that held the remaining drums, more and more crates could be seen.

"Must be hundreds of the damned crates," the diver observed. "I'm at the wall. The cable comes through a small opening in it. And it's . . . it goes right into one of the crates . . . It's . . . it's firmly fixed to it.''

''Red Diver. Control. Art. Where does the cable go to on your side?''

''Hold on.''

Silence.

''Control. Red Diver.'' The bantering tone of voice had long since disappeared. ''Cable goes to a drum. It is connected to a metal box welded on to it.''

''Red Diver. Understand . . . Green Diver. Control. Any clues to what's in the crates? Any markings on them?''

''Control. Green Diver. Stand by.''

On the monitor the picture swam toward one of the crates, showing it close up on the monitor.

Einar watched the screen, increasingly perturbed, as the diver's hand came into the picture and started to brush off the accumulated deposit on the crate. He felt Birte's hand steal into his.

A few letters and numerals appeared on the crate, apparently a serial number. And a word: HEXOGEN.

An icy chill shot through Einar. He had suspected it—but seeing it was still a shock.

HEXOGEN.

And at the same time, the gritty voice of the diver cracked out of the speaker.

''Holy shit! Explosives! *High explosives!* There must be—thousands of pounds of the damned stuff!''

There was a taut pause. Then—

''Oh, dear God! That box on the drum. That cable. The explosives. The drums are booby-trapped!''

41

Admiral Reed at once took charge.

''Get the chief of the *Coral Sea* Explosive Ordinance Disposal over here!'' he barked. ''Now!''

Nelson hurried to obey. Reed turned to the other officers assembled in the room.

''Analysis?'' he snapped.

''It is rather obvious, I should say,'' Admiral Stirling observed. ''The explosives were clearly meant to scatter the contents of the drums over as large an area as possible, when they were detonated.''

''Agreed,'' Reed nodded. He turned to the toxicologists. ''Comments?''

Erlanger nodded. "The greater the area . . . eh, seeded with the poison crystals, the greater the mobility; that is to say, the greater the ultimate cloud of poison gas."

"Quite," Stirling said. "As I see it, it would have been quite impossible to offload that rather large amount of drums into rubber rafts, as the Nazis attempted to do with their ultimatum drum. I submit that the U-boat commander had orders to blow up the entire submarine with the drums still on board, after he and his crew had been taken off by another sub, what? Exploding the U-1000 while surfaced would most certainly provide optimum dispersal of the toxic crystal. And, under the circumstances, the U-boat certainly was expendable."

"It makes sense," Commander Cannon said.

"And the—booby trap?"

Stirling shrugged. "It was quite mandatory in the war—World War II, that is—to booby-trap heavy loads of explosives. As a safeguard against unauthorized tampering, don't you know. Rather a lot of the unexploded bombs dropped on London were booby-trapped. Our sappers were quite busy fellows."

Lieutenant Commander Dedham entered the room. Reed at once turned to him.

"Commander," he said, "what's the situation below?"

"One of the remaining six drums is connected to an extremely large cache of high explosives, sir."

"How large?"

"In excess of ten thousand pounds, we estimate." He looked gravely at the admiral. "And at least one drum is definitely booby-trapped. What's more, it is positioned in such a way that it effectively locks the other drums in place, blocks any access to them. We can't reach them to secure them without moving the booby-trapped drum, and we do not know if by moving it, we will set off the trap. And the entire bulk of high explosives with it."

"Any idea what . . . what kind of booby trap it is?"

"No, sir. No one in my crew is familiar with World War II–type booby traps."

"Commander Cannon?"

"I doubt it, sir. The men hadn't even been born then."

Lieutenant Commander Nelson came hurrying into the room, followed by a lieutenant. The man came to attention before Admiral Reed.

"Lieutenant J. G. Nevins, sir," he reported. "Explosive Ordinance Disposal Detachment, *Coral Sea.*"

"At ease," Reed said. "Lieutenant. What do you know about an explosive called hexogen?"

"Sir," Nevins frowned. "Hexogen is the German name for RDX. We call it cyclonite."

"Describe it. Its properties."

"It is a hard, white crystalline solid, sir," Nevins answered. "It was developed around 1900. By a German. But it wasn't much used until World War II when a lot of it was produced by both them and us. It's probably the most powerful of all nonatomic military explosives, sir."

"How powerful?"

"It can develop a detonation power of four million pounds per square inch, sir, and it is used primarily when the highest shattering power is needed. It is insoluble in water, and—"

Reed looked up sharply. He interrupted.

"Being submerged would not have hurt it?"

"No, sir."

"Go on."

"The stuff is very sensitive to percussion, and it's used in blasting caps, for instance," Nevins continued. "It's sometimes mixed with other substances to reduce the sensitivity. It's a real corker of an explosive, sir."

"Thank you, Lieutenant," Reed said. "For your information, there is a large amount of hexogen stored in the U-boat down there. And—it is booby-trapped."

Nevins stared at the admiral, wide-eyed.

"What do you know about booby traps, Lieutenant? World War II vintage?"

"Sir," Nevins said, fighting hard to keep his voice steady. "Nothing, really. I only know they could be set off in all kinds of ways, and you never knew what it would be. They could be pretty complicated." He swallowed. "Those things were never actually manufactured, sir. They were sort of improvised, with whatever you had available. I . . . I don't really have any knowledge of World War II booby traps."

"Can we get someone who does know?" Commander Cannon asked. "An explosives expert? Perhaps someone who has personal experience with the damned things?"

"Those detonator mechanisms can be deucedly ingenious," Admiral Stirling said. "It would take ages for an expert in booby traps even to begin to reason it out. Still—we might find a sapper," he suggested. "An old-timer. Or reservist. A bomb disposal squad veteran, perhaps."

"Where'll we find him?" Reed asked.

"I will contact the Admiralty. Have them search their files. Quite extensive, you know. When we locate the blighter, we can have him flown out here at once.''

"But that will take days. And we have only hours. Perhaps minutes. The weather will not hold much longer, and we can't take the chance of not being able to fly your man out here, after having waited for him to be located. If he's found at all.''

"That weather business,'' Stirling nodded. "That is a point.''

"We will have to deal with the situation ourselves. Here and now.''

"Admiral,'' Einar said. "I have experience with World War II booby traps. I both set them and disarmed them. And I attended a special course in booby traps. Allied and Axis. In England. While we were waiting for the invasion to kick off. It was at ASC at Shrivenham. I graduated in the eleventh CI class . . .''

For a split moment he let his mind flit back. Forty-one years. It had been quite a course. Combat intelligence, they had called it. And it included booby traps. Each graduating student had been given a load of wires, springs, batteries, and miscellaneous junk, and assigned a two-hundred-meter-long strip of land running through a heap of ruins and other debris. Each was instructed to set at least eight booby traps along his assigned route—and when finished, turn around and make his way back along the route of one of his classmates, discovering and disarming every trap *he* had set, while he deactivated yours. Quite a course. He'd nearly blown off a finger when he detonated a trap with a cherry bomb that had been used instead of high explosives.

He looked at the British admiral. "The admiral may be familiar with the course,'' he said.

"Indeed,'' Stirling nodded. "I have heard about Shrivenham. A top-rated course.''

"Excellent,'' Reed said. "I'll have the divers describe the booby trap on the drum down there. In detail. The—''

"Excuse me, sir, but that won't do.''

"What do you mean, won't do?'' Reed snapped.

"Trying to describe a booby trap to someone would be like trying to describe the color red to a blind man.''

"You'll be able to see it on the monitor.''

"Still not good enough, sir.''

"You know another way, mister?'' Reed asked bitingly.

"Yes, sir,'' Einar said firmly. "Let me go down there.''

"Impossible!'' the admiral snapped. "We cannot allow a civilian to—''

"Sir. I am not a civilian. I am in the intelligence reserve. I hold the rank of major!'' Einar flared.

"Of course. I know. It is still impossible. You have no experience in deep-sea diving."

"I can learn."

"No. It is out of the question. I cannot take the responsibility. We will have to find an alternative."

"What? You can't just cut the damned cable, Admiral. That would be suicidal. It would trigger an explosion immediately."

"Admiral." It was Henderson. "Major Munk is right, sir. Our only chance is to let him try to disarm the booby trap himself. We cannot wait for a possible British sapper. We have to retrieve the remaining drums. Now. Or it will be too late. I understand there is a storm about to break. We can't leave the drums down there and wait for that storm to blow itself out. Those drums are so close to rupturing now, that there is no time for further delays. At the risk of coining a phrase, Admiral, we are already living on borrowed time."

"And if the booby trap is sprung?"

"At least we have a *chance* to prevent the V-3 poison from being released, if we try to disarm the trap," Henderson ventured. "If we don't try, there is no chance at all. Even six drums would wipe out a catastrophic number of people."

Reed looked at the man, his eyes hard.

"Sir," Henderson went on. "As you know, I am representing the White House. The President. If there is any responsibility to be shouldered, I will do it." He glanced quickly at Einar. "I . . . I have the authority to do so," he said firmly. "I know Major Munk. I have the greatest confidence in his abilities."

Einar all but gaped at him. I'll be damned, he thought. The bastard is sticking his neck way out. Coming through . . .

"If there are any responsibilities to be shouldered, mister, *I* will shoulder them!" Reed said curtly. He turned to Einar. "Can you do it, Major?"

"I sure as hell can give it my best try," Einar said soberly. "But—I can give you no guarantees. No one can—when it comes to booby traps. There are too many types, too many variations. But I am familiar with most of them. Push, pull, cut, pressure applied, pressure released, you name it. And there are as many variations on those types as there are traps. Each one is unique. And there are different detonating mechanisms and methods. When you try to disarm a booby trap, Admiral, there is only one certain fact, and that is—you never know."

For a moment Reed contemplated him solemnly. Then he turned to the dive officer.

"Lieutenant Avellino," he said. "Can it be done? Can a . . . a nondiver make a successful dive?"

"It can be done, sir."

"What will be needed?"

"Major Munk will have to undergo a pressure-and-oxygen-tolerance test, sir."

"Which is?"

"The major will enter a decompression chamber. He will be briefed by an inside tender. A diver. He will be pressurized to 165 FSW—that's feet of sea water—for a period of twelve minutes. He will then be decompressed to 60 FSW. He will hold an oxygen mask over his mouth and nose and breathe pure oxygen for thirty minutes. The DDC will then be decompressed to the surface."

"How long does all that take?"

"An hour and a half, sir."

"And compression for the dive itself, assuming he passes the test?"

"Emergency compression—one hour."

"That's an elapsed time of two and half hours, Lieutenant."

"Yes, sir. DDC time only. But it would be the same for anyone else."

Reed nodded slowly. He looked at Einar.

"Major Munk?"

"Any time," Einar said.

Reed turned to the salvage master.

"Commander," he said. "He's all yours."

Birte's eyes never left her husband's. She wanted desperately to hold him, to beg him not to undertake such a dangerous task, to keep him near her, away from harm. But she also knew he had to do what he was doing. And she said nothing.

After all, she thought ruefully, I've seen enough movies with weepy, whining wives seeing their husbands off on a difficult and perilous mission—imploring them not to go when they damned well know their men have no choice, and thereby making it even more difficult and perilous for them—for me to fall into that mold myself.

Her eyes met Einar's. He smiled at her. He knew how she felt. And it warmed him. She walked over to him and confidently took his arm.

As Einar and Birte left the wardroom with Dedham, Reed addressed Commander Cannon.

"Is the *Cormorant* capable of storing the last container after bringing it up, Commander?"

"Yes, sir. No problem."

"Good. I'm going to move the task force upwind. Fifty miles." He turned to his aide. "Send this message," he ordered.

"From CTF-49 to TF-49, info CINCLANT/SACLANT/CINCWESTLANT. Paragraph one. Upon receipt, TF-49 except USS *Cormorant*, ASR-23, will get underway immediately and proceed to position latitude 48 degrees north, longitude 13 degrees west. Upon arrival report to Rear Admiral Everett Stirling, Royal Navy, designated CTU, 49.1. . . ."

It was 1621 hours, one hour and four minutes after the cache of high explosives and the booby-trapped drum had been discovered in the U-1000 below.

All the other vessels of TF-49 had departed the area, leaving the USS *Cormorant*, ASR-23, alone, webbed in her four-point-moor over the diving site. The divers had been brought up.

Henderson and Dedham had walked Einar through his preparations for the tolerance test and the ultimate dive, and Einar had been sent off to be outfitted with the special clothing he was to wear under the neoprene rubber diving suit.

The test was scheduled to commence at 1630 hours, and Henderson was waiting with Birte at the DDC for Einar to return from supplies, when a seaman came hurrying up to him.

"Sir," he said. "Urgent message. From Washington."

Henderson grabbed the paper the man held out to him. His eyes raced over the content.

It was from CID/FBI. It contained further, urgent information about one of the subjects on whom in-depth investigations had been conducted.

His eyes raced to the name.

And with a chill he knew who the saboteur was on board the USS *Cormorant*. . . .

Einar and the seaman assigned to him as guide were walking down a corridor on their way to the DDC from supplies. Einar was clad in a tight-fitting fire-retardant garment, much like a jumpsuit. He felt keyed up. He knew the task that lay before him would be the most crucial he'd ever faced. And he prayed he wouldn't blow it. No pun intended, he thought sardonically. He carried his own bundled-up clothing in his arms as he hurried down the passageway toward a ladder to the deck below.

As they passed a side corridor, they suddenly glimpsed the furtive figure of a man ducking into an open doorway.

The seaman stopped. He frowned. That security alert was still in effect, wasn't it? He turned to Einar.

"That's the winch room," he said softly. "For the SPCC. Now what? Please, sir, wait here for a moment."

Cautiously he started toward the open doorway.

Einar followed.

The compartment behind the door was dark except for the strip of light from the corridor, which spilled across the deck.

The seaman stepped into the room.

There was a short, sharp crack. The seaman jerked spasmodically. He wrenched his face toward Einar—surprise dying in his one remaining eye. The other had been splattered across his cheek by the dumdum bullet that had torn through the thin bone behind it and gouged a searing path through his brain.

He was dead before he lurched against the bulkhead and slid to the deck.

Einar had no chance to move before a man stepped into the light.

In one hand he held a small, open bottle.

In the other a gun.

42

Einar at once recognized the gun held in the man's hand, the gun that had just killed his companion—and now was pointed unwaveringly at his face.

It was a Lilliput. German made. A gun developed for the Nazi Werewolf terrorists: 4.2mm, magazine load; the smallest effective automatic ever made, so small it could be concealed in a man's palm.

But at close range, firing dumdum bullets, as lethal as the best of them.

He stared at the man before him, his eyes riveted on his. For a split moment he had the illusion that he was staring into jet black pits.

"Dr. Hart!" he breathed.

"Allow me to correct you, Professor Munk," the toxicologist said, his voice an icy rustle. He drew himself up. "Hartmann. Dr. Maximilian Hartmann. Former director of the *Sudeten Chemiewerke;* creator of the Führer's, Adolf Hitler's, V-3." He smiled an arctic smile that sent a chill through Einar. "A substance you so whimsically call 'brown sugar'!"

Suddenly it all tumbled into place.

He stared at the man standing before him, the moving force behind it all. Hart—or Hartmann. The mainspring behind the attempts to kill his Birte. And him. As they came too close to his obscene secret: to ensure the ultimate success of Adolf Hitler's insane vengeance scheme . . . The man behind Operation V-3. The terrible poison was *his!*

It made sense. Wierdring and the other U-1000 survivors would have reported to Hartmann when their mission failed. And Hartmann, obviously a fanatical Nazi ideologist, would have had no choice but to safeguard his secret and impatiently wait for the day his and his Führer's vengeance against their archenemies would burst from the sea—and to make certain that it happened.

It had been them against Hartmann all along.

And Hartmann had won.

Einar was at this moment perhaps the only hope of having even a chance to disarm the booby trap below in time.

And he stood staring at death.

The V-3 horror would exact the Führer's final vengeance.

Any day.

Any hour . . .

His eyes were inexorably drawn to the little open bottle in Hartmann's hand.

Was it . . . ?

Hartmann followed his gaze. Again he smiled his ghastly smile.

"You are curious, Professor Munk?" He held up the little bottle. "No. Let me put your mind at ease. It is not what you fear it is. It is not 'brown sugar'!" He coughed an unpleasant little laugh. "It is sulphuric acid. Highly concentrated, fuming sulphuric acid, Professor. I am certain you are familiar with it." The sarcasm in his voice was oily and derisive. He was obviously enjoying himself.

Einar looked uncomprehendingly at him.

"Acid?" he said dully. He was suddenly uncomfortably aware of the cold sweat trickling from his armpits down his sides.

"Come now, Professor," Hartmann mocked him. "Use your imagination. The whole ship's company has avidly been hunting a saboteur. Give me credit for not wanting to disappoint them forever. And what more fitting act of sabotage than causing the loss of an entire diving capsule? With the divers in it, of course. With *you* in it, Professor."

He suddenly spilled a little drop of acid on the steel deck.

Instantly it seethed and bubbled as it burned into the metal.

Mesmerized, Einar watched the fuming acid eating into the steel, his senses—supercharged in the face of death—excruciatingly aware of the roiling ferment of the acid burn.

"I am certain you also know the highly corrosive powers of the acid, Professor. Or—you need only look. When poured on the main cable supporting the diver capsule, any visible action would slowly subside. No one would know. But the action of the acid would weaken the cable to the point of snapping when enough weight was applied to it. Such as a diver capsule being lowered into the deep.''

An icy coldness darkened Hartmann's eyes. This time the smile was a mere vicious slit.

''Of course,'' he rasped. ''With you here—all that is a mute question.''

His eyes met Einar's.

''Good-bye, Professor Munk,'' he said. ''I salute you. You have been a worthy adversary.''

Einar's world was filled with only one thing—the sight of a tiny gun, and a finger tightening on the curve of a trigger.

No!

He would not die!

Anger exploded in him.

Suddenly he hurled his bundle of clothing at the hand holding the gun. In the same instant he dropped to one knee—and felt a lance of white-hot heat knife across his left ear.

Hartmann, taken by surprise, instinctively raised his hands to ward off the flying bundle of clothes. The bundle struck the hand that held the bottle, slammed it upward—and the acid flew from it to drench the ex-Nazi's face.

His shriek came from the abyss of hell itself.

Instantly his flesh began to boil. Erupting in sizzling bubbles, it writhed with a sudden, grisly life of its own. His eyes split open and added their horror and fluid to the dissolving skin of his face. In abject agony and terror, bellowing in blinding torment, the man clawed at the searing, roiling pain that was his face, and the fulminating acid at once attacked his gouging fingers that tried to tear the torment from him, consuming their flesh.

Appalled, rooted to the spot in horror, Einar watched the fuming flesh peel off the man's face like paper from a wall aflame, as his mutilated hands clawed at it in a frenzy of soul-searing torture, the flesh dripping from them.

Hartmann's strident screams became a ululating moan. It stopped. As did the motion of his crippled fingers.

Dr. Maximilian Hartmann, former director of the *Sudeten Chemiewerke,* creator and protector of Adolf Hitler's V-3, was dead. . . .

Einar did not know how long he stood staring in shock at the gruesome remains of Hartmann, crumpled grotesquely at his feet. He suddenly knew what it was that had bothered him, and bitterly he cursed himself. He should have known. Dammit! He should have known! And acted on it. If he had, two young men would still be alive.

Two hundred and fifty kilograms per drum, Hart had said—long before a diver had read it on a drum! How could he have known?

He'd missed it when Hart had said it during the meeting in the command center. So had everyone else. But he kicked only his own ass for missing it. Dammit to hell! He could have called the bastard on it—and exposed him then and there.

Or—could he?

It could have been a guess on the scientist's part. From the size of the drums. An educated guess. It had been, after all, the expert speaking. And one does not question what an expert says.

A piss-poor rationalization at best.

He was abruptly yanked out of his state of shock and self-incrimination by the urgent voice of Henderson.

"Munk! Are you all right? Munk?"

Einar started. "Yeah," he mumbled. "All right."

Henderson looked at the twisted, unrecognizable body of Hartmann. He shuddered visibly.

"Hart?" he asked hoarsely.

Silently Einar nodded.

Birte came running up to him, her face white.

"You're hurt!" she cried in alarm. "You're bleeding!"

Unconsciously Einar touched his ear. The blood had run down his neck and soaked the collar of his jumpsuit. "It's all right," he said. He brought his hand down and—preoccupied—looked at the blood on his fingers. "It's just a scratch."

"Scratch or no scratch," Birte said firmly, "you are going to have a doctor look at you before you go gallivanting around on the ocean floor."

Einar nodded. Mentally he shook himself. But the hellish sight of Hartmann's face was forever etched on his sickened mind.

"Are you able to go on with the dive?" Henderson asked.

"Of course. It is really only a scratch."

"What . . . what happened?" Henderson asked. He deliberately kept his eyes averted from the remains of Hartmann.

Einar told him.

"He killed the boy," he said bleakly. "Just—like that. There was nothing I could do."

Other members of the *Cormorant* crew, who had arrived with Henderson and Birte, were already removing the body of the young seaman. Someone threw a small tarpaulin over Hartmann.

"I . . . I had no idea Dr. Hart was . . . was . . ." Einar let the sentence trail off.

"I only found out myself a few moments ago," Henderson said. He fished the Pentagon report from his pocket and handed it to Einar. Einar glanced through it. He was slowly regaining his full composure.

Hartmann had left Germany via the ODESSA escape route immediately after the war. He had gone to South America and entered the United States illegally from Mexico. He had built himself a new identity under the name of Hart, using false papers supplied by one of the SS forgery mills. It had obviously not been an easy task to unravel the man's past. After various jobs in industrial and manufacturing organizations, he'd entered the academic field and gradually risen to become a leading toxicologist. When the urgent call for top toxicologists went out from the Pentagon, a colleague of Hart's had actually been chosen from the respondents, but the man at the last minute had been the victim of a freak laboratory accident that had temporarily blinded him. The accident was under investigation. Dr. Hart had at once volunteered to take his colleague's place, and had been accepted.

"The bastard did some fancy footwork to get himself involved in the operation," Einar said as he returned the report to Henderson.

Einar gave a last look at the tarpaulin-covered body of Dr. Maximilian Hartmann.

A deadly enemy had been eliminated.

But the greatest adversary still waited below.

His creation—V-3 . . .

The personnel transfer capsule was slowly descending toward the wreck of the U-1000. The descent to 650 feet would take one hour. There were four men in the PTC, three divers and Einar, two of the divers outfitted with Man-Amplifiers.

Einar had passed his tolerance test without problems. There had been a quick, tender embrace by Birte and a bright "thumbs up" kind of smile, and Einar had once again entered the deck decompression chamber to undergo the one-hour emergency compression for the dive.

Einar had never done any deep-sea diving, only some scuba diving along the southern Florida coast, and diving on a reef off Bermuda wearing a bell-type, glass-faced helmet at a depth of thirty to forty feet, all several years ago. He had found the underwater world fascinating, filled with color and frisky life.

He was fully aware that the world he was about to enter now would be one of Stygian darkness—and life-threatening dangers.

He sat quietly with his companions in the cramped iron bubble that was the PTC. He was grateful he had no tendencies to feel claustrophobic, or he'd have been clawing the steel walls already—especially when he contemplated the fact that at the depth to which he was descending, the pressure on him would have been 290 pounds per square inch. He wondered how it would feel. They'd told him he wouldn't know it at all. Yeah?

He had trouble getting used to his own voice and those of his teammates, made high-pitched and squeaky by the helium in the breathing gas, and he realized the necessity for the electronic devices that somewhat converted their shrill chatter into something like normal speech.

He fingered the bonded umbilical that entered his diving suit, suddenly in awe of it. On its strength, his life would depend. It would be his sole, tenuous communication link with the world above. And with Birte. Through it would flow the heated air he'd breathe and the warmth that would sustain him. The umbilical.

How terrifyingly apt the name.

For the hundredth time he dwelled on the myriad bits of information that had been crammed into his mind in the last few hours. He suddenly realized that he remembered not one of them. He had an instant of panic—then he knew it was only the tension. It would all come back to him when he needed it. It always did.

He'd spent the compression time in the DDC, learning the fundamentals of using his neoprene rubber diving suit and his MK 1 MOD S helmet, with its little TV camera mounted on it, and its built-in communications capabilities. It had been the strangest schoolroom he'd ever attended. Four bunks and a tiny work space in the main chamber; shower, sink, and toilet in the outer lock; and a separate little lock through which their food and other necessities were supplied. He did not look forward to the seven days he'd have to spend there; that was how long it would take to decompress from the 650-foot depth. Hell—it still beat the alternative.

The PTC came to a stop a few feet above the ocean bottom. Two of the divers remained in the capsule to provide backup and feed the umbilicals as Einar and one of the divers exited through the hatch in the bottom, which automatically had cracked open when the outside pressure equalized that to which the PTC had been pressurized.

And Einar found himself in an alien world. Hostile, cold, and shrouded in inky blackness. Nothing at all like the friendly, luminous waters off Bermuda, he thought. The only illumination was provided by the bumper ring lights installed on the PTC. The buoyancy he experienced, however, was familiar to him. It at once gave him a feeling of freedom—and curtailment.

He and his companion turned on their work lights and with molasses movements started for the U-1000, the diver leading, Einar carrying his little box of tools, straining against the drag of the umbilical.

The passage through the jagged gap into the innards of the wreck was an eerie experience. Einar was startled when his light picked up a gleaming heap of bones topped by a hollow-eyed, grinning skull, which once had been one of the U-boat crewmen. Uniform tatters still hung from the bleached bones. Undulating gently in the water, they gave the apparition an eerie life. There had to be others, he thought. Many others. No one had mentioned that.

And finally he stood before the fateful drum, the solid metal box that held the booby-trap mechanism securely joined to it. Rusty, dull, and encrusted, it did not look like a deathtrap, a killer able to snuff out many thousands of lives in unspeakable agony.

He knew it was.

Cautiously he began to examine the booby-trap housing. It was a box about nine by six inches and four inches deep, welded to the drum. A thick lid was held on it with sturdy screws. Rusted in place, it would be difficult to remove. The MAM diver would have to help. A heavy, insulated cable ran a couple of feet out from the box, disappearing through the bulkhead into the adjoining compartment.

Einar knew what that compartment held.

Thousands of pounds of high explosives.

He let his hand glide along the cable.

"Let's take a look at what's on the other side," he said.

"You got it."

The diver turned away and carefully led the way back. At the hatchway to the explosives compartment, they encountered the bleached remains of two more submariners. Einar carefully skirted them.

Although he had known what to expect, the sight of the hundreds of crates of high explosives sent a chill through Einar. Looming in squat stacks, like stolid executioners they had been waiting forty years to blow the world asunder. Despite the hot water that coursed through his suit to keep him warm, Einar felt dead cold. There seemed to be an aura of taut anticipation in the gloomy hold, where the crates surrounded him in brooding silence as if they knew that today was to be their day.

Einar made his way to the crate next to the bulkhead, into which the cable ran. Warily he began to examine it.

In the command center on board the *Cormorant*, there was not a sound to be heard as the officers, the two scientists, and Birte followed the work below.

Henderson came up to Admiral Reed.

"Admiral," he said. "I am about to transmit my report to the White House."

"Of course," Reed said, his eyes glued to the monitor screens. "Go ahead."

"I should like to include in it how you propose to dispose of the poison, once it is all retrieved," Henderson went on. "In response to a query, sir."

Reed turned to him in annoyance. "I wish they'd leave us in peace until the damned job is done," he snapped.

"Yes, sir. What shall I tell them?"

Reed glared at him, his jaw clenched.

"Tell them this," he growled. "I shall make my proposal to SACLANT. I propose to take no chances whatsoever. I propose not to open any of the sealed engine containers, to analyze the poison or for any reason. And you can tell them their toxicologist experts agree with me. I propose to dispatch the LPD with all the containers filled with the drums to the Pacific Missile Range in the South Pacific. I propose to close the entire area, as is often routinely done, and I propose to blow the damned LPD and its damned cargo to hell! Let the cloud of poison gas sweep out over an empty sea and dissipate itself, as it will, endangering no one. The area is big enough for the job. It was once used as a test site for nuclear weapons." His eyes bored into Henderson. "And tell them if they have a better idea to let me know. Understood?"

"Yes, sir."

"But, dammit! Let us retrieve and secure all the drums, and not go off half-cocked," Reed finished. He turned back to the monitor.

The lid was off the crate. Through his face plate, Einar peered at what it held.

Mated to the connector cable from the booby trap on the drum was another metal box, sitting in the middle of the crate with blocks of high explosives packed around it, each block wrapped and sealed in heavy wax paper, making water penetration practically nil.

It was the main load detonator mechanism.

The thoughts in Einar's mind churned as he tried to recall every minute bit of knowledge he had stored somewhere in the deep recesses of his mind. He stared at the box. On top of the device was a small window. Carefully he cleaned it of sediment. Below, he could make out the disc of a small wheel. With a sinking feeling he realized he had no idea what it was. The entire mechanism was foreign to him. He only knew he could not touch it; he could not take the chance and disturb the detonator device on the main load. It would instantly trigger an explosion. Neither could he move the booby-trapped drum without first disarming the trap with its separate charge of explosives.

The trap was the key.

He motioned to the diver to return to the drums.

On the monitor screens at the main control console, Reed watched as the two men began to make their way back to the cargo hold where the last few drums were still lashed down.

Impatience tingled in him, but he knew he could not hurry the procedure. Haste in this case would not only mean waste. But annihilation.

For a moment, earlier, he had contemplated ordering the entire ship's crew to wear their protective gear—but he'd quickly realized that no amount of protection would save them if the trap below was sprung.

In the wreck the divers had reached the booby-trapped drum again.

Minutely, area by area, touching nothing, Einar began to inspect the trap. From the connector cable, taut wires went to the hidden interior of the device. The central core of it seemed to be crimped to a detonator cap.

Primacord!

The core of the insulated cable was a wire-bound, waterproof detonating cord, insensitive to temperature and shock, with a tensile strength of 222 pounds, which when initiated would explode instantly along its entire length. It was usually used to connect several charges for simultaneous detonation.

If the booby trap was set off—the entire main load would explode in the same instant!

He studied the wiring.

It was probably a release device. Try to move the trap, or cut one of the wires, and a spring-operated plunger would slam into a detonator that would set off the explosives on the drum, scattering its deadly contents—and also fire the primacord, which would detonate the main load.

There were two wires. One of them would be a safety; when cut, it would probably cause the detonator cap to be moved out of reach of the plunger, if it was released.

Which one?

And which one would set off the explosion?

He bent over the device, studying it minutely. How would the safety work? He wracked his brain for long-hidden knowledge. Neutralize the trap in some manner? Pull the detonator out of the way? So that if the plunger *was* released, it would not connect? That could be it. He peered at the two wires. If he was right, one of them would release the plunger, the detonator pin, and the other would release a spring that would pull or push the detonator to a safe position. It would be logical to assume that such a safety device did, in fact, exist in the mechanism. So that the trap could be rendered harmless if for any reason it became necessary to move the booby-trapped drum. And there *were* two wires.

Two wires: one safe, one deadly. And it was up to him to decide which one was the safe one, which one would trigger the trap.

And the main load of thousands of pounds of high explosives.

What else could he do? Should he take the chance and select one of the wires? Or should he not? It was not an either-or question. That decision had already been made for him. By the Führer, and by time. If he did not make a try, the drums would soon split open and spew out their lethal poison, and the cloud of death would become a reality. If he did try—at least there was a fifty-fifty chance he might make the right choice.

Again he gazed at the exposed wiring. One of the wires seemed to angle a little downward. The other ran straight, at least as far as he could follow it with his eyes.

The one that angled down could well be the one that would release the spring to pull the detonator to its safe position. It would make sense. That spring would probably be located somewhere below the detonator.

Once again he studied the wiring. He was suddenly back at Shrivenham. And the booby-trap course. It was the old game of second guessing: you know the would-be disarmer of your trap will realize there has to be a safety wire; it was required. So you make the detonator wire *look* as if it were the safety wire, hoping he will cut it. But you will also realize that he may see through that ruse and decide that what *looks* like the safety wire is really the detonator, and so select the one that looks like the detonator wire to cut. However, you may figure that he might think just that way, and therefore keep the safety wire looking safe and the detonator wire appear to be the trigger. Already confusing, but the game never ended. It was the old truism: the only thing you know for sure about a booby trap is, that you never know.

And yet, he had to make a decision.

And he had to make it now.

Why was the drum booby-trapped at all? There could be many reasons. As a hands-off safeguard, a warning, against possible tampering? Perhaps. If so, would they have gone to the trouble of playing the second-guessing game? Probably not. The trap was really more a matter of routine than an attempt to trick an enemy.

He stared at the mechanism.

He made up his mind—shutting out the voice that clamored in the back of his mind: you are wrong! You are wrong!

He reached for the wire he had decided was the safety wire to hold it steady while he cut it with his clippers.

Suddenly he was jerked violently off his feet.

There was a sickening, scraping sound. His umbilical pulled him helplessly across the cargo hold deck. He felt the whole wreck shudder and pitch as it shifted its bulk on the rocky, uneven sea bottom.

It jarred to rest. Einar tried to get up. He could not move. Somewhere his umbilical was caught . . .

Topside, in the control room, the men at the console stared in shock at the wildly gyrating pictures on the television monitors.

"Commander!" Reed cried to the salvage master. "What's going on?"

White-faced, Dedham answered. "The wreck is settling, sir. We have removed a lot of heavy drums. The weight has shifted. The U-1000 is changing position."

"What about the men?"

"It depends. If the wreck rolls over, or if the shift is severe enough, their umbilicals may be severed. Or their suits ripped open. They would not survive five minutes."

"Anything we can do?"

"Nothing, sir. Just . . . hope—"

In the wardroom command center, Birte sat stiffly before the monitors, tightly gripping the edge of the table. She did not move. She made no outcry. She said nothing. Her very being was with her husband far below the ocean surface. She heard the voice of the capsule operator squawk from the speaker in alarm.

"Green Diver. Capsule. Are you all right? What is happening? Your umbilical jerked taut!"

"I'm . . . caught—" Birte at once recognized the strained voice of Einar, even over the tinny unscrambler device. "I am . . . okay. But—I can't move."

"Red Diver. Capsule. You okay?"

"Capsule. Red Diver. Okay. Banged up a bit. No damage. The damned wreck is settling!"

"Red Diver, assist Green Diver. His umbilical is fouled."

"Understand. Will assist."

Birte sat totally motionless. She dared not move lest she should miss hearing the voices from below. She stared fixedly at the monitors. The sudden motion of the wreck had disturbed the sediment and muddied the water. The pictures were cloudy and indistinct.

In the control room a seaman came up to Admiral Reed. "Message, sir," he said. "From Lieutenant Craig."

Reed at once grabbed the paper handed to him. It was from the meteorologist officer on board the *Coral Sea* fifty miles upwind from the dive position. The storm was worsening. It was bearing down on the *Cormorant.* It would be only a matter of hours before the dive would have to be aborted.

With angry worry Reed glared at the cloudy monitors. Dammit! he thought. What next? Weather above, explosives and a shifting wreck below. What the hell next?

Einar felt his umbilical slacken. He struggled to his feet. The Red Diver stood before him.

"You okay?" he asked.

"Okay," Einar croaked. He dared say no more. He did not trust his voice. It had been close. Too damned close. He thanked God that the explosives and the poison drums were tied down, or the settling of the wreck might have set off the detonators.

He at once turned back to the booby-trapped drum. The deck was tilting. The submarine was lying at a different angle. He prayed it wouldn't shift any farther. Or topple over.

He had a sudden disquieting thought. The drums. The remaining drums, still lashed down. Had they been damaged during the shift of the wreck? Were any of them leaking? Quickly he and his fellow diver looked them over. They were okay. Einar at once returned his attention to the booby trap.

He again located the wire he had selected to cut. He reached for it, his rapid heartbeat loud in his ears.

Clumsily, trying not to disturb anything in the unknown mechanism that might set it off, he attempted to get a good hold on the wire. It was impossible. His heated neoprene rubber gloves were too cumbersome to get into the cramped space.

"Capsule," he said. "This is Green Diver. Is it . . . is it possible for me to take my gloves off?"

There was a brief pause.

"Yes. But—it will hurt like hell. Don't keep them off too long. It'll be damned cold."

"Got you."

Einar removed his gloves.

Instantly the cold bit into his flesh. A sharp pain pricked his hands. He'd felt that pain before, he realized. When for a few moments he'd put his hands into the icy slush in the freezer compartment when he was defrosting the old refrigerator back home. Only here he couldn't pull his hands back out when they started to hurt.

He took hold of the wire.

He held the clippers to it.

The agony in his hands was quickly getting worse. His fingers were growing numb.

He thought of Birte. His mind was filled with her. The beauty of her the first time he saw her in her little apartment . . . Her flushed excitement during the war plant sabotage raid . . . How she had saved his life when he hadn't been able to kill his erstwhile friend, turned traitor . . . Making love with her the first time, that magical moment in the rain on the beach . . . Her tenderness with the terrified Siemens woman in Germany . . . Her courage in the china factory and in the Irish icehouse . . . Her constant support and belief in him. And her love. In a fraction of a second, it all shone in his mind.

He cut the wire.

43

The wire tore from his numb fingers. With the hand that rested on the booby-trap housing, he felt a sudden tiny vibration. The release of a spring? Wildly the thought cascaded through his mind. Nothing had happened! Nothing! No explosion! He was safe. Had he cut the safety wire? Had the plunger mechanism misfired? Or had the efficiency impairment of the waterlogged explosives reached the point of nonexplosion? Even as he thought it, he knew that could not be. The booby trap had been sealed dry until he had opened the box. He *had* cut the right wire! He exulted.

Birte! I did it!

The booby trap was disarmed.

Quickly he cut the second wire so that the explosives could be removed from the drum.

He looked at the cut end of the wire protruding from the connector cable.

Harmless now.

He suddenly frowned. *One* wire? There should be two. He had cut *two* wires. What had happened to the cut end of the first wire he'd clipped?

He suddenly stiffened in shock.

He knew what had happened to it as it had been ripped from his fingers. It had been yanked into the connector cable. There had been a spring not only on the booby-trap end—but also in the mechanism in the main detonator box!

Why? And why only on that one?

An icy thought lanced through his mind. At once he turned and began to fight his way to the explosives compartment. His fellow diver followed.

Einar went straight to the open crate that held the detonator box.

He squinted at it. And at the little window on top.

The wheel below it was turning. A red disc had become visible beneath it—slowly moving to fill the circle with crimson. And with chilling certainty he knew.

The detonator mechanism was a delayed-action device.

And it had been activated.

The main load—the thousands of pounds of powerful high explosives—would be detonated. And there was no way to stop it.

Only one question.

How long?

"Control Room," he croaked. "Green Diver—" Even as he was reporting what had happened, his mind was awhirl. It was a delayed-action device utilizing chemicals. Had to be. When he cut the booby-trap safety wire, it had also released a spring-operated piston in the main load detonator mechanism that rammed into a glass vial with a strong acid, shattering it. The released acid had already begun to eat through a wire that, when weakened enough to break, would allow the firing pin to ram into the detonator and set off the explosion. The time delay would depend on the acid and the thickness of the wire. It was the kind of delayed-action device often used in the war, and he was thoroughly familiar with it. And he knew there was no way to control or stop the action once started. And there was also no way to determine the length of time it would take before the explosion occurred. The little red moving disc could measure seconds. Or minutes. Or—hours . . .

"—the delayed-action detonator device has been activated," he finished. Cold fear was eating into the marrow of his bones.

In the brief moment of silence, he could almost feel the stunned shock topside.

Birte. He suddenly ached to hold her. He did not want to be apart from her, when—

"Diver Team A." The dive supervisor's voice seemed to explode in Einar's helmet. "Abort! Repeat—*abort!* At once. Divers return to the capsule. Capsule! Ready to ascend."

"No! Wait!" Einar shouted inside his helmet.

"Green Diver. This is Admiral Reed," the words crackled in Einar's ears. "Abort at once! That's an order!"

The thoughts tumbled and whirled in Einar's brain. There was something. What? Dammit! *What?*

"Admiral," he said urgently. "We *can't* abort. We *must* bring the rest of the drums to the surface before the charge blows." He hurried on, afraid not to have enough time to finish his say. "The explosion is delayed. We may have enough time to—"

"It will take an hour just to get you up!" Reed's voice snapped. "Return to the capsule. Now!"

Reed felt the pressure on him as an almost physical force. He was suddenly face to face with the most crucial decision he'd ever have to make. . . . He could cut the capsule loose and steam away. Sacrifice the divers below to save the ship and crew? He rejected the thought even as it was born. No. He would get under way as soon as the capsule was back on board. The amount of poison that would be scattered now to form the deadly poison gas cloud had been diminished. Greatly diminished. It was his only choice. Staying would be a useless sacrifice. He only hoped there would be enough time to get the PTC up from below.

"Major Munk," he said heavily. "You have your orders. We will retrieve the capsule—with or without you in it. Is that clear? I must save the ship's crew."

Suddenly Einar knew what it was that had been trying to surface from his unconscious mind.

"Would not the captain of the U-1000 have had the same thought, Admiral? The explosion *is* controlled by a delayed-action device. Would that delay not have to be long enough for the German skipper and *his* crew to reach safety? *Let us use that time!*"

There was silence from above.

"Wierdring, or Mahler, one of them said they'd be long gone before the explosion occurred. Dozens of kilometers away, he said. Dozens, Admiral. That's . . . that's perhaps three hours. Or four. We can do the job and get away in that time."

Still there was silence.

"What if we leave? Now? And it turns out there would have been ample time to bring the last drums to the surface? How many hundreds of thousands will die, Admiral? Needlessly."

Suddenly Reed's voice crackled in Einar's helmet.

"Make it fast!"

They did.

Einar quickly returned to the capsule, and the other MAM diver took his place.

The two divers went to work at once, securing and loading the remaining drums in the last aircraft engine container. How long did they have? They did not think about it. . . .

The drums were loaded. The *Cormorant* had retrieved both the full container and the capsule with the divers in record time. Forty-two minutes . . .

Commander Cannon watched the capsule and the container hurriedly being secured aboard the *Cormorant.*

It was time to get the hell out of there. "Ready emergency breakaway!" he ordered. There was no time to follow any SOP in unrigging the moor. The four nylon hawsers that led to the mooring buoys would have to be severed, cut at the deck line, the buoys abandoned. It was simply a matter of taking an axe to the lines.

"Break moor!" he ordered.

The restraining hawsers fell away. The *Cormorant* was free to move.

At once she got under way at full speed.

Einar and the other divers had transferred to the DDC, and Birte was speaking to him over the communication system.

She felt as if a weight the size of the *Coral Sea* had been lifted from her shoulders. It was over! Einar was safe. Everyone was safe. The terrible poison had been rendered harmless.

They had won.

Suddenly there was the distant sound of a violent thunderclap coming from the depth below, growing with frightening power. Miles of ocean rumbled, shuddered, and shook as the sea-bottom blast of tons of high explosives tore the sea apart.

And all at once, just off the port side of the *Cormorant,* the ocean erupted in an ear-piercing roar and a gigantic column of raging water that shot high up into the air, mushrooming out in a cascade of solid foaming sheets of green water that deluged the ship.

For a moment it seemed as if the entire ship were being lifted up out of the water—then the shock force of the monstrous explosion hit.

The steel plates of the helo deck buckled with the banshee shriek of tortured metal. The port lifeboat instantly splintered into a myriad jagged pieces that were hurled through the water-drenched air. The massive loading arms, the heavy booms that had been used to hoist the filled engine containers up from the ocean bottom, were twisted and bent. Water geysered up through the center well, and there was a sharp, twanging sound as the underwater stabilizer beam between the two hulls cracked. A seaman caught on deck was lifted up and savagely slammed against the crane gantry, his head smashed open like a shell, his back wrapped around a steel beam. A PTC, stored on its aft stowage stand, was buffeted loose. It toppled off the stand and rolled forward like a three-thousand-pound bowling ball, crushing and mangling everything in its path, and demolishing the essential deck decompression chamber/personnel transfer capsule mating clamps, as the *Cormorant* violently heaved and rolled and pitched in the turbulent water.

In the confinement of the DDC, Einar was thrown sharply against the worktable, the edge of it gouging him painfully in the back. He grabbed hold of it and hung on as the chamber bucked and pitched. What was happening outside, he thought? To Birte? To the ship? The lights flickered and went out—then came back on as the emergency power system cut in.

Birte was on the floor of the command center, clinging to the frame of a hatchway. She had been thrown from her chair at the com system table and had slid across the deck, scraping the skin off her knees and elbows. The temporary television monitor sets had crashed in a shower of sparks, and the shards of coffee cups and saucers rattled through the wardroom. She tried to shut out the clanging, booming noises that reverberated through the ship and terrified her. She felt utterly helpless. Her thoughts flew to her husband, imprisoned in a sealed iron tank, depending on delicate life-sustaining systems for his very existence. Please God, she prayed, let him be all right. . . .

Gradually the frothing, bubbling boil and churning around the ship subsided.

The *Cormorant* was still afloat. Pounded, battered, and devastated by the mammoth explosion in the U-1000 below, she rode heavily in the still-seething water.

Had she been directly over the mammoth explosion, she would have been torn apart.

But she was still afloat.

The container with the last drums of Adolf Hitler's final vengeance weapon was still intact, secure on board.

The Führer's V-3 had failed its mission.

EPILOGUE

July 1985

"Birte! Where's the double-stick tape? You got it?" Einar's voice sounded slightly aggrieved.

Fifty-seven, fifty-eight, fifty-nine, sixty, Birte counted to herself, as she stirred the fixings of the Danish red pudding in the saucepan.

"Haven't touched it!" she called. "Look in your left-hand drawer!"

"Oh . . . I found it!"

Birte poured the gelatinous red mass over a layer of fresh strawberries in a deep dish. She plopped in a few bleached almonds, sprinkled a fine covering of powdered sugar over the surface of the junket, and placed it in the refrigerator to set. Served with cream poured over it, it would be the evening's dinner dessert, the popular *Rødgrød med Fløde* that appeared on every Danish menu, but that was impossible to pronounce for someone not brought up in the Danish language. Even though she'd heard it a hundred times, she looked forward to hearing Einar explain to their guests how the dessert helped catch spies.

In both World War I and II, he'd tell them, whenever they were unsure if a subject under investigation was a native Dane or a spy, they'd give the man a Danish menu to read, and when he came to *Rødgrød med Fløde* and it didn't come out right, he would be up against the nearest wall! She always suspected he romanticized that last bit.

She walked into Einar's little office. He was sitting at his desk, which was cluttered with clippings, snapshots, and other paper items.

“How’s it coming?” she asked.

“Nearly done,” Einar said. “The best damned US book special yet. Commander Cannon sent me a great photo of the *Cormorant.*”

“Well, don’t be too long. The Hendersons will be here at seven.”

“I know. I want to have the album done so I can show it to Jonathan. I’m sure he’ll recognize a few things in it.” He looked up at Birte with a grin. “I put that cartoon in.”

“What cartoon?”

“You know. The one that shows a little boy playing soldier, being dressed down by a chicken colonel with insignias on his shoulders the size of vultures.”

“I’m sure he’ll love it,” Birte said dryly. “Are you putting in that nice letter from the President? It sounds so mysteriously romantic. *For extraordinary services rendered in the interests of your country.*”

“You bet. It’ll be next to the last item in the book.” He picked up a small newspaper clipping. “This’ll be the last.” He handed it to Birte. “It was in this morning’s paper.”

She read:

> WASHINGTON, D.C. (AP) The Navy Department today announced that the Pacific Missile Range has been reopened to commercial shipping as of yesterday. The special operations under the command of Rear Admiral Benjamin Reed, USN, which kept the South Pacific range closed for several weeks, have been successfully concluded.

Birte gave the newspaper clipping back to her husband. It was a fitting epitaph for the final act of insanity in the history of the Third Reich and the Führer, Adolf Hitler.

The V-3.

LIST OF ABBREVIATIONS AND ACRONYMS

General

BMW	Bavarian Motor Works
IOU	I Owe You
NATO	North Atlantic Treaty Organization
PA	Public Address System
st.tv.	Stuen til venstre (Ground floor, left) Danish
TAT	Transatlantic Telephone Cable
UCLA	University of California in Los Angeles

Medical

Bp	Blood pressure
ID	Identification
IV	Intravenous
MAST	Military Antishock Trousers
OR	Operating Room
PA	Physician's Assistant

Military—British

Asdic	Anti-Submarine Detection Investigation Committee
HMS	His (Her) Majesty's Ship
RAF	Royal Air Force
SOE	Special Operations Executive

Military—German and Danish

BOPA	Borgerlige Partisaner (Citizen Partisans) Danish
E.T.	Efterretnings Tjeneste (Espionage Service) Danish
HIPO	Hilfspolizei (Danish-German Auxiliary Police)
LI	Leitender Ingenieur (Chief Engineer)
NAPOLA	Nationalpolitischen Erziehungsanstalten (National Political Educational Institutions)
ODESSA	Organisation der Ehemalige SS Angehörigen (Organization of Ex-SS Members)
OT	Organisation Todt
SS	Schutz Staffel (Literally: Defense Echelon—Nazi Elite Troops)
PPK	Polizei Pistole, Kriminal (Police Pistol, Criminal)
V-1	Vergeltungswaffe 1 (Reprisal Weapon 1—buzz bomb)
V-2	Vergeltungswaffe 2 (Reprisal Weapon 2—rocket)

Military—U.S. Army

AA	Antiaircraft
AC of S	Assistant Chief of Staff
AIC	Army Interrogation Center
B-2	OSS Camp
CI	Combat Intelligence
CIC	Counter Intelligence Corps
CID	Counter Intelligence Directorate
CO	Commanding Officer
CWS	Chemical Warfare Section (Service)
DIA	Defense Intelligence Agency
ETO	European Theater of Operations
GI	U.S. infantryman
G-2	Intelligence
HQ	Headquarters
ID	Identification
JCS	Joint Chiefs of Staff
MG	Military Government
MIS	Military Intelligence Service
NTK	Need to Know
OCS	Officer Candidate School
OSS	Office of Strategic Services
OSS-SI	Office of Strategic Services, Secret Intelligence
OSS-SO	Office of Strategic Services, Special Operations
PI	Photo Intelligence
SHAEF	Supreme Headquarters Allied Expeditionary Forces
TDY	Temporary Duty
TWX	Teletypewriter

Military—U.S. Navy

ASR	Auxiliary Submarine Rescue
BMC(DV)	Boatswain's Mate Chief (Diver)
CINCLANT	Commander in Chief, Atlantic
CINWESTLANT	Commander in Chief, West Atlantic
COMNAVAIRLANT	Commander Naval Air Force, Atlantic
COMSURFLANT	Commander Naval Surface Force, Atlantic
CTF	Commander Task Force
CTU	Commander Task Unit
CV	Aircraft Carrier
DDC	Deck Decompression Chamber
DDS	Deep Diving System
DSRV	Deep Submergence Rescue Vehicle
EN1(DV)	Engineman First Class (Diver)

ETA	Estimated Time of Arrival
FSW	Feet of Seawater
LPD	Landing Platform Dock
MAM	Man-Amplifier, Marinized
MCC	Main Control Console; Mixmaker Control Console
MK	Mark
ML	Medical Lock
MOD	Model
NATO	North Atlantic Treaty Organization
OPS	Operations
PO_2	Partial Pressure of Oxygen
PTC	Personnel Transfer Capsule
SACLANT	Supreme Allied Commander, Atlantic
SOP	Standard Operating Procedure
SPCC	Strength, Power, and Communications Cable
TF	Task Force
TT	Transfer Trunk
UQC	Underwater Telephone
VIP	Very Important Person

AUTHOR'S NOTES

Poison Gas

Although poison gas was not used in World War II as it had been in World War I, both the Allied and the Axis powers had large stockpiles of conventional poison gases such as chlorine, mustard gas, lewisite, and phosgene; and experiments on new and even deadlier toxic weapons were carried out, such as nerve gases, notably the German *Soman, Sarin,* and *Tabun,* the latter reportedly used by Iraq in 1984 during the war against Iran—the first time a nerve gas was ever employed in combat. A blood gas that interfered with the function of the blood and the utilization of oxygen by the body tissues, as well as bacteriological agents such as anthrax, code-named N, were also developed.

During World War II the British tested anthrax on the small island of Gruinard in Scotland; the island will be contaminated for another hundred years. In July 1944 the Joint Chiefs of Staff were asked by Churchill to consider using poison gas against the Germans in retaliation for the V-weapons, but such measures were ruled out.

Toward the end of the war, I—as a CIC agent in the U.S. Army—had a case of a foreign forced laborer who stated he had worked on a new poison gas being produced at a secret plant, the properties of which were said to be horrendous. The information obtained was forwarded to Army Interrogation Center of the Third Army.

After World War II the Germans dumped at least one hundred thousand tons of mustard gas weapons in the Baltic Sea. Early in 1984 this act extracted its terrible toll. Twelve fishermen, including seven from the Faeroe Island trawler, the *Heldarf Tendur,* were blinded and horribly burned when they hauled in the badly deteriorated poison gas containers and shell casings. It was one of the worst of such incidents, and the waters of the world still hold dumps of such lethal poison-gas time bombs.

The U-1000

According to *Navies of the Second World War: German Submarines 2,* by H. I. Lenton, published by MacDonald & Co., Ltd. and other works on German U-boats during World War II, the U-1000 was one of sixteen type-XX, oceangoing submarine transports primarily intended to carry rubber and other priority materials to Germany from the Far East. With a displacement of 2,700-plus tons, eight cargo compartments capable of carrying either dry or oil cargo, a cargo deadweight of eight hundred tons, and a complement of fifty-eight, the sub was built by Blohm and Voss in Hamburg in 1943–44. The U-boat was active in mining the Baltic Sea in August 1944, but on September 29, 1944, the sub—for unknown reasons—was "salved and paid-off."

Of the approximately fifteen hundred Nazi U-boats active during World War II, the fates of only five are unknown. One of them is a type-XX cargo transport sub.

The U-1000!

The Man-Amplifier

The Man-Amplifier, or exoskeleton, is not a figment of sci-fi imagination. The device *does* exist.

Initiated some years ago, the research project, carried out at the Cornell Aeronautical Laboratory in Buffalo, New York, was then under the supervision of project director Neil Mizen and was supported by the Office of Naval Research.

The operator of the Man-Amplifier was strapped into an elaborate steel harness, worn as a full-body brace. Sensor instruments would detect any muscular exertion by the man, and his efforts would be amplified as needed by small, powerful, individual, electrically driven hydraulic booster engines located on the exoskeleton at the appropriate joints of the wearer inside. For instance, if the operator flexed his elbows or his knees in order to lift a heavy object, the Man-Amplifier, its electrical sensors detecting the effort, would activate and use its own power to do the job. Thus heavy loads could be handled that otherwise would break a man's bones. The power supply was worn as a backpack, and the effects of using the device is exactly as described in *V-3.*

The U.S. Navy especially intended to use the Man-Amplifier to perform heavy and difficult work in tight shipboard quarters and in special salvage operations. A team of "supermen" wearing exoskeletons, able to lift thousands of pounds and to operate in remote and cramped spots where heavy machinery can't be used, would obviously be of enormous value.

The Danish Resistance

The Gestapo chief of Copenhagen bitterly complained that the Danish resistance movement was the most difficult encountered by German occupation forces anywhere, and British Field Marshal Bernard Montgomery described the valiant efforts of the freedom fighters as second to none.

In addition to carrying out countless daring sabotage actions against the Nazis, the Danish underground published approximately twenty-five million issues of "illegal" papers. The sabotage action described in *V-3* is based on an actual raid reported in one such publication, DANSK DAAD #3, Land Og Folk Forlag, Danmark, 1943. This action was actually filmed by the resistance fighters and became part of the nearly half a million feet of film chronicling the activities of the resistance organizations, shot by their own cameramen, often literally under the noses of the Gestapo.

There were several resistance organizations throughout the country, including one consisting of young boys, who were responsible for numerous successful raids against Nazi installations and transportation.

The incredible Shell House raid and the tragic French convent school crash happened as told in *V-3,* and the notorious HIPOs—established in October 1944 as an auxiliary Nazi police force under a former Danish police officer, the traitor Erik V. Petersen—did exist, although they numbered a mere handful compared to the Danish patriots who, in spite of enormous obstacles, refused to bow to the occupying forces.

The record of the Danish resistance is a proud one.

BIBLIOGRAPHY

In addition to the author's personal records and several works in foreign languages, the following English-language books have furnished information and facts for *V-3*.

Allen, Robert. *Lucky Forward: The History of General George Patton's Third Army*. New York: The Vanguard Press, 1947.

Atkinson, Bruce W. *The Weather Business*. New York: Doubleday, 1969.

Bauer, Eddy, et al. *Encyclopedia of World War II*. New York: Marshall Cavendish, 1972.

Botting, Douglas. *The U-boats*. Alexandria, VA: Time-Life Books, 1979.

Brower, J. S. *Guide to Underwater Explosive Excavation*. Pomona, CA: J. S. Brower, 1977.

Cohen, Paul. *The Realm of the Submarine*. London: Collier-Macmillan, 1967–69.

Cousins, Geoffrey. *The Story of Scapa Flow*. London: Frederick Muller, 1965.

Cruichshank, Charles. *Deception in World War II*. New York: Oxford University Press, 1979.

Dyer, George. *XII Corps: Spearhead of Patton's Third Army*. Washington, D.C.: XII Corps History Association, 1947.

Fitzsimons, Bernard, ed., et al. *The Illustrated Encyclopedia of Twentieth Century Weapons and Warfare*. London: Purnell & Sons, 1967–69.

Flender, Harold. *Rescue in Denmark*. New York: Macfadden-Bartell, 1963.

Garlinsky, Josef. *Hitler's Last Weapons*. New York: Times Books, 1978.

Garrison, Peter. *CV Carrier Aviation*. San Rafael, CA: Presidio Press, 1980.

Hjersman, Peter. *The Stash Book*. Berkeley, CA: And/Or Press, 1978.

Hymoff, Edward. *The OSS in World War II*. New York: Ballantine Books, 1972.

Jennett, Sean. *Cork and Kerry*. London: B. T. Batsford, 1977.

Jones, Joseph C., Jr. *Ice Boxes*. Humble, TX: Jobeco Books, 1981.

Koster, D. A. *Ocean Salvage*. New York: St. Martin's Press, 1971.

Lampe, David. *The Danish Resistance*. New York: Ballantine Books, 1960.

Langer, Walter C. *Hitler Source Book*. Washington, D.C.: National Archives of the United States, Declassified, 1968.

Lenton, H. T. *Navies of the Second World War: German Submarines 2*. New York: MacDonald, 1965.

Limburg, P. R. and Sweeney, J. B. *Vessels for Underwater Exploration* (Doubleday edition, 1965). New York: Crown Publishers, 1973.

Martin, Robert C. *The Deep-Sea Diver*. Cambridge, MD: Cornell Maritime Press, 1978.

Mentze, Ernst. *Five Years: The Occupation of Denmark in Pictures*. Malmö: A. B. Allhem, 1946.

MIS. *Order of Battle of the German Army*. Washington, D.C.: Military Intelligence Service, 1943.

Morgan, William J. *The OSS and I*. New York: W. W. Norton, 1957.

Morison, Samuel Eliot. *The Two-Ocean War*. Boston: Little, Brown, 1963.

Parrish, Thomas, ed., et al. *Encyclopedia of World War II*. New York: Simon & Schuster, 1978.

Preston, Anthony. *Aircraft Carriers*. Greenwich, CT: Bison Books, 1982.

Robertson, Terrence. *Walker, RN*. New York: Bantam Books, 1979.

Roosevelt, Kermit, et al. *War Report of the OSS*. New York: Walker, 1976.

Smith, R. Harris. *OSS*. Berkeley, CA: University of California Press, 1972.

Taylor, Sybil. *Ireland's Pubs*. New York: Penguin Books, 1983.

U.S. National Oceanic and Atmospheric Administration. *The Complete Underwater Diving Manual*. New York: David McKay, 1982.

ABOUT THE AUTHOR

Ib Melchior, as well as being a best-selling author, is also a motion picture writer-director-producer in Hollywood, with some twelve feature films and numerous TV shows and documentaries to his credit.

He was born and educated in Denmark, majoring in literature and languages, and graduated from the University of Copenhagen. He then joined a British theatrical company, the English Players, with headquarters in Paris, France, as an actor. He toured Europe with this troupe, becoming stage manager and co-director of the company. Just prior to the outbreak of World War II in Europe, he came to the United States with this company to do a Broadway show.

Then there followed a stint in the stage-managing departments of the Radio City Music Hall and the Center Theater ice shows in New York. When Pearl Harbor was attacked, he volunteered his services to the U.S. armed forces. He served with the "cloak-and-dagger" OSS for a while and was then transferred to the U.S. Military Intelligence Service. He spent two years in the European Theater of Operations as a military intelligence investigator attached to the Counter Intelligence Corps. For his work in the ETO, he was decorated by the U.S. Army as well as by the king of Denmark and was subsequently awarded the Knight Commander Cross of the Militant Order of St. Brigitte of Sweden.

After the war he became active in television and also began his writing career. He has directed some five hundred TV shows, both live and filmed, ranging from the musical "The Perry Como Show" on CBS-TV—on which he served as director for three and a half years—to the dramatic documentary series "The March of Medicine" on NBC-TV. He has also served as a director in a production capacity on eight motion-picture features in Hollywood, including AIP's unusual *The Time Travelers,* which he also wrote.

In addition to this extensive career as a director, Ib Melchior's background as an author and writer includes over a million words published in story and article form in many national magazines including *Life,* as well as in several European periodicals, some of which have been included in anthologies. He has also written legitimate plays for the stage, one being *Hour of Vengeance,* a dramatization of the ancient Almeth legend that was the original source of *Hamlet.* This play was produced at the Globe Playhouse in Los Angeles, and Melchior was honored with the Shakespeare Society of America's Hamlet Award for Excellence in Playwriting, 1982.

Melchior has also won several national awards for TV and documentary film shorts that he wrote, directed, and produced, and he has written several scripts for various TV series, including "Men Into Space" and "The Outer Limits." Among his feature films are *Ambush Bay,* a motion picture with a World War II background, filmed in the Philippines for United Artists, as well as the notable *Robinson Crusoe on Mars* for Paramount and several other films with a science fiction theme.

In 1976 he was awarded the Golden Scroll for best writing by the Academy of Science Fiction.

Ib Melchior is the author of the best-selling, critically acclaimed novels based on his own experiences as a CIC agent, *Order of Battle*, *Sleeper Agent*, and *The Haigerloch Project*, as well as *The Watchdogs of Abaddon*, *The Marcus Device*, *The Tombstone Cipher*, and *Eva*. His novels are now published in twenty-five countries.

Ib Melchior lives in a two-story, Mediterranean-style home in the Hollywood Hills. He is an avid collector of military miniatures and historical documents. He is married to the prominent designer, Cleo Baldon, and has two sons. He is the son of the late Wagnerian tenor, Lauritz Melchior.